BECAUSE YOU'RE MINE

by

Nan Ryan

A TOPAZ BOOK

TOPAZ
Published by the Penguin Group
Penguin Books USA Inc., 375 Hudson Street,
New York, New York 10014, U.S.A.
Penguin Books Ltd, 27 Wrights Lane,
London W8 5TZ, England
Penguin Books Australia Ltd, Ringwood,
Victoria, Australia
Penguin Books Canada Ltd, 10 Alcorn Avenue,
Toronto, Ontario, Canada M4V 3B2
Penguin Books (N.Z.) Ltd, 182–190 Wairau Road,
Auckland 10, New Zealand

Penguin Books Ltd, Registered Offices:
Harmondsworth, Middlesex, England

First published by Topaz, an imprint of Dutton Signet.
a division of Penguin Books USA Inc.

ISBN 0-451-40595-1

For

My six nieces:
A half dozen of the sweetest,
prettiest young women I know.

Helen Hull Clayton

Susan Ford Hull

Jennifer Jonas Leggett

Sarah Allen Soisson

Kate Marie Allen

Chris Mahler Allen

Prologue

The last days of the Mexican War—a field hospital outside Mexico City's Chapultepec Castle—dusk on a late September evening, 1847.

"Who goes there?"

"Colonel Raleigh Burnett. Adjutant, Western Border Battalion."

"Advance, Colonel, and be recognized."

Colonel Raleigh Burnett quickly stepped into the light of the swaying battle lantern. His injured right arm was tied up in a sling, his uniform jacket draped over his right shoulder. Left-handed, he saluted youthful Victor Rivera, the captain of the guards.

"Colonel Raleigh Burnett," he repeated his name. "General Patch sent for me."

"Yes, Sir, Colonel Burnett. The general's waiting." Victor Rivera stepped aside, motioning the tall, dark-haired officer into the large hospital tent.

Colonel Burnett came forward, pausing for a second just outside the tent's open flap. In a voice low and soft, he asked, "Is the general expected to . . . ?"

The muscular young captain of the guards shook his dark head sadly, then respectfully lowered his eyes. The message was plain. The wounded general was dying. Colonel Raleigh Burnett nodded, removed his dusty blue forage cap with his good left hand, drew a deep slow breath, and ducked inside.

Lamplight flickered and danced, casting shadows on the canvas walls of the noisy field hospital. Wounded men, their faces sweating and contorted in agony, writhed on rumpled cots lined up in rows. The smell of death was heavy in the close, stuffy air. Moans of pain were constant.

Colonel Raleigh Burnett, poised just inside the hospital tent's opening, had seen so much of death and war he was almost immune to the horrible scents and sounds around him.

But not quite.

Not when his oldest and dearest friend was now one of the war's casualties. Raleigh Burnett gripped his forage hat in stiff fingers and slowly looked about.

General Norman Patch, his eyes closed, lay unmoving on a cot set apart from the others in a secluded corner of the hospital tent. Situated to afford the mortally wounded general a small degree of privacy in these, his final hours, the cot was but a few short yards from where Colonel Burnett stood.

The colonel stared in horror at the silent soldier lying deathly still on the narrow cot. Burnett's heart slammed against his ribs. The prostrate general was barely recognizable as the old comrade he had known since their early days at West Point. Raleigh Burnett found it impossible to believe that this ashen-faced casualty, lying helplessly on the cot, was the same man.

Could it be possible that only a few short days ago—not even a full week—this now war-ravaged soul had been the fiery, vibrant, robust commander whose supreme confidence and daring had so successfully rallied his admiring troops against Santa Anna's army?

Colonel Raleigh Burnett swallowed hard, and set his forage hat on a nearby table. He shrugged his soiled blue fatigue jacket off his right shoulder, let it slide down his good left arm, and placed the jacket alongside the hat. Then gathering himself, he moved forward to face the sad task of saying good-bye.

When he reached the cot, his shadow fell across Norman Patch's sweating, chalky face. The general's pale eyes opened. He blinked to focus and saw Raleigh Burnett standing above. The wounded man smiled weakly and lifted a hand in greeting.

Colonel Burnett seized the proffered hand in his good left, smiled, and said, "You old gold brick. Couldn't you think of some other way to get a furlough?"

Wounded and weak though he was, General Patch chuckled. Or tried to. But the effort made him cough and choke. Colonel Burnett released Patch's hand, dipped a cloth into a basin of water, and bathed his friend's shiny face.

"Anything I can get you, Norman? Do for you?" He sponged the fevered cheeks, the glistening forehead, the lank sun-streaked hair.

"Yes, old friend," the general responded, pushing the damp cloth away. "Pull up a chair. I must talk to you."

Colonel Burnett laid the cloth beside the basin of water, drew up a folding chair, and sat facing Norman Patch. "I'm here." He again took the general's hand, squeezed it gently. "I'm listening."

General Patch began by saying, "You remember my beautiful wife?"

Burnett nodded. He had first met the blond, aristocratic Castilian, Dona Constancia Carrillo at the couple's wedding a decade ago. He had been Norman Patch's best man. He'd seen the beautiful Constancia on several other occasions before her untimely death in the summer of '43.

"I remember her," he said softly.

"As you know our large ranch in Spanish California came from a land grant through Constancia's father, Don Pascal Antonio Carrillo. When Constancia died, I fell heir to the land."

"Yes. Of course," Colonel Burnett said. "And in a few days, old friend, you'll be back on the ranch, resting in your own bed."

"No," said Patch. "I won't."

"Nonsense, as soon as you—"

"I'm not going to make it," the general interrupted. "We both know it."

The smile left Burnett's face. "I'm sorry."

"Don't be," said Patch and sighed wearily. Then the general called up his last reserve of strength. His eyes cleared and focused on Raleigh Burnett. He struggled up onto his elbows. "There is something you must do for me. It's very important."

"Name it and it's done."

"Little Teresa, Constancia's sister and my ward, is my only living heir. At ten years of age, she's too young to inherit, isn't she?"

An attorney by profession, Raleigh Burnett knew the law. "She is. Any inheritance meant for Teresa would have to be held in trust until she turns eighteen. Or, until she marries, in which case her husband could take title to the land on her behalf."

"That's what I thought. You handle it, Raleigh. Draw up the necessary documents. See to it the child's interests are protected. Hold the land in trust for Constancia's little sister, Teresa, until she turns eighteen. Or marries, whichever comes first. Since Constancia's death, little Teresa has been at the Sacred Heart Convent outside Tucson in the Arizona Territory."

The two friends continued to talk quietly, planning for the inevitable, ensuring the future of the dying man's ten-year-old sister-in-law, Teresa Carrillo, and sole heir to the vast Spanish California ranch. Patiently, Raleigh Burnett explained, in laymen's terms, exactly how the trust would work. Satisfied, the rapidly tiring general thanked his dear old friend who, only two days ago, had risked his own life in a valiant attempt to save his. That was the kind of man Colonel Raleigh Burnett was. Brave. Dependable. Trustworthy.

Now Patch could die in peace.

"You need to rest, Norman." Colonel Burnett rose to his feet. "Be assured your behest will be honored. I'll see to it that Teresa Carrillo is taken care of."

"I know that, my friend," said General Patch. "And I thank you for this final courtesy."

Colonel Burnett, blinking back tears, raised his good left hand and saluted his commanding officer one last time; then he returned to his post.

At the hospital tent's opening, young Captain Victor Rivera continued to stand silent sentinel as the hot September dusk deepened into a still summertime darkness.

The dying general felt relieved. He had seen to it that Constancia's totally dependent little sister would one day take title to the vast cattle and silver empire in Spanish California. Her life would be one of ease and splendor. She would take her pick of her many acceptable suitors. She and her husband would dwell in the magnificent Carrillo mansion and mingle with California's wealthy landed gentry. The sound of children's laughter would echo throughout the many rooms of the big ranch house.

It was a pleasing vision and General Patch was filled with a sense of well-being.

But almost immediately uneasiness claimed him again. What if something happened to Raleigh Burnett? Teresa wouldn't reach her maturity for another eight years. Much could come to pass in that length of time. Burnett could be shot and killed in these final days of the war. And Teresa would be left unprotected. The child might never know about the trust deed, might never lay claim to her land.

With effort, the general struggled to again lift his head from the perspiration-drenched pillow. Focusing with difficulty, he saw the captain of the guards standing a few short yards away, arms crossed over his chest. He summoned the young officer to his bedside.

"Captain Rivera, I understand you are from the Arizona Territory."

"Yes, sir," Victor Rivera confirmed. "Fort McDowell. Born and raised on the nearby Verde River."

"Good, good. You know Tucson?"

"Yes, sir, General, I do. How may I be of service?"

"I want you to write a letter for me. Two letters, in fact," said General Patch, inclining his head toward the nearby battle desk, atop which rested a neat stack of cream vellum stationery, and a plumed pen and inkwell.

While the general dictated, Victor Rivera wrote out the message addressed to the Mother Superior of the Sacred Heart convent in Tucson, Arizona. The terms of the trust for young Teresa Carrillo were spelled out precisely. Instructions to contact Raleigh M. Burnett, the California attorney, were included, along with a Los Angeles address.

When the message was concluded, folded, put into a vellum envelope, and sealed with candle wax, the general had Victor Rivera write a letter to his sister-in-law. In it he told the young Teresa Carrillo that he loved her as Constancia had loved her, was sorry he had to leave her alone, but that he had ensured her future. Briefly explaining that the vast acreage in old California which had belonged first to her father, Don Pascal Antonio Carrillo, then to her older sister, Constancia, would one day be hers. He repeated the instructions on how to get in touch with Raleigh Burnett to claim her rightful inheritance.

"Give me your word, Captain," said the general, his pale eyes intense, "that you will deliver these letters as soon as this war has ended."

"I solemnly promise, sir."

"The letters are confidential. Do not allow either of them to fall into the hands of anyone other than to whom they are addressed. Do you understand me?"

"You have my word, General Patch."

The general released a deep sigh of satisfaction. "Carry on, Captain!"

PART

1

PART
1

Chapter One

A ranch six miles south of San Juan Capistrano, California—sunset on a perfect spring day in 1880

A slender young rider sat astride a dancing chestnut stallion outside the whitewashed fence boundaries of one of Southern California's largest working cattle ranches. The rider, squinting against the lowering sun, was dressed in the unique garb favored by Mexican *charros*—leather trousers, white shirt, scarlet butterfly necktie, scuffed ankle boots, and a broad-brimmed straw sombrero.

The rider's narrowed, unblinking gaze slowly lifted to the hammered silver sign mounted from the tall crossbars above the rancho's main gate. The shimmering silver letters spelled out simply LINDO VISTA—beautiful view. The rider, whose dark eyes quickly turned as hard and cold as onyx, had no doubt that the view from inside the imposing ranch house located on an elevated rise was indeed beautiful.

Soon, very soon, the rider would know for certain.

As unmoving as a statue, the long-legged, leather-trousered rider stayed resolutely in place for the next hour. It was not the first time the rider had been there. It would not be the last.

Since arriving in San Juan Capistrano, California, two weeks ago, the slim young rider had ridden *El Rancho*

Lindo Vista's vast expanse daily, exploring every far-reaching acre, systematically becoming acquainted with every unique landmark.

The rider eagerly learned the location of each hidden trail or secret footpath or abandoned silver mine and all the towering trees and rich grassy ranges and sandy desertlands and towering mountains and rushing streams and rugged coastline.

Carefully keeping out of sight, and avoiding the legions of ranch hands working the big spread, the rider ended each long tiring ride at this same well-concealed vantage point in front of the huge white ranch house. Field glasses raised. Watching. Waiting. Hoping for even the slightest glimpse of the rich, powerful man who called the white, red-tiled roofed house home.

The young one.

Not the old one.

The rider had seen the old one that very first day in California. A frail, sickly old gentleman with silver hair, he'd been out taking the afternoon sun on the southern flagstone patio. He had been there most days since, slight shoulders and thin arms covered with a bulky sweater, knees hidden under a lap robe.

No, it was not for him the rider restlessly hunted. Through the powerful field glasses, the rider's dark gaze searched anxiously for a strong, vigorous, totally healthy man who at thirty-one was but seven years the rider's senior. It was for him the rider waited. It was for him the rider watched.

For the ailing old man's idolized only son. And sole heir to *Lindo Vista.*

Burton J. Burnett.

The rider didn't give up the fruitless quest until the blood-red sun had slipped below the western horizon and into the sea behind the imposing many-roomed ranch house. Finally, disappointed once more, the rider lowered the glasses, turned the chestnut stallion about and rode away.

The rider put the stallion into an easy lope for the six-mile journey back to the sleepy village of San Juan Capistrano. The rider lifted a hot, sun-reddened face to the cooling evening breezes.

The wind soon picked up, pressing the tight leather trousers against the rider's lithe long legs, billowing the blousey white shirt out in back, and tossing the ends of the scarlet necktie up against a full-lipped, but set, unsmiling mouth.

The rider laid big roweled silver spurs to the chestnut stallion's flanks and the powerful beast instantly shot into a fast, ground-eating gallop.

Hugging the galloping stallion with leather-clad knees, the rider solemnly resolved to come back again tomorrow. Back to the vast rangelands known as *Lindo Vista*. Back to stand sentinel at the hidden command post behind a towering oak across from the white-washed ranch house on the cliffs. Back to hopefully see the elusive Burton J. Burnett.

Beginning to relax and enjoy the ride, the determined young rider raced the dying sun back to the village.

As the young rider on the chestnut stallion thundered northward toward San Juan Capistrano, a train snaked toward the very same destination, moving steadily southwestward.

In the very last car—a private Pullman—on the slow-moving train, a lone passenger was sprawled comfortably on a plush, pearl-gray sofa. He lounged lazily, his dark head resting on the sofa's plush back, his long legs stretched out before him, booted feet propped carelessly atop a gilt-inlaid rosewood table.

He held in one tanned hand a tall crystal goblet of iced Kentucky Bourbon, half full, and in the other a fragrant Cuban cigar, blue smoke curling up from its glowing tip. Totally relaxed, pleased with his successful business trip to Chicago, and even more pleased that it was ended, Burt Burnett was smiling.

As usual.

Burt smiled a lot.

People who knew him well said that they had never seen him without a warm smile on his face. The men of the village swore that even when conducting business, no matter how hard a bargain Burt drove, his engaging smile never left him. The town's older ladies said that Burt had an adorable, boyish smile, so guileless and open it made them want to give him a big warm motherly hug.

That famous Burnett smile had a similar effect on younger

women. They, too, had a strong desire to hug him, but not in a motherly fashion. Burt Burnett had been, since he turned eighteen, San Juan Capistrano and southern California's most eligible bachelor. A good-looking, sensual man with warm humorous gray eyes, that compelling, ever-present smile, and a natural easy charm made him a favorite. And not only with the local girls, but with women down in sunny San Diego, up in lazy Los Angeles, and as far away as the bustling Bay city of San Francisco.

Burt Burnett was playful, irreverent, and incredibly attractive. With the upbringing of a gentleman and the charm of a rogue, he knew how to show a woman the time of her life and keep his mouth shut afterward. Never one to kiss and tell, he was a sought-after lover, a man who was as discreet as he was passionate.

And Burt Burnett was indeed a passionate man. A fact of life which had been attested to by more than one beautiful, starry-eyed, well-sated woman who couldn't keep from boasting about her own unforgettably torrid trysts with the amazingly ardent, darkly handsome lover.

As the train wound its way homeward in the setting California sun, Burt Burnett smiled with guilty pleasure, recalling the pair of fun-loving twins he had met in Chicago.

The gorgeous Todd twins, Hope and Faith, had shown him unlimited charity. The girls were identical. He couldn't tell them apart, so he never really knew which one he was with. But then it hadn't mattered. Not to him. Not to them. Both were fantastically gifted in the finer points of lovemaking.

For Burt it was his swan song. The final romp before settling down to domestic bliss. So he had made the most of it. Thanks to the accommodating, acrobatic Todd twins, his last hurrah had been memorable.

The train was beginning to slow.

The tiny depot was coming up in the near distance. Burt took another swig of his iced bourbon, swirled it around in his mouth, and swallowed. He drew on his cigar and blew a well-formed smoke ring. Then he set the goblet aside, snubbed out the cigar in a crystal ashtray, and lowered his booted feet to the carpeted floor. He rose, moved unhurriedly to the window, lifted the shade, and looked out.

The lights of Capistrano were twinkling on, one by one,

as the sun disappeared completely, leaving only a wide ribbon of red-gold light in the far west behind the ocean. Smiling as he studied the familiar landmarks of home, Burt's attention was suddenly drawn to a slim, sombreroed rider galloping headlong toward the approaching train.

Burt's smile broadened.

He knew exactly what the dashing, leather-trousered *vaquero* intended to do. He knew, because he had done it so many times himself.

It was the kind of senseless, daredevil stunt wild young men enjoyed. Only the most experienced horseman would attempt such a dangerous feat. It took a great degree of bravery and was considered a true mark of manhood.

Burt had been just fourteen the first time he had tried it.

Burt raised the window all the way and stuck his dark head out. He whistled and applauded as the brave, foolish rider raced his chestnut stallion across the tracks just a split second before the train's engine, whistle blowing loudly, reached the crossing.

The slim, *charro*-clad rider yipped joyfully as the chestnut's rear hooves cleared the railroad tracks a half second before the big black steam engine reached the crossing. The train roared past with its whistle blowing frantically, and its heavy wheels screeching and grinding on the steel tracks as it attempted to stop.

Burt laughed as the rider disappeared from sight.

The rider galloped on, ignoring the raised fists the ashen-faced engineer shook out the window from his perch at the engine's throttle. Never looking back, the rider cantered directly to the little village's stables as total dusk descended.

Dismounting, the rider threw a long leg over, dropped to the ground, and patted the winded chestnut's sleek neck.

"That's a mighty fine stallion you have there," said Paxton Dean, the stable owner, again admiring the mount.

"The best," said the rider. "Trained him myself. He does anything I ask of him."

"You'll be wanting him again in the morning?" asked Paxton Dean, as he took the reins and began removing the lathered chestnut's bridle.

"By all means. Look for me around sunup." Patting the big stallion's velvet muzzle and cooing to him, the rider said,

"You are the best, aren't you big boy." The chestnut whinnied and blew, answering his master. The rider laughed and
gave the stallion's jaw a gentle slap, then heading for the
open door, said, "See you both tomorrow."

"I'll have him saddled and ready for you," said Paxton
Dean. "Night now."

"Good night." The rider walked away, but stopped suddenly and paused in the doorway, pondering. Then turned
back and said, "I've changed my mind. I won't be needing
my horse tomorrow."

"You won't?"

"No. I won't be riding after all."

The rider immediately stepped outside, looked both ways,
then crossed Camino Capistrano, the village's main thoroughfare. Casting a covetous glance, as usual, up the street
toward the stately white Mission Inn, that grand, obscenely
expensive hotel built on the cliffs adjacent to the old Spanish
Mission, the rider went directly to the much more modest
little Inn of the Swallows.

A small, unimpressive hostelry sandwiched between the
silent undertaker's parlor and the noisy Balboa Saloon, there
was nothing grand about the inn. All the small, colorless
rooms were identically furnished with iron bedsteads, wash-
stands, an armoire, a small round drum table, and a worn
horsehair sofa. No pictures graced the plain white walls, no
curtains covered the window shades.

But the place was clean and the price was right.

The rider climbed the stairs to the second floor and threw
the door open to a pair of connecting rooms at the end of
the hall.

"I'm back! Where are you, Carmelita? I'm finally back."

A short, stocky Mexican woman with dark flashing eyes
and thick black hair shot through with strands of silver entered from the adjoining room, her hands on her spreading
hips.

"Do you know what time it is? I was ready to send out
the sheriff to look for you!"

"You worry too much," said the smiling rider and swept
off the big sombrero, allowing an abundance of luxuriant
long blond hair to cascade down around slender shoulders.

Chapter Two

Burt was still laughing when he pulled his head back inside the train window. The wheels ground to a screeching halt while he buttoned his half-open white shirt and reached for the dark suit coat lying across the pearl-gray velvet sofa. He shoved long arms into the jacket's dark sleeves, reached up behind his head to adjust the stiffly starched white shirt collar, then shot his arms forward to display an inch of snow-white cuff.

The train stopped.

A uniformed conductor jumped down, reached up for the set of deboarding steps, and placed them on the ground. Then he stood aside, hands folded before him.

Smiling sunnily, Burt swung down from the train and spotted Cappy Ricks waiting beside the black, open carriage. Cappy's roan gelding was tied to the back.

Cappy Ricks, *Lindo Vista*'s head ranch foreman, had turned sixty-six on his last birthday. His full head of hair was totally gray and his six-foot-two frame stooped a mite, but he was still a remarkably strong, fit-looking man.

Burt called to the aging ranch foreman.

Cappy's craggy features tightened into a brief smile and he started forward. The two men shook hands warmly.

"Good to have you back, Burton." Cappy affectionately patted Burt's muscular shoulder.

"Good to be back," Burt said. Then he asked immediately, "How is he, Cappy? How's Dad?"

"Holding his own," Cappy assured him. "Actually, he's been feeling a little better for the past couple of days."

"Good! Any chance he'll feel like attending the big shindig Saturday night?"

"He's not feeling *that* good, son," Cappy said. "But don't be worrying about that. I'll stay home with him Saturday night, keep him company."

"You're a good man, Cappy Ricks," said Burt with gratitude and affection.

"Well, now, I don't know about that." Cappy ducked his head, half embarrassed, yet pleased. Clearing his throat needlessly, the aged ranch foreman looked up again. "So . . . how did it go up there in Chicago? Your trip worthwhile?"

"In more ways than one," Burt said, and winked, his sunny smile broadening mischievously.

Reading his meaning, Cappy shook his gray head, clapped the younger man on the back, and warned, "All that's behind you now, my boy. I hope you fully realize that and are willing to—"

"I do and I am," Burt said, nodding. "So stop your preaching. From here on out, you won't know me."

Cappy looked skeptical. He had known Burt Burnett since Burt was just a year old. He knew Burt as well as Burt's own father knew him, maybe even better. He knew Burt's strengths as well as his weaknesses. One of his weaknesses was women. Cappy didn't blame Burt, knowing the fault wasn't entirely his.

Since back when he was just a young strapping boy of fifteen, Burt had drawn women to him without even trying. And the strangest thing was that Burt was not some soft, suave, insincere ladies' man. He was a man's man. As rugged and rough as the toughest California cowhand, and he never lied or made deceitful promises to woo a woman.

But then, he didn't have to. They were willing to take him any way they could get him and then savor the memory of the brief encounter ever after.

"I believe you really mean it," Cappy finally said, idly patting Burt's back again.

"I do, my friend. You'll see. I'll walk the line."

"Well, that's a load off my mind," Cappy said and meant it. "Your daddy's gonna' be mighty glad to see you, boy."

"He'll have to wait 'til tomorrow." Burt grinned.

"Yep. He knows." Cappy inclined his gray head to the waiting carriage. "I did what you asked, Burt. Brought the open carriage in for you. I'll ride Dusty on home and tell your daddy you made it in okay."

"I sure appreciate this, Cappy." Burt nodded yes to the uniformed porter. While the porter loaded the matching leather valises onto the floor of the carriage, Burt shrugged his wide shoulders and, smiling, said to Cappy, "You know how Gena is about horses. Can't stand the smell of them. If I rode Sam over to see her, she wouldn't have anything to do with me."

"Now ain't that a heck of a note," said Cappy, frowning. "A gal that'll be spending the rest of her life on *Lindo Vista* and she don't like horses or cattle. Why, she don't even like the land or the sun or the—"

"She likes me, Cappy," Burt smilingly interrupted the older man.

Cappy laughed then. "Lord, I guess she does." He shook his gray head. "I'll have to hand it to Miss Gena. She's shown the patience of Job, if you ask me."

"I didn't."

"Yes, siree," Cappy continued as if Burt hadn't spoken, "waiting around all these years for you to settle down and finally marry her. She's one understanding and tenacious gal."

"Gena's been a good sport," Burt agreed, nodding. "And she'll be a good wife, you wait and see."

"I suppose," admitted Cappy dubiously. Then—"But you better be getting on over to her place. The train was two hours late getting in, you know."

"Was it?" Burt sounded surprised. "So Gena was expecting me at ..."

"Six p.m. It's almost eight."

Burt climbed up onto the carriage's leather-padded seat and took up the reins. "I'm off then. See you tomorrow. Thanks again."

"Say hello to Gena and the senator."

Burt waved a hand in the air as he drove away, signaling

that he would. He wasn't worried about Gena being upset. She would be glad to see him, no matter how late he arrived.

Gena de Temple was pretty, dark-haired, and twenty-seven-years old. She lived with her widowed father, State Senator Nelson de Temple on a long, narrow piece of land that was the northern border of *Lindo Vista.*

It had been understood, for as long as anyone could remember, that Burt and Gena would one day marry. It had suited Burt fine. It still did.

He and Gena enjoyed a fond, familiar, comfortable closeness, despite the fact they were, in most ways, direct opposites.

Gena didn't ride; had never been on a horse. She couldn't stand the smell of horseflesh. If Burt had been out riding, Gena refused to let him touch her until after he'd had a bath. She had no interest in the land, had never been off the main road leading into the village. She assiduously avoided the harsh California sun. She detested the arid deserts, the forbidding mountains, and the pounding coastal surf equally.

The only rugged thing Gena de Temple loved was Burt Burnett.

Which was fine with Burt. She might never share his love of the rough, wild land, but then what woman would? Educated, intelligent, the consummate hostess, Gena would make him a good wife, be a caring mother to his children. Since foolish, storybook romance didn't actually exist, Burt saw no reason to wait any longer to marry Gena and make an honest woman of her.

His wild oats had been freely sewn. Gena was tired of waiting. His father was slowly dying and Raleigh Burnett's greatest wish was to see his first grandchild. So with all parties in agreement, it had been decided. Burt Burnett would—at long last—marry Gena de Temple. Tonight, at dinner, they would finalize the wedding plans.

Burt turned the matched blacks into the circular drive outside the large de Temple mansion. The carriage wheels had hardly rolled to a stop on the pebbled drive before the front door opened and Gena stepped out into the fast-fading twilight.

Burt bounded out of the carriage, turned the reins over to a waiting groomsman, and went to meet his fiancée. Gena

paused on the porch steps and watched the man she openly adored come toward her.

He was smiling, naturally.

His perfect white teeth flashing in the darkness of his tanned handsome face, he moved quickly, with a catlike certainty. When he reached her, Gena stood on tiptoe and threw her arms around his neck, eagerly lifting her lips for his kiss.

Burt kissed her once, twice, then raised his dark head.

"Miss me?" he teasingly inquired.

"I did. And you? Did you miss me, darling?"

Burt buried his face in Gena's dark hair as a sharp pang of guilt shot through his chest. An incredibly graphic vision of the naughty naked Hope Todd—or was it Faith?—well, anyway, one of the tantalizing Todd twins rose up to remind him of his recent infidelities.

"Mmmmm," he murmured into Gena's perfumed hair and felt heat rise to his face.

"Good!" said Gena, pulling back to look up at him. "I was terribly lonely, so I'm glad you were, too."

Burt just smiled at her.

Arm in arm, Gena chattering happily, they went inside, where they were met by a beaming Senator de Temple. The distinguished silver-haired senator shook the younger man's hand, welcomed him home, and within minutes, the three retired to the high-ceilinged dining room to enjoy a long, leisurely dinner.

The conversation was of the wedding plans. An official engagement party was set for Saturday evening. Tiffany-engraved invitations had been sent out a month ago. RSVPs had been received. There had been no regrets. Everyone who had been invited would attend.

Senator de Temple, proud father, would host a crowd of three hundred in the mansion's marble-floored ballroom. A church wedding and extravagant reception would follow at Christmastime.

After dinner, the trio enjoyed brandy and coffee in the library. And more talk of the nuptials.

"I *must* have the largest, most elaborate wedding in Sout ern California history," mused Gena aloud. "I am, after the daughter of the powerful Senator Nelson de Tem

And I shall be marrying the most eligible bachelor in the entire state!"

"And so you will have the biggest and best wedding, my darling," said the doting senator. "I'll see to it."

"I'll have my wedding gown made in San Francisco," Gena said, squeezing Burt's hand. "And I know of a very special florist down in San Diego who promises he can deliver hundreds of white orchids even in December. Daddy, you recall that caterer we used for your induction party back in ..."

And so it went.

Burt listened politely, secretly wishing that Gena and he could quietly elope and avoid all the folderol. But Gena had waited a long time. The least he could do was to go along with her plans with good grace.

"I do hope we haven't left out anyone whom we should have invited to the engagement party," said Gena, troubled.

The silver-haired senator smiled indulgently at his daughter. "Dear, I'm sure we've thought of everyone. Do stop worrying. You'll make yourself ill."

Burt seconded her father's mild warning. His arm around Gena's shoulders, he gave her a gentle squeeze. "The senator's right, Gena. Relax. The engagement party will be all you ever dreamed of." He drew her closer. "Everything is going to be perfect."

Chapter Three

I'm sorry, Carmelita. I didn't realize it was getting so late," the slender, leather-trousered Sabella Rios said apologetically as she ran slender fingers through her heavy blond hair. "I won't stay away this long again."

Carmelita Rivera's hands stayed on her hips, but the frown on her face dissolved with the relief of having Sabella back, safe and sound.

"Any luck today?" Carmelita asked, beginning to smile at the beautiful, headstrong young woman whom she couldn't have loved more had Sabella been her own flesh and blood.

Sabella shook her head and flung herself down onto the horsehair sofa. "None." Pulling her right knee up to her chest, she tugged off her brown leather boot, dropped it to the threadbare carpet, and began rubbing her cramped toes.

"I will do that for you," said Carmelita. The older woman groaned slightly as she lowered herself to the footstool directly in front of Sabella.

She removed Sabella's remaining boot, drew both her feet up onto her lap, and massaged them with strong, nimble hands.

Sighing, moaning, nodding her thanks, Sabella leaned back, threw her arms up behind her head, and said, "I can't understand it. How can a man *never* be on his own property? Isn't there work he should be doing? Is he so lazy he never helps the cowhands out? Could it be that something is wrong with him? Perhaps he's sickly and can't ... what if he's an invalid who never sets foot outside the ranch house?"

Carmelita gently scolded, "You know better than that. If something were wrong—if he'd been in an accident or any-thing—you would have read about it." Her knuckles knead-ing the tender sole of Sabella's left foot, she voiced her thoughts aloud, "We should never have come here. It is not too late. No one knows yet. Why don't you give the whole thing up and let's go home."

Sabella snatched her foot from Carmelita's hands. Her arms came down from behind her head, and she leaned for-ward until her set, determined face was mere inches from the Mexican woman's.

"Never!" she said through clenched teeth. "Never. I am staying. You're free to go back to the Arizona Territory if you wish, but you'll go alone. I'm not leaving until I have what I came here for."

Her dark eyes clouded with worry, Carmelita said, "I wouldn't leave you but, Sabella ... *nena, nena* ... this can only lead to more heartbreak and tragedy. What you are doing ... what you aim to do ... it is not right. It is not right and I—"

"Not right?" Sabella's tone was brittle. "It's not right?" she repeated, incredulous. "What *I'm* doing is not right? Have you forgotten what they—"

"No, no. I have forgotten nothing. But I pray each night that you will one day forget."

"Save your prayers, Carmelita." Sabella abruptly shot to her feet. "I don't need them. I know exactly what I'm doing."

"No," Carmelita said firmly, sadly, "you do not. You are too young to know some things. Too inexperienced to fathom the kind of tragic consequences your actions will bring to all involved. Including yourself."

Yanking the long tails of her white shirt out of her tight leather trousers, Sabella laughed away Carmelita's concerns. "Carmelita, dear, dear, Carmelita. Certainly there will be consequences. I realize that I will pay a price, and a high one, but I'm perfectly willing to do so." Her dark eyes turned a shiny, polished obsidian and she added resolutely, "It will be worth it."

"I hope so," said a defeated Carmelita, shaking her head.
A silence. Then: "You'll be riding back out there in the
morning?"

Sabella shrugged slender arms free of her shirtsleeves, and
idly blotted the beads of perspiration from her throat and
shoulders with the soiled white shirt.

"No. I won't be returning to the *rancho* tomorrow. I've
decided to try another tack. I'll stay close to the inn all day.
I'll get dressed up. Do a bit of shopping here in the village."

Carmelita's dark eyebrows knitted together. "Have we
enough money for . . . ?"

"I won't spend any money."

"Then why go shopping?" Carmelita slowly rose, putting
a hand to the small of her back.

"To meet people. To make friends. To see what I can find
out about Mr. Burton J. Burnett."

She pinched her cheeks. She bit her lips. She twisted her
clean, shining hair into a thick golden rope and pinned it
atop her head. She ran her hands over her slender waist,
smoothing down the gathers of her freshly laundered, pink
cotton dress. She plucked at the high, white lace collar, and
touched a tiny white button at her throat.

She grabbed up the straw bonnet with the pink satin ribbon around the crown and hurried from the bedroom. Kissing Carmelita's cheek and telling her not to worry, Sabella
Rios left their small suite.

She descended the stairs in such a ladylike manner, no one
would have recognized her as the same young woman who
had raced down the steps yesterday in trousers and boots.
Heads turned when Sabella reached the tiny lobby, and when
she stepped outside, a couple of prosperous-looking gentlemen stared openly in frank admiration.

Sabella was pleased.

It wasn't because she wanted to attract the attention of
these particular gentlemen. She didn't. But she was relieved
to see that here—just as in the Arizona Territory—she could
spark swift interest in the most sophisticated men. Her physical attributes, the immediate attraction she held for the opposite sex was extremely gratifying to Sabella.

But it wasn't shallow vanity that made her glad so many men found her appealing.

It was much more.

It was a necessity that she be attractive if her well-thought-out plan were to work.

She *had* to be pretty. She *had* to be alluring. She *had* to be mysterious.

And she *had* to attract Burt Burnett's attention on their very first meeting.

Smiling, Sabella strolled along in the warm California sunshine. More heads turned. Men, young and old, noticed the tall, slender blonde in the pastel pink dress and saucy straw hat. They speculated on who she was, what she was doing in Capistrano. Gentlemen nodded and tipped their hats as Sabella walked leisurely past.

She wondered as she glanced at their faces: Was one of them Burton J. Burnett? Could it be the tall, blond man with the handlebar mustache who was grinning so foolishly at her? Or the short, brown-haired young fellow who was a half a head shorter than she and already developing a paunch beneath his custom-tailored clothes? Or the skinny, lank-haired man with the gaunt, Lincolnesque face, and the funeral-drab frock coat?

Sabella released a soft sigh of relief when finally she had gone past the entire knot of men and was alone on the sidewalk. She felt the wispy hair on the nape of her neck rise and her stomach reflexively turn at the unpleasant prospect of marrying any one of the men she had just passed.

Dear God, she silently prayed, *please don't let Burton Burnett be too repulsive.*

Sabella immediately felt guilty for calling on the Almighty with such a selfish and sinful request when the reason behind her wish was so unforgivably sinister. Hoping the Lord wouldn't strike her dead, Sabella swept through the door of a millinery shop.

It was empty, save for a thin, middle-aged woman placing gloves in a glass-topped case near the back of the store.

The woman looked up as Sabella entered. She smiled and said in warm, friendly tones, "Good morning, Miss. Is there anything special you're looking for?"

"No. Not really. I'll just browse around for a bit, if I may."

"For as long as you like," said the congenial clerk. "Call me if you need help. I'll be back in the storeroom." Smiling, she turned then, ducked through a curtained doorway, and disappeared.

Sabella had been milling about for only a moment when she saw, stopping just outside the millinery shop's front windows, a couple of women. Young women. Neither looked to be more than twenty years old. The well-dressed pair came hurrying inside, talking excitedly.

Sabella swiftly removed her straw bonnet, snatched an absolutely atrocious-looking hat from a nearby pedestal, slammed it on her head, turned to the chattering girls, and asked, "What do you think? Should I buy it?"

The girls looked at her. They looked at each other. Then back at her. And they burst out laughing. Sabella laughed with them, picked up a long-handled hand mirror, and mugged at herself, sticking out her tongue and crossing her eyes before she took the hat off and returned it to the pedestal.

In minutes all three young women were trying on hats— every kind of hat, every cap and bonnet in the store. When they had exhausted the supply, they all fell down in a giggling heap atop the ruby-red loveseat at the center of the small millinery shop. Clutching their stomachs, tears rolling down their cheeks, Janie Desmond and Cynthia Douglas took an immediate liking to Sabella Rios.

The trio left the millinery shop together, walked one block up the street, and went into a ladies' ready-to-wear. They spent the remainder of the morning trying on dresses. None bought anything.

Back out in the warm sunshine, Cynthia Douglas said, "My stars above, it's almost noontime. Mother'll have a walleyed fit if I'm not home by straight up twelve." She grabbed Sabella's hand. "Janie's having lunch at my house. You come along, too."

"You're sure I wouldn't be imposing," demurred Sabella.

"Good grief, no!" assured the green-eyed, auburn-curled Cynthia. "Say you'll come. Please, please. After the meal, we'll go up to my room. Janie and I are going to practice our dancing. Do you dance beautifully, Sabella? I just know you do. Maybe you can show us. What do you say?"

Sabella accepted Cynthia Douglas's invitation. Cynthia's parents were gracious and cordial, and far too well-mannered to quiz her about her background.

But after lunch, when the young women retired to Cynthia's big upstairs bedroom, Sabella came under rapidfire questioning from both the inquisitive Cynthia Douglas and the talkative Janie Desmond.

Nonetheless, Sabella revealed very little. She told them that both her parents were dead and said that she had come to San Juan Capistrano to check on a possible inheritance, but did not elaborate.

"My traveling companion and chaperon, Carmelita Rivera, and I are presently in residence at the Inn of the Swallows," she said. "We'll stay on for an indefinite period of time until we—"

"The Inn of the Swallows?" Cynthia interrupted. "Why, that's a dreadful place. You should have chosen the Mission Inn! It's a splendid hotel; the rooms are gigantic and the best ones face the ocean and . . . and . . ." She caught the look on Sabella's face and immediately began apologizing, "Sabella, how thoughtless of me. I am sorry. The Mission Inn is terribly expensive and if you're staying for several weeks—"

"Exactly," said Sabella.

Cynthia frowned. "If only it were fall instead of spring."

Nodding, Janie hurried to explain Cynthia's meaning. "Both our families—Cyn's and mine—spend the entire summer up in San Francisco every year. Otherwise you could stay with one of us."

"It's very kind of both of you to worry about me." Sabella smiled at the auburn-haired Cynthia Douglas and the brunette Janie Desmond. "But Carmelita and I are actually quite comfortable. The inn isn't so bad."

"The worst thing is we'll hardly have time to get to know you," Cynthia lamented. "We leave bright and early next Monday morning for San Francisco."

"And we won't be back to Capistrano until September," Janie sadly concurred. "By then you'll be gone back to the Arizona Territory."

"That's true," Sabella said, thoughtful. She brightened and said, "But we have until Monday, so let's enjoy ourselves while we can."

"You're right. We'll spend as much time together as possible!" said Cynthia.

"Yes! You'll have dinner at my home tonight. Then tomorrow we'll go on a picnic at the beach and then . . . oh, I almost forgot! Saturday night! Promise you'll go to the big party with us this Saturday," enthused Janie.

"A party?" Sabella said, dark eyes lighting with interest. "I do love parties. Is it some special occasion?"

Janie let out a loud Indian whoop while Cynthia, shaking her head piteously at Sabella, declared, "Special? I guess it is. Only the biggest event in Capistrano history!"

"Oh, my yes!" trilled Janie excitedly. "It's Gena de Temple's long-awaited engagement party! You must come with us, you simply must!"

"But I wasn't invited. I don't even know Miss de Temple."

Cynthia waved a dismissive hand in the air. "Our engraved invitation was addressed to the entire family, which of course includes any houseguests."

"But I'm not a houseguest."

"We won't tell if you won't," Janie said, and Cynthia nodded.

"Well, all right. I'll attend Miss de Temple's engagement party with you," Sabella laughingly replied. "Who is the lucky groom?"

"Only the most eligible bachelor in all Southern California," Cynthia stated emphatically, a dreamy expression coming into her green eyes, a foolish little smile to her lips.

"Really?" Sabella said, amused, and turned to Janie.

"Oh, absolutely!" agreed Janie, pressing folded hands to her breasts as if in prayer and closing her eyes.

Laughing, Sabella asked, "Does this wonderful man have a name?"

In unison the girls sighed, "Burt Burnett."

Chapter Four

The day had been a gratifying one for Sabella. Everything was falling into place sooner than she had hoped.

Back at the inn late that afternoon, Sabella stripped off her straw hat and pink cotton dress. Wearing only her chemise, she climbed atop the bed and folded her long tanned legs beneath her.

She reached under the pillow and withdrew a worn, leather-bound journal. She flipped past the pages filled with large, distinctive handwriting to the journal's back where she had tucked several carefully saved newspaper clippings. Some were long, in-depth articles. Others contained but a few lines. Several of the clippings were brittle and yellowed with age. A few had been only recently pasted in.

One name prominently dominated each and every article in Sabella's leather book.

BURNETT.

Solemnly, Sabella reached for the folded copy of the morning's *San Diego Herald* which Carmelita had left there for her. She unfolded the newspaper and her dark eyes narrowed as she searched anxiously for the name.

BURNETT.

It didn't take long to find it. The Burnett name headed up

an article on the front page of the society section. Bottom
lip caught behind her top teeth, Sabella read:

Wealthy young cattle baron, the handsome Burton J. Burnett, is due
back at his palm-shaded palace after a ten-day stay in Chicago, Illinois.
Burnett, son of the aging patriarch, Raleigh Burnett, traveled to the big
Midwest city to meet with a team of hydrology scientists. The Burnett
family is one of the main underwriters of a hush-hush hydrology research
program currently underway. Burt Burnett arrives back in San Juan
Capistrano just in time for his Saturday engagement party to . . .

Sabella read the entire article. Then read it once more.
She then took a pair of small embroidery scissors, snipped
it neatly from the paper, and placed it in the back of the
leather-bound journal with the other clippings.

She closed the book, lifted it from the bed, folded her
arms around it, and pressed it to her breasts.

Her dark eyes staring into the past, she said softly, "I
will definitely be present at Burt Burnett's engagement party.
Nothing could keep me away. After all, if I'm to be Mr.
Burnett's wife, I really should attend."

Saturday evening.

The fifteenth day of May.

Lights blazed in every window of the two-story de Temple
mansion. A steady stream of carriages rolled up the circular
drive to discharge arriving guests. Music floated out over
meticulously landscaped grounds of neatly trimmed lawns
and rare exotic shrubbery and ornamental waters.

Inside the roomy, opulent de Temple mansion, ladies in
extravagant gowns and gentlemen in custom-cut evening
wear moved down the wide corridor toward the marble-
floored ballroom. There at the arched entrance to the gigantic ballroom stood the hosts, the silver-haired Senator Nelson
de Temple and his lovely daughter, Gena.

Senator de Temple was impeccably groomed and distinguished looking in a dark tuxedo, pleated white shirt, and
white kid gloves. The regal, dark-haired Gena was radiant
in a low-cut, stylish, one-of-a-kind ball gown of rustling gold
taffeta. A dazzling necklace of gold and diamonds glittered
at her pale, bare throat. Matching earrings winked from be-

neath a mass of dark springy curls dressed into an elaborate, upswept hairdo.

The senator and his daughter smiled and warmly welcomed their guests. The callers shook hands with the senator, hugged Gena or kissed her cheek, asked where Burt was, and were waved away with a laugh and directed on into the rapidly filling ballroom.

Inside, Latin waiters dressed in tight black trousers and waist-length, white starched jackets moved unobtrusively among the crowd, carrying round silver trays in white-gloved hands. Atop the trays were fragile-stemmed glasses filled with fine, sparkling champagne.

At the far end of the long rectangular ballroom, a ten-piece orchestra played waltz music for dancing. In a large, spotless kitchen on the far side of the house, a harried French chef and his crew of six labored over culinary masterpieces.

By shortly after nine that evening, all the invited guests had arrived.

And one who hadn't actually been invited.

Sabella Rios stood stiffly under the thousand karats of faceted chandeliers in the magnificent flower-filled, gilt-and-marble ballroom. Awed by a display of wealth and opulence far grander than anything she could have ever imagined, she smiled wanly in an attempt to appear self-possessed and at ease.

She was anything but.

Never in her life had she felt so out of place, so inadequate. The dress she wore was the best one she owned, and until tonight she had thought it elegant and beautiful. Now she realized that the white silk ball gown, lovingly hand-sewn by the goodhearted Carmelita, appeared dismally plain and woefully out of fashion amidst the costly and stylish satins, taffetas, and laces swirling so colorfully all around her. No sparkling diamonds flashed at her throat, no string of pearls or even a modest gold locket. She possessed no jewelry of any kind and had nothing to enhance either her plain dress or bared flesh.

The simplicity of her inexpensive ball gown was not Sabella's only concern. As she watched the elegant dancers spin gracefully about the polished floor, she worried that she would be found out for the imposter she was. She had danced her share in her twenty-five years but never in a great hall such as this. At *fandangos* and carnivals and *Cinco de Mayo* celebrations she had danced madly and merrily in the streets. The music had been lively, loud, and brassy. Here in this grand ballroom, violins played smoothly, sweetly, setting a slow restrained tempo for a dance step with which she was unfamiliar. Sabella's only hope was that no one would ask her to dance.

Pretending to listen as Janie and Cynthia gossiped about this guest or that, she heard nothing they said.

Coolly—she hoped—she searched the sea of faces before her. She looked intently for that one important guest, the man she had come here to find. The man who had no idea she existed. The man who would soon be her husband.

Not Gena de Temple's.

Sabella's gaze returned to the dark-haired woman in the gorgeous gold taffeta ball gown, who had, moments ago, shook her hand and welcomed her warmly. Gena de Temple was now graciously circulating among her guests, a stemmed glass of bubbling champagne in her satin-gloved hand, a radiant smile on her pretty face.

Sabella suddenly experienced a terrific pang of guilt as she looked at the happy, unsuspecting Gena. She hated the thought that she must hurt badly the gracious young woman who had never done her any harm. But it couldn't be helped. Gena would have to go.

Sabella was sorry that she hadn't gotten to Burt Burnett before Gena de Temple had fallen in love with him. Before he had asked Gena to marry him. It would have been so much easier. Then no one would have gotten hurt except those who deserved to suffer.

Sabella gritted her teeth and hardened her heart.

Wondering why the eager fiancé was not at Gena's side, Sabella looked away from the dark-haired woman. Again her eyes moved slowly, questioningly over the well-heeled crowd, searching for Burton J. Burnett.

She hadn't seen him yet, although he must surely be present. The thought occurred that perhaps she *had* seen him. Maybe she was looking directly at him this very minute and just didn't realize it.

All at once there was a disturbance at the big ballroom's arched entrance. A strange hush fell over the filled room. Conversations lowered and died away. A low buzz of twittering excitement seemed to spread quickly through the crowd.

Curious, longing to find out what all the commotion was about, Sabella, whispering "excuse me, please," moved in front of two stocky, diamond-draped women.

A tall, broad-shouldered man stepped into view. He paused directly beneath one of the many-faceted chandeliers. Sabella's dark eyes widened and her lips fell open in astonishment.

She stared helplessly at the compelling latecomer whose well-brushed hair—gleaming in the light from the chandelier above his head—was as midnight black as the smartly tailored tuxedo draping his tall, lean frame. A stiff-collared shirt of fine white cotton contrasted sharply with the darkness of his smooth, suntanned face.

Towering giantlike over all the others, the strikingly handsome man easily eclipsed everyone around him. All were lost in his large shadow. Obscured by the magnetic force of his strong masculine presence. Forgotten in the electric flurry of excitement he so effortlessly aroused.

Without being told, Sabella knew.

This big, darkly handsome man exuding power, wealth, and poise was Burt Burnett.

Late for his own engagement party!

Chapter Five

Burt flashed a quick grin, his twinkling, slate-gray eyes burning into those around him, and all was instantly forgiven.

In apology, Burt bent to kiss the soft pale cheek Gena turned up to him, whispering softly, "Sorry, darlin.' I'll explain later. Forgive me?"

Gena simply nodded, her eyes aglow with adoration and relief. Burt's long arm went around her slender waist and he moved with her through the crowd, smiling that celebrated Burnett smile, shaking hands, greeting old friends, bringing his own special brand of excitement to the occasion.

Now the party could really begin, everyone happily agreed.

But even as he left admirers thoroughly charmed in his wake, Burt Burnett's attention was not really on the obligatory task at hand. He was nearly oblivious to the throngs of glowing guests, many of whom had traveled great distances for this gala event.

Burt was barely aware of Gena clinging to his arm and guiding him through the crush of well-wishers eager to see him, talk to him, touch him. Distractedly, he nodded, continued to smile, and made easy conversation with the guests.

Burt Burnett saw only one guest, had eyes for only one stunningly beautiful young woman. She stood across the crowded ballroom, but Burt saw her. Only her.

An exquisite young goddess with silky blond hair and golden tanned skin and a slender, feminine figure swathed in shimmering white silk. A real heavenly body.

From an incredibly lovely face, the largest, darkest eyes he had ever seen were looking boldly at him. Each time he stole a quick glance at her, those gleaming black eyes were on him, a strange fever-hot light burning brightly in their dark depths.

Burt was drawn to her as though she were sending out a silent signal to him. *Come to me,* she seemed to be saying. *Come closer if you dare.* Desperate to reach her, Burt impatiently shook reaching hands without knowing or caring whose, and anxiously gravitated toward the beautiful blond vision in white.

He became unreasonably irritated as Gena kept tugging on his arm and stopping him for more hellos. His chest tight, his legs weak, he felt as though he were swimming against the tide and in imminent danger of drowning.

"Mrs. Dorsey, so good to see you. . . . Why, Teddy Campbell, you old reprobate, how in the world are you? . . . Miss Eller, you're looking well. How's your mama? Good, good. Thank you so much for coming. . . ." Burt continued the pleasantries, all the while making sure he was heading directly toward the one guest whom he longed to greet.

He was almost to her.

Only a few more steps and he would be facing her, standing so close he could reach out and take her hand in his. His fingers tingled with anticipation at the thought.

Another round of regards offered and accepted, and Burt looked up again. Then did a double take.

She was no longer there.

Sabella knew instinctively from the first moment when he looked up and saw her that she had so thoroughly captured Burt Burnett's attention that he was drawn to her, would come to her. The message was written clearly in his flashing eyes and in the aggressive attitude of his big, sleek body.

The crowd slowed his progress. Which made him all the more eager, edgy. Halfway to her, he began tossing his dark head back and forth, like an impatient thoroughbred at the starting gate.

She knew to stand her ground until the last possible second.

Sabella was totally confident of her effect on Burt Burnett. She was confident, as well, that none of the other guests were aware of the secret drama unfolding before their very eyes. Not even Gena de Temple. No one knew except the two who were the major players. She and Burt Burnett. They might as well have been alone in that crowded ballroom for all the seeming attention he paid the others. She alone knew his heart wasn't in it. It was to her he genuinely wished to speak. It was her hand he wanted to shake. Her eyes he longed to look into.

Chin lifting slightly, breasts rising and falling against the soft fabric of her white silk ball gown, Sabella purposely waited until Burt was only a few steps away. She allowed her dark gaze to clash with his one last time before someone grabbed at him, distracting him for a second.

Sabella seized the time to hurriedly make her exit through the open double doors directly behind her. Cynthia Douglas followed, puzzled and concerned.

"Are you all right, Sabella?" her new friend asked worriedly.

"Actually I feel a little faint," said Sabella, pressing the back of her hand to her brow. "Would you think me terribly rude if I returned to the inn?"

"Certainly not." Cynthia was understanding. "Shall I go with you and—"

"No, no, you stay and enjoy the party."

"You sure? I could easily—"

"I insist. It's nothing, really. I've just been getting too much sun lately."

Cynthia patted her hand. "I'll have our driver bring the carriage around. Old Roberto will take you back to the inn immediately."

"Thanks, so much. If you'll kindly make my apologies to our host and hostess, I won't bother to go back inside."

Burt finally freed himself from a grasping, slightly tipsy guest. He turned and shot an anxious look at the spot where his blond dream girl had been standing. And stood no more.

Feeling almost panicky, Burt searched, his gray gaze roving

restlessly over the crowd like a moving beacon, searching for a sign of the glorious golden hair, the shimmering white dress, the dark, dazzling eyes.

But the beautiful woman was gone.

With Gena still clinging to his arm, Burt reached the two young girls he had seen near the blond beauty. Burt had known Cynthia Douglas and Janie Desmond all their lives. Since both were barely twenty, he thought of them as cute little girls, just children really. He always teased and flirted with them, all in good fun. Like children, they always giggled and blushed and hit at him with their fists, loving every minute of his attention.

Tonight was no exception. He kidded the girls, gave each a big hug and a kiss on the cheek, and assured them he would miss them something awful when they reminded him they'd be leaving early Monday morning to spend the summer in San Francisco. And he attempted, as smoothly as possible, to find out who their new friend was. And where she was.

But an uncharacteristically jealous Gena dragged him away before Burt could learn anything. Even her name. Cynthia was about to tell him, but she never got the chance.

Burt spent the remainder of the long, frustrating party searching for the elusive blonde in the white silk gown. Wondering who she was, where she had come from, Burt knew better than to ask any further questions and risk exposing his unreasonable interest in her.

He continued to quietly, hopefully search for her throughout endless dances, turning about on the polished, white marble floor with a wide variety of partners in his arms. While countless champagne toasts were proposed to Gena and him, each one punctuated with a kiss between them, his gray eyes fitfully drifted over the crowd, searching for her. When a tempting midnight feast was served, Burt held a filled china plate in his hands, but barely touched the food. He was too preoccupied with looking for the mysterious, beautiful woman in white.

He didn't see her again.

But he didn't forget her.

Chapter Six

When the engagement party finally broke up, it was well past three a.m. As soon as the front door was closed behind the last revelers, the tired senator, yawning, said good night to Gena and Burt, and climbed the stairs to his room.

Wishing he could leave, knowing he couldn't, Burt allowed a mellow, happy Gena to draw him into the dimly lit drawing room. They sat on the long, cream brocade sofa before the cold fireplace. Burt put a long arm around Gena's pale bare shoulders.

"So lovely, don't you agree?" Gena said, pressing her dark head to his shoulder.

"Perfect," said Burt in low, level tones and realized guiltily he meant the mysterious woman, not the party.

Hoping Gena hadn't read his thoughts, he put a hand under her chin, tilted her face up to his, and kissed her. When their lips separated, Gena playfully tugged on his black silk tie. It came undone. She finished untying it while Burt sprinkled kisses over her bare shoulders and up the side of her throat. Gena sighed and squirmed happily as his lips spread heat over her sensitive flesh. Her nimble, long-nailed fingers flipped open the tiny buttons going down the center of Burt's white dress shirt.

"I wish," she said dreamily, pushing the open shirt apart and raking her nails down his naked chest, "that we were

already married so we could go upstairs to bed." She leaned
to him, bent her head, and kissed his chest. "What hypocrites
we are, darling," she breathed, then bit him gently. "We've
been intimate for years. Why skip the night we've finally
become officially engaged?" She lifted her head and looked
into his gray eyes.

"Because," said Burt, with a straight face, "there are still
some rules of decorum that must be obeyed."

Gena sighed with frustration. It was true. They couldn't
sleep together in her own house with her father just down
the hall. But, oh, how she wished they could. She wished
with all her heart she could get Burt upstairs tonight and
make love to him until he was totally drained and spent.
She had a nagging premonition that it was dangerous to let
him leave.

Instinctively she felt that she needed to put her stamp on
him tonight of all nights. She could read it in his smokey,
heavy-lidded eyes, could feel it in the coiled tenseness of his
body: a potent sexual hunger. A hunger far wilder, stronger
than any she'd sensed in him for ages.

It frightened her.

She was hesitant to let him go without satisfying that raw
need. She was almost frantic to keep him here with her. She
fought the strong impulse to scrape her long nails down the
bare flesh of his chest until she drew blood. She hated that
she had to let him get away without leaving her scent on him.

"You're right, of course," Gena finally murmured, but she
again bent to his chest, pushed the white shirt aside, and
licked a wet, warm circle around a flat brown nipple. She
felt a responsive little shudder surge through Burt's tensed
body, and was then determined, decorum or no, to satisfy
his animal hunger.

"Damn it, Gena, don't," Burt whispered into her dark
hair.

"Shhhh," she murmured, her lips and tongue playing on
his chest. Her hand touched his knee, slid up the inside of
his lean thigh to his groin. Her breath caught when she felt
the half-hard flesh straining the fine fabric of his tuxedo trousers. She couldn't let him leave like this. She wouldn't.

Gena began to stroke him through his trousers, coaxingly
toying with him, tenderly molding the beautifully growing

erection. Even as she caressed him, felt his male flesh expanding to enormous proportions, she had the nagging suspicion that the throbbing tumescence beneath her possessive fingers had little or nothing to do with her.

The terrible uncertainty escalated when Burt drew her hand away and he again said, "Don't, Gena. Stop now." Smiling, he tried to make light of the situation by teasingly adding, "You want me to go home suffering?"

"No, my love," Gena told him huskily, "I don't. And I won't let you suffer. Not ever."

Her lips went back to his naked chest, while her dexterous fingers unbuttoned the fly of his black trousers.

"Oh, Jesus," moaned Burt as his straining masculinity sprang free.

He put a covering hand on the thrusting flesh, but didn't fight her very convincingly when Gena brushed his hand away.

"Allow me," she said, wrapping soft white fingers around him, feeling her feminine power return as he surged within her gentle grip. She kissed his mouth while she manipulated him with her hand, sliding her stroking fingers up and down the pulsing shaft until she was absolutely certain he wouldn't be able to get up and walk away from her.

It took only seconds until he was powerless. Putty in her hands. Hers to do with as she pleased. Hers to either pleasure or punish. It thrilled her so totally she trembled with excitement. For now, she, only a small, soft, defenseless woman had complete domination over this big, strong, rugged man.

Feeling almost giddy with triumph, Gena tore her lips from Burt's. Her hand never leaving him, she slid off the brocade sofa to the plushly carpeted floor. She turned about in a swirl of rustling gold taffeta and was between his spread legs. She sat back on her heels, smiled wickedly up at him, licked the tip of her forefinger, and ran it over the smooth rocket-shaped head of his impressive erection.

"Know what would feel really good to you, darling?" She put out her tongue and licked her lips wetly.

"Christ, Gena, the servants . . . your father . . ."

"Are asleep. No one is awake but the two of us. And

this," She nodded to the swollen flesh she cupped in her hands. "Shall I put it to sleep?" She laughed sexily.

She bent quickly to him, pressed a kiss to the engorged flesh, then opened her mouth wide, and took him inside.

"Aaaah," Burt groaned involuntarily in surrender, clasped the sides of her head in his hands, and began to lift his hips rhythmically, surging up to meet the wet warmth of her drawing mouth.

Heart hammering, Burt sat there on the brocade sofa in the elegant de Temple drawing room, looking down at the dark, moving head of Gena who, because she loved him so much, was on her knees between his legs, eagerly providing him with lusty carnal pleasure. Burt watched for a long moment, then guiltily closed his eyes against the dark head and imagined a golden head in its place.

The beautiful stranger in the white silk gown was now gloriously naked and kneeling between his spread knees, her unbound blond hair spilling over his bare thighs, and her warm lips tugging sweetly, sensuously on him.

The fantasy was too real, too potent.

Burt shuddered with a deep, wrenching climax, unable to stop himself. Spent, he collapsed against the high-backed sofa, his spine limber, his limbs limp, his eyes tightly shut.

Jubilant in her conquering, the sly, smiling Gena lifted the rustling taffeta hem of her full skirts and wiped her mouth, uncaring that she soiled the expensive designer gown. She rose to her feet as Burt's glazed gray eyes came slowly open.

"Now, darling," she said, looking down at him lovingly, "you may go if you really must."

Swiftly adjusting his trousers, Burt didn't bother with his open shirt. Shakily he rose to his feet, and followed Gena out into the silent corridor where she turned to face him.

"You must be exhausted," she said. He nodded sheepishly. "Are you staying in town at the Mission Inn?"

"No," Burt said, choosing to eschew the convenience of the empty suite at the nearby Mission Inn lest Gena insist on slipping down to join him. Inexplicably anxious to leave, he looked forward to driving the six long miles to *Lindo Vista* in the moonlight. "I'll go on home."

He took her bare arm, drew her close, bent and kissed her, biting for an instant on her full bottom lip with sharp white teeth. "Will you be all right?" He whispered. "I mean you got cheated while I ..." He shrugged wide shoulders.

"No, darling, I didn't. Satisfying you satisfied me."

Burt grinned, kissed her again, turned her about, pointed her toward the grand staircase, and said, "Then go up to bed." He gave her taffeta-covered bottom a harmless little swat with his open hand.

Gena laughed, kicked off her dancing slippers, lifted her long rustling skirts, and started up the marble stairs. But she paused a few steps up, turned to look down at him, and said, "I love you, Burt. I love you, and now that we are engaged, I refuse to share you. You belong to me, darling." She kissed her fingertips, blowing him a kiss. "Never forget that."

"Get to bed, Gena," Burt said, smiling easily.

His smile fled the moment Gena was out of sight. Oddly, her little lovey warning—although she had meant nothing by it—rankled him. He wondered why. She'd said those same teasing words to him a thousand times and it had never bothered him before.

Burt shook his dark head, let himself out the heavy front door, and immediately drew in a long, slow breath of clean night air.

He still didn't bother buttoning his half open white shirt. Instead he took off his dark tuxedo jacket, hooked it on a thumb, and slung it over his shoulder.

He drove himself home, glad to be alone. The matched blacks pulling the open carriage were strong and spirited, so Burt let them have their head. In perfect stride they raced down the deserted coast road, the carriage wheels spinning rapidly, the wind blowing forcefully against the speeding carriage.

Burt lifted his face into the strong cooling winds. His hair blew wildly around his head and into his eyes. He smiled with pleasure. One-handed, he finished unbuttoning his white dress shirt, yanked on it until the long tails came up out of his tuxedo trousers. The wind immediately caught the freed shirt and pushed it back from his bared chest. Burt felt the winds slam against his heated flesh, eddying and swirling the crisp dark hair on his chest. He laughed with delight. Wind tears stung his gray eyes, but he wasn't bothered by them. He could have ridden forever in the cool spring night, letting the wind drive out of his brain the indelible image of a beautiful young woman with blond hair and golden skin and soft feminine curves.

Burt reached the tall, crossbarred gates of *Lindo Vista,* feeling relaxed and calmed by the long, fast ride. He nodded to the night guard, drove through, and turned the carriage over to a sleepy, yawning attendant. Thanking the young boy, Burt went up to the silent, darkened house and slipped in the back door. He was yawning with fatigue as he climbed the stairs to his room. He grinned. After what Gena had done to him on the drawing room sofa, he would have no trouble sleeping.

In his spacious bedroom at the far end of the long hall, Burt didn't bother lighting a lamp. In the shadows he hastily stripped down to the skin and climbed naked into the soft bed which a servant had turned down earlier.

Stretched out on his back, hands folded beneath his head, Burt closed his gray eyes, squirmed about until he found just the right spot on the mattress, sighed, let his muscles relax, and waited for sleep.

But sleep didn't come.

He couldn't get the blond stranger off his mind. Restlessly, he tossed and turned, seeing her beautiful face, those fathomless dark eyes, that golden-hued skin.

"Jesus Christ, what's gotten into me?" he finally muttered aloud.

Sure, she was beautiful, but so what? The world was full of pretty women. What was so special about this one? Nothing. Not a thing. He wouldn't even have noticed her if she hadn't been a stranger. The fact that he didn't know her, had never seen her before, was the reason she had stood out from the crowd.

The only reason.

He laughed at himself then, making fun of his foolishness. Everything was fine. He was engaged to a very pretty, dark-haired woman who loved him. Chances were he would never see the blonde again. He knew everyone in Capistrano. She had to be visiting. In a few days, she'd be gone and that would be that.

Rolling his broad shoulders up off the bed, Burt agilely turned onto his stomach, slid a cocked knee halfway up the

mattress, and wrapped his muscular arms around a couple of fat, fluffy pillows.
Into their downy softness, he murmured, "Sorry, baby, you're too late. I'm afraid I've been spoken for."
His heavy-lidded gray eyes closed and he yawned drowsily. Still, it was a long time before Burt finally fell asleep.

Chapter Seven

Burt rose with the sun. The minute his gray eyes opened on a brand new day, he was wide awake, full of energy, his old easy-going self. He bounded eagerly out of bed, feeling totally rested despite the lack of sleep. He sang at the top of his lungs as he bathed, hummed tonelessly as he shaved, and whistled merrily as he dressed.

In half an hour he was out of his room and descending the grand redwood staircase which angled down from the open upstairs hallway. Sniffing the pleasing aroma of freshly brewed coffee when he reached the wide downstairs corridor, he inhaled deeply and headed toward the back of the house and the big white kitchen.

Adjusting the yellow silk bandanna at his throat, he pushed the swinging kitchen door partially open with the toe of his boot, stuck his dark head inside, and said, "Reckon a starving man could get a biscuit around here?"

The kitchen girls giggled. The short, corpulent woman standing at the cookstove jumped, startled, and her gray head snapped around. She saw the big, tall, black-haired cowboy and her blue eyes immediately twinkled, her stern mouth turned up into a wide smile.

Waving him in with a long-handled wooden spoon, the stout-bodied cook said, "Good Lord, are we glad you're home. Aren't we, girls?" Smiling, the two young helpers nodded, their eyes clinging to the tall man. The cook turned back to her skillet. "I swear, Burton, it's been so quiet around here I nearly went nuts."

"Why, Martha, my only love," Burt said, winking at the girls as he clomped across the spanking-clean kitchen floor, "you've been crazy for as long as I can remember."

Chuckling happily, the rotund cook warned, "You better watch your mouth, boy, or you'll be riding the range on an empty stomach."

Burt stepped up behind Martha, put his hands on her rounded shoulders, and leaned his chin atop her head. "You don't mean that. You'll fix anything I want."

"That's what you think." Martha elbowed him in the ribs. "Get back. Stop your foolishness, I've got work to do." But she beamed, fond of the tall young man who never failed to praise her cooking.

Burt lifted his chin from the cook's gray head and let his arms fall to his sides. Looking over her shoulder at the thick-sliced ham sizzling in the skillet, he said, "Looks good. I'll have a half dozen eggs with it and maybe a couple of—"

"You'll have what I put before you," Martha told him. Then she squealed in outrage when Burt growled like a bear, grabbed her up, and lifted her off the floor. Stretching his strong, muscular arms almost to their full length, he held the shrieking, laughing cook in the air as he calmly recited what he wanted for breakfast. What he had better get.

"You going to give me what I want?" he asked calmly.

"Yes, yes! Put me down, you big fool," Martha scolded.

Burt promptly lowered her to the floor and released her. "That's more like it." He planted a kiss to her flushed, fleshy cheek and said, "And make it snappy. I'm as hungry as a wolf."

"Get out of here!" Martha hit him on the arm with her wooden spoon. But, as he turned and walked away, she called after him, "I heard you come in this morning, Burton"—a gray eyebrow lifted—"it was after four o'clock. Must have been quite a party."

Burt reached the door, and turned back. That familiar grin flashed across his dark face. Filling the doorway, he said, "The guests seemed to enjoy themselves and I . . . I . . ."

His words trailed away. He frowned. Out of the blue he

was struck with the vivid recollection of looking up to see a mysterious blond beauty across the crowded de Temple ballroom. Now he experienced again that curious and electrifying sensation he'd had when he felt the pressure of her fixed dark gaze upon him.

Burt shrugged and shook his head, as if to clear it. He walked away with Martha firing questions at him.

He found his father and Cappy Ricks on the south flagstone patio. Before going out to join them, Burt paused on the threshold. He silently studied his father.

Raleigh Burnett appeared older than his seventy-four years. His profile outlined by the pink light of morning, he looked gaunt, his cheeks sunken, the wide slash of his mouth drooping downward at the corners. His hair, a snowy white, lay against his narrow skull like a downy cap.

His shoulders in the worn gray sweater were stooped and his hands were heavily veined, the knuckles knotted with arthritis. His once massive frame, now shrunken, emaciated from long years of pain and suffering, was that of a frail, feeble old man.

Cappy Ricks was only eight years younger, but his demeanor belied his sixty-six years. He sat erect, walked briskly, and could stay in the saddle all day. The contrast between the two men was monumental.

Burt drew a deep breath and called out to them.

At the welcome sight of his tall son approaching, Raleigh Burnett smiled broadly with delight.

"Well, well," he exclaimed when Burt reached him, "damn if it doesn't give my old eyes pleasure to see you."

"Same here, Dad," Burt said, patting the old man's thin shoulder and nodding to Cappy. He took his place at the table where coffee steamed in a silver urn and cutlery lay in neat array. "How you feeling?"

"Better, now that you're back," said the elder Burnett.

Burt poured himself a cup of strong black coffee and draped a large white napkin across his knees. Silver-domed platters of ham, bacon, sausage, eggs, and hot cakes were soon brought out to the table. He helped himself to large portions of everything.

Full of farcical stories, Burt entertained the two older men with tales of his adventures and misadventures in far-off Chicago. Embroidering slightly to make some of his escapades even more colorful, omitting, of necessity, some of the highly personal exploits, he regaled them throughout breakfast.

Cheered by the comical tales, the elder Burnett's pale face turned crimson and he went into spasms of ribald laughter more than once during the meal. And he listened raptly, his eyes shining, as Burt talked of last night's engagement party.

The time went by too rapidly to suit Raleigh Burnett. Soon Burt was pushing his plate away, patting his full stomach, and reaching inside his black cowhide vest for a cigar.

"Have another cup of coffee, Burton," urged his father. "Stay and enjoy your cigar."

Burt nodded and poured himself more hot black coffee. Knowing how his father longed for company, he leisurely smoked his cigar and drank his coffee. It was Cappy Ricks who finally fished his gold-cased watch out of his vest pocket, looked at Burt, and said, "Burton, if we're going to get that corral ready on time, we'd best get to it."

"He's right, Dad." Burt pushed back his chair, tossed his napkin on the table, and rose. He put a hand on the old man's shoulder. "You gonna be okay out here? Want me to take you inside?"

"No, no, I'm fine, son." Raleigh Burnett affectionately patted the strong brown hand resting on his shoulder. "You two go on." He looked up and smiled. "Good to have you home."

"Good to be home, Dad," Burt replied, and he and Cappy left the old man to his memories and daydreams.

Burt worked hard throughout the day. And as he worked, he joshed and cut up with the ranch hands just like always. He was, as usual, full of mischief and laughter.

But secretly, silently, down deep inside, Burt felt strangely keyed up, anxious almost. He was fidgety and distracted. Late that afternoon, when hours of manual labor hadn't rid him of his restlessness, he decided to take a long relaxing ride. That would do the trick.

He enlisted Cappy to accompany him. The ranch foreman was glad to go along. Shortly after six p.m., the mounted pair set out toward the close coastal ranges. Knee to knee they crossed the wide green valley of rich grazing grounds, heading toward the foothills where a sea of yellow lupines and orange poppies drowned the sloping hills in blazing color.

The warm California sun shone down on their backs and lit the tops of the mountain peaks far out in the distant inland ranges. Down into shaded canyons and up steep rocky hills they rode, and along the grassy banks of the gurgling Coronado creek. Below the broken rock dam at Dreamy Draw, they stopped and watered their horses.

After zigzagging in and out of the rolling hills, they turned back toward home. Topping a rise, they saw in the distance a lone rider astride a big chestnut stallion silhouetted against the setting sun.

Both Burt and Cappy drew rein, exchanged puzzled glances, and looked back at the lone horseman.

Squinting directly into the bloodred rays of the dying sun, Burt watched as the slim rider lifted an arm, swept off a big straw sombrero, and shook out an abundance of long golden-blond hair.

"Jesus, it's her!" Burt exclaimed and kicked his paint stallion into a gallop.

Puzzled, Cappy Ricks followed.

But they were too late. The elusive rider swiftly wheeled the chestnut about, dropped below the horizon, and disappeared.

Burt, then Cappy, reached the spot where the rider had been. With Sam, his paint stallion, dancing nervously beneath him, Burt shaded his eyes and anxiously looked in all directions. No sign of her. It was as though she had never been there.

"Are my old eyes deceiving me, or was that a woman I saw?" Cappy said.

"It was a woman."

"What you reckon she was doing way out here?"

"I don't know," Burt said. His tone was tranquil. But his thoughts were in a turmoil and silently he added, *But I intend to find out.* Wheeling the big paint around, he called, "Let's go home. I'm due at Gena's in an hour."

The next afternoon Burt again went for a ride. This time alone. He anxiously searched for her—for the blond rider in the tight leather trousers who was one and the same with the blond beauty in the white silk ball gown. Mile after mile he rode until his back ached from too many hours in the saddle and his eyes burned from relentlessly sweeping the endless horizon.

Then finally, he caught a fleeting glimpse of her.

But just as yesterday, she vanished before he could reach her. Cursing under his breath, Burt raced the winded Sam over fallen boulders and up a craggy butte to the flat mesa where she had been. He plunged the paint down into a deep, steep-sided canyon in a desperate attempt to find her.

But to no avail.

The mysterious woman was beginning to become an obsession with Burt. He had to find her, meet her. He couldn't rest until he did. He wouldn't stop until his search was successful. Until he caught up with her and learned who she was and what she was after.

No one suspected that anything was bothering Burt.

Except Gena.

Highly intuitive, at least where Burt was concerned, she sensed something was wrong. When he was with her, he seemed distracted, as if his mind was somewhere else. Even when his arms were around her and his lips were on hers, it was as if they were not alone. Someone was with them. Something was coming between them.

Gently, she questioned him. "What is, darling? Have I done something? Are you upset for some reason? What's wrong? Please, tell me."

"Nothing's wrong," Burt smilingly assured her.

"You sure?"

"Positive."

Unconvinced, Gena said anxiously, "Burt, kiss me. Kiss me, darling."

Chapter Eight

It happened when he least expected it.

Exactly one week after he'd first seen her at the engagement party, Burt was alone out on the far eastern reaches of the vast Burnett range. He had been riding all day. At dawn he had filled a canteen, packed a lunch in his saddlebags, and set out. He had ridden more miles in one day than he had ever covered before.

When the sun began to wester and still he hadn't seen her, Burt was ready to concede defeat and head back. He had been behaving like a fool and it was high time he called a halt. This was it—the last excursion. No more searching for her. No more thinking about her.

Burt patted the tired Sam's lathered neck and said, "I'm sorry, boy. I know I've punished you today. How about a nice long drink of water and then we'll go home?"

The stallion blew and snorted as his master turned him about and guided him slowly up a narrow rock path into the foothills of the southernmost tip of the Santa Ana mountains. The reins loose in his hands, Burt carefully maneuvered the big steed along the jutting ledge of a timbered hillock. Rounding the conical slope and urging Sam down the hillside, he found a rushing brook fed constantly by the snow melt from high up in the mountains.

He found more than water.

Wondering if he was seeing things, terrified it was only an illusion, Burt pulled up sharply on Sam's reins and stared at the golden-haired, leather-trousered woman standing on the bank beside the flowing stream.

For a long moment she stood with her back to him, unmoving. Then she heard his approach, slowly turned, and looked directly at him. Her dark flashing eyes holding his, she said nothing. She stood with her booted feet slightly apart, the brown leather of her trousers hugging each long leg like a second skin. Her scarlet butterfly tie was untied and hanging loosely around her neck. The white shirt she wore was undone down to the swell of her breast. Her hair—that glorious golden blond hair—tumbled wildly around her face and down her back.

She was even more beautiful than he had remembered. More tempting in her revealingly tight pants and man's white shirt than she'd been in the shimmering white silk ball gown. She would, he knew instinctively, be even more ravishing if she wore neither. Naked, she would surely be the most exquisite creature on earth.

His pulse racing, his heavy, rapid heartbeat pounding in his ears, Burt dismounted, and hurried toward her, but stopped a few yards away, afraid she would flee. Leave him. Vanish like the lovely dream she was.

When, miraculously she didn't move, made no attempt to escape, Burt flashed her a wide smile, moved slowly closer, and said in low, teasing tones, "This is private property, Miss." His smiling eyes locked with hers. "You're trespassing."

Sabella smiled seductively back at the tall, dark man in the snug-fitting Levis and yoked sky-blue shirt, whose warm gray eyes clearly revealed his attraction to her. "Really? Well just what are you going to do about it? Kill me?" She raised her perfectly arched eyebrows, put her hands on her trousered hips, swayed a step closer to him, and tilted her head back. "Or kiss me?"

Burt didn't hesitate.

His long arm shot out with lightning speed, his lean fingers curled around the belt loop of her tight leather pants, and he pulled her to him.

"I don't kill women," he said as his smiling mouth descended to hers and his long lashes swept down over his gray eyes.

Sabella turned her head at the last possible moment, evading his kiss. His eyes blinked open in surprise and disappointment. The sound of her tinkling, teasing laughter mocked him. Mildly annoyed, Burt didn't allow her to get away with her little prank.

His fingers still hooked around her belt loop, he drew her closer and she was the one to gasp in surprise when he swiftly, forcefully took her chin in his hand, turned her laughing face up to his, and arrogantly predicted, "You're laughing a little too soon, sweetheart."

"Am I?" she challenged, determined to appear totally calm.

But she winced softly when she felt an arm of steel go around her as he drew her closer still. He held her so close, Sabella could feel the length of his tall rock-hard body pressed intimately against hers, from knees to chest. His lips hesitating an inch from her own, he whispered, "Let's see if you laugh *after* the kiss."

Giving her no opportunity to pull away, Burt kissed this mysterious game player. And it wasn't a friendly little peck. He kissed her. Really kissed her. His mouth took total possession and his tongue skillfully parted her lips and slipped between her teeth. He kissed her as though they were lovers, not strangers, brazenly seeking out and tasting all the sweetness of the soft, trembling mouth now opened wide to him.

When finally he ended the long, drugging caress, Sabella wasn't laughing. Shaken more than she wanted to be by his alarmingly intimate and undeniably exciting kiss, Sabella began immediately pushing on Burt's broad chest. He released her.

"Well, what's this?" he said, as if surprised. "You're not laughing." A muscle twitched in his tanned cheek and his gray eyes flashed with mischief.

"Cherish the memory of that kiss," she coolly advised, wiping her mouth on the sleeve of her shirt as though the kiss had been distasteful. "You'll never get another."

"Oh, I don't know about that," Burt said, eyes twinkling.

"Well, I do. I must go." Sabella retreated, pretending a

nonchalance she didn't feel, quietly struggling to regain her equilibrium.

Intrigued, Burt followed. "Stay. I won't hurt you."

"I know that." She continued walking.

"Do you? How can you be sure?"

She glanced over her shoulder at him. "You'll never get the chance."

"Will I get the chance to know you?" She didn't answer, just kept walking. "Who are you?" Burt said, frowning, and stopped.

Sabella paused, too. She turned slowly to face him and suddenly favored him with a full-lipped, teasing smile. "Who do you want me to be?"

"Mine," Burt said, lifting a hand to fiddle with the collar of her shirt.

"Am I supposed to be flattered with that answer?" Sabella tilted her head to one side.

"Many women would be," Burt informed her.

Sabella rolled her eyes heavenward, brushed his hand from her collar, and again marched toward her grazing chestnut stallion.

Laughing, Burt waited a second, then caught up with her in a few long strides, and took hold of her arm. "I saw you at the party last Saturday night."

"I know," she said. "I saw you seeing me."

"Why did you leave? Why did you call me over, then go before I could reach you?"

"I didn't call you over. I didn't even speak to you." She started to take a step forward.

"You asked me with your eyes." Burt stopped her, pulled her back. "No, that's not right, you didn't ask."

"No, I most certainly didn't, I—"

"You insisted. Ordered. Commanded me to come to you."

"I'm afraid you've had too much sun," she said. "Maybe you'd better—"

"Stop it," Burt warned, his gray eyes darkening to a deep smokey hue. "You summoned me at that party. You know it and I know it. The question is why?"

Sabella shrugged, but didn't answer. Burt clasped her shoulders, turned her to fully face him. "All right, sweetheart, you've had your fun. Now tell me, what's this all about? You didn't just happen to ride way out here today. You've been riding every day on this *rancho.* My *rancho.* Why? What do you want from me?"

"What have you got?" Sabella replied teasingly, boldly meeting his narrowed gaze, an enigmatic smile playing on her lips.

"Everything you need. Everything you could ever wish for," Burt informed her, his hands tightening their grip on her upper arms. Warmth again creeping into his gray eyes, he said softly, "Everything. Let me give it to you."

"The sun is setting," Sabella again said, "I must go."

"Not until you've told me your name," Burt said.

Holding her easily in his firm grip, Burt raised a hand, touched her full bottom lip with the tip of his lean forefinger, then let the finger trail down over her chin and come to rest directly in the delicate hollow of her throat. Sabella swallowed convulsively when that suntanned hand, warm and calloused from hard work, casually slid inside her opened collar and flattened on her breastbone.

"Let me go," she demanded.

"Tell me your name and I will."

"Sabella," she said, her breath short, her heart beating erratically. "Sabella Rios. Now release me."

"Sabella," Burt softly repeated the name, a wide smile on his handsome face. He withdrew his hand from the opened collar of her blouse, but immediately captured her slender fingers, drew them up to his chest. Pressing her small spread hand directly over his heart, he said her name again. "Sabella. Sabella, you already know who I am, don't you?"

"Yes, of course."

"Say it for me," he coaxed and Sabella could feel the heavy cadence of his heartbeat against her open palm. "Say my name. Call me Burt."

"Burt," she said, her lips parting, as she purposely pitched her voice low, making the tone softly sweet. "Burt, I really must go. And so must you." Her dark eyes slowly lowered from his, focusing on his wide, sculpted mouth. "After all, you are an engaged man."

"When? When will I see you again?" he asked, as if she hadn't spoken the last sentence.

"Tomorrow." Her eyes lifted to meet his.

Burt shook his dark head. "I can't wait that long."
"Tonight then." Sabella pulled her hand free, turned away, put a booted foot in the stirrup, and felt his strong hands immediately encircle her waist to lift her into the saddle. Settling herself astride the big chestnut, she smiled down at Burt and said, "Midnight. The old mission in the village."

Chapter Nine

Sabella laughed and kicked the chestnut into motion the minute the words were out of her mouth. Burt had to step back quickly to get out of her way. She dug her booted heels into the stallion's flanks again and shot up the gentle, wooded slope of the hill, knowing the tall, dark man she was leaving behind was watching her every move.

Since he was, she put on a show solely for his benefit. She urged the powerful chestnut steed into a froglike leap onto a narrow jutting ledge of rock suspended from the wooded hillside. Once the horse's hooves had gained tentative purchase on the slippery shelf of sandstone, she reined him about in a tight semicircle and held him in place.

Seventy-five feet below, at the rippling stream where she had just left him, Burt Burnett stood nailed in his tracks. His booted feet apart, hands balled into tight fists at his sides, he stood looking up at Sabella, an anxious expression on his handsome face.

"Jesus, sweetheart," he shouted, "be careful!"

Sabella called down, "Don't worry about me, Burnett."

And knowing that he would worry and that she had the well-trained chestnut positioned exactly in the right spot, she yanked up firmly on the reins, making the startled stallion whinny and rear onto his hind legs. With the chestnut's front hooves pawing at the air, Sabella kissed her hand and waved to Burt.

"Nooooo! Sabella!" Burt roared, an edge of panic in his booming baritone. "God Almighty, stop it!"

When she saw him break and start running up the hill toward her, Sabella brought the chestnut back down on all fours, turned him, and quickly traversed the narrow ledge around the hill. She reached the other side and started down into the valley with the sound of Burt shouting her name echoing in her ears.

That pleased her.

Sabella was laughing when she reached the valley floor and put the responsive beast into a full, all-out gallop. She had clearly won the first round with the unsuspecting Burton J. Burnett. But she would have little time to savor the small triumph.

The second round was coming up at midnight.

Sabella's laughter quickly died away. Her night-dark eyes lost their brilliant, flashing light. A shiver skipped her spine at the vivid recollection of Burt Burnett's hot, aggressive kiss. And it wasn't a shiver of revulsion.

No use denying it, the man was not exactly repulsive. He was, in fact, strikingly handsome. He was awesomely tall— he had to be at least six-foot-two or three. His broad shoulders and massive chest were of hard, beautifully sculpted contours tapering perfectly into an incredibly trim waist. His hips were slim, but his lean buttocks and long muscular legs had that same fashioned-from-granite appearance as his deep chest and clefted back.

Self-deception had never been one of Sabella Rios's faults. She wouldn't deceive herself now. Burt Burnett was a good-looking man of impressive stature with an arrestingly handsome face. His physical attributes were many. Rich, raven-black hair, worn a shade too long, curled appealingly over his starched blue shirt collar. A smooth olive complexion was further darkened by the constant California sunshine. Heavily lashed gray eyes could change dramatically from pale silver to smokey charcoal. A straight, well-shaped nose gave him a proud, noble appearance. And a full sensuous mouth knew all too well how to make a woman respond to his fiery kiss.

Burt Burnett was not only undeniably handsome, he was a compelling, magnetic man who possessed generous helpings of charm, wit, and a passion for living.

Sabella's delicate jaw hardened and her cold eyes grew colder still.

That great zest for living which Burt Burnett and his monied friends shared wasn't too remarkable considering the manner in which they lived. It was quite easy, she imagined, for the wealthy, landed gentry to find their existence endlessly exciting when everything there was to be had on this earth was theirs. Who wouldn't be gay and charming and happy with a life of such splendid ease?

Her brows now knitted together in a deep frown, Sabella thought of the woman so dear to her whose zest for life and youthful good looks had faded much too soon. How well she remembered the constantly tired, sad-eyed woman who scrubbed endless floors and cooked countless meals and ironed mountains of clothes.

The floors she had scrubbed, the meals she had cooked, the clothes she had ironed were for someone else's family, not her own. The thin, uncomplaining woman labored in other people's homes for the few coins she could earn to care for her crippled, despondent husband and totally dependent child.

The once pretty woman grew old before her time. Her pale flawless skin wrinkled too quickly from the harsh Arizona sun. Her dark, glossy hair lost its lustre and turned prematurely gray. Her lithe body lost its supple softness and she became thin and brittle looking as if her very lifeblood had dried up, leaving her withered and old and beaten.

And finally dead. As dead as her lost dreams.

She too could have stayed young, healthy, and beautiful had she been allowed to lead the kind of life Burt Burnett and his friends casually took for granted.

The kind of life *she* should have had.

The kind of life that was in fact her birthright.

Sabella blinked away the tears that were starting to sting her eyes. She squared her shoulders and reaffirmed her resolve. She couldn't change the past. But she *could* fix the future.

And she would.

*   *   *

Burt's evening with Gena was agonizingly long.

While she spoke excitedly of the flurry of activity surrounding their upcoming December wedding, her fidgety fiancé kept casting covert glances at the ornate French clock atop the marble mantel. Anxiously he counted the minutes until he would again be with the mysterious blond beauty who hadn't been out of his thoughts since the minute he had looked up to see her standing across the de Temple ballroom.

"Well . . . ?" said Gena, looking at him as if she were waiting for an answer. "Will you?"

Burt had no idea what she'd asked. "I'm sorry, dear. What was that?"

Gena sighed and shook her head. "Really, Burt, sometimes I think you don't pay one bit of attention to anything I say."

"Ah, now that's not true. Come on." Burt gave her his best Sunday smile and gently tugged on a dark springy curl lying on her pale left cheek. "Give me another chance. Just repeat the last—"

"I said, 'Do you think I look best in beige or pale lavender?' You know, for my traveling suit . . . the suit I'll be wearing to the depot spur after the wedding to begin our honeymoon trip."

"Yes," Burt said, smiling, nodding. "By all means."

Gena's green eyes flashed with annoyance and she clicked her tongue against the roof of her mouth. "That's no answer. You're *not* listening!"

Caught, Burt said, "I'm sorry, truly I am. I'm just awfully tired. I had a long, tough day at the ranch." He rubbed an eye, and added, "In fact . . . would you think me unforgivably rude if I said good night and left a little early?"

"For heaven sake, it's only a few minutes past eleven." Gena was incensed. "It's not like you to be so tired. Especially on Saturday night."

Burt grinned and pointed an accusing finger at her. "You weren't listening. I repeat, I had a really hard day."

"I *was* too listening!" Gena exclaimed. Then finally she smiled. "All right, all right. Go on home. And take it easy tomorrow."

"Yes," Burt was quick to agree. "I will. What I need is an entire day of rest."

"Be here at seven tomorrow evening," Gena reminded him, toying with his tie. "The dinner party for Judge Fite, remember? Some of Father's dearest friends will be here. Tom and Vivian Gentry, the Roberts, Don Miguel Andres Amaro—"

"I'll be here," Burt interrupted, springing to his feet, forgetting that he was supposed to be tired.

When they said good night at the door, Gena's arms went up around Burt's neck. She said, "Sleep well, my love. And dream of me."

Burt grinned. "Who else?"

Gena smiled as she watched him cross the stone terrace, skip down the steps, and hop into his carriage.

As soon as the carriage rolled away, Gena's smile became a frown. Her tone unpleasant, she immediately summoned a servant. "Julio! Julio, where are you? Get in here this minute!"

The aging little Mexican came at once. "*Sí, Señorita* Gena. You need something before I go to bed?"

"Yes." Hands on her hips, green eyes narrowed, she ordered, "Get me Cisco and Santo!" Julio's gray eyebrows rose in puzzlement and he stared speechlessly at his mistress. "Well, what are you waiting for?" she snapped.

Backing away, Julio raised his open palms, shrugged his stooped shoulders, and said, "*Señorita* Gena, is Saturday night. They are not here. Probably in town, no?"

Gena exploded with anger, causing the old servant to cringe. "Well, go get them! I want Cisco and Santo! Here! Now!"

Burt raced into the village.

He drove straight to the Mission Inn, rolled to a stop before the sprawling cliffside hotel, whose architectural design was a strange but eye-pleasing mixture of Spanish Gothic and Italian Renaissance. Burt bounded out of the carriage. Quickly, he withdrew a couple of coins from his pocket and handed them to a waiting attendant. When asked, he told the boy no, he wouldn't be needing the carriage again tonight.

The boy looked puzzled when, instead of going into the

inn, Burt turned and hurried away. Smiling, Burt rushed eagerly toward the Mission San Juan Capistrano a short block away. A spring to his step, he optimistically considered the possibility that later tonight when he retired to that giant mahogany bed in the suite maintained by the Burnett family at the Mission Inn, he might not be in it alone.

A golden-skinned beauty with pale blond hair might well be there with him.

Burt reached the old mission. It stood silent and placid in the moonlight, a magical place of great beauty and peace. Burt made his way through the fragrant flower-filled gardens and around the fountain-fed ponds. He passed the tumbledown ruins of the old stone church, destroyed in an earthquake long before he was born. He skirted the boundaries of the Indian cemetery where the slaves who built the mission now rested. He stopped before the gleaming white chapel.

Burt swung open the heavy, carved door and ducked in out of the moonlight. Inside the magnificent structure, the oldest mission in all of California, Burt waited impatiently for the bewitching beauty he prayed would show up.

Minutes dragged by.

Burt paced nervously, his hands in his pockets, his teeth grinding together so forcefully his jaws ached. She would come, he told himself. She would come, but she'd make him wait until the last possible minute. She'd know he had arrived early and she'd torture him by staying away until the stroke of midnight.

Or later.

Burt stopped pacing. He took off his tailored, navy linen suit jacket and tossed it over a wooden pew. He loosened his wine silk tie, unbuttoned his shirt collar. He shoved his hands back down into his pants pockets and rattled the loose coins he carried.

He began pacing again, jingling the silver coins.

He took his hands out of his pockets and began snapping his fingers. He prowled restlessly, snapping his fingers and telling himself she would come. She'd be there any minute.

Quickly tiring of the finger snapping, he switched to popping his knuckles. He paced and popped, popped and paced. Muttering to himself, he pulled forcefully on each long finger in turn until the knuckle loudly popped. Then he started over again.

At last came the sound of someone approaching—soft footfalls, the rustle of long skirts.

Burt's arms instantly fell to his sides and he released a long, deep sigh. Then smiling broadly, he moved across the shadowy chamber to the very front of the building. There he stood, completely still, concealed in deep shadow, waiting beside the door, his back against the mission's rough interior wall.

The bell in the tower was chiming the witching hour when Sabella pushed open the mission's heavy wooden door. She stepped into the darkness and quietly closed the door behind her. She advanced a few feet, then paused to stand unmoving for a long moment in a pool of moonlight.

Her blond hair was unbound and flowing down her back, held off her face with a blue satin ribbon. Her dress was a cool summer frock of sky-blue organza, its bodice tight over her full, high breasts, the ruffled, low-cut neckline falling appealingly down around bare, golden shoulders.

Sabella felt Burt's presence, although she couldn't see him. She had no idea if he were in front of her or behind, but she knew he was here, knew he was looking at her. She could feel those glittering gray eyes resting on her, assessing her, undressing her.

She smiled and her own eyes closed in victory as a pair of strong, suntanned hands came out of the darkness from behind and lean fingers gently clasped her bare shoulders. She was drawn slowly back until she was pressed flush against the hardness of a tall male frame. Strong, muscular arms went possessively around her waist, and an almost imperceptible movement of his powerful right shoulder urged her head to drop backward against its firm support.

A deep, masculine voice said softly just above her ear, "I was afraid you wouldn't come."

Chapter Ten

Her musical laughter filled the silent sanctuary as Sabella slowly turned in Burt's embrace. She tipped her head back and lifted her hands to the broad expanse of his chest.

"You're a liar, Burt Burnett," she softly accused, gazing directly into his flashing silver eyes, "and here in this holy chapel, of all places."

"Am I?" he said, his gaze locked with hers, his hands spanning her narrow waist.

"Yes. You knew very well that I would come." She smiled engagingly at him and softly added, "Just as I knew you would be here waiting."

Burt smiled, too.

"Kiss me," he whispered, his lips lowering to hers until they were almost—but not quite—touching. Again he said, "Kiss me. Kiss me, Sabella Rios."

Burt kissed Sabella with a surprisingly slow, sweet tenderness that left her half stunned and speechless. When the devastatingly gentle, caring kiss ended, his lips, warm and smooth, stayed on hers. His breath became hers as he murmured into her mouth, "You're very beautiful. You look like an angel who belongs here in this hallowed place. Are you, Sabella? Are you an angel?"

"I'm no angel," she warned, her lips brushing his. "Far, far from it."

"Thank God," he said.

And he kissed her again.

In the darkened old chapel, Burt stood with his back against the thick adobe wall, his feet apart. His hands cupping Sabella's hips, he drew her to him, and pressing her soft, slender curves to his tall, solid frame, he kissed her through several breaths.

Minutes passed as they kissed hotly until finally Sabella tore her mouth from his.

"Please," she whispered breathlessly, her lips against Burt's tanned throat, "you must stop. Don't kiss me anymore. If you do, I shall surely faint."

"Just one more," Burt murmured against her sweetly scented silken hair. "One more little kiss. Then I'll stop."

He didn't wait for permission. He placed both hands in her hair, tangling the long luxuriant locks around his fingers and urging her head back. He looked at her gleaming lips for a long moment before he bent his head and kissed her.

Knowing this was to be the last she would give him tonight, Burt wanted a special kiss—a long, passionate kiss he could savor through the sleepless hours that surely awaited him.

He began the kiss slowly, lightly, barely pressing his closed lips to the left corner of Sabella's mouth. Then he rained a shower of soft, brief little kisses back and forth over her parted lips until her lips were sweetly and spontaneously responding: clinging, plucking, attempting to fully capture his.

Burt teased her.

He drew her soft bottom lip into his mouth and gently sucked it. Then the top one. He tormented her further by nibbling on her lips in a prolonged prelude to the coming kiss. Throughout the deliberate dallying, he whispered to her that all he ever wanted to do, now and for always, was to kiss her.

Flustered, her entire body tingling, Sabella warned herself about the dangers of standing in the darkness with this handsome, hedonistic man. The way he looked at her. The inflection of his voice. The flash of his smile. Hard to resist. The mastery of his heated lips. The mystery in his smokey eyes. Impossible not to feel their effects.

Burt ran his tongue along the seam of Sabella's lips and

over her teeth. Sabella shivered. At the same time, she reminded herself that she hated Burt Burnett's arrogance in
assuming she would hold still for this conscious dawdling,
this intentional trifling with her lips as though she belonged
to him.

But more than his arrogance she hated the scary, hot-cold
sensations that surged through her as his mouth toyed and
played with hers.

His smoldering gray eyes slowly closing, Burt wrapped
lean fingers around the delicate nape of Sabella's neck beneath the heavy blond hair. His other hand touched her
waist, moved to the gentle flare of her hip, stayed for a
second, then slid down and around the curve of her buttocks.

Sabella struggled in silent protest to the unauthorized lib-
erty. But not for long. Burt's lips stopped their teasing and
claimed hers in a hot, commanding kiss. His tongue thrust
brazenly into her open mouth, touched her tongue, and
stroked it sensuously. Sabella felt her knees buckle. She
would have fallen if not for the fact that Burt held her fast
in his powerful arms.

While his lips and tongue did magical things to the sensitive insides of her mouth, Sabella became aware that her
breasts had swelled and were flattened against the hard muscles of Burt's chest. Even more alarming, his spread hand
was firmly cupping her bottom and he was pressing her pelvis
to meet the slow, rhythmic thrusting of his own.

Horrified, Sabella nonetheless allowed this new intimacy
to continue for another moment. She had no choice. She had
to make Burt Burnett desire her so that he would want to
see her again. Would *have* to see her again.

So she remained pliant and receptive in his arms until she
was satisfied he was on fire for her. Then she pushed anxiously on Burt's chest and struggled to free herself from his
suffocating embrace. Burt's lips reluctantly released hers.
Breathing hard, his chest heaving, he let his head fall back
against the wall and closed his eyes.

"Burt, I have to go," Sabella whispered, laying her head
on his chest. Against her cheek she felt the rapid, heavy
beating of his heart and was half frightened at the depth of
the passion she had stirred in him. "I must leave."

"Baby, no," Burt groaned. "Don't go. You just got here."

"My chaperon . . . she'll be worried."

"No, she won't," he argued. "She's sound asleep. She'll never know. Stay with me, sweetheart." His arms tightened around her.

"I can't." Sabella lifted her head, looking up at him. His eyes were closed as though he were in pain, his head turned to one side, a muscle throbbing in his jaw. "I will meet you tomorrow," she whispered comfortingly.

Burt's eyes opened. His strong arms and clasping hands still pressing her to the granite hardness of his tall, tense body, he said, fighting for breath, "There's a . . . place a half . . . mile south of the village. It's called The Point."

"I know where it is. Is it safe for us to meet there?"

Burt swallowed hard, lifting his head. "At dawn it is."

"I'll be there," she promised.

"You better be," he said, then finally an infectious grin crinkled the corners of his sultry gray eyes.

"Where will we go?" Sabella asked, squirming to be free of his encircling arms.

"I know the perfect spot," he said. She nodded and he added, "Will you kiss me good morning the way you just kissed me good night?"

"Better," she promised.

Burt hugged her to him one last time, then released her. He stayed where he was as she danced out of reach, yanked open the heavy carved door, and hurried outside, leaving him dazed, confused, and aroused.

And totally enchanted.

Sabella hurried through the large, moon-dappled church-yard. Half afraid Burt would catch up and start kissing her again, and half afraid she would let him, she didn't dare slow her pace until she had left the mission, the manicured grounds, and the amorous Burt Burnett behind.

Only then did she begin to relax. Soon she began to smile. Satisfied with the evening's success, she strolled leisurely back toward the Inn of the Swallows.

The little village was quiet at this late hour, the streets nearly deserted. All was still and peaceful, a warm beautiful spring night in coastal Southern California.

The scent of the sea was carried on the rising night breezes and below the cliffs, the dark waters of an endless ocean glinted silver in the bright moonlight. The faint sound of hauntingly romantic guitar music drifted from a walled courtyard of a nearby dwelling. Blooming bougainvillea covered the home's high adobe walls and sweetened the sea-scented air.

Farther down Camino Capistrano, the village's main thoroughfare, a loud shout of male laughter suddenly shattered the nighttime stillness. The loud laughter came from the Balboa Saloon two blocks away. As Sabella drew nearer to the bar's swinging batwing doors, she heard the clink of glasses, the rattle of poker chips, the low drone of men's voices, and the shrill laughter of a woman.

She was less than half a block from the tavern when a tall, spare man stepped through the swinging doors and out onto the wooden sidewalk. He struck a match with his thumb, lifted it to a thin brown cigar between his teeth, and the tiny orange flame lighted his face.

Sabella stopped short.

An unsmiling, sinister-looking man dressed entirely in black, he was Latin with a gaunt, sunken-cheeked face, cold black eyes, a drooping black mustache, and a whiplash scar on his right jaw. The newly lit cigar dangling from his lips, the Mexican lifted a booted foot up to the hitching rail and pulled a dark trouser leg up a few inches.

A black leather scabbard was strapped to his hairy calf. The Mexican flicked a knife out of the leg scabbard. The long blade glinted menacingly in the moonlight. Smoke drifting up into his narrowed black eyes, the Mexican lowered his foot to the wooden sidewalk and began casually cleaning his fingernails with the knife blade's tip.

Making a face, Sabella automatically began backing away. The Inn of the Swallows was located on the other side of the saloon. She shook her head, backtracked, and ducked in between two buildings, choosing to walk down the dark, narrow alley rather than risk an unpleasant encounter with the man standing before the Balboa Saloon with a long-bladed knife in his hand.

She hurried through the alley, circled around behind the inn, went quickly inside, and climbed the back stairs. She slipped silently into the second-floor suite. Careful not to awaken Carmelita Rivera sleeping soundly in the adjoining room, Sabella undressed in the darkness.

Naked, she pulled a batiste nightgown over her head, raised her arms and let the gown's soft fabric whisper down over her tall, slender body and fall to her knees.

The Mexican already forgotten, she got into bed and lay awake for the better part of an hour, painstakingly reviewing the tension-charged events of the past week.

So far, all had gone pretty much as expected.

Only one week after his seeing her for the first time, Burt Burnett desired her, had slipped away early from his fiancée to meet her. Already he was edging dangerously close to falling into the trap she had cautiously set for him.

Plotting her strategy with the deliberation of a battlefield commander, Sabella lay in bed and pondered her next crucial moves. She would, she knew, be walking a tightrope for the next few days and weeks. It was absolutely necessary that she exercise sound judgment in handling Burt Burnett.

If she played her hand very carefully and very wisely, within a month Burton Burnett would come to the decision that the only honorable thing to do would be to break his engagement to Gena de Temple.

Sabella sighed and stretched in the darkness like a great cat. She was pleased with the timetable she had laid out well in advance of coming to California. She had figured on it taking two months from the day she arrived in San Juan Capistrano until Burt Burnett realized he couldn't live without her. And that was *before* she had known he was engaged to another.

She had now been in Capistrano three weeks. Unless she missed her guess, it wouldn't take more than another full week, perhaps two, before he was falling in love with her. Sabella's dark eyes flashed.

Soon he would propose.

She wouldn't accept his proposal of marriage right away. She'd let him worry and wonder for a while. But not for long. The small sum of money that had taken her years to save would last only a few months. She had to become his wife before her meager funds ran out. Besides, waiting was dangerous. The risk too great that she would be found out.

By summer's end she would exchange the holy vows of matrimony with Mr. Burton J. Burnett and then ... then ... Sabella's dark eyes narrowed with cold, cunning purpose. Then all her carefully laid plans for the greedy, thieving, powerful Burnett family would become reality!

Shivering involuntarily with a mixture of dread and excitement at what she would have to go through before it was finished, Sabella solemnly vowed—as she had at least a thousand times in the past—to make the Burnett men pay for their sins.

Both Burnett men.

What better payment could be extracted from the old man than for him to lose his idolized only son. And to her of all people!

The same could be said for the old man's arrogant son. What more fitting retribution than to take *his* only son from him!

The son—their son, hers and Burton Burnett's—who would be the next and only heir to *Lindo Vista.*

Chapter Eleven

Sabella wasn't the only one who had plans.

Burt had a few of his own. But his had nothing to do with long-term commitment or marriage. At least not marriage to Sabella Rios.

He stayed on at the mission after Sabella had gone.

He had to. He had no choice.

What she had done to him in the seductive darkness had left him with a temporary physical condition which made it embarrassingly *hard* to follow her.

So Burt stood there where she'd left him, sagging against the mission wall, waiting for his hot, heavy blood to cool. And for his rapid heartbeat to quit slamming forcefully against his ribs. And most importantly for the throbbing erection straining the tight confines of his navy linen trousers to go away.

Teeth gritted, a vein pulsing in his high forehead, Burt stood there in that house of God, feeling like the very devil. All because of a woman.

A woman he knew absolutely nothing about. A mysterious blond beauty who could make him weak in the knees just by touching him or saying his name. He had no idea who she was, where she had come from, or what she wanted from him.

But he knew what he wanted from her. And the sooner

he got it, the sooner he would get her out of his system and put an end to this risky business. His only interest in the beautiful, enigmatic Sabella Rios was physical. He wanted her. He was hot for her. Fever hot. Burning up with desire. He had a hunch it was pretty much the same with her.

She had come to Capistrano with her *duenna*, saw him at the engagement party, their eyes had met and held. He was instantly attracted. She was instantly attracted. Now she was sneaking out at night, risking getting caught, solely to see him. Her purpose in coming, he felt certain, was not for the stimulation of his clever conversation. They hadn't said a dozen words to each other.

Unless he missed his guess, she was after the same thing he was after. A few stolen hours of forbidden passion. A couple of rollicking rolls in the old hay with a hot-blooded stranger who had as much, if not more, to lose as she did should they be found out. Since that was the case, surely he would be successful in seducing her—or was it vise versa? within the next few days. Or nights. He would make love to her until they'd both had their fill and then that would be that. Nobody the wiser. Everybody happy. It's been great fun. No hard feelings. Bye, bye, baby. *Adios, querida.*

The blond temptress would move on to her next adventure and he would marry Gena de Temple and be a devoted, faithful, content husband.

Burt finally pushed away from the wall and exited the chapel. Whistling a mellow love song, he walked through the silent churchyard in the moonlight. He momentarily considered walking down to the Balboa Saloon for a nightcap, but decided against it.

Instead he went directly to the nearby Mission Inn. There in the Spanish wing of the grand hotel, on the very top floor, the Burnett family maintained a suite. A lavish suite kept always at the ready. The suite was a necessary convenience. Like his father before him, Burt stayed at the inn when he didn't feel like making the six-mile trek home to the ranch.

Burt walked unhurriedly through the hotel's well-tended grounds where Spanish garrison cannons, their huge steel barrels gleaming in the moonlight, stood harmless and quiet beneath the towering oaks. Lemon and orange trees, in full bloom, lined wide stone walkways leading up to the imposing inn on the cliffs.

Burt reached the inn's front entrance, climbed the stone steps, and went inside.

When he walked into the spacious, high-ceilinged lobby, he glanced at the open doorway of the hotel's little chapel. Inside the tiny chamber diffused moonlight spilled through a half dozen Tiffany stained-glass windows, softly illuminating a massive, seventeenth-century gold-leaf altar brought from Mexico.

Burt moved quickly through the deserted lobby where clustered leather chairs and long comfortable sofas were empty, and a Steinway grand piano sat silent. He stepped up to the marble-topped counter, behind which stood a dignified desk clerk.

"Sorry to bother you at this hour, George," Burt said to the uniformed employee.

"No trouble at all, Mr. Burnett," said George Wilde, smiling pleasantly. "Always glad to be of service, sir." He reached for the key to the Burnett suite, and handed it across to Burt. "Anything else I can do for you?"

Burt nodded. "Have a fresh saddled mount waiting for me in back of the inn at five a.m. tomorrow." He grinned and amended, "Make that this morning."

"It's as good as done," said the efficient George Wilde.

Upstairs, in the roomy suite's master bedroom, Burt threw open the heavy gold-velvet curtains, then raised the row of tall windows fronting the ocean. Night breezes immediately stirred the heavy curtains and ruffled the turned-down silken covers on the massive mahogany bed.

The big bed sat squarely in the center of the room. Moved there at Burt's instructions, the bed gave its privileged occupant—or occupants—an unobstructed view of the endless Pacific ocean, silvered now in the spring moonlight.

Burt inhaled deeply, stripped to the skin, and crawled into bed. Disappointed that he hadn't managed to get the beautiful Sabella Rios into this big bed with him, he sleepily promised himself she would be here soon.

Naked and hot and his.

She was, he mused, sleeping right now on a narrow iron

cot in a drab little room at Inn of the Swallows. Such a shame, when she could be here in this big soft bed with him. Burt smiled and closed his eyes.

Lulled by the night sounds and the cool sea breezes stroking his long, lean body, he fell asleep.

Down the street, in her second-floor room at the Inn of the Swallows, Sabella was also asleep.

While she slept, a lone man dressed all in black still stood below on the wooden sidewalk outside the Balboa Saloon. He held the knife in his hand, its blade flashing in the day-bright California moonlight.

A thin brown cigar clamped firmly between his white teeth, he ran his thumb lovingly along the razor-sharp blade as though he were caressing a cherished lover. As he idly toyed with the knife, a young, pretty Mexican woman with thick dark hair and large brown eyes pushed open the swinging batwing doors, walked up behind the man, and eagerly wrapped her plump, bare arms around him.

"Coming back inside, *querido?*" she murmured.

"Por supuesto," said the Mexican and flicked his cigar away into the street. "Of course." But he didn't move. He didn't bother turning to look at her.

The woman kept pestering him. She pressed her ample bosom against his slender back and hugged him tightly. She wedged a leg between his, and tormentingly rubbed her dimpled knee up and down the inside of his thigh. She squealed with surprised delight when the silent, black-clad man grabbed her by her colorful cotton skirts and yanked her around in front of him.

In the blink of an eye the woman found herself facing him, pinned up against the hitching rail with his knee between her legs and the long blade of his knife pressed against her bare throat. Half frightened, half excited, she looked into his cold black eyes when he asked, "What is your name, *querida?* I forget."

Clinging to his black shirtfront with plump, red-nailed fingers, the tipsy woman said, "Is Ramona! Don't you remember how you make your Ramona moana!" She laughed. He didn't. She said, "What is wrong? Are you angry with your Ramona?"

The thin lips beneath the sleek black mustache finally turned up into a wicked smile and the whiplash scar on his right cheek pulled tight.

"Angry?" he said flatly. "You will know it when I am angry."

"Then come back inside," she said, relieved. "We drink and play, have good time."

The knife's blade pressed slightly against the woman's bare brown throat and the man's bony knee lifted higher between her parted legs. "You want to play, *querida?*" Anxiously, she nodded. "We will play. We will play here," he said, sliding the tip of the knife blade slowly back and forth across her throat and rubbing his knee hard against her groin through the gathers of her skirt.

He ordered, "Moan for me. Let me hear my Ramona moana."

"Stop," warned the woman, her eyes round, her big breasts rising and falling rapidly against his black shirtfront. "*Por favor!* No. No! Ohhhhh. Ahhhhh," she moaned with a mixture of fear and sexual arousal.

The cold-eyed Latin took the blade from her throat. He smiled sadistically when he saw the pinpoint of bright red blood appear on her fleshy brown throat. He watched, entranced, as the tiny scarlet droplet slowly grew into a dark wine blossom. He dipped his finger into the blood, smeared it on his bottom lip until it was gleaming wet. Then his tongue darted out and licked the blood away with such relish it might have been rich sweet cream he was tasting.

Watching him, the woman frowned, but sighed happily when he put the knife away and wrapped his ropey arms around her. Bending her backward over the hitching rail, he kissed her throat, his lips plucking forcefully at the minuscule knife prick. He was sucking greedily when a gig rolled up to a dusty stop directly before the saloon.

A graying, aged Mexican climbed down out of the gig, hurried up onto the wooden sidewalk, and grabbed at the shirtsleeve of the black-clad man.

"Cisco! Cisco!" Julio Valdez shouted.

Cisco slowly raised his head, saw who was calling his name, scowled, and bent back to woman's bare throat. His thin lips closing over a portion of brown satin flesh, he made slurping sounds as he sucked.

"*Por favor*, Cisco," said a worried Julio Valdez, "you must come—"

"Get away from me, old man." Cisco's head snapped up. His black eyes slitted, he said, "Whatever it is can wait. I am busy." The woman in his arms giggled.

"No, Cisco, wait," Julio rushed his words. "You must listen. *Señorita* Gena, she send me and say to—"

"Gena?" Cisco's head again came up as he instantly lost interest in the woman. "Gena needs me?"

"*Sí Sí.* She say to me, 'Julio, get Cisco and Santo!' And I say 'Now?' And she say, 'Now. Tonight. I want them here!' " Bobbing his gray head up and down rapidly for emphasis, Julio added, "I have been looking for you and I did not know where—"

"I was right here all evening, you old fool," said Cisco, irritably, releasing the stunned woman so quickly she was off balance.

Stumbling, she frantically grabbed at him, throwing her arms around his neck again. "Don't leave me, Cisco," Ramona begged. "We go to my place. You can keep your knife out and ... make your Ramona moana all night long!"

"Shut up, bitch!" said Cisco, working to peel her clinging arms away from his neck.

"*Sí, sí.* All right. I will not say a word." Ramona stubbornly clung. "I do anything for you—"

"How long ago?" Cisco asked Julio. He managed to unhand himself from Ramona, and shoved her so forcefully, she fell to her knees. Arms outstretched to him, she sobbed and pleaded. Annoyed, Cisco cruelly kicked her, the toe of his black boot catching her under the chin and knocking her over backward.

Horrified, old Julio quickly bent down to her. "Ramona, you hurt? *Dios!* Are you okay?"

Without even glancing back, Cisco stepped down off the sidewalk and hurried to the gig.

"Wait, Cisco!" Julio called, on his knees beside the weeping Ramona. "What are you doing? Take your own horse! I will drive Ramona home and then—"

"You know Gena can't stand the smell of horses," Cisco

shouted, unwrapping the long reins and releasing the brake.
"You ride my gelding back to the ranch."
"But what about Ramona . . . aren't you going to . . . to . . ."
Cisco never heard him.

His mind was not on Ramona. It was on the rich, refined
woman for whom he worked. The pretty, green-eyed woman
who had sent for him late on a Saturday night.

Anxious to reach home and her, Cisco took up the long
black buggy whip and repeatedly lashed the back of the
blowing steed pulling the gig. Within minutes he was leaping
down and tossing the reins to a sleepy attendant in back of
the de Temple mansion.

He hurried toward the terraced yard, smoothing down his
slick black hair with both hands, and licking his thin lips to
be sure there was no blood left on them. He opened the
black wrought-iron gates and went into the courtyard. As he
circled through the big hedge-bordered yard, he began
sniffing at himself to make certain he didn't carry on his
person the offensive scent of horses. He checked as well for
any telltale sign of Ramona's cheap perfume.

Satisfied he was presentable, Cisco tiptoed across the stone
patio, silently climbed the outside staircase to the mansion's
second-floor balcony, and moved toward the lighted suite he
knew belonged to Gena de Temple.

He knocked softly at the door and waited.

Moments passed before the frowning, sleepy woman who
was Gena's personal maid opened the door. Petra Gabriel
said to the tall, spare man standing before her, "You know
better than to come here again knocking on these doors! Get
on down to your 'dobe and sleep it off! You are drunk."

"Ah, Petra, my pet, I love you, too," said Cisco sarcastically.

"Don't get smart with me, you skinny, reptile-eyed *bas-
tardo*! Go on! Get away from here before I—"

"It's all right, Petra," Gena's cultured voice came from
behind Petra. "I asked Cisco to come here this evening."

The indignant Petra continued to block his way. She turned
and said, "It is not evening. It is almost two o'clock in the
morning and he is not coming in this house if I have to—"

"Go back to bed, Petra," Gena calmly ordered.

Muttering to herself in rapid Spanish, the incensed maid

stalked out of the peach-and-white salon, slamming her bedroom door behind her.

"Come in, Cisco," Gena said cordially. "Close the door behind you."

She stood before a white marble fireplace with her arms crossed over her breasts. She wore a long, loose dressing robe of pale peach satin trimmed in cream Belgian lace. Her hair was unbound and brushed down around her shoulders, a thick wedge falling provocatively over her left eye.

With only one eye Gena could see the naked hunger in Cisco's. Poor Cisco. He wanted her. He always had. Burt frequently warned her about Cisco, said he was a dangerous man, that he couldn't be trusted. But she was not afraid of him. He would not harm her. He would do anything she asked of him.

Gena had to turn away quickly so that Cisco wouldn't see how amusing she found him. Her back to him, she said, "Where's Santo?"

"I do not know," Cisco lied. "Whatever it is, you do not need Santo. I will handle it for you."

Gena turned back around and smiled at him. "Yes, of course, you will. Sit down, Cisco."

He dusted off the seat of his black trousers, rubbed his palms on his thighs, and took a seat on the peach brocade sofa facing the cold marble fireplace. Gena moved gracefully forward and sat down close beside him.

"I need a favor, Cisco."

"Tell me, Gena. Whatever it is, whatever you want, I will do it for you."

She smiled and crossed her shapely legs. Her satin robe fell open to reveal the matching nightgown beneath. The lace bodice was very low over Gena's full breasts and the gown's biased cut fit tightly at her waist and across her hips. She leaned back comfortably and placed a hand in her lap.

Cisco's narrowed black eyes watched her slender fingers toy idly with the slippery satin fabric covering her thighs.

"It's Burt," Gena said as the slippery satin of her gown eased up a trifle so that her shapely ankles and small delicate feet in their high-heeled satin bed slippers were exposed. "Something is wrong with Burt."

"What has this to do with me?" Cisco's dark, gaunt face tightened with displeasure at the mention of Burt's name.

His deep dislike of the Burnetts was no secret. He had been born on *Lindo Vista* back in '45. When he was ten years old, he, his younger brother, Santo, and his parents had been banished from the *rancho* simply because they were Mexicans.

Cisco began to stroke the white whiplash scar on his cheek. "Cisco, can I trust you?" She touched his knee. Cisco tensed and swallowed hard. Before he could answer, Gena said, "I want you to trail Burt." Her hand lifted to her hair and she twined a long dark curl around her finger. "I want to know where he is and what he's doing every hour of the day and night. Will you do it?"

Reluctantly lifting his slitted black gaze from a small beauty mark in the shadowed valley between her full pale breasts, Cisco said, "If that is what you wish. But I do not understand." He lifted black-shirted shoulders, lowered them. "I was under the impression that Burnett is most always with you."

"Do you see him here now?" Gena swept a hand about in an encompassing gesture. "He left me hours ago. Said he was tired. I don't believe him." She wet her lips with the pink tip of her tongue. "Do you?"

"I will find out."

"Good, good. I knew I could count on you."

Gena rose, signaling that the meeting had come to an end, it was time for him to leave. Cisco got up and moved toward the door. Gena followed, the long, parted robe flowing out behind her. When he reached the door and opened it, she touched his back lightly. He turned to look at her.

"Tell me something, Cisco," she said, the expression on her face somber, "and don't lie to me."

"I never lie to you, Gena."

She swayed a hairsbreadth closer to the tall, mustachioed Mexican in black, allowing her unfettered breasts to press lightly against his corded ribs.

"Do you suppose ... could it be that"—she bit her lip, lowered her lashes, then slowly raised them—"I am no longer desirable?"

"You are the most desirable woman alive," said the dazzled Mexican.

"Why, thank you, Cisco," said Gena, smiling again, urging him out the door. "Whatever would I do without you?"

Chapter Twelve

Burt Burnett stood on the rocky summit of The Point in the cool Sunday morning dawn. Thick swirling mists rolled in off the dark ocean, kissing his smoothly shaven face. Gusts of wind tousled his carefully brushed black hair and pressed the fabric of his blue chambray shirt against the muscles of his chest.

He stood facing the sea with his hands in the back pockets of faded Levi's, his gray eyes squinted against the stinging wind. The toes of his scuffed black-leather cowboy boots were mere inches from the cliff's jagged edge; it was a hundred foot sheer drop to the strip of sandy beach below.

The fog was so thick Burt couldn't make out the shoreline beneath him, but he knew the morning tide was coming in. He could hear the loud breakers crashing far out offshore, then rolling in to pound the beach and splash foam at the base of cliffs.

The Point could be a dangerous place on a morning such as this. One misstep in the murky morning light, one careless movement on the slippery rocks and it was all over.

A sudden chill skipped up Burt's spine as if someone had walked across his grave. The unsettling thought flashed through his mind that this familiar place was unsafe for him on this cool, gray morning.

The danger, however, had nothing to do with falling to his

death from the bluffs. The danger was falling for a mysterious blond woman about whom he knew absolutely nothing.

"Burt? Burt, are you there?"

The warm, pleasing voice came to him from out of the swirling mist and any misgivings about his own safety vanished.

Burt turned and anxiously warned, "Sabella, stop right where you are! Don't take another step. I'll come down to you."

Sabella didn't obey. As agile and unafraid as he, she moved quickly toward the sound of his voice. In seconds she stepped out of the fog and into his sight. Burt, scrambling down to meet her, stopped short, and stared.

The heavens parted and she was perfectly framed in a narrow shaft of sunlight piercing the dense gray fog. While dark rolling mists spiraled about, enveloping everything else, she was gloriously illuminated. Her loose blond hair, gilded by the sun, blew around her beautiful face, and the skirts of her pink summer dress billowed out from her slender body like a colorful bell. Captured as she was by that lance of light, she appeared to be otherworldly, like an angel flying too close to the ground.

Burt's heart stopped beating for a second, then started again, pounding fiercely in his chest.

He smiled with frank admiration of her beauty.

Sabella looked at the tall, dark man above, his handsome face registering guileless delight.

She returned his smile. "Aren't you proud of me?" she called. "I successfully made it to the top before sunrise."

Burt reached her. Grinning, he stood facing her in the shaft of streaming light. He lifted a hand to her face. With his little finger, he pushed back a strand of shimmering blond hair that had blown across her smiling mouth.

"You call yourself successful," he said, staring at her lips, "when you haven't even kissed me yet?"

Laughing, Sabella placed her hands on his shirtfront, stood on tiptoe, and pressed a quick, glancing kiss to his mouth. Then she said, "May I ask you something?"

His flashing gray gaze touched her hair, her face, her body. His eager hands touched her cheeks, her shoulders, her waist.

"You may ask me anything," he assured her, gently drawing her closer.

"Do you always smile?" She tilted her head to one side. "Are you never unhappy?"

Continuing to smile, Burt shrugged wide shoulders. He said, "I don't have time to be miserable unless it's absolutely necessary." His smile broadened as he added, "Long ago I pledged all my energies to living life as well as I can."

Sabella nodded. "Ah, yes, a man after my own heart."

Burt slid his arms around her, locking his wrists behind her waist. "I thought as much. What do you say we dedicate ourselves to enjoying this morning to the fullest?" He lifted an inquisitive dark eyebrow.

Sabella's hands slid slowly up over his chest. "And why not? Isn't that what we're both here for?"

Burt happily shook his head. "You bet it is."

And he meant it.

He reasoned that one more quick fling wouldn't hurt anything. Or anybody. Especially since this beautiful woman apparently viewed this budding sexual relationship exactly the same way he did. As a pleasurable, enjoyable game. An amusement. A diversion of no lasting significance.

His kind of woman!

Burt bent and kissed Sabella's mist-moistened lips. And he kept on kissing her until the kisses became long, deep, arousing caresses. The pair were still kissing there on the rocky pinnacle of The Point when the misty fog lifted and the sunrise turned the deep waters of the Pacific ocean from a cold, dead steel to a hot, molten gold.

When the sun grew warm on his back, Burt tore his lips from Sabella's, grabbed her hand, and drew her along with him down the rocky path. When he reached the tethered mount below, he untied the roan and looped the reins over the creature's neck. He climbed on the roan's back, smiling down at Sabella.

Her cheeks were flushed pink and it wasn't from the sun. Her lips were bee-stung, swollen from his kisses. Her large, dark eyes flashed with an appealing mixture of promise and challenge.

Half in jest, half not, he said, "I shouldn't take you with me. I should just leave you here."

"You definitely should," she said, then added saucily, "but you won't."

"You're mighty sure of yourself, Miss Rios."

"No," she said, her heavily lashed lids lowering flirtatiously over dark, gleaming eyes. "I'm mighty sure of you, Mr. Burnett."

Burt loved it. He threw back his dark head and laughed. Then he reached down and grasped Sabella beneath her arms, lifted her, and placed her in the saddle before him.

"What am I going to do with you?" he said.

"You could start by kissing me again."

The passion in his kiss took Sabella's breath away. Withholding from this determined, sexually experienced man the only thing he wanted from her would not be easy.

But she would do it.

Today and every day until she became his wife.

That Sunday sunrise began a whirlwind week for the passionate, impatient Burt. As the mission bells rang and the villagers gathered for worship services, Burt whisked Sabella down to the beach and into a secluded cove. While above in the old chapel the padre admonished his flock to "yield not to temptation," Burt was down below doing his dead level best to persuade Sabella to "yield to temptation."

She didn't.

But she did lie in his arms on a spread blanket in the dim cool interior of the concealed cove. Just yards from the crashing surf, they spent the warm spring morning there together, laughing, kissing, sighing, touching, and teasing.

At noon Sabella abruptly pulled from Burt's embrace and sat up, leaving him blinking in confusion and dazed with passion. She rose to her knees, sank back on her heels, and announced, "I can stay no longer." She smiled apologetically and stood up.

Burt's hand shot out, moving quickly under her long skirts. His lean fingers encircled her left ankle.

"Yes, you can."

He lay stretched out on his back, his black hair disheveled, his blue chambray shirt half open down his dark chest. His hand moved aggressively up over Sabella's shapely calf as he warned, "I won't let you go. Not yet." His thumb made coaxing little circles on the ticklish back of her knee. "Stay awhile. Please."

Sabella adamantly shook her head. "All we ever do is kiss and hug," she complained, crossing her arms over her chest. "If I stay, can we talk for a change?"

"Why, sure, sweetheart. Absolutely!"

Burt's fingers tightened around the back of her leg and he urged her slowly back down to kneel beside him. He rolled up into a sitting position facing her. His hands lifting to span her waist, he drew her forward and buried his face in the softness of her pink-covered bosom. His breath hot, it penetrated the fabric of her dress, scorching her flesh.

She shivered.

Her hands going to the thick raven hair at the sides of his head, Sabella warned, "You promised. You said if I'd stay, we would talk."

"We'll talk, honey," Burt murmured, pressing an open-mouthed kiss to the swell of her breast through the thin fabric of her clothing. "We'll talk about making love."

"Oh, you!" She forcefully shoved him away, shot to her feet, and fled.

By week's end, Burt knew he was pretty much a goner.

The beautiful, elusive Sabella Rios was in his blood and under his skin. She drove him half crazy. He was helplessly attracted. He was endlessly fascinated. He was constantly tortured by his growing hunger to possess her.

Unfulfilled and unsatisfied desire fueled the striving and the passion. He let his work go at the ranch and spent the lengthening spring days with Sabella. He made outlandish excuses to Gena in order to spend the warm starlit nights with Sabella.

The fever in his blood grew steadily hotter and he took the object of his fierce desire to secret, romantic places in an all-out attempt to sweep her off her feet and out of her clothes.

Sabella would not be swayed.

She was not blinded by passion or by love. While she couldn't deny that his skillful, drugging kisses made her pulse race erratically and elevated her body temperature, her heart remained chilled through and through, her mind alert and of a single purpose.

Beneath the magnetic charm and masculine beauty of the man, Sabella saw Burt Burnett for what he really was. A cunning swindler. A heartless thief. The despised enemy.

"Let me," Burt murmured, his lips hot against her throat, "let me, baby."

"No, Burt. No," Sabella found herself repeating those oft-used words again. If she had said no once in the last few days, she had said it a thousand times.

It was Sunday. Again. A full week had passed since that misty dawn at The Point.

They stood now embracing on the brow of a green, velvety-topped mesa at sunset. They were miles from the nearest house, had ridden hours to reach this place.

Burt was barechested. His discarded shirt lay on the ground at their feet. Sabella's white blouse was open down the front, the long tails outside her tight leather trousers. She wore nothing—no chemise, no camisole, nothing—beneath the open shirt.

So she was saying no and frantically trying to rebutton the blouse that Burt had so skillfully unbuttoned. While she was attempting to button the blouse, he was attempting to push it apart. Sabella managed to get a couple of buttons buttoned as his heated lips moved over her face.

Kissing her cheeks, her eyelids, he whispered coaxingly, "Ah, Sabella, just take your shirt off, that's all." He kissed her top lip, bit it gently. "Nothing else. Just your shirt."

Before she could reply, his mouth took hers in a spine-melting kiss that was instantly so hot and overwhelmingly sexual it loosened raw emotions in them both. Within seconds they were too weak to stand. They sank slowly to their knees, their mouths fused, their hearts pounding. Caught up in the lingering kiss, Sabella temporarily forgot the buttons of her blouse.

Burt didn't forget for a second.

Sabella wound her weak arms around Burt's neck and clung to him. Her tongue plunged boldly into his mouth, pleasing him, thrilling him. She felt him shudder against her and her own body involuntarily shuddered in return.

Since first they met they had kissed dozens—hundreds—

of times. But this kiss was different somehow from all of others. The reasons were many. For one thing, they had never been together this far from civilization before. In this beautiful, desolate spot in the remote foothills of the Chocolate Mountains, it was as if no one had ever been here before, as though they were the only two people alive. A safe, rugged place of primitive beauty, it did things to the senses.

Sabella knelt there on that velvet-topped mesa in the dying sun, with her dark eyes closed, sighing, wondering at the indescribable pleasure of the prolonged kiss, the tingling joy, the incredible warmth enveloping her.

Slowly it began to dawn.

It wasn't just the splendor of this private wilderness paradise or the heat of Burt's lips that were responsible for the feverish flow of blood through her veins. It was more. All at once she became vitally aware that the blouse she had struggled so hard to button was once again completely open and pushed back away from her body.

Her bared breasts were touching Burt's naked chest. Her nipples had turned into twin points of fire, stinging with hot burning pain. The only hope of extinguishing the fierce flame was to press closer to that hard-muscled male flesh. The only soothing balm for such sweet agony was to bury the aching points of pure sensation more deeply in the dense growth of crisp black hair covering his broad torso.

Instinctively, Sabella arched her back, pressed her swelling breasts intimately closer to the hot haven of Burt's muscular chest.

He sighed with pleasure.

While he feasted on the honeyed mouth opened sweetly to his, Burt slid a hand up Sabella's back, underneath the open shirt, and drew her closer still. Blood pounded in his ears and he groaned with ecstasy at the feel of her diamond-hard nipples gouging into his chest. He was sure it was only a matter of minutes before his eager lips were at her breasts, kissing their soft creamy fullness, sucking on the tight sensitive nipples.

He was equally sure they were all alone here on this distant mesa, that they could do anything they pleased right out in the open and no one would see. The prospect was tremendously exciting—making love to this fiery beauty atop this isolated tableland with the old Sun God their only witness.

Their lips separated at last and, breathing hard, Burt sank back on his heels, bringing Sabella with him, cradling her against his chest.

"Ah, yes, baby," he murmured huskily, "yes."

Chapter Thirteen

"Burt ... ooooh, Burt," Sabella whispered dreamily. Burt's arms tightened around her. He held his breath, waited, every muscle in his long, lean body tensed and straining. Her flushed cheek was against his bare, heaving chest. She turned her face inward, kissed his madly beating heart, and said breathlessly, "No. No, we ... can't."

She scrambled out of his arms and out of his reach with a swiftness that surprised him and left him grasping at thin air. Her back to him, she sat on her heels and quickly buttoned the blouse.

A long silence.

"Jesus Christ!" Burt finally exploded and fell over flat on his back, his hands first clasping his throbbing temples, then clenching into tight fists at his sides. His stomach muscles were pulled so tautly, his faded Levi's fell away from his belly, exposing his navel.

He wanted her badly. Never had he wanted a woman so much. She loosed in him a raw emotion hidden even from himself, and in his deep frustration, he was tempted to grab her, tear the clothes from her body, and take her whether she wanted it or not.

Burt was jolted back to reality when, as if she had read his darkest thoughts, Sabella said softly, her back still to him, "Go ahead if you're determined." She finally turned to look at him. Her large dark eyes were those of a frightened child. "You're bigger, stronger than I. I couldn't stop you."

Burt's jaw was tightly clenched and his half-closed eyes were a wintry gray. His fists flexed and unflexed. At last he exhaled heavily.

"I don't rape women, Miss Rios," he said coolly. He lifted his arms, folded them beneath his head. "Not even tempting, tormenting golden-haired witches who delight in pushing me past the edge of my endurance."

"You think that's what I'm doing?" Sabella crawled closer, sat down, and laid a soft hand on his ridged belly. Burt winced involuntarily.

"No, I don't think that," he muttered, a muscle working furiously in his jaw, "I *know* that."

Sabella's expression became one of wounded innocence. Her fingertips traced the thick line of jet black hair going down the center of Burt's flat stomach.

"Now why would I do such a cruel heartless thing?"

Burt closed his eyes against the dying sun's harsh glare and against the wily seductress toying so mercilessly with him. "You tell me, sweetheart," he said curtly. "Maybe just because you're a woman." His eyes opened, he looked up at her. "Back in the days of the Roman Empire, a wise man named Juvenal wrote, and I quote, 'Cruelty is natural to women; they torment their husbands, whip the housekeeper, and enjoy having slaves flogged almost to death.' Unquote."

Sabella remained silent for a long uneasy moment, wondering if he suspected the truth about her; knew what she was really up to. But she felt the tensed muscles beneath her hand slacken and saw the corners of Burt's full lips start to turn up in the beginnings of that easy, familiar smile.

Quick as a wink she rose to her knees, threw a leg over his supine body, climbed astride him, and sat down atop him. She looked at him, smiled, and said, "Since I have neither husband, housekeeper, or slave, that leaves only you for me to torture."

Burt finally laughed. "At least you're honest."

Sabella made no reply. She leaned down, started to kiss him, but Burt stopped her. "No, baby, don't. Not now. I've had enough torture for one afternoon."

"Then talk to me," she coaxed, "and *not* about making

love. Tell me all about you. About your family, your ranch, the land."

"Honey, I can't think with you straddling me," Burt said candidly. "You want anything out of me other than groans of agony, you'll have to get up." He winked at her, grinned impishly, and added, "So you won't get me up."

"Burt Burnett!" she scolded him for his crudity, but promptly moved. Seated crossed-legged beside him, Sabella again gently prodded him to talk, to tell her something about himself.

Burt just smiled lazily, rolled up into a sitting position, draped his long arms over his knees, and said, "Ladies first. You came to Capistrano to investigate an old inheritance. That's all I know about you. Fill me in. Tell me about your home in Arizona. About your family. Your life there. Tell me which side of the bed you sleep on. How you like your eggs in the morning. Where you got that pale blond hair and those dark eyes." He paused, turned his head, rested his chin on his bare upper arm. "How many lovers you've driven mad. Tell me everything."

Laughing now, Sabella carefully revealed only as much as she wanted him to know. She pulled up a blade of grass, twisted it between thumb and forefinger and blew on it before she spoke.

"I was born and raised in the Arizona Territory," she began. "My parents are both dead."

"Honey, I'm sorry," Burt said sympathetically. "That's really tough."

Sabella continued as if he hadn't spoken. "My father, a Spaniard named Tito Rios, worked on a small cattle ranch owned by Victor and Carmelita Rivera. Carmelita is the dear friend and chaperon who is with me in Capistrano."

"I see," said Burt, his narrowed gray gaze resting on Sabella's beautiful face.

"Teresa, my mother, was orphaned when she was a child and placed in a convent. When she turned eighteen, she came to live at the Rivera ranch. She met my father, they fell in love, got married, and I was born within a year. My pale hair came from my blond, blue-eyed father. My dark eyes and olive skin from my mother. I sleep in the middle of my bed. I don't eat eggs." Smiling, she tickled his bare arm with the blade of grass. "Long ago I lost count of how many lovers I've driven mad."

Burt grinned. "You have lots of younger brothers and sisters?"

"No. No, I don't. I'm an only child."

"Ah, ha! That's it. That's why you're so spoiled," accused Burt, lifting his chin from his arm, his gray eyes twinkling.

"Me?" She made a face. "What about you? I don't have to ask if you are an only child."

"You don't?"

"No. It's evident you are. So arrogant, so demanding, so persuasive. Tell me, do you always get your way?"

Burt chuckled good-naturedly. "I did until you came along." He placed a hand on her knee, fiddling with the inside seam of her leather trousers. "Go on, tell me about—"

"There's really not much more to tell," Sabella said. "I have Carmelita—she's widowed now—and she's family to me." Sabella shrugged her slender shoulders. "As I've told you, we came here to check on a possible inheritance and . . ."

"Anything I can do to help? Dad's an attorney. Of course, he hasn't practiced in years, but—"

"No, thanks all the same." She pushed her hair from her eyes. "Enough about me. Let's talk about you. Have you always lived here in Southern California?"

"Born right here on *Lindo Vista*," Burt said, nodding, and his forefinger started sliding slowly up her inside trouser seam. Sabella swiftly caught his hand, held it in both of her own. "Except for the four years I was away at the university," he went on, "I've been right here at the *rancho*."

"You say right here. Do you mean that this mesa where we are now—way out here—is all part of the *rancho*?"

"Yes, indeedy."

"But we're miles from . . ." She looked all around. "Your ranch must be very large."

"Thirty-three square leagues." He withdrew his hand from hers.

"Thirty-three square leagues?" Her well-arched eyebrows lifted.

"146,000 acres," he said, smiling. "*Poco mas o menos*. A little more or less."

"That's enormous."

"One of last coastal tracts of its size between the Oregon border and Baja, California," stated Burt proudly. "Back in its heyday *Lindo Vista* supported ten thousand head of cattle and half as many horses."

Sabella mused aloud, "It must have been difficult drawing an accurate *diseno* for such a huge tract."

"So you know about the old maps of Spanish California?"

"A little," said Sabella, noncommittal. "Were your ancestors Spanish?"

"No."

"I thought most of the acreage in Southern California was deeded to Spanish families through land grants from the throne of Spain."

"That's true. You're absolutely right. Most of *Lindo Vista*—twenty-two square leagues—was originally owned by an aristocratic Spanish family."

"Oh, really?" Sabella commented, purposely keeping her tone casual. "What was their name? Do you recall?"

"Sure. Carrillo," Burt was forthcoming. "The land was granted to Don Pascal Antonio Carrillo many years ago and he in turn passed it on to his descendants. We bought the *rancho* from Carrillo's heirs and paid off the outstanding taxes back in '48—just after the war. The same year Dad married my mother."

Burt didn't notice the narrowing of Sabella's dark eyes as he spoke, was unaware that her teeth were firmly clenched, her jaw set.

"As soon as they married, Dad brought his new bride to *Lindo Vista* to live in the *rancho*'s hacienda. The house dates back to 1830; the elder Carrillo built it. I was born there a year after the wedding. We still live there."

Sabella sounded calm, but silently seethed when, already knowing the answer, she asked sweetly, "So the old ranch house is still livable?"

"Honey, it's a mansion. Built to last forever. A large, handsome old house filled with the finest of furnishings."

Burt continued to tell her things, to talk openly, as if he had nothing whatever to hide. He told her about the terrible droughts of the sixties when many of the California cattle ranchers lost everything. Said it was during that period that

they bought additional acreage at rock-bottom prices, adding
to the vast empire that was *Lindo Vista.*

As he spoke of the ranch, a look of pride came into his
gray eyes. It was obvious he loved the land, that his roots
were deep, that he meant to live out the rest of his days on
Lindo Vista.

"*Lindo Vista* boasts every kind of terrain under the sun,"
he mused thoughtfully. "The western boundary is several
miles of rugged, untouched coastline. Then south down to
the banks of the Santa Margarita River. North up to Trabuto
canyon. And east across the wide rolling valley, up into the
Coastal Ranges and the Santa Anas, and down into flat, hot
deserts beyond."

The look of pride and satisfaction on his handsome face
as he spoke of the ranch both angered and sickened Sabella.
He was so smug, so totally comfortable in his envied role as
the rich young lord of *Lindo Vista.*

She supposed she should be grateful. It was this supreme
arrogance which made her plan possible. Burton J. Burnett
was accustomed to taking anything he wanted as though it
were his due. He was used to having beautiful women throw
themselves at him. He supposed that she was just another of
the multitude hoping for a few magical nights in his arms.

How wrong he was.

Constantly coddled and catered to, he had likely never had
a bad day in his entire life. Well he would have several before she was through with him!

Carefully maintaining an air of nonchalance, Sabella gently
prodded Burt to tell her more, to talk about his parents.

He told her that his father was an old man, seventy-four,
and very frail and sickly. Said he really knew very little about
his mother, that she had left them when he was just a boy.

"Your mother left you?" Sabella was honestly taken
aback. She had never read anything about a Mrs. Raleigh
Burnett in the newspapers, but she had assumed that the
woman was dead.

"My mother was more than twenty years younger than
Dad," Burt said in low, level tones. "When they met she was
barely twenty, he was forty-two." With the setting sun turning his smooth brown shoulders the color of brick, Burt
stared unblinking toward the west, and said, "Mother was a

young, beautiful San Francisco aristocrat. She had the reddest hair, the greenest eyes, and the whitest skin you've ever seen. Naturally, Dad worshipped her. Couldn't rest until she agreed to marry him."

"Did it take him long to persuade her?"

"Not long. They married a few weeks after meeting. He brought her down to *Lindo Vista* and he gave her anything she wanted; did everything he could think of to make her happy."

Burt reached for his discarded shirt, took a cigar and a tiny box of matches from the breast pocket. He stuck the cheroot in his mouth, bit down on it with sharp white teeth. Before he could light it, Sabella took the matches, struck one, and held the tiny flame to the tip of his cigar.

Looking directly into his gray eyes, she said, "But she wasn't happy?"

Burt puffed the smoke to life as she shook out the match. "Apparently not. The summer I was six years old, Mother— Dana was her name and it fit her perfectly—went to San Francisco for a month-long holiday. Dad and I stayed behind at the ranch. While there, she met a handsome Mexican grandee at a Nob Hill soiree." Burt puffed on the cigar, leaned back on a stiffened arm. "It must have been love at first sight. She divorced Dad immediately, married the Mexican, and went with him to his home in Mexico City."

"No!"

"Yep. Broke Dad's heart. He was never quite the same after that." Burt chuckled suddenly and shook his dark head. "He banished anyone with a Mexican or Spanish surname from *Lindo Vista*. Old *compadres* who had worked for him for years. Whole families that lived in adobes on the ranch; children who were born there. Dozens of *vaqueros*, the best horsemen in the Southwest. The entire staff of the house. The cooks, the maids, the housekeeper. Everybody."

"That seems a bit unjust," Sabella said. Not that she was surprised to hear that the old man would do such a hurtful thing. She knew exactly how unjust both father and son could be.

"It was. Sure, it was," said Burt. "Unfair. Illogical. Foolish. Sometimes when people are badly hurt they do senseless things. Who knows how we might behave in similar circumstances." Sabella remained silent. "And, I suppose, the same could be said for Mother. People thought she acted unfairly. But maybe she couldn't help herself."

"Maybe," agreed Sabella. Then, thinking aloud. "But how could a mother leave her six-year-old son?"

"For love, I guess." Burt shrugged bare shoulders. "Didn't the poet say, 'It is impossible to love and be wise.' "

Nodding, Sabella replied, "The poet also said, 'Pleasure of love lasts but a moment/Pain of love lasts a lifetime.' "

"I'll try and keep that in mind," Burt said, starting to grin. He flicked his cigar away. "And speaking of love . . ." He put his arms around Sabella, deftly laid her back on the grass, and followed her down, "Let's make some."

He kissed her before she got the chance to object.

And kept on kissing her as a dexterous hand slipped between them and went about the pleasant task of again unbuttoning her white blouse.

As they lay there kissing in the dying sunlight, a spare, black-clad, stony-faced Mexican sat on the shaded rim of a rocky rampart high above them, out of sight. The powerful field glasses raised to his dark eyes were trained on the embracing couple stretched out below on the velvety mesa.

The man's thin lips, beneath his sleek black mustache, slowly turned up into a pleased smile. The whiplash scar on his dark right cheek puckered and pulled. His hands began to shake with building anticipation.

"Ah, *Sí, sí,*" Cisco silently encouraged. "Go ahead, Burnett. Make love to the beautiful *señorita.* I won't tell Gena." His smile became lewd and evil. "*Mi palabra de honor.* You have my word."

Chapter Fourteen

Gena de Temple was aware, with a kind of nagging clairvoyance, that she was in real danger of losing Burt. Forever.

She was worried as she had never been before. Through the years she had, more than once, laughed and looked the other way when tales of Burt's dalliances reached her ears. She had told herself repeatedly that his sexual escapades had nothing to do with his devotion and commitment to her. She had reasoned that what there was between the two of them could not be threatened by a nameless parade of morally loose blondes, brunettes, and redheads.

All his brief, meaningless affairs had been conducted in a clandestine, gentlemanly fashion. Out of respect for her, he had spared her hurt and embarrassment by misbehaving only on those occasions when he was out of town. To the best of her knowledge, Burt had never had an affair with a woman she knew, a woman who lived in or around Capistrano.

Not that he hadn't been offered many an opportunity from the local ladies. She had seen the blatant invitations flashing from the eyes of females from fifteen to fifty whenever they looked at the irresistible Burt.

It had never bothered her. It had, in fact, pleased her very much. She was envied and she gloried in it. She enjoyed being the object of their jealousy, delighted that they coveted her handsome lover, wishing he belonged to them.

And *she* had him!

Or did she?

Gena's exalted position had always been secure until now. Something was very wrong. Someone was luring her lover away. Somehow she had to put an end to it.

These distressing thoughts plagued Gena as she waited impatiently for Cisco. It was evening. Sunday evening.

Again.

A week had passed since she had summoned Cisco to her suite and ordered him to trail Burt, to find out what Burt was up to, if anything, and then to come straight back and report only to her. Say nothing to anyone else.

Gena was alone in the mansion on this warm Sunday evening except for the servants. Her father, Senator de Temple, was in Los Angeles. He, Don Miguel Andres Amaro, and a host of important dignitaries were to participate in a ribbon-cutting ceremony for a newly constructed state building. Don Miguel and the senator had left on the noon train. Gena had spent the long, miserable afternoon worrying and waiting for Cisco.

When was he going to bring her some news?

Gena glanced at the delicate white porcelain clock on the marble mantel. Nine p.m. She sighed wearily. What was keeping Cisco? Had he again failed to find Burt? Was he searching still, unwilling to give up? Had he found out something so disturbing he was reluctant to tell her?

Gena's heart lurched in her chest when finally she heard the distinctive sound of booted feet on the wide balcony outside her upstairs suite. She instinctively started toward the tall double doors which stood wide open to the balmy night. Halfway across the spacious salon, she caught herself. She mustn't let even Cisco know how upset, how frightened she was.

Gena drew a steadying breath, hastily sat down on the peach brocade sofa, smoothed the skirts of her yellow silk gown, and picked up a book from the nearby table. Hurriedly flipping it open, she was pretending to read when the tall, spare Cisco stepped into the open doorway and softly said her name.

Gena looked up and smiled easily at Cisco. She noted, with a quick appraising glance, that he had, before coming here, taken the time to bathe, shave, and change clothes. His inky black shirt and trousers were freshly laundered and neatly pressed. He was hatless; his longish black hair, brushed straight back, was still damp from his bath.

Her searching gaze went to his dark, narrow face. His black eyes held a somber look and a muscle twitched spasmodically in his scarred cheek. He knew something. Something bad.

Purposely making herself remain cool and collected, Gena said, "Do come in, Cisco." She laid the unread book aside, rose to her feet. "Let me pour you a drink."

Cisco slipped into the room like a dark specter, looking, as usual, strangely evil and forbidding. Gena felt the wispy hair on her nape rise. She appeared totally composed as she crossed to an inlaid satin commode, atop which several carved crystal decanters were lined up in a neat row. Not bothering to ask what Cisco wanted to drink, she poured two glasses of madeira.

She smiled warmly at the black-clad man sprawling on her peach brocade sofa, and bent from the waist to hand him his wine. She caught the quick flash of fire in the depths of his black eyes as he stared hungrily at her decolletage. Her fashionable yellow silk gown was so severely cut that her full, high bosom was barely concealed when she stood completely erect. Bending in such a daring dress courted disaster.

Gena didn't care.

She was far too preoccupied with worry over Burt to concern herself with Cisco seeing too much naked flesh. Besides, she derived a bit of perverse pleasure in allowing this scarfaced, mustachioed Mexican to steal glimpses of her breasts, although she would have hotly denied it had anyone suggested such a despicable thing. It was, she knew, a rather dangerous, depraved kind of game she played with Cisco. She wasn't sure why she did it. Certainly it wasn't that she was attracted to such a man; a common laborer, a Mexican vaquero, a lowly, uneducated hired hand without fortune or future.

A fixture on the de Temple *rancho*, Cisco lived with his brother, Santo, in a small adobe out back of the stables.

Gena had heard whispered tales from the house servants about Cisco's sadistic treatment of the many women in his life.

He was, it was said, mean and brutal when drunk on tequila, and many a night, a sobbing female had fled his adobe in fear and shame. But, oddly enough, they always returned, as if something he did to them made them want more.

The scar on his cheek, so it was said, had been carved there by a jealous Mexican sweetheart who came to his adobe unannounced late one night and found him with a rich railroader's beautiful redheaded daughter.

As Cisco sat there now on her peach brocade sofa, his dark, long-fingered hand trembled so badly he spilled a few drops of the madeira on his clean black trousers. Pretending she hadn't noticed, Gena inwardly gloated.

She started to sit down beside Cisco, but changed her mind. Instead she tugged a French empire chair up directly before him and sat down facing him. Anxious to hear what he had learned about Burt, she never realized that her yellow-gowned knees were touching his.

Gena made herself leisurely sip her wine as if she were in no particular hurry to hear what Cisco had to say. In a way she wasn't. Instinctively she knew he had brought her bad news. She was almost tempted to shout at him, "Don't tell me! Please don't. Forget that I ever asked you to follow Burt. Drink your wine and go!" She said nothing. She heard nothing but the ticking of the clock and the pounding of her heart.

Cisco drank his madeira down in one long thirsty pull and placed the empty glass on the table at his elbow. His eyes lifted to meet hers.

He said, "*Señorita* Gena, I had rather have my tongue torn from my head than to have to tell you all the shocking, disgusting things I have seen today."

In truth, Cisco had a hard time suppressing a smile of satisfaction when he saw the lovely Gena flinch as if he had struck her. It was exactly the reaction he had counted on. He knew enough about women—especially this spoiled, beautiful, unattainable one—to realize that just such a statement would make her beg him to tell her everything.

Every little dirty detail.

Gena took another quick sip of her wine, swallowed convulsively, put a hand on her rapidly falling and rising bosom and said, "Please, Cisco, you must. You must tell me everything. Everything. I must know the truth."

Sadly shaking his head, Cisco's hollow-cheeked face looked tortured. He laid a spread hand on his shirtfront and said, "It is like a knife thrust deep into my heart to hurt you, my gentle dove."

Touched by his compassion, Gena leaned close, held out her hand to him. He took hold of the pale, fragile fingers, held them firmly, tightly in his. He leaned up from the sofa so that their faces were only inches apart. And the sight of her exposed breasts was his to enjoy anytime he lowered his eyes.

"Just as you suspected, *cara*," he said softly, "Burnett has been with another woman. He is with her this very minute."

"Oh, God, no," Gena half sobbed, expecting to hear those very words, yet hoping against hope it wasn't true. "How could he do this to me? We are engaged. We're planning a Christmas wedding." Her green eyes closed in genuine agony.

Cisco was pleased. "I cannot understand," he bit out the words, "how any man could want another woman when he has you."

Gena's eyes slowly opened. Heartsick, she said, "Thank you, Cisco. You're very kind. But you must not spare my feelings. I want to know everything that you know."

"*Sí.* I will start at the beginning. The woman is a young, beautiful Spaniard named—"

"A Latin?" Gena interrupted, shocked, horrified. "Burt's sleeping with a dirty peasant girl? Someone's paid servant?"

Pride mixed with anger flared in Cisco's black eyes, but Gena didn't notice. "No, *señorita*, the woman is neither peasant nor servant. Her name is Sabella Rios and she came here from Tucson in the Arizona Territory several weeks ago. She is with her *duenna* and they are staying at the Inn of the Swallows." He paused, waiting.

"What is she doing in Capistrano? Where did Burt meet her? How long has this been going on?"

"I do not know what she is doing here. I have dispatched Santo to Tucson to learn what he can of *Señorita* Rios. It is unclear where or when Burnett met the young lady, but from what I saw this afternoon"—here he paused, bit his lip, closed his eyes, slowly opened them—"they have apparently known each other well for some time."

"You mean she knew Burt before coming here? Was he expecting her then? Have they been . . . they were together today?" Cisco nodded. "You saw them together? Where? What were they doing?"

Cisco wore a pained expression when he said, "You sure you want to hear this?"

"I command you tell me!" Gena snapped irritably. "Leave nothing out."

He sighed, rose to his feet, crossed the room, and poured himself another glass of madeira. His back to her, he began, "Burnett again spent last night alone at the Mission Inn. He went home to *Lindo Vista* around noon today and left again shortly before two p.m." Cisco turned and walked back to the sofa. He glanced at the twin mounds of creamy flesh exposed by the low-cut yellow dress. He licked his lips and sat back down. He scooted forward on the peach sofa, trapping her crossed legs inside his spread knees. "The young lady in question—*Señorita* Rios—left the Inn of the Swallows at approximately three o'clock. She took a saddled chestnut stallion from Paxton Dean's livery stable and took the coast road south out of town."

"To meet Burt?"

Cisco nodded. "Burnett, on that big paint he rides, was waiting for her inside that grape arbor on the southern outskirts of town. Together they rode off toward the southeast, supposing that they had not been seen."

"But you were there. You followed them."

"*Sí.* All the way across the valley and on up into the foothills of the Chocolate mountains. When finally they stopped, dismounted, and ground hobbled their mounts, I wound my way up to a rocky ridge directly above the small mesa where they were. You sure you want me to go on with this?"

"Absolutely. I have to know."

Cisco could hardly contain his excitement. He was eager to tell what he had seen. Actually, he was going to tell *more* than he'd seen. He had no intention of admitting the couple hadn't made love. Damn them both! He had watched their every move for hours through the field glasses and nothing had happened other than some fierce kissing and thrashing about. Apparently Burnett wasn't much of a lover. He sure hadn't managed to get in the blonde's leather britches.

"The minute they laid down on the grass," he began softly, "they were kissing as if starved for each other." Gena let out a little sob of despair. "Never have I seen a pair so hot for each other. In seconds they had torn off their clothes and were naked right out there in the open. Then Burnett was positioning himself between the willing blonde's long tanned legs and they were going at it. The woman cried out in climax almost immediately."

Her pale, lovely face screwed up into an unhappy frown, Gena said, "Did you leave then? Or did you wait while they got dressed and—"

"Ah, *Señorita* Gena, they didn't get dressed. They were just getting started."

"You mean they . . . they . . . more than once?"

"*Mucho más.* Many, many times." Cisco set his empty wineglass aside and began to count on his fingers. "First with her stretched out on her back beneath him. Then, her seated astride him as he lay on his back. That's twice. Next they lay down on their sides facing in the same direction and he took her from behind."

"Dear God in Heaven!" Gena wailed.

"That is three times, no? Then, let me see . . . oh, now I remember, Burnett stood flat footed, lifted the blond beauty off the ground, wrapped those long golden-tan legs around his waist and eased her down and impaled her. She seemed to like that very much, she moaned and called his name again and again. How many times is that? Four. Next he laid the woman down on the grass, and she was so exhausted, she could not move, could not even lift her arms. So Burnett made love to her with his hands and with his mouth. He kissed her while she sighed and I watched as his face moved down her body and went between her—"

"Hush!" Gena shouted, jumping to her feet. "Don't say another word! Not one more word!" She was trembling violently with emotion, her hands curled into fists at her sides, tears spilling from her eyes.

Cisco quickly rose. He had never seen Gena de Temple

so upset before. Which was just as he had planned. She was, at this minute, very vulnerable. Badly in need of comfort and affection. He quickly put his arms around her and pulled her to him, hoping she was hurt enough to be persuaded to retaliate against Burt, to turn the tables and give Burnett a dose of his own medicine. Tit for tat.

Over her head, he glanced at the massive mirror mounted above the fireplace. Reflected there he saw the two of them with a huge, comfortable-looking bed directly behind them. Visions of making love to Burnett's fiancée in that bed on this balmy night filled his head.

"Oh, Cisco," Gena sobbed, clinging to him, burying her face on his chest, "what shall I do? I can't stand to lose Burt. I can't. How can I keep him? I don't know, I don't. Tell me what to do!"

Cisco wanted to cry out, "Come to bed with me this minute, *mi cara*! Do this and you will never think of the *gringo* again."

He said nothing.

"But wait . . . wait . . . I do know!" Gena's dark head suddenly shot up and she forcefully pulled free of the startled Cisco's embrace. Pointing impatiently toward the open doors in a gesture that clearly meant he was to leave her at once, a bright light came into her tearing eyes and she said aloud, "I know exactly what to do!"

Chapter Fifteen

"This is good-bye. I have decided not to see you again."

"Jesus, sweetheart, you don't mean that! I know you don't."

"But I do." Leather creaked as Sabella turned slowly in the saddle, looking directly at Burt. "This has to end and we both know it."

"No." Burt shook his head fiercely. "No. I won't let you go."

It was nearing eleven p.m. The pair had spent the warm, lazy Sunday afternoon and evening together in the rugged foothills of the Chocolates. After the long ride back, they were now nearing the village, approaching the far eastern outskirts of San Juan Capistrano.

Sabella abruptly pulled up on her mount when they reached an elevated spit of land above the valley floor and Capistrano's twinkling lights.

It was then and there she announced that she was ending their relationship. Burt, reining in his chuffing paint beside her, was caught completely by surprise.

Again he said, "Sabella, you can't leave me. I refuse to give you up."

"You have no choice," Sabella stated flatly. "The decision is mine to make."

Burt swung lithely down from Sam's back and tossed the

reins to the ground. With a swiftness that startled her, he lifted Sabella out of the saddle, set her on her feet, and pressed her up against her big chestnut stallion.

"You're right, sweetheart," he said, "it is your decision." He flashed that devastating Burnett grin then and added, "But I can help you make it. And I will."

He drew her hands up, placing her palms flat against his chest. Sabella felt the heat of his body, the heavy beating of his heart. His gray eyes gleaming in the starlight, Burt told her honestly, "If I knew that you would never again touch me this way"—the smile left his face and his silver gray eyes became hooded—"my heart would stop its beating."

Sabella was delighted by his touching confession. She could hardly hide her glee. Her timing had been perfect. Had she threatened one day sooner to never see him again, he might have let her go without a backward look. But he wouldn't now. She was sure of it.

He would never let her go.

She would be the one to let him go. And she would, but not now.

For a long moment Sabella said nothing, just looked into his gleaming gray eyes. Then: "That's very sweet. Very flattering, but I really doubt that—"

"Shhhh," Burt warned and gently lowered her hands from his chest. Quickly he flipped open two buttons of her white shirt, slid long, lean fingers inside, and placed his hand on the undercurve of her left breast. Sabella softly winced, struggled a little, then stilled as he gently stroked her and said in a low, level voice, "Tell me you never want me to touch you this way again." He lifted and pressed her bare breast slightly upward, so that his palm could more fully feel her heart rhythmically beating.

"I can't," she lied softly, convincingly, carefully concealing her true feelings.

If he only knew. But he must not know. Not now.

Inhaling deeply, purposely causing her soft full breast to swell against his caressing hand, she said again, "I can't, Burt. I admit it. I don't think I could stand it if you never touched me again."

"Ah, baby, I know, I know," he said and quickly kissed her, his mouth hot and eager. His lips sliding over her cheek to her ear, he whispered coaxingly, "Come with me to the Mission Inn. We'll slip up the back way. Nobody will know." He kissed the pulse point below her ear. "On the top floor there's a room facing the ocean. In that room there's a great big old bed with cool silky sheets and—"

"No," she softly interrupted, shaking her head. "Not yet."

Burt lifted his head. Agonized, he said, "When, sweetheart?"

"Not," she told him, her arms going around his trim waist, "until you have broken your engagement to Gena de Temple."

Chapter Sixteen

Gena de Temple hummed as she sat in the huge, gold-veined, peach-marble bathtub which was filled to the brim with thick, foamy bubbles. Her personal maid, Petra, was in the next room, laying out the clothes her mistress had chosen for the first ensemble of the day. There would, Petra knew, be several changes of clothing before the day ended.

Petra was still in a state of shock that the late rising Gena was out of bed before nine on this warm Monday morning. It wasn't like her. Gena rarely woke before ten and even then she stayed at least another hour or two in her four-poster, lolling lazily and enjoying a leisurely breakfast from a bed tray.

"Petra!" Gena called as she carelessly tossed the bar of perfumed soap and soggy washcloth into the depths of the tub. "Come quickly. I'm finished. I'm ready to get out now."

Petra walked into the large bathroom as Gena rose to her feet in the massive marble tub. Watery bubbles sliding down her pale slender body, Gena allowed the big Mexican woman to swirl a thirsty white towel around her and lift her out of the tub.

As if Gena were still a small child, Petra stood the naked, dripping Gena on a peach velvet rug beside the tub. A neat stack of white towels was at the ready. Petra used a half dozen. Carefully, meticulously, she dried Gena until not one bead of moisture remained on her bare body. Gena stood still dutifully while the luxuriant towels blotted and rubbed and patted at her clean, tingling flesh.

Gena didn't think of herself as spoiled. She was of the uppercrust, a true patrician. A gentlewoman who naturally had her own personal maid. So why on earth would she want to tackle the tedious task of drying herself after her baths when Petra would do it for her, had done it for her since the day she was born?

Naked, Gena strolled into her big sunny bedroom with Petra trailing closely behind. Here, again, Gena saw no reason to expend precious energy on getting dressed. After all, she was just out of her bath, she wanted to stay fresh and cool. Dressing could be hard, hot work; she might actually perspire with the struggle of it.

Petra dressed her.

Every article of clothing that went on Gena's body was put there by Petra's able hands. The process took a good twenty minutes, beginning with sheer silk stockings and ending with a saucy straw hat. The finished package was quite delectable.

Pleased, Gena admired herself in the free-standing mirror. She looked very young and innocent, which was exactly her intent. The dress she had chosen had never been worn. Bought impulsively on a shopping foray last spring in San Francisco, she had decided, the minute it had been unpacked, that it didn't suit her image.

The frock was of yellow organza and the skirts were too full and too frilly. The tight bodice buttoned all the way up to a high round collar that almost choked her. The wide silk sash going around her small waist reminded her of the dresses she had worn as a child.

The girlish dress was perfect for today.

Smiling at herself in the mirror, Gena said, "Has the brougham been brought around? I'm ready to leave." She pinched her pale cheeks.

Petra nodded. "Gilberto has been waiting down front for the past half hour."

"Ask Julio to go down and tell Gilberto he won't be driving me this morning. Get me Hank Brody."

"But, why?" Petra frowned. "Gilberto always drives you."

Gena whirled to face the puzzled maid. "Not when I go out to *Lindo Vista.* You know very well that Mr. Burnett doesn't like Latins on his property."

Petra rolled her dark eyes, but hurried to do Gena's bidding. Minutes later the stocky Mexican woman stood on the front steps waving as the shiny black brougham rolled down the graveled drive.

Inside the roomy covered carriage, Gena relaxed against the lushly padded, wine-velvet upholstery. The matching side curtains were tightly shut against the harsh morning sunlight. On the seat beside her lay a yellow silk parasol to be unfurled and held over her head when she reached her destination.

It was Monday, the seventh day of June.

The day after Cisco had told her of watching Burt make love to another woman. Earlier this morning, a wire from Santo in Tucson had arrived. He had learned only that the young woman, Sabella Rios, was twenty-five and had lived in Tucson all of her life. Her parents, Tito and Teresa Rios, were both deceased. She had lived, since their deaths, with Victor and Carmelita Rivera on their small ranch. Victor Rivera had died several years ago, and since that time, the young woman, Sabella, had supported herself and Rivera's widow by doing a man's work. She could ride, rope, brand, and herd cows with the best of the *vaqueros* and cowhands.

Why had she come to Capistrano? Folks in Tucson said it was the matter of an inheritance.

Gena didn't believe it. Not for one second. Armed with the sparse information Santo had supplied, Gena knew it was time to call on Mr. Burnett.

The old one.

Not the young one.

It was nearing noon when the black brougham approached the tall ranch gates of *Lindo Vista.* The guard on the gate recognized the gleaming coach. He smiled warmly and swept off his hat when Gena pulled back the side curtain a few inches and greeted him.

"Miss Gena, I'm afraid you've come all the way out here on a wild goose chase," said the keen-eyed sharpshooter. "Burt ain't here. Him and some of the boys'll be gone all day. They're far out at the line shacks doing some repair work."

"Well, it isn't Burt I came to see, Calvin," Gena said. "It's been a while since I visited Mr. Raleigh. I thought he might be glad to see me."

"Why he sure will. He'll be tickled pink, that's for sure." He signaled the brougham's driver through. "Go right on in. Nice to see you, Miss Gena."

Gena had known, before coming, that Burt would not be at home. Which is why she had chosen to come.

Raleigh Burnett's pale blue eyes lighted with surprised pleasure when he looked up to see the pretty dark-haired woman in the frothy yellow dress step into the book-filled library.

Gena de Temple was, and always had been, the apple of his eye. He had, along with Senator de Temple, purposely seen to it that Burt and Gena were thrown together often.

Cleverly, quietly, through the years, he had manipulated his handsome son and the senator's pretty daughter, putting the idea of marriage into their heads, making them think it was their own. Sensing a few years back that the two had become intimate, he was not shocked, he was overjoyed. But he had, on more than one occasion, subtly reminded Burton that intimacy with a young lady of Gena's class carried with it responsibility, duty, commitment.

Raleigh Burnett had always had his heart set on having Gena de Temple for a daughter-in-law. There was no one else acceptable for his only son. No other young woman he wanted giving birth to his grandchildren.

"Gena! My dear child," he said cheerily, lifting gnarled, shaky hands, "what a pleasant surprise!"

Smiling at the frail white-haired man, Gena swept across the room in a swirl of frothy yellow skirts and flashing lacy petticoats. When she reached the wheeled chair where the old gentleman sat, she grabbed both chair arms, bent, and gave his withered cheek a kiss. She laughed then, gaily, warmly, and danced around to stand directly behind the chair. She threw her arms down around his neck and placed her spread hands on his thin chest. Kissing the top of his snow-white head, she said, "How would you like to have lunch with me? Just the two of us. All alone."

Pleased, thrilled she had come to visit, he clutched at the soft hands resting on his chest and said, "I can think of nothing I'd enjoy more. Ring for Blanton, my dear."

Gena crossed the room, yanked decisively on the corded bell pull and in seconds Raleigh Burnett's manservant stood in the doorway.

"Blanton, I have a beautiful guest for lunch. We won't be dining on the south patio. It's sunny there and the young lady has skin of priceless porcelain."

The servant nodded to Gena. "Very well, Sir. Where shall I serve you?"

"You choose, child." Raleigh Burnett, smiling, looked up at Gena.

"Mmmmm. Let's see . . . what about Burton's card room? We'll be well out of the sun there, yet we'll be able to see the ocean."

"You heard the young lady," said the old man to his servant. "And, Blanton, hop down to the cellar and bring up one of my hoarded bottles of Romanee Conti '55. This calls for a celebration!"

In the little-used room where a redwood bar stretched the length of the entire northern wall, round gaming tables covered in green baize were interspersed with square card tables of polished redwood. Carved redwood pillars supported the high ceiling and the paneled walls were of redwood as well, save for the back one.

The card room's choice location was at the far rear of the big L-shaped house. The very last room in the mansion's north wing, it was directly below Burt's upstairs bedroom. A row of tall glass doors served as its west wall, offering to any who might care to look, a spectacular view of the manicured grounds and the azure Pacific Ocean beyond.

For today's lunch, one of the square redwood tables was draped with an ivory damask cloth. A silver bowl filled with pink Castillian roses was placed at its center.

When Blanton pushed Raleigh Burnett's wheeled chair into the paneled room, the old man said happily to Gena, "I am so glad you came. This is going to be the most pleasant lunch I've had in ages!"

Gena didn't reply. It was, she knew, going to be far from pleasant.

When the wine and the meal had been served and they were left alone, Gena slowly pushed her plate away, bowed her head, and began to softly cry.

Raleigh Burnett was astounded. "Child, what is it? Are you ill? Shall I ring for a—"

"No." Gena raised her head, looking directly at him from tear-bright eyes. "You are the only one who can help me."

"Me? I'll do anything for you, child. But I don't understand."

Gena dabbed at the corners of her eyes with her dinner napkin. "Mr. Burnett, Burt is being . . . unfaithful to me."

"No!" His pale blue eyes widened. "That worthless whelp!"

"He's seeing another woman and . . . and . . . I'm afraid it might be serious."

"Oh, now, Gena, you know better than that." He patted her hand. "While it's despicable of him to . . . to . . . who is she? An actress from San Francisco? A lonely San Diego divorcée looking for a good time?"

Gena shook her head. "She is single. She's twenty-five years old. She's staying right here in Capistrano. Her name is Sabella Rios."

"A Mexican!" Raleigh Burnett's white eyebrows shot up and his face flushed red with anger. "My boy's carousing with a Mexican girl?"

"She's Spanish, so she says. She showed up here several weeks ago from the Arizona Territory to settle an inheritance. But her story doesn't check out. No attorney has anything pertinent in probate that I can find. But she found Burt, and he found her. I'm not sure how long their affair has been going on, but I suspect it began the minute she came to town. Looking back, I vaguely recall her coming to the engagement party with the Douglas family. But Burt never even met her that night, so I don't know. . . ."

Gena continued, speaking rapidly, excitedly, telling all she knew of Sabella Rios to the attentive old man. She admitted she was very worried and she needed his help. She told him that for the past few weeks, Burt had been handing her the flimsiest of excuses for not coming to see her.

"Do you know why? He's been with her! With that Spanish girl. With that . . . that . . . cheap peasant who wears pants like a man! Mr. Burnett, I will not be made a fool of nor will I . . ."

Gena continued to rage. Her stunned companion listened intently, sympathized, and assured her that he would straighten Burton out but good.

Gena felt relieved when she kissed the old man good-bye around three that Monday afternoon. She knew she could count on him to swiftly solve her problem. Everyone was aware of Raleigh Burnett's deep hatred for Latins. He would very likely demand that Burt drop the Spanish woman immediately or risk being disinherited.

In no time the whole unpleasant affair would blow over and Burt would be back in her arms where he belonged.

The placated Gena had no idea that she had left Raleigh Burnett far more upset than she herself had ever been.

After Gena had gone, Raleigh Burnett stayed on in the paneled card room alone, angrily waving Blanton away when an afternoon nap was suggested.

"Leave me alone!" he shouted, his pale eyes wild. "Get out! Get out of here and shut the door!"

Puzzled, concerned, Blanton did as he was told.

Long minutes passed.

Raleigh Burnett trembled violently despite the comfortable warmth of the card room.

"Could it possibly be?" he asked himself in horror. "Twenty-five years old, Gena had said. That would be about the right age and she had come here from the Arizona Territory. Could it be . . . ?" His bony fingers gripped the wooden arms of his wheeled chair and his heart squeezed so painfully in his narrow chest he could scarcely breathe.

"Was this Sabella Rios the daughter of . . . of . . . Merciful God, no!"

Chapter Seventeen

Alone in that silent handsomely paneled room overlooking the vast Pacific ocean, Raleigh Burnett felt ill.

Sick with worry.

Secrets from his long-buried past came flooding back to overwhelm him, to plague and threaten him.

His thoughts tumbling, the years fell away. Time sped swiftly backward.

It was again that hot September sunset in 1847. He had been summoned to the field hospital tent of his fellow officer, General Norman Patch. He sat at his dear friend's bedside and solemnly vowed to honor the dying general's last wish. To hold in trust for his ten-year-old sister-in-law, Teresa Carrillo, the Southern California *rancho*, which he, General Patch, had fallen heir to upon the death of his wife, Teresa's older sister, Dona Constancia Carrillo Patch. The vast acreage was to be turned over to Teresa when she reached eighteen or married.

Looking back on that day the now aged Raleigh Burnett squeezed his tortured pale blue eyes shut for a second and laid a hand on his hurting heart.

Shaking his white head, he opened his eyes and stared unseeing at that restless sea. He murmured aloud, "Norman, Norman, my friend, I *meant* to keep my promise, so help me God." Raleigh Burnett ground his teeth and shuddered. He'd had every intention of honoring the vow. Had never meant to break his word. And he wouldn't have if it hadn't been for . . . if he hadn't met. . . .

The vision of a young, beautiful red-haired woman sweeping gracefully down a grand staircase in a San Francisco mansion came back as vividly as if it had happened yesterday. It had been almost thirty-two years.

Out of the army, back at his law practice in Los Angeles, Raleigh Burnett had traveled that chilly November of '48 to San Francisco to settle a disputed mining claim for a client. The client had insisted he come that evening to a gala party. Reluctantly he went and for a long, unpleasant hour stood awkwardly about, tired, half bored, considering how he could manage, without being detected, to steal away.

He was about to do just that when, starting across the wide, silent corridor, he looked up to see, coming down the stairs, a tall, slender woman with the fieriest red hair and the palest white skin he'd ever seen.

Awed, he stood rooted at the base of the stairs, speechless, watching her come slowly down, the lush, full skirts of her emerald velvet dress brushing the marble stairs behind her. A youthful, elegant creature of incredible beauty, she never once looked at the steps as she descended.

She looked directly at him.

When she was two steps from the bottom, she paused, smiled, and extended her hand to him.

He took it and looked into a pair of large arresting eyes the exact color of the emerald green gown she wore.

"I'm Dana Hart," she said, moving one step lower. "Were you waiting here for me?" She smiled flirtatiously then, her pale cheeks dimpling prettily. "Or were you going to slip away before I had the chance to meet you?" She moved down another step.

His hand holding hers firmly, he said, "I'm Raleigh Burnett, Miss Hart, and I've been waiting all my life just for you."

"You're a charming liar, Mr. Burnett," she said and her voice was as warm and pleasing as her smile. "If you're bored and wish to leave, I can well understand." Her green eyes sparkled. "Now's your chance to slip out. I won't tell."

"Come with me," he said impulsively.

She laughed. "I wish I could, but my father would never forgive me."

Then it registered. She said she was Dana Hart. He was in the home of a Mr. and Mrs. Connor Hart. "Good Lord, you're—"

"The host's daughter," she admitted cheerfully. "I promised Daddy I would come down for a few minutes." She took the final step, stood directly before him, looking up into his eyes. "Will you dance with me once before you leave, Mr. Burnett?"

She possessively took his arm. Together they went into the crowded ballroom. As they turned about on the floor, he learned that she had just turned twenty. That she had spent four years in a finishing school in Boston. That she had recently returned from a grand tour of Europe. That she hoped he intended to stay in the Bay City long enough to take her to the theater and the opera and the many fine restaurants.

He did.

He stayed long past the time he should have gone back to Los Angeles and his neglected law practice. He was afraid to leave. Afraid someone would steal her away. Someone younger, handsomer, richer than he. He told her of his fears.

Dana laughed and said, "Younger? Raleigh, you're being foolish. Let me assure you that I don't mind your being old enough to be my father. I've always been attracted to mature men. Handsomer? Why I think you're quite the handsomest of men with your raven black hair and sky blue eyes." Then, totally innocent, completely sincere, she said, "Richer? Darling, aren't you terribly rich? I naturally assumed that you're wealthy like everyone else we know."

Raleigh Burnett realized then that without a great personal fortune he couldn't hope to win and wed the enchanting red-haired twenty-year-old aristocrat with whom he was madly in love.

An outlandish idea instantly flashed into his mind. A devious decision was quickly made. He held in his own name— in trust for the eleven-year-old Teresa Carrillo—the deed to exactly twenty-two square leagues of rich Southern California rangeland. *Lindo Vista* was a working, well-run ranch where thousands of cattle and horses grazed and dozens of employees worked and an empty many-roomed white mansion sat on a cliff overlooking the ocean.

A vast empire worth untold millions.

"Ah, love, sweet love," he said, laughing easily, "I suppose I couldn't exactly be called poor. Besides my law practice, I have a little place down in Southern California. You may have heard of it. *Lindo Vista.*"

Dana's large emerald eyes widened. "Why, Raleigh Burnett, what a modest man you are. Of course, I've heard of *Lindo Vista*! The old Carrillo land grant. You own that *rancho*?"

"I do," he said, forcing himself to sound nonchalant. "How would you like to be mistress of *Lindo Vista*?"

"Darling, are you proposing to me?"

"Yes. Marry me, Dana."

Remembering now how the deceitful scheme had came about, the aging Raleigh Burnett relived—as he had so many times—the day of the fateful decision. Once he'd told Dana the monstrous, unforgivable lie, there was no turning back. No making amends. No confessing that the property was not really his.

Not if he wanted to keep her.

So he had officially made it his. Then and forever. Any and all legal documents naming Teresa Carrillo as heir to *Lindo Vista* were destroyed. Sworn statements, credentials, records, and charters were taken from the files and burned.

With the defeat of Mexican California, many land titles were in dispute. As a colonel of the victorious Union forces, his hold on *Lindo Vista* was more firm than any *alcalde*. Possession was nine-tenths of the law.

A smart, knowledgeable attorney, he knew exactly how to clean up any traces of evidence that the land rightfully belonged to the little Carrillo girl. He didn't worry that he would ever be caught. Young Teresa Carrillo was the only living member of either the Carrillo family or the Patch family. There were no relatives on either side, which was the reason she lived in a convent. She had no one, not even a guardian.

Raleigh reasoned that she was only a child who had no idea that her dying brother-in-law had set up the trust for her. When her older sister had died in 1843, Teresa had been placed in the convent at the tender age of six. She probably remembered very little about living at *Lindo Vista.* She likely didn't recall where the *rancho* was located.

Telling no one of his terrible duplicity, Raleigh Burnett married the beautiful red-haired Dana Hart and brought his bride home to *Lindo Vista.* The next two or three years were the happiest of his entire life. Pushing his guilt aside, refusing to think about the little girl he had so callously wronged, he showered his adored young bride with Paris gowns and luxurious furs and expensive jewels. Within a year she bore him a son and his happiness was complete.

And if the beautiful Dana was less than a devoted mother, Raleigh couldn't fault her for it. She was, after all, only a child herself. There were plenty of servants to care for Burton. A young maid who was weaning her own child was happy to serve as wet nurse. The young mistress of *Lindo Vista* didn't wish to spoil her fine figure, her high, round breasts. That was understandable. Raleigh didn't want them spoiled either.

Worshiping her as he did, he never once considered that his darling Dana neglected their son. She was simply a little overwhelmed, which was natural. In time she'd grow used to being a mother and would love the boy as he did.

Blind to her faults, he was content just to be in the same room with her. Often she treated him more like a father than a husband, but he was charmed when she sat on his lap and teased him and went through his pockets looking for trinkets he'd brought her as if she were a little girl.

Many was the night he carried her up the redwood staircase to their room in the mansion's southern wing, thinking he was the luckiest of men. And sometimes in the darkness when his beautiful wife slept sweetly beside him, he felt so thankful he was almost afraid. He was *too* happy. *Too* content. Could anything so wonderful last?

For more than a half dozen years Dana was rarely out of his sight. If she wanted to go into the village, he drove her. If she expressed a desire to go on a trip, he traveled with her.

Then came that summer he would never forget. Burton was six years old and all boy, a real outlaw, cute and precocious, and full of mischief. Dana confessed to her husband that she needed to get away from their rambunctious son for a while. She loved him dearly, of course, but she hadn't had a moment to herself since his birth.

"Sweetheart, how thoughtless of me." Raleigh was understanding. "Burton is a handful I know. My sweet angel needs a rest." Smiling, he said, "I can't get away from the ranch right now, but you go to San Francisco. Spend a week or so with your folks. It'll do you good."

"Sure you don't mind?"

"I insist on it!"

She went and never came back. Not even to say good-bye to her son. Their son.

Raleigh was shocked and devastated. For love of her he had betrayed a sacred trust, stolen a fortune, become a thief. And still she had left him. Ran away to Mexico with a rich, handsome grandee who was only a few years older than she.

Raleigh had forgiven her long ago. She was young and beautiful and spirited. She had longed for romance, adventure, excitement and he couldn't blame her for that. Grateful for those few wonderful years she had given him, he cherished the son she had borne him. In Burton, he still had a part of her.

After she'd gone, every dream, every hope, every plan he had was for his son, Burton. And now all those dreams, hopes, plans were in danger.

Again.

He had reasoned wrongly about the young Teresa Carrillo never learning of the trust. He hadn't figured on the dying General Patch telling anyone else about their agreement. But the general had told the young captain of the guards, Victor Rivera. He had apparently also written the young girl a letter telling her of her inheritance. When Teresa Carrillo turned eighteen, Rivera took her from the convent. On her behalf, Rivera had contacted him, Raleigh Burnett, to inform him that Teresa Carrillo was now of age and ready to take title to her land.

Remembering the terrible unpleasantness that followed, Raleigh Burnett drew a ragged breath. The girl Teresa soon married a *vaquero*, Tito Rios, and Rios and Rivera both took up the cause. Years of bitter accusations, legal hassles, and angry threats followed. Then Tito Rios was crippled in an accident and gave up the fight. So did Teresa. Finally, even the stubborn Vic Rivera realized there was nothing he could do.

Teresa Carrillo Rios had been swindled out of her fortune. "You'll pay for this, Burnett!" Rivera angrily threatened the last time they met. "You won't get away it, you greedy unprincipled *gringo* bastard! Mark my words, one day you'll get what's coming to you!"

That day, Raleigh Burnett realized, had finally come.

He needed no one to confirm his worst suspicions. Instinctively he knew that this mysterious young woman, Sabella Rios, was the daughter of Teresa Carrillo Rios. He knew as well why she had come to Capistrano.

She was here to pay him back for what he'd done to her mother.

He didn't blame her. He deserved it. But his much-deserved retribution could be exacted in one way and one way only.

By destroying his beloved son, Burton.

Chapter Eighteen

Feeling faint and short of breath, the troubled Raleigh Burnett struggled to wheel his chair the few feet to the bell pull. The effort left him perspiring, wheezing, and so weak he had to wait several minutes to get his breath and regain enough strength to pull the cord.

Blanton appeared almost immediately. He took one look at Raleigh Burnett and his brows drew together in concern. Crossing quickly to the white-haired old man, the worried servant said, "You are going to your room right now and nap until dinnertime."

"I'm going nowhere," Raleigh Burnett stubbornly declared. "I'm staying right here! As soon as the boys get back, send my son in here!"

"You can speak with Burton at dinner, but now—"

"You heard me!"

Shocked, baffled, Blanton said in low, controlled tones, "What is it, Raleigh? What did Miss de Temple do to upset you?"

Raleigh Burnett sadly shook his white head. "It isn't Gena . . . it's . . . oh, God . . ."

He said no more. He waved his servant away. Blanton left, but remained in the wide corridor just outside the open door, considering whether or not he should immediately send for Doctor Ledet. Against his better judgment, he delayed.

Burt and the hands got in early. It was shortly after four in the afternoon when Burt and Cappy Ricks came up to the house. Blanton heard them, cast a quick glance inside at Raleigh Burnett, then hurried down the long corridor to the main section of the house.

Cappy Ricks stood at the base of the redwood staircase, slapping his gloves against his trousered leg and announcing to no one in particular that he thought he'd go on out to the kitchen for a cup of coffee. Paying no attention, Burt was already climbing the stairs.

"Burton," Blanton called to him, "your father wants to see you in the card room."

Burt turned on the stairway, smiled, and gestured to his sweat-stained shirt and dusty Levi's. "Ten minutes. Soon as I get cleaned up."

"I think you'd best come now," said Blanton.

Burt frowned, but came back down the stairs, running a hand through his dirty, disheveled black hair. Motioning Cappy to follow, Burt hurried around the corner. The two men walked fast down the long wide corridor to the card room. Blanton was close on their heels.

Just outside the door, Burt lifted a tanned forearm, blotted away beads of dirt and perspiration from his forehead, gestured for the other two to remain outside, and stepped into the doorway, smiling.

"Say, Dad. How you doing?"

Raleigh Burnett's pale blue eyes narrowed at the sight of his tall, imposing son. "Come in and close the door behind you."

Burt shrugged wide shoulders, stepped inside, and shut the door. "You look tired," he said, moving closer to the old man's wheeled chair. "Miss your afternoon nap?"

Raleigh Burnett glared at Burt and clenched his arthritic hands together in his lap. "I had a guest for lunch today."

"Good for you. Who was it?"

"Your fiancée, Gena." He scowled. "Or have you forgotten about Gena?'"

"No. I haven't," Burt calmly replied, pulling out a straight-backed chair from one of the green baize gaming tables, turning it about, and straddling it, folding his long arms over its back.

His father's face turning a fiery red, he said, "Well, you're damned well acting like it!"

"Jesus Christ, what's Gena been telling you? And why the hell is she bothering you with her problems?"

"Her problems?" Raleigh Burnett snarled. "Her problems? How about your problems? Seems to me you're the one with the problems!" His face was now flaming red.

"Better calm down, Dad." Burt's tone was tranquil. "You know Doc Ledet said you're not to get overly excited."

The old man leaned a little forward in his chair. "Well, by God, you should have thought about that before you started playing around with a cheap Spanish whore!"

Burt's tanned face became almost as red as his father's. He shot to his feet, twirled the chair out of his way, and ground his even white teeth, a muscle twitching in his clenched jaw.

"Never," he warned, his voice icy cold, "call Sabella Rios a whore again! You don't know what you're talking about! You know nothing about her!"

"You're wrong!" shouted his father, a vein standing out and throbbing on his pale forehead. "I know more about that woman than you'll ever learn!"

"Really?" Burt said sarcastically, and cocked his dark head to one side. "Then suppose you tell me what you know." He crossed his long arms over his chest. "Go ahead. Recite all the dirty, damaging lies Gena fed you along with your lunch. I'd like hear to them."

Raleigh Burnett shook a bony, arthritic finger at his son. "Don't you be trying to lay this blame on Gena. She was right to come here. Right to let me know what's going on."

"The hell she was! She knows very well that—"

Interrupting, Raleigh said, "Damnit, boy, when are you going to grow up? Not even engaged for a full month and already sleeping with another woman! Isn't one woman ever enough for you?"

"Yes," Burt calmly told him. "I've finally learned that one woman is all I want. All I ever really wanted."

"Then why in heaven's name—"

"Dad, I have fallen in love for the first and the last time. I didn't plan it, I didn't mean for it to happen, but it has happened and nothing can change that fact. I'm in love with a sweet young woman who, by the way, refuses to sleep with me."

"Do you know why?" Raleigh Burnett howled, his eyes practically popping out of his head. "Know why? Let me tell you why, it's because she wants—"

"It's because she is a good, well-brought up, decent young woman. That's why! She's beautiful, intelligent, and warm-hearted. She happens to be Spanish, so I know for that reason alone you hate her before you've even met her."

"No, that has nothing to do with it!"

"Come off it, Dad. If the young lady's name was Smith or Jones you wouldn't be half this upset."

"Oh, God, that's not it . . . you don't know. . . ." Raleigh Burnett's words trailed away. His stricken expression, his sudden silence, made Burt wish he had waited, had broken the news of his intention to marry Sabella in a softer, more tactful way. But it was too late.

"I'm sorry, Dad," he said gently. "I know this is hard on you."

"Hard on *me*? Are you out of your mind? What about Gena de Temple? The woman who has loved you all these years?" Raleigh Burnett shouted. "The woman you promised to marry!"

"I feel terrible about hurting Gena," said Burt. "I'm going this very evening to break off the engagement. The senator will be there, so I'll inform him as well. I'm sure he'll take out his anger and indignation on me alone. At least I hope it will not alter your friendship with the de Temples."

"You'll be damned lucky if the senator doesn't try to kill you!"

"That's a chance I'll have to take," said Burt. "I'm breaking the engagement. I'm marrying Sabella Rios. If she'll have me."

"Oh, she'll have you all right! She'll have you in more ways than you ever . . ." he caught himself. Desperate, he tried another tack. He held out a bony, arthritic hand to his son. "Burton, listen to me, please listen to me. Gena's a very wise, very understanding woman. I'll talk to her, fix it up, tell her everything's okay. Ask her to give you a just little more time." He smiled weakly, hoping he had come up with a solution. "Meanwhile, you take the Rios woman to San

Diego or Los Angeles. Check into a fine hotel. Romance her, dazzle her, ply her with champagne and caviar until she gives you what you're after. Stay a week, two if necessary. Keep her in bed until you get her out of your system. Then come on back home and marry Gena."

"You haven't been listening, Dad," Burt said, refusing to take the hand reaching out for him. "I am in love with Sabella. I mean to marry her."

Fear gripping his weak heart, Raleigh Burnett said plaintively, "Burton, from the night you were born you've been more precious to me than you can possibly imagine. Everything I've ever done has been for you. Everything that I own, the fortune I've accumulated, this mansion and all the land of *Lindo Vista* . . . everything . . . all of it is to be yours." Tears filled his pale blue eyes and he choked back a sob. "Don't throw it away. I'm begging you, Burton, don't do this to me. I've lived all my life for you, so please, won't you . . ."

Burt decisively shook his head. "I love you, Dad, and I'd die for you. But I will not live for you." He took a couple of steps backward. "I'm going now. I have to clean up before—"

The distraught old man threatened, "I'll disinherit you, so help me I will! You won't see a penny of money nor an acre of land!"

Burt nodded. "Fine. You do what you must. But it won't change my mind. I *am* going to marry Sabella Rios. Nothing will stop me."

He turned then and started to walk away.

Raleigh Burnett was trapped and knew it. He saw no way out. If he were to save his son from the vengeful Sabella Rios and certain heartbreak, he would have to tell Burton the truth. The awful, unforgivable, damning truth.

All of it.

In defeat and resignation, he shouted at his tall son's retreating back, "No! Burton, wait, come back. There are things you don't know about this woman! Things you don't know that I . . . That I . . . uhhhh . . . arrgh. . . ." Raleigh Burnett began to choke and struggle for breath.

"Dad!" Burt shouted and whirled about to see his father clutching his chest in pain and starting to pitch forward. His heart hammering, Burt raced back across the room. He reached the wheeled chair in time to catch his father before he crashed to the floor.

"Cappy! Blanton!" Burt shouted, cradling his sick, perspiring father in his arms. "Damn that Gena! Coming out here, burdening you!" The door burst open and Cappy and Blanton anxiously rushed in.

Burt scooped his father up in his powerful arms, and running out into the corridor, called over his shoulder, "The sofa in the music room is closest, I'll take him—"

"No ... no ... my own ... my ..." Raleigh Burnett murmured, grasping at Burt's soiled shirtfront.

"He wants you to take him to his room," Cappy interpreted.

So Burt raced down the long corridor of the mansion's northern wing, rounded the corner, dashed across the wide foyer and straight to the first door down the hall in the southern wing.

His eyes rolling back in his head, choking and gasping for breath, Raleigh Burnett cried out in excruciating pain before blacking out completely. He went limp then, his head lolling against Burt's chest.

"Jesus, he's passed out. He's not conscious!" Burt shouted in alarm.

Blanton hurried past Burt into Raleigh Burnett's room, threw back the covers on the big four-poster.

Burt gently placed the seemingly lifeless man on the bed, saying, "I'll go for Doc Ledet!"

"Send one of the cowhands," Blanton said, starting to undress the clammy, pallid man.

"I'll go, Burton." Cappy touched his shoulder.

"No!" Burt violently shook his head. "Sam can get me there faster! You stay and watch over Dad. He needs you!"

The household had heard the commotion and servants were already gathering outside Raleigh Burnett's room. Burt anxiously wove his way through the throng, telling them, as he went, that his father was indeed very ill.

Blanton and Cappy exchanged worried glances as they looked at Raleigh Burnett lying pale and lifeless-looking in the big bed, his frail frame swallowed up in a fresh white night shirt, his arms outside the covers.

Cappy tiptoed closer to the bed. To Blanton, he whispered, "What do you think it is?"

Blanton replied, "I'm not sure. I suspect he's had a heart attack, or perhaps a stroke."

"Will he . . . ?"

Blanton simply shook his head. He bent, picked up Raleigh Burnett's discarded clothes from the rug, straightened, and backed away, saying respectfully, "I'll be right outside the door."

Alone with the sick man, Cappy Ricks stood for several long minutes beside the bed, staring down at Raleigh Burnett's chalky face. Finally Cappy pulled up a chair.

He was starting to sit down when Raleigh Burnett's translucent eyelids began to flutter weakly. Cappy's own eyes widened. He moved closer, and patted a limp, thin hand lying on the mattress, and said, "It's Cappy, Raleigh. I'm here, right here."

"B-Bur-Bu . . ." The sick man's lips tried to form the name of his son.

"Burt's gone for Doc Ledet," Cappy told him. "He'll be back here with the doc any minute."

The paper-thin eyelids lifted and a pair of glassy, pale blue eyes looked up, trying to focus. "Cappy, that you?"

"It's me, old friend. Right here with you."

Raleigh Burnett sighed softly and said resignedly, "Cappy, I'm dying."

"Naw, no such thing." Cappy's gruff voice sounded strained even to himself. "Why, you're just a little wore out and—"

"Please . . . listen to me," rasped Raleigh Burnett. "There's something I have to tell you before it's too late."

"I'm listening, Raleigh."

"There's something you must know so that you can warn Burton." Raleigh Burnett licked his dry lips and drew a shallow, painful breath and began, "A long time ago I committed a terrible sin."

PART
2

Chapter Nineteen

An enormous peppermint-striped tent stretched the width of the entire back courtyard, shading a throng of laughing, chattering guests from the hot September sunshine. Beneath the huge tent a sumptuous buffet was laid out on a long, linen-draped table. The table was crowded with an assortment of dishes and delicacies meant to tempt and please every palate.

Huge silver platters held sliced, smoked ham and succulent roast beef and juicy barbecued ribs. For those who preferred seafood, there were boiled shrimp on beds of shaved ice, smoked oysters, and grilled salmon steaks. Fowl aplenty, too—tender pheasant, crispy fried chicken, and baked duckling.

The deep round bowls of silver epergnes overflowed with sweet California oranges and tart yellow lemons and bunches of sun-ripened purple grapes. There were sweets of every kind imaginable, in addition to the huge, white three-tiered wedding cake.

The giant cake stood at the long table's center. Beside it a massive crystal punch bowl was filled to the brim with a rosy pink liquid. Floating atop the chilled savory lake was a graceful swan carved from ice.

The liberally spiked pink punch was not the only liquid libation available. Jeroboams of chilled Piper Heidricks and

Niagaras of Mumms filled and refilled fragile long-stemmed glasses of the thirsty guests. Claret, port, and madeira were on hand as well, as were bourbon, scotch, and brandy.

On the clear September air the sweet aroma from bowers of colorful, fresh-cut flowers mingled with the subtle, ever present scent of the sea.

At five p.m. the wedding party was in full and noisy progress at *Lindo Vista*.

A cortege of carriages had been arriving throughout the sunny September afternoon. Discharged passengers streamed through the old hacienda's foyer, out the back door, across the flagstone patio, down the steps and into the peppermint-tented courtyard. As the crowd grew larger, people spilled out onto the vast manicured back lawn on the cliffs overlooking the ocean. The size of the crowd, the wide smiles on the faces of those present, the amount of food and liquor consumed, and the frequent bursts of hearty laughter signaled that the wedding reception was a grand success.

Neither the proud, handsome groom nor the glowing, beautiful bride had been sure how this party would turn out. Nonetheless, they had invited the entire population of the village to come to the *rancho* and join them in celebrating their wedding day. Elaborate plans had been made and executed. Preparations to host an enormous crowd of guests had been meticulously carried out. Enough rich food to feed every man, woman, and child in Capistrano had been ordered. Oceans of champagne had been chilled and enough hard liquor had been purchased to inebriate every hollow-legged drinker in southern California.

While the plans were being made, while the tent and the flowers and champagne and the foods were being ordered, Burt and Sabella wondered if they might end up toasting each other alone beneath a large tent where no one had gathered at a party to which no one had come.

Their concerns, as it turned out, had been completely unfounded.

Strong sentiment had at first been with the wronged Gena de Temple when news of the broken engagement spread quickly among the many mourners at Raleigh Burnett's funeral in June. It was, all agreed, just as well that Raleigh Burnett had gone on to his final reward before this sad turn of events. Lord knows if he hadn't already been dead, this would have killed him!

The gentry was absolutely outraged.

Poor, dear Gena! She had their full sympathy and support. That support grew every time she tearfully repeated her heartbreaking tale of how Burt Burnett had suddenly, coldly jilted her! How, they ask themselves, could he be such a callous cad? Shock spread through the village like a tidal wave sweeping in off the ocean. That shock increased when they learned Burt had thrown the senator's patrician daughter over for another. A young Spanish woman without relatives or background and a stranger to them all!

Those who liked Burt best looked for a logical excuse for his abominable behavior. Some blamed it on the wretched Santa Anas. The hot dry winds from the desert had blown throughout the first part of summer. Not a drop of rain had fallen during the entire month of June. It had been too hot to eat or sleep much less think straight. There were no cooling breezes from the ocean to offer relief. For weeks on end there was the taste of dust in everyone's mouth.

Maybe those constant blowing Santa Anas had made Burt go a little soft in the head. Had caused him do things he wouldn't normally do. Make some idiotic decisions. Act in such a rash way as to bring harsh criticism down on his dark head.

But even as the relentless hot, dry Santa Anas continued, the winds of forgiveness began to stir in the village. Despite his questionable behavior, it was next to impossible to stay permanently angry with Burt Burnett. Old friends who had known Burt all his life soon began to come around. In no time they reasoned he had every right to change his mind about marrying Miss de Temple. It was a free country, wasn't it?

Besides, who could stay put out with Burt Burnett for long, no matter what he did? He was an outgoing, likeable man whom they had known and loved since he was a chubby toddler with big gray eyes and a big wide smile. He would ride, astride his own gentle mare, into town with his father when he was barely two years old. He had a big hug and bigger grin for everybody he met on the streets. They had watched the adorable dark-haired tot grow into a tall, handsome man who still had a big hug and bigger grin for everyone he met.

Then too, Burt had not, as some might have been tempted to do, hidden out after the breakup with Gena de Temple. Knowing full well that everyone was talking, he rode into the village daily for all to see and point at. And he was as friendly and as outgoing as he had ever been. Choosing to ignore the frowns of disapproval and whispered gossip his presence incited, he'd stroll down the wooden sidewalk straight to the Inn of the Swallows, smiling easily and nodding to all passersby.

The romantics of Capistrano understood Burt better when they saw him with the beautiful young woman who had unseated Gena de Temple. In Burt's eyes, when he looked at Sabella Rios, was such an expression of adoration it was clear she had completely captured his heart. He was a man who was totally, helplessly, finally in love!

Every woman who saw the handsome pair together wished secretly that she herself were half so adored by a man half so handsome as the jet-haired, silver-eyed Burt Burnett. Likewise every man wistfully wished that he were half so in love with a woman who was half so pretty as the golden-tressed, dark-eyed Sabella Rios.

And now, on this warm September afternoon, the eternal romantics—and those who were not—had happily accepted the invitation to come to *Lindo Vista* in celebration of Burt Burnett's marriage to Miss Sabella Rios.

Everyone showed up en masse.

Everyone except Senator de Temple and his daughter, Gena.

In the midst of all the frivolity, Cappy Ricks stood alone and apart from the crowd. One hip pressed up against the old, stone wishing well, he stood leaning back, arms crossed over his chest, his squinted eyes seeking out and following the white-gowned bride.

Cappy suddenly shivered in the warmth of the afternoon sunshine.

Amidst the loud laughter and talk, the feasting and the drinking, the music and the merriment, the troubled ranch foreman wondered—for the thousandth time—if he had done the wrong thing by not telling Burt about Raleigh Burnett's shocking confession in his final hour of life.

Should he have warned the unsuspecting Burt about this beautiful young woman who was now his wife?

He had meant to do just that—but had never gotten around to it. He had fully intended to tell Burt everything once Raleigh Burnett's funeral was over. He had figured it was best to wait until after the elder Burnett had been laid to rest. Then he would tell Burt. As soon as they got back from the cemetery, he would tell him.

Everything.

He had sure meant to do it.

But he hadn't. He couldn't. Burt had just buried his father. Surely that was no time to reveal what he knew would inflict even more pain on the grieving son. He'd wait a week, two at the most, then have a long private talk with the boy.

It never happened.

Two days after the funeral Cappy met Sabella Rios and that changed everything. Despite who she was and what he knew about her, he was instantly charmed. He couldn't keep from liking her. He could not believe that she was anything other than exactly what she seemed: a very sweet, very pretty young woman who was totally in love with Burt.

Right from the start she had seemed so open and so honest. She didn't act like a woman with something to hide. He had attempted, in an offhand, casual manner, to find out what she was up to, what was going on.

Instead of dodging his questions, she seemed to genuinely appreciate his taking an interest in her, asking about her family, etc. She talked at length about her mother, her father, and her life growing up on a small Arizona ranch. She freely revealed all kinds of personal information without the slightest hesitation.

On occasion he had purposely tried to trip her up. Other times he attempted to get a rise out of her. He would brag mercilessly about *Lindo Vista*, go on and on about the vast acreage the Burnett family owned. All the while searching her pretty face for the slightest change of expression.

There was none.

Still Cappy was worried as he looked now at the glowing and gorgeous young woman in her long white-satin dress.

Mrs. Burton J. Burnett. The troubled foreman shook his silver head, disgusted with himself. Fool that he was, not only had he not tried to stop the wedding, he had walked Sabella down the aisle.

"I have no one," she had told him with poignant honesty, her large dark eyes burning directly into his. "You'd be the next best thing to having my own father give me away."

Today at the noontime nuptials in the old mission's chapel, it had seemed almost as if he actually were her father.

Toward the end of the brief ceremony, the padre had asked, "Who giveth this woman away?"

Cappy recalled that a slight lump had formed in his throat when he replied, "I do" and placed her hand in Burt's.

Cappy sighed heavily. Then he smiled, shoved his nagging doubts aside, and loosened his choking tie. He reached out and took a glass of champagne from a passing waiter's tray and began to relax.

Everything would work out. Maybe Sabella Rios and Burt Burnett hadn't met through pure happenstance. Maybe fate hadn't tossed the two them together. Maybe the angel-faced blonde had searched Burt out with ulterior motives in mind. But maybe, just maybe, she had fallen in love with Burt, just as he had with her. And maybe Burt need never know. . . .

"Cappy? Cappy Ricks, where are you?" Sabella's warm, musical voice pulled him from his reverie. He looked up. She stood smiling in the sunlight, Burt at her side, a possessive arm around her waist. Motioning with her hand, she called, "Come on over here, Cappy. We're about to cut the cake!"

Chapter Twenty

She could delay no longer.

The hour had finally come. The hour which she had dreaded for the past ten years.

The sun had long since slipped into the Pacific Ocean and bright stars had come out to wink in the dark night sky. Colorful Japanese lanterns, strung out over the sprawling grounds of the estate, illuminated the peppermint-striped tent and the big yard beyond.

At the center of the large manicured lawn, a three-tiered fountain splashed cool clear water down into a circular pool at its base. A couple of laughing young ladies, who'd had a touch too much champagne, were wading about in the crystal-clear pool.

Sabella envied them their carefree, childish fun. She longed to join them. She wished she could step into the fountain, and kick and laugh and play until it was time to go home.

Only *this* was her home.

She wouldn't be leaving with the rest of the crowd.

She would be spending the night here with . . . with . . .

Sabella smiled wistfully as she watched the laughing Cynthia Douglas and Janie Desmond, the friendly pair she had met in the millinery shop last spring, splash about in the fountain.

Only recently they had returned from their summer in San Francisco. Before they were even unpacked, they had learned of Burt's switch from Gena de Temple to her. Both swore to her that they were delighted. Enjoying themselves now, they giggled and squealed and waded about in the water, their dresses hiked up past their knees. A group of approving young men circled the fountain, clapping and egging them on.

The dancing had begun shortly after dark on a specially constructed outdoor dance floor on the oceanside of the splashing fountain. The loud, brassy band which had played fast-paced tunes throughout the warm sunny afternoon had been replaced by a small string orchestra whose members were elegantly attired in dark evening clothes.

The tempo was slower. The music more mellow. The tone half dreamy.

Sabella had been turned about on the dance floor by so many pairs of arms, her head was spinning and her slippered feet were sore. Still, she wished she could stay there all night, dancing, laughing, talking. Safe in the crush of people.

She couldn't.

She had made her bargain with the Devil and the first of many payments was now coming due.

Swaying to a slow, romantic ballad in the arms of her new husband, Sabella pulled her attention from the laughing girls in the fountain, lifted her head from Burt's chest, looked into his silver gray eyes, and calmly said, "Darling, give me half an hour."

The simple statement sent a shudder through Burt's tall, lean frame. While Sabella faced the hours ahead with dread and apprehension, Burt looked forward to them with expectation and anticipation.

He squeezed her hand gently, smiled, and pressed a soft kiss to her temple. His lips against her forehead, he whispered, "My love, I'll give you the rest of my life."

He hugged her tightly to him one final time, then released her. He stayed where she left him, standing in the middle of the dance floor, his arms at his sides, his hands balling into fists. His admiring gaze following her every graceful movement, he watched as she lifted the long satin skirts of her wedding gown and weaved her slow, sure way through the crowd.

Pride and love swelling in his heart, he saw her approach the hacienda with a growing group of excited young women following closely on her heels. The excitement seeped through the crowd as the departing bride disappeared into the striped tent and then reappeared on the other side.

She had reached the flagstone patio. Regally she climbed the steps, then turned about. In her hand was the slightly wilted bridal bouquet fashioned of ivory orchids and roses.

Every unmarried girl and woman eagerly pressed up close, hands outstretched, hoping to be the lucky one. Cynthia Douglas and Janie Desmond, barefoot and giggling, managed to maneuver themselves up to the front.

Sabella smiled brilliantly at all the females gathered before her. She teased them by making a couple of false starts, then tortured them no more. She tossed the bridal bouquet high into the air, whirled about, and hurried inside the hacienda with the sound of feminine screams, squeals, and laughter following her.

Once inside the safety of the house, Sabella's bright smile vanished.

Sweeping through the wide, silent corridor, she climbed the grand redwood staircase as if she were ascending to her doom. Wondering miserably if she could survive the terrible ordeal ahead, she told herself she had to, there was no choice.

She reached the second floor landing, hesitated, closed her eyes for a second, and nervously bit the fleshy inside of her bottom lip. Her eyes opened, she drew a shallow breath, and forced herself to move. At the head of the wide corridor leading down the mansion's northern wing, she paused again.

She began to tremble so violently her teeth chattered, and she felt icy cold and faint. She clamped her jaw down tight, gritted her chattering teeth, and narrowed her dark eyes in determination.

She lifted the long flowing skirts of her white-satin wedding gown and marched down that long silent corridor. When she stood directly before the very last door, she lingered for a long moment outside, waiting, putting off entering. Postponing her entrance into the luxurious quarters which, this night, would be for her a frightening chamber of horrors.

Her cold hand slowly reaching for the gleaming silver doorknob, she was struck anew with the terrifying realization that she would be spending the agonizingly long night on the other side of the door. Unable to get away. Trapped like a condemned prisoner. Locked up with a dark, amorous stranger of superior physical strength who, in his eagerness and lust, might well behave more like an animal than a man.

Sabella turned the silver knob, pushed open the heavy door, and stepped inside.

"*Madre de Dios!*" muttered Carmelita, hurrying toward her. "Where have you been? I expected you to come up ages ago." Shaking her graying head, the stocky Mexican woman took Sabella's elbow, turned her about, and began undoing the tiny hooks going down the back of the satin wedding gown.

"It's still quite early," Sabella defended herself.

"It's nearly nine o'clock! Are you forgetting all the years you spent teaching yourself the rules of proper etiquette for such occasions? You know very well the guests cannot leave before the bride and groom! Why, some of the older ones must be completely worn out."

"They're not the only ones," said Sabella.

The dress unhooked, Carmelita peeled it down Sabella's slender arms to her waist, pushed it over her hips, and said, "There, now, step out." Sabella took Carmelita's offered hand to steady herself, and stepped free of the mushrooming satin gown. "Your bath has been drawn for so long it's probably cold. I'll ring for—"

"No, don't." Sabella shook her head. "It'll be fine."

Carmelita saw the anxious look on Sabella's face and softened. "Oh, my little *nena*," she said, wrapping comforting arms around the slender Sabella, "you don't have to go through with this! There's still time. We could slip away while everyone's—"

"No," Sabella pulled from Carmelita's embrace. "We are not leaving here until I can take with me Burt Burnett's only son!" Tugging at the tape of her full, lace petticoats, she said, "Since that is impossible without first . . . without allowing . . ." She swallowed hard. "I just pray that I will be one of those fortunate women who gets pregnant on my wedding night!"

Older, wiser than her young charge, Carmelita frowned. "Do not count on such quick results. It may take weeks, months, even years before—"

"No!" Sabella said forcefully. "Don't say that! My mother got pregnant with me as soon as she was married. The same thing will happen to me. I know it will. It has to."

While Sabella took her bubble bath, Carmelita turned back the champagne-colored counterpane of the massive bed. She folded the downy matching coverlet to the bed's foot, and peeled back the cool, silky top sheet of the same hue. She fluffed several matching lace-edged cased pillows up against the tall solid headboard, then lowered the light in the frosted-glass-globed lamp on the bedside table. She moved a crystal bowl of ivory roses from the bureau to the night table.

She then went about the spacious bedchamber, checking to see if everything was ready, if all the windows were open as Mr. Burnett had requested. They were. She crossed the plushly carpeted room and opened the tall glass-paned doors leading onto the balcony. Breathing in the cool night air which carried the scent of the sea, she crossed the wide balcony, looked down, and saw dozens of guests milling about, laughing, talking, drinking.

Her gaze sweeping over a sea of faces, she easily picked out the bridegroom. He was taller, bigger, handsomer than any of the other gentlemen. A fine-looking man in Carmelita's opinion. Watching him closely, she saw Burt say something to a circle of friends, laugh heartily, then begin making his way through the throng. She turned away and hurried back inside.

The men in the crowd started to whistle and roar as Burt moved determinedly toward the hacienda, a bottle of champagne tucked under each arm and mischief in his eyes.

"Name the first one after me, Burt," someone laughingly said.

"Hey, Burt, want us to wake you at sunrise for breakfast?" teased another.

It was all in fun and Burt took it good-naturedly. When he reached the steps of the back patio, he pivoted, grinned boyishly, and said, "Good friends, Mrs. Burnett and I thank you all for coming. There's plenty of food and liquor, the orchestra's still playing. Stay as long as you like." He grinned, winked, and said, "But it's time for me to bid you all good night!"

Piercing whistles and thunderous applause followed him into the silent house. Burt's bright smile didn't disappear once he got inside. He was beaming when he made a detour by the kitchen. He snagged a couple of stemmed glasses in his lean fingers, nodded yes when a white-jacketed waiter quickly produced a silver bucket of ice. The smiling servant took both bottles of champagne from Burt, set one aside, shoved the other down into the depths of the ice, and handed the silver bucket to Burt.

"You're a good man, Thomas McGuire. Remind me to give you a raise tomorrow," Burt said, smiling as he backed away.

Carmelita hurried back inside to warn Sabella that she had to hurry, Burt was on his way up. Sabella had barely shoved her arms into the long gossamer sleeves of her filmy white negligee before a firm knock sounded on the heavy door. The women temporarily froze, and looked at each other. Then Carmelita gave Sabella one last reassuring hug, hurried to the interior door leading into the suite's sitting room, dashed through it, and waited there until she heard Sabella say, "Come in, Burt."

Carmelita stepped out into the corridor and fled as Burt opened the door and went inside the bedroom.

Burt nudged the door shut with his muscular shoulder, then stood there against it for a long moment, unmoving, the silver champagne bucket in one hand, two stemmed glasses in the other, helplessly staring at the young woman who was now his wife.

She was covered from her graceful throat to her cute little toes in a flowing, long-sleeved negligee of ivory satin trimmed in delicate lace. Her blond hair was unbound and spilling around her slender shoulders and down her back. The lamplight, coming from behind, made a halo of the lustrous golden locks. Her eyes were fixed on him and in their dark luminous depths was an oddly appealing mixture of virginal anxiety and challenging boldness. She was, without doubt, the most exquisitely beautiful woman Burt had ever laid eyes on. He wanted her with such a blinding passion he could hardly keep from dropping the champagne bucket and rushing forward to pull her into his eager embrace. His hands trembled with the need to immediately sweep away her covering nightclothes and have her naked in his arms.

"Sweetheart, I hope I didn't rush you," he said, his tone low, caressing.

"No, not at all," Sabella told him, her knees trembling, her heart pounding in her chest.

With quick catlike grace Burt moved into the room. Nervously observing his approach, Sabella thought he had never looked so big, so dark, so frightening before. He was a giant of a man and she felt small and defenseless in his intimidating presence. He walked directly toward her. When he was less than two feet away, he placed the silver ice bucket and the stemmed glasses on the night table by the bed.

He turned to face her, stepped closer, smiled, and placed his hands on her upper arms.

"Will you join me in a toast, darling?"

"Yes, of course," she said, nodding, swallowing convulsively. If only she could drink the entire bottle. Maybe then she could stand what was in store for her.

Burt shrugged out of his dark suit jacket and tossed it onto a nearby chair. He stuck his middle finger beneath the neat knot of his black silk tie, and yanked, loosening it. Then he unbuttoned the top button of his white dress shirt.

Sabella closely watched the quick, impatient way he removed his jacket, the way he decisively pulled at his tie and swiftly flipped open the collar of his shirt. Would he be that reckless and hasty with her? Would he snatch away her robe and toss it aside, then immediately tug her gown off, leaving her stark naked and miserably embarrassed?

Burt handed Sabella a glass of champagne. He picked up his own, held it out, looked straight into her dark flashing eyes, and said, "May all our bright tomorrows be half as sweet as this first night together."

Chapter Twenty-one

His champagne flute touched, clinking musically against hers. They raised the stemmed glasses to their lips. Burt took one generous swig of the chilled wine, then lowered his glass. Sabella gulped thirstily, swallowed anxiously, then immediately took another large drink. Unnerved by the hot light shining in Burt's smokey eyes, she was bent on consuming as much of the bubbly champagne as possible. She drank until she had drained the last drop, took a quick, anxious breath, and held out her empty glass to him.

"May I have another?" she asked, so jittery she felt like snatching the bottle and turning it up to her lips.

"Of course, you can," Burt replied, both his tone and his smile tolerant, understanding. "You may drink all the champagne on *Lindo Vista* if you so desire."

He pulled the heavy bottle from its icy depths. Sabella locked her knees so they wouldn't tremble so violently and eagerly held out her glass. But Burt didn't pour. He realized she was so nervous she could hardly stand. Withholding the bottle, he grinned devilishly at her, and teased, "If we're to do some serious drinking, sweetheart, why don't we get comfortable? I never did like standing to drink. Did you?"

Before Sabella could answer, Burt scooped her up into his powerful arms, the champagne bottle still clutched tightly in his fist. Sabella quickly closed her eyes in horror as he turned and started to move. Held firmly against his broad, solid chest, the empty glass gripped in her cold fingers, she buried her face in his shoulder and tried to slow the hammering of her racing heart.

She couldn't.

This big, dark man who held her in his arms was a thief without conscience whom she would despise to the end of her days on earth. But he was now also her legally wedded husband. The one she had vowed this very noon to love, honor, and obey. Any second he would toss her onto the bed, rip off her robe and gown, and force himself on her without preliminaries. And she would have no choice but to meekly submit.

Sabella's eyes opened and her head came up off Burt's shoulder in surprise when she saw that he had not taken her to the bed after all. He had carried her across the dimly lit room to a big, well-worn brown leather chair and matching ottoman. While she gave him a puzzled look, he sank down into the soft depths of the armchair, settling her comfortably on his lap.

"Now, Mrs. Burnett," he said, smiling so broadly his teeth gleamed white in his tanned face, "if you'll hold your empty glass slightly down so that I can pour without shoving your knees up to your chest, I'll fill it."

Sabella released a caught breath and nodded, relieved that they were not in the bed. She flung her hand out and lowered her glass so he could reach it. His arms trapped beneath her legs, he leaned a little forward, peered down, and poured. Pouring from such an awkward position was no easy feat and neither he nor she were surprised when the fizzing champagne hit the shallow glass and splashed up and out onto the back of his hand. A few dewy drops spilled as well on the lacy hem of Sabella's satin negligee.

"Sorry, honey," Burt said, not really sounding as if he were. "Tell you what, next time you marry, the fancy gown for your wedding night will be on me. How's that?"

"I think," she said, adopting what she hoped was a teasing tone, "that you have no intention of buying me a new nightgown." She relieved him of the champagne bottle, carefully placing it on the table beside the chair.

"Ah, you're a smart as well as a beautiful woman," Burt

said. "No more wedding nights for you, Mrs. Burton J. Burnett." He squeezed her narrow waist possessively. "You belong to me. I will never let you go."

"I see," Sabella replied playfully after another large, anxious swallow of champagne. "Does this mean I will have no more new nightgowns? That I must take very good care of this one?"

Burt shook his dark head. "No, sweetheart, it doesn't mean that at all." Smiling warmly, looking straight into her dark, flashing eyes, Burt lifted a lace-trimmed panel of her ivory satin negligee and carelessly dried off his champagne-wet hand on the expensive garment.

"Burt Burnett!" she scolded, "you've ruined my . . ."

"Have I?" He grinned. "Well it doesn't matter. After tonight, you won't be needing it."

"I won't?" She tried to keep her tone modulated, to sound and appear completely calm.

"Nope. You may buy dozens, hundreds if you wish"—he brushed a long silky strand of golden hair back from her face—"so long as you leave them in the bureau drawer when you come to bed."

"Now, Burt, I—"

"Kiss me," he interrupted, knowing he shouldn't have made such a bold statement on this first night, "kiss me and we'll argue the point later."

Sabella automatically tensed for the deep, probing kiss of passion she expected. She closed her eyes and waited. And waited. Finally her eyes opened, she tilted her head to the side, and said, "Aren't you going to kiss me?"

His dark head pressed against the old leather chair's cushioned back, his long, lean body in a relaxed attitude, Burt said, "No, I'm not. I asked you to kiss me." His hand touched her wrist, moved caressingly up her arm to her elbow, then fell away. "I'm waiting, sweetheart."

Sabella was quickly becoming confused. She was thrown off balance, baffled by his behavior. She had dreaded this hour for so long, had supposed that she knew exactly what would happen. She had steeled herself to endure devastating embarrassment, humiliating shame, and agonizing pain. And she had assumed that by now—after they had been alone for several long moments—she would be experiencing all three horrid sensations.

She knew what a passionate man Burt Burnett was. She had spent the summer fending off his unflagging attempts to seduce her. So she had imagined that tonight he would be such an anxious, aggressive lover he would already have her stripped naked and lying helpless beneath him in that big bed.

Grateful she had misjudged him, but frankly puzzled, Sabella took another drink of champagne, then leaned to him, and brushed a soft, moist kiss to his smooth, warm lips. Burt's head never left the chair back. He never reached for her. Both his hands remained resting on the chair arms.

"That was awfully sweet," he praised, lips stretching into a wide, boyish grin. "I liked it. Will you do it again? Please."

Sabella stared at him, wondering if maybe he was as nervous as she. Could that be possible? Were men afraid their first time, too? Not that this was his first time. Lord knew how many women he'd had. It would be his first time with her. Was he tense because of it? Fearful he wouldn't please her? Foolish though it was, the thought that this big, handsome, cocky man might be apprehensive just as she was, touched a soft spot in her woman's heart.

"Share my champagne," she invited, raising her glass to his lips.

Burt took a drink, and almost before he could swallow, her lips were back on his. She kissed him tenderly, sweetly, molding her soft, wine-wet lips to the wide, smooth contours of his, instinctively attempting to illicit a response. It took a while, but in time she got it. After pressing dozens of varying kinds of kisses to his warm, sculpted lips, Sabella realized that his head was no longer resting against the chair back and his hands were no longer on the leather arms.

He was kissing her as she was kissing him and his arms were around her, pressing her close. At last, Burt's lips momentarily left hers. He lifted his head, looked at her somewhat dreamily, and said a very odd thing.

"Baby, do you like this chair?"

The pulse leaping in her throat, her dark liquid eyes glowing from the drugging, champagne-laced kisses, Sabella touched the knot of his loosened silk tie with her forefinger, and said, "I hadn't given it a great deal of thought. Why? Does it make any difference? It's just a chair and—"

"No, darlin', you're wrong there," Burt gently corrected her. "It isn't *just* a chair. It's a very special chair. I call this old chair my 'Happy' chair."

She lifted a well-arched eyebrow. "Your Happy chair?"

"That's right. You see, when I'm really happy, I sit here in this chair."

"That's absurd." Sabella was skeptical, sure he was teasing her.

"No, it's not. Not at all." He smiled and she had to admit he looked very happy at this particular moment. "I like to sit here when I'm completely happy. Anytime I'm sitting in this old beat-up chair, I'm one happy man." He sighed contentedly, reached out, plucked a strand of her long golden hair off her shoulder and idly twisted it around his finger. "I have a Worry chair too. It's in the library downstairs. It's a burgundy-colored wing chair with a tall, straight back and wood-trimmed arms. Most uncomfortable. I sit there to do my worrying."

"You worry?" she said, charmed in spite of herself by his lovable foolishness. "I can't imagine you worrying about anything."

Burt grinned and admitted, "The burgundy chair is in mint condition. Looks brand new, whereas you can see for yourself that this one has had a lot of wear." Impulsively, he bent his dark head and kissed the swell of her breast through the sleek covering of her lace-trimmed negligee, surprising her. Ignoring her little wince and her sharp intake of air, he kissed her a second time, opening his mouth a little, then lifted his head, and told her, "From now on, you may sit here in my Happy chair when you're happy."

"Thank you," she said for want of something more appropriate. She knew she would never be happy enough to sit in his Happy chair, but she didn't want him to know it.

Burt lifted a lean, dark hand, slid long fingers into her flowing golden hair at the side of her head.

"I have never allowed anyone else to sit in my Happy chair," he stated as if it were gospel truth. "Never." His mouth lowered toward hers and then hesitated, hovering inches away, so close she felt his warm breath when he told her, "Nor, sweetheart, has anyone else slept in that great bed behind us. Just me.

Only me." His lips brushed a kiss to hers and he murmured against her mouth, "Now you will sleep in that bed with me tonight and every night. I love you, Sabella Rios Burnett. I love you more than you'll ever know."

Then his mouth took hers again and he kissed her, urgently but gently, tenderly exploring, caressing and nibbling until he could feel her starting to relax, starting to respond. His lips moving across her cheek, he said, "More champagne, sweetheart?"

Sabella breathlessly nodded. Burt promptly poured more chilled golden wine into her glass and urged her to drink, assuring her that he'd have another bottle sent up when they finished this one. A dozen bottles if need be. Sensing that she was slowly, steadily becoming more at ease and comfortable with him, he kept her right there where they sat, in his old leather Happy chair. He knew she wouldn't feel threatened so long as they weren't on the bed.

That suited him fine.

He could think of no better place to begin their first night of lovemaking than here in his Happy chair.

So there they stayed, drinking champagne, sharing one glass in their building intimacy. Between sips, they kissed hotly, they touched each other through the barrier of their clothing, they heard faintly mellow romantic music, muffled voices, and occasional laughter drifting up from below through the open balcony doors.

Sabella soon became wonderfully relaxed. In time, surprisingly, she became aroused as well. She didn't know if it was the effects of the champagne flowing through her bloodstream or Burt's heated, probing kisses or the sensuous slither of lush satin against her sensitive flesh, but she was growing warmer with every beat of her heart.

She didn't fight what was happening to her or make any attempt to hold back her newly awakened passions. Heartened to find that she could respond—after a fashion—to this man with whom she *must* make love, Sabella willed herself to let go, to surrender fully, to derive pleasure if possible.

Her thoughts fuzzy, her body tingling, she kissed Burt with total abandon, her lips almost as hot and as eager as his. As their mouths melded and clung, his hand slipped inside her negligee and cupped her left breast through the satin of her low-cut nightgown. His touch made her sigh in startled joy, and when his thumb brushed back and forth over her nipple through the thin, slick covering, coaxing it into a throbbing point of pure sensation, she shuddered.

Burt's kisses grew steadily more intoxicating, his caressing hands more enthralling. He was probably, she pondered dreamily, a masterful lover who knew well how to please a woman. He was, in fact, thrilling her, pleasing her. What sweet sensual pleasure it was to sit here on this darkly handsome man's lap and share wine-flavored kisses with him while he urged the slinky fabric of her long satin nightgown to glide slowly up, up, up her legs. When the hem of the shimmering white gown reached her dimpled knees, Burt released it, allowing it to pool there in her lap.

Dropping his dark head back against the chair, he took her champagne glass away, set it aside, then drew her hand to the open collar of his shirt where the loose knot of his tie rested. Her brain a trifle fuzzy, Sabella smiled, looked into his silver-gray eyes, and read the clear message in them. Swept away by the romantic milieu, she was amenable to his implied suggestion.

Placing both hands on the tie, she deftly undid the loosened knot, then yanked on one end of the silk neckpiece until it was freed from his stiff, white shirt collar. She playfully trailed the pointed tip of the tie up over his handsome face, tickling his chin and nose and forehead, before laughing softly and tossing it to the floor.

"From the first time you ever touched me," Burt said, his voice low, rough with emotion, "every nerve and muscle in my body has ached for you." His smoldering gray eyes held an endearingly pleading look. "Touch me, sweetheart. Unbutton my shirt and touch me."

Nodding, Sabella began unbuttoning his white shirt. Her dark gaze held his as she deftly slipped button after button through the buttonholes. When she reached his waist, she pulled at the shirt's long tail until it came up out of his dark trousers. She made a face of frustration when the stubborn bottom button refused to slide through its buttonhole.

"Let it go. I've a better idea," Burt said and lifted his right wrist to her so she could remove the gleaming gold cufflink.

Sabella plucked the heavy gold link from the shirt's cuff and immediately turned her attention to his left wrist. She held the matching links in the palm of her hand as Burt, in a purely masculine gesture, leaned forward and anxiously pulled the shirt up over his dark head and off. He dropped it to the floor. Sabella held out her hand. He took the gold cuff links and laid them aside.

He waited, tensed, while her inquiring gaze slid over his bared torso. Openly, thoughtfully she appraised him. He was indeed handsome, his suave, dark masculinity potently appealing. Sabella licked her kiss-swollen lips when she laid her hand on him and fanned her open palm slowly across his wide chest. Then she raked her long nails through the dense, dark, curling hair and giggled delightedly when he groaned.

Burt let her play for a time, the flat hard muscles of his chest quivering in response to her warm, soft touch.

His breath growing short, he finally captured her roving hand, drew it up over his shoulder, and kissed her. Then it was Sabella who quivered as the crisp black hair of his broad, solid chest tickled her sensitive skin in a most delightful way. It felt so good she caught herself growing anxious for the moment when her breasts would be totally bared against him.

She wondered dreamily if he had read her mind when she felt his fingers on the tiny lace frogs at her throat, unfastening her negligee. His burning mouth never leaving hers, Burt pushed the opened negligee apart. He drew her hand down from his neck and gently pushed the flowing sleeve of the negligee down her arm. Her lips clinging anxiously to his, Sabella helped all she could, dropping her arms to her sides and shaking her slender shoulders to free herself of the robe.

The burning kiss never ending, the negligee fell away forgotten, trapped beneath Sabella, spilling over Burt's bent knees in a shimmering white curtain. Sabella's bare arms went around Burt's neck and she pressed him back against the worn leather chair, kissing him wildly, eagerly, as she had never kissed him before. She made a little sound of protest deep in her throat when Burt tore her arms from around his neck, his lips from hers, and sat her back a little.

But she purred like a kitten when, looking directly into her shining eyes, Burt began to urge the narrow satin straps of her nightgown off her shoulders as he said in a low, gentle voice, "Let me love you, Sabella. Let me show you just how sweet love can be."

Chapter Twenty-two

Burt carefully lowered the gown's snug-fitting bodice. Sabella's lips fell open and her breath became shallow as she felt her breasts surge against the slowly sliding satin. When at last the slippery confinement fell away and her swelling breasts sprang free, she and Burt simultaneously sighed.

Until that moment they had been looking into each other's eyes. Now, as if on cue, both lowered their gaze to the creamy, pink-tipped peaks, standing out bare and beautiful, as if proud of their round fullness. The lowered gown straps trapping her arms at her sides, Sabella continued to watch, just as Burt did, as slowly he drew her flush against him.

The last thing she saw was her tight, aching nipples disappearing into the thick black hair covering his chest. Then her eyes closed as the feel of that crisp curling hair tickling her sensitive nipples brought instant electric joy. She arched her back and pressed herself as close as possible to the pleasing texture and incredible heat of him.

His hand dexterous, Burt quickly freed her arms from the fallen straps, but Sabella was only vaguely aware of it. For the moment her arms were of no particular importance to her, so long as she could press her stinging nipples against his hard, hair-covered chest, nothing else mattered. The excitement she felt was almost unbearable. There could be no greater joy than this.

But in only a matter of seconds, she found out there could be. His hand wrapped around the back of her neck beneath her long flowing hair, Burt captured her mouth and kissed her, his tongue thrusting deeply, touching hers, stroking all the dark, wet recesses of her mouth. When his lips left hers abruptly, he said huskily, "Sweetheart, open your eyes. Look at me, Sabella?"

Her lips parted, her face flushed, she opened her passion-glazed eyes. Her lids lowered, long lashes fluttering nervously, she watched entranced as Burt put both hands to her waist, lifted her slightly, and bent his dark head to her bared torso. His mouth a hot searing brand on her naked flesh, he kissed a path from the delicate hollow of her throat down to her bursting breast. When he reached the tightened, desire-darkened nipple, he pressed the softest, gentlest of closed-mouthed kisses to the tight little point. The feather-light caress was enough to send a deep shudder of pleasure through Sabella's slender body. She whispered his name in desperate entreaty for him to continue.

"God, you're so beautiful, so sweet," he murmured, brushing his hot face back and forth over her naked breasts. "You make me so happy, Sabella. I'll make you happy, too, if you'll let me."

"I . . . I'll let you," she said anxiously, eager to have his mouth back on her yearning breasts.

"Will you, sweet?" he whispered and placed a dark, lean hand beneath her bare left breast, urging it upward as he bent to it.

"Ahhhhh," Sabella sighed involuntarily when his warm lips opened over the straining, throbbing nipple and his tongue began to make licking, loving strokes across the taut point of pure sensation.

Her freed hands went into Burt's dark hair at the sides of his head and she impatiently drew him to her, pulling his hot, handsome face closer, thrusting her torso forward, frantically urging more and more of her bare throbbing breast into his hot sucking mouth as it opened wider and wider to accept her.

Sabella was so caught up in this delightful procedure in

pleasure of which, until now, she had been totally ignorant, she was no longer concerned with what was expected of her tonight. She didn't dread what Burt would do to her in his big bed. Sighing and squirming and drowning in physical joy, she no longer thought past the moment. This exquisite experience, the strong, flexing pull of Burt's lips at her breasts drew from her all thought of the future.

So enraptured was she, Sabella didn't mind a bit when Burt laid a warm, caressing hand on her knee. She did not object when he snagged the hem of her nightgown and began slowly pushing it up, his hand stroking the golden tan flesh of her thighs.

Sabella had no idea how long they stayed in the leather Happy chair, kissing, touching, enjoying the increasingly thrilling journey toward that final destination of all-out lovemaking. It seemed at once like a long time and yet it was as though it passed in a heartbeat. Perhaps that was because she relished every new thrill, each novel sensation she experienced at the hands of this skilled, patient lover who was her husband.

"Burt, Burt," she whispered and trembled.

She buried her face in the curve of his neck and shoulder when his hand, which had been lying unthreateningly atop her bared leg, slipped slowly down to the warm inside of her thigh. He touched the damp, curling triangle of blond hair between her legs and she gasped.

"Shhh, baby," he said, his hand doing nothing more than cupping her possessively, gently pressing the springy golden curls against the moist flesh. "Kiss me, Sabella."

He turned his head and captured her mouth with his own. He kissed her and throughout the long, hot, sexy kiss his hand stayed where it was, carefully covering the crisp blond curls which protected that most feminine part of her. That possessive hand stayed completely still, the lean fingers at rest. For that reason, because he made no attempt to stroke or probe or rush her, Sabella relaxed and her quivering thighs, tightly pressed together, fell naturally apart.

By the time Burt rose from the Happy chair and carried her across the room to the big waiting bed, Sabella was more than ready to go. She wasn't quite sure when it happened, or exactly how, but she realized when Burt stood up that she was no longer wearing her satin nightgown. She was completely naked in his arms, her gown and negligee lying in a shimmering white pool on the darkness of the rug.

She didn't care.

She sighed with sensual pleasure when Burt put his knee on the mattress, leaned over, and gently laid her in the very center of the big, silk-sheeted bed. Almost all her inhibitions had been discarded along with her nightgown. She lay stretching and squirming, enjoying the feel of cool silk against her hot skin. She hadn't realized she was still wearing one of her house slippers until Burt removed it, leaning down to kiss her bare instep before sliding the slipper off and tossing it to the floor.

She smiled dreamily when he said in a low, baritone voice, "I told you I would kiss your feet."

"Mmmmm," she responded then turned her head to watch as he kicked off his own shoes, dropped down on the edge of a chaise lounge, and took off his dark stockings.

He rose and his hands went to his belt buckle. Sabella wondered idly if she should turn away, not look.

She watched as he unbuttoned his trousers, shoved his thumbs into the sides of the waistband, and sent both dark trousers and linen underwear to the rug.

Sabella drew a quick, shallow breath and stared in wonder at his glorious physique. He was truly magnificent in his naked glory, an Apollo—a veritable god. His broad chest and smooth back were matched in their masculine beauty by the rippling muscles of his tight belly, the strong, sleek muscles of his thighs and long lean legs.

She could no longer avoid staring at that part of his anatomy about which she was the most curious. As if he knew exactly where her questioning glance was focused, Burt came to the bed, wrapped a hand around the intricately carved post of the bed's tall headboard, and stood proud and still for her to leisurely examine him.

His pulsing erection, thrusting upward out of the dense growth of black hair covering his groin was awesome in size and shape. Sabella had never in her life seen a naked man. But she had been raised on a ranch, had watched horses mate. Involuntarily, she shivered. The naked, fully aroused Burt put her in mind of a mighty stallion, ready to mount a mare. A small degree of her earlier fear returned. Would he behave as a stallion? Would he climb into bed, flip her onto her stomach, yank her up onto all fours, and shove that huge member into her, deaf to her cries of disgust and pain?

Burt released the bedpost.

Gracefully, as he did all things, he slipped into bed and quickly drew the champagne-colored sheet up over his nakedness to his waist. He turned onto his side, raised up and supported his weight on his elbow. He reached out and laid a gentle hand on Sabella's tense face.

His fingers stroking her cheek, he looked into her large, frightened eyes, and said, "Come into my arms, sweetheart. Let me hold you."

His fingers moved down the side of her throat and out across her bare shoulder. Slowly, surely he pulled her into his embrace, lying back flat on the bed, drawing her against his side. He felt a tremor surge through her naked, slender body. He put a thumb beneath her quivering chin, turned her face up to his, and kissed her.

He kept kissing her until she was again warm and pliant in his arms. He purposely turned onto his side as he held her so that his straining erection could press against her belly. His lips feasting on hers, his arms around her, he allowed her to acquaint herself with his body. He let her feel the throbbing flesh against her, to become comfortable with the size, the texture, and the hardness of him. To experience the powerful palpitations surging through him while he was still outside her body, before he buried himself deep inside her.

He could tell by the way she was pressing herself to him that she was eagerly familiarizing herself with him. He wasn't surprised. Sabella was a healthy, curious, hot-blooded woman and he looked forward to the long, lovely nights ahead teaching her how to make love.

After a time Burt pressed Sabella down onto her back and leaned over her, his lips still playing with hers. He kissed her temples, her eyes, her cheeks, and then moved to her mouth again. When his lips slid over her chin to brush a kiss to the hollow of her throat, Sabella sighed. He nibbled and nuzzled his way down to her breasts and she sighed more heavily when his mouth covered a straining nipple.

Burt sucked on her nipples until she was writhing and squirming and whispering his name. At the same time his hand began to stroke her bare belly, her shapely thighs. When his fingers went to the golden triangle this time, they did not stay still.

Burt lifted his dark head and watched Sabella's beautiful face as he carefully, gently slipped the tips of his fingers through the blond coils until he touched the sensitive female flesh. Her back arched and her breath caught in shock when he touched her where no man ever had before. She wasn't sure she liked having his fingers there. She didn't, she decided. Not at all.

Sabella fidgeted in an attempt to get him to stop what he was doing and she glared at him, making a face. But Burt simply smiled at her, began to gently stroke her, and promised, "Soon, sweetheart, it will feel good."

And he was right.

Before she knew it Sabella was sighing and writhing with excited pleasure. It felt to her as if his caressing fingers were spreading liquid fire and that any second she would burn completely up. And the strangest thing was, she welcomed the coming blaze, could hardly wait for it to happen.

"Burt, Burt," she was breathless, her gaze was locked with his, "it's so . . . so . . ."

"Yes, yes," he murmured. "Feels good, doesn't it, sweetheart?"

"It . . . it . . . feels so . . . so good I can't stand it any longer."

He whispered, "Just a few more seconds now . . . just a little while more."

Throat dry, blond head tossing frantically on the pillow, Sabella licked her lips, and asked, "How do you know when to stop? How will I know when I—"

"You'll know, sweet," he softly assured her.

"Will . . . will . . . you know, too?"

"I think so," he said, the timbre of his voice low, soft, carefully hiding his amusement at the innocence of her question.

His eyes filled with love and tenderness, Burt continued to patiently guide his beautiful virgin bride ever closer to her first climax. Her long slender legs parted, her breath coming

in rapid little gasps, Sabella lay there glassy-eyed, feeling as
though were Burt to take his hand away, she would surely
die. At the same time feeling she would surely die if he
did not.

Just when the wild new pleasure escalated to the point
were it was so intense it was painful, Sabella felt a great,
mysterious explosion of heat where Burt's fingertips were
touching her. A blinding, throbbing ecstasy transported her
upward to an undreamed-of level of rapture and kept her
there for several long frightening seconds.

Left shaking and stunned by the experience, Sabella was
grateful when Burt's arms went around her and he held her
tight. She clung to him for dear life, her heart pounding in
her chest, her eyes wide with wonder. Burt held her, murmured endearments, kissed her flushed face, and soothingly
stroked her bare back until she had calmed.

He gave her time to lie back and relax, allowed her to rest
on the pillows. She drew deep breaths and sighed, her arms
and legs gone totally limp, a wonderful sense of well-being
enveloping her. She had absolutely no energy, but she didn't
care. There was nothing she wanted to do. She had no desire
to move, to change positions, just wanted to lie here flat on
her back forever.

When Burt began kissing her forehead, her cheek, her ear,
she didn't mind, but neither did she respond. Eyelids drooping with total relaxation, she lay there lazily accepting the
soft, gentle kisses he brushed to her open lips. As if he didn't
realize that she was not interested, he continued to kiss her.
His mouth kept moving warmly on hers, forcing hers to open.
His tongue played over her lips, licking and teasing. At the
same time his hand caressed her breast, the thumb rubbing
back and forth over the sleeping nipple.

Quite unexpectedly Sabella felt herself beginning to come
alive, to respond to his kiss, his touch. Soon her lips were
clinging to his and the thrusting tongue inside her mouth
thrilled her, pleased her just as it had before. Her arms went
around his neck and she pulled him closer. He put a hand
to her rib cage and, rolling back up onto his side, brought
her with him. They lay facing each other and Burt drew her
leg up over his hip and around his back.

It was then Sabella realized fully that Burt was still very

much erect. Thoughtlessly she had forgotten that he had not yet known the kind of wild, beautiful release she had experienced.

Burt's dark hand spread on the rounded cheek of her bottom and he urged her pelvis to meet his rhythmically in a simulation of the act of love. That hot, hard power against her bare belly was electrifying and Sabella immediately wondered if it would feel that good when it was inside her.

Burt's spread fingers left her buttocks, captured her wrist, and drew her hand between their pressing bodies, placing it on his rigid flesh. He released her hand, looked into her eyes, and said, "I caressed you, sweetheart. Do it to me."

"I ... I don't know how," she admitted, her fingertips barely touching him. She moved her leg from around his back and looked at him.

Burt showed her. With his hand coaxing hers, he showed her what to do, how to wrap her fingers not-too-tightly around him and slowly move them up and down the length of him. Sabella learned quickly. In minutes she shook off his helping hand and took over on her own. She was warming to the intriguing exercise when Burt abruptly grabbed her hand to stop her.

She frowned. "It doesn't feel good?"

"It does, but I ..." He smiled, drew her down, and kissed her. He didn't want to say it out loud, to tell her that he was going to explode in her hand if she continued touching him.

Their kisses were instantly fever hot. So were their bodies. With his mouth fused to hers, Burt pressed Sabella over onto her back. Their lips separated as his hand swept over her belly and urged her legs apart. His touch found her wet and hot and ready. He moved between her open thighs, lowered his dark face to hers and kissed her, his long, lean body pressing against hers, his weight supported on his elbows.

He slid downward a little to let the tip of his blood-filled tumescence press and rub against the slick, burning spot which was the true key to all her carnal joy. After only a few seconds, he lowered his hand between them, dipped his fingers into the wetness flowing freely from her and spread it on himself so that he would go in easier.

Sabella knew the moment had come and couldn't keep from tensing, tightening her muscles against the invasion. She shut her eyes as tightly as possible and gritted her teeth. One second passed. Two. Three. The tip of his maleness was pressing into her, seeking entrance.

She heard Burt's low, compelling voice saying, "Open your eyes, darling. Look at me so I'll know if I'm hurting you."

Sabella's dark eyes reluctantly opened. She clasped Burt's hard biceps with clawlike hands, her nails biting into his flesh. She looked into his eyes.

"Now, my love, relax," he said. "Let yourself go completely limp."

Sabella nodded, swallowed convulsively, and forced her body to go slack. Burt felt the change and thrust swiftly into her. She released one little involuntary moan at the shock of it, but then no more. The pain was brief and bearable and much sooner than she had expected the discomfort had passed and it started to feel good.

She soon began to move in rhythm with Burt, to lift and lower her pelvis to meet the roll and thrust of his. Pleasure began to spread in an ever-widening arc outward from that fiery place where his body was joined with hers. She was beginning to experience that same wonderful sensation she'd known earlier when his hand had so lovingly caressed her.

Only this was better.

This was unbelievably wonderful. She realized with surprise that a fine sheen of moisture covered her naked body and that Burt's muscular shoulders and clefted back were glistening with perspiration despite the coolness of the room.

Her hands slid down his slippery arms, moving to his hard, trim waist. She smiled dreamily recalling how she had wondered earlier, when she felt his throbbing power pressed against her stomach, if it would feel that good inside her. How foolish she had been, how utterly ignorant of her own body as well as his.

She realized now, moving with her dark, handsome lover as if she had been born to do nothing but this, that she'd had no conception of what it was like to make love. It was, she decided, a purely physical act that had little or nothing to do with being in love. It must be so because in the part of her brain that was still capable of logical thought, she was fully aware that she did not love this man, did not even admire or respect him. He was her enemy.

She hated him.

Yet here she was, naked in his bed, her body if not her soul laid wide open to him. And it was pleasurable, no use denying it. Wonderful, breathtaking pleasure unlike any other pleasure on earth.

Already Sabella had learned enough about this new pleasure to know that they were joyously striving together, ascending toward that longed-for burst of blinding ecstasy she now knew awaited. Faster and faster became their rhythm. Deeper and deeper were his filling, stretching thrusts. Hotter and hotter grew their sweat-slick bodies. Harder and harder beat their racing hearts.

"Burrrrt . . . Burrrrt . . . I . . ." she murmured breathlessly, feeling her climax beginning.

"Yes, baby," he whispered, driving into her, feeling himself expanding to that aching fullness which could only end with total emptying release.

Together they attained a deep, shuddering rapture, that sweet gift of passion liberated, the wondrous explosion of ecstasy that seemed to go on and on with such devastating magnitude that Sabella cried out loudly and bit Burt's slick shoulder with sharp, punishing teeth.

As they slowly, tiredly drifted back to reality, Sabella became vaguely aware of music and of voices carried up from below on the cool ocean breezes. She turned her head on the pillow and looked across the shadowy room. The tall doors all stood open, had been open the entire time they were making love.

Her head snapped around and she opened her mouth to speak, but before she could say a word, Burt told her, "They didn't hear you cry out, sweetheart. I'm the only one and it was the sweetest sound I've ever heard."

He then collapsed flat on his back, put a long arm around her, and drew her close. Her head cradled on his shoulder, she snuggled tiredly to him, and draped an arm across his chest.

"Burt?"

"Hmmmm?"

"Is . . . is making love always . . ." her words trailed away and she sighed.

"Always what, sweetheart?" Burt coaxed. "Go ahead. You can ask me anything. I'm your husband."

"Well, I was just wondering if making love will always be as good as it was this time?"

Delighted, happy as he'd never been in his life, Burt laughed heartily and hugged her tight. "No, honey, not really."

"No?"

"No." He kissed her soundly. "Next time it will be even better!"

Chapter Twenty-three

S *ilver Lining*, the Burnetts' personal Pullman car, waited on the private railroad spur. The long, silver-gray car gleamed brightly in the September morning sunlight. At dawn, the car's sleek body had been freshly washed and meticulously polished by a trio of Burnett ranch hands, while the interior was thoroughly cleaned and tidied by a pair of Burnett house servants.

The railcar's larder was stocked to overflowing with every imaginable fancy food and edible delicacy. Fine champagne and vintage wines filled the liquor cabinet. Scarlet, long-stemmed Happiness roses bloomed from every crystal vase, their delicate bouquet sweetening the fresh air.

This grand-hotel-on-wheels was ready, inside and out, for the journey.

Fancy script letters of hammered silver spelled the name directly beside the Pullman car's door: *Silver Lining*. Raleigh Burnett had chosen the title, saying the unexpected rich veins of silver discovered in the coastal ranges on *Lindo Vista* had afforded this expensive folly.

And it was a folly.

Raleigh Burnett had traveled in the *Silver Lining* only two times after ordering it from the Pullman Palace Car Building Company in the autumn of '71. Soon after that, his health began to fail and the operation of *Lindo Vista* and overseeing all the other holdings were turned over to his only son.

Burt had made good use of the luxury railcar. He had traveled across the country in the *Silver Lining* more than once; had taken it up the coast to San Francisco on numerous occasions, enjoying the privacy and comfort it provided.

Inside the specially constructed car, a parlor with satin-wood walls, a lush wine hand-loomed carpet, and comfortable sofas and chairs of pearl-gray velvet made rail travel homelike and restful. Even more restful was the large, opulent bedroom/observation compartment aft of the parlor.

Under a vaulted ceiling with Gothic fretwork, a large square bed covered with a pearl-gray velvet counterpane, was topped with mounds of pillows. On either side of the bed were matching onyx night tables atop which were lamps with shiny gray shantung shades muting the light from their balloonlike globes. Across the room, a floor-length, gray damask cloth draped a square table. The flatware service was of silver gilt, the dishes of ivory porcelain banded in silver. Four straight chairs, their backs and seats covered in gray velvet were pulled up to the table. The heavy drapes gave the bedroom total privacy. Black velvet cloth had only recently replaced the gray to insure no light came through the many windows.

Between the salon and the bedroom, a bath with a square, gray marble tub, shiny silver fixtures, stacks of thirsty towels, and rows of expensive oils and soaps made bathing at any hour of the day or night convenient and enjoyable.

Those fortunate enough to travel in such grand style reached their destination a great deal fresher than the masses who could barely afford a ticket to ride in one of the train's hot, dusty chair cars.

Carrying charges for a private car were the price of eighteen first-class rail tickets. That's what it cost to have the northbound California Starlight hook on the *Silver Lining* and pull it to San Francisco. Those first-class tickets had been purchased. The train, steaming up from San Diego, would be stopping at the rail spur at approximately eleven a.m.

It was now twenty minutes of.

The pair of privileged passengers who were to travel aboard the sleek *Silver Lining* were nowhere in sight.

At *Lindo Vista*, three quarters of a mile from the rail spur and the waiting private Pullman, Cappy Ricks paced nervously back and forth in the wide downstairs corridor of the hacienda. Twisting his hat brim in his calloused hands, he glanced up every few seconds, then shook his gray head.

Finally he heard a high squeal followed immediately by tinkling feminine laughter, and then Burt's deep voice. Cappy looked up. The newlywed couple appeared on the upstairs landing, Burt carrying Sabella in his arms, both of them laughing at some private lovers' joke.

Despite his irritation at their tardiness, Cappy began to smile when he saw them. They looked young and happy and very much in love. The sight of them brought back that day a long time ago when he himself was a happy, young bridegroom. The vision of his sweet, dark-haired young bride, Geneva, came back as vividly as if it had been yesterday instead of forty-three years ago.

Smiling now, Cappy thought the new Mrs. Burnett was as pretty as a picture in a traveling suit of copper-colored cotton. She had that fresh, glowing radiance of a woman who has just found out the sweet mystery of married love. Cappy told himself he'd been foolish to worry so. If she wasn't in love, he'd eat his hat!

Halfway down the grand staircase, Burt stopped abruptly to kiss his bride.

"Enough of that foolishness," Cappy called to them, jamming his sweat-stained Stetson on his head, "you're gonna' miss that train north if you don't get a move on."

"What time is it, Cappy?" Burt asked, unruffled, looking into Sabella's eyes.

"A quarter til," said Cappy. "Mornin', Mrs. Burnett."

"Good morning, Cappy." Sabella turned her head, and beamed down at him. "It's my fault, I'm afraid, I was late getting dressed." She blushed immediately and wondered if her face were bloodred. She *had* been late getting dressed, but it had hardly been *her* fault. Burt had caught her as she got out of her morning tub and one quick kiss had led to lovemaking, though she'd warned him throughout that they didn't have the time.

"Yeah, blame her," said Burt, nodding his dark head, grinning mischievously. Then: "What are we waiting for? Let's go." He skipped the rest of the way down the stairs and dashed across the foyer, running out the door a helpful servant held open for them.

By the time Cappy reached the waiting carriage out front, Burt and Sabella were seated comfortably inside. One arm around his bride, Burt impatiently drummed long fingers on his knee.

"What kept you?" he asked, frowning, then winking at Sabella. "If you don't hurry, we'll miss our train!"

Cappy paid him no mind. The big ranch foreman swung up onto the high seat, unwrapped the long leather reins from the brake handle, and immediately put the matched blacks in motion. The open carriage sped down the palm-lined avenue to the ranch gates, passed under the tall cross bars, and turned into the lane.

Heading north, Cappy urged the team into a full, fast gallop, the carriage's quickly turning wheels churning up a thick cloud of dust that hung in the still September air.

It was two minutes until eleven when the carriage rolled to a stop at the private rail spur.

A staff of Burnett employees were assembled there, waiting to make the journey with the golden couple. Two cooks, one of whom was the stocky, good-natured Martha, Burt's own personal favorite. Two maids—one to keep the lavish quarters neat, the other to keep the couple's clothes clean and pressed. Blanton, who since Raleigh's death had become Burt's manservant. And Carmelita Rivera, Sabella's old friend and personal maid.

The entourage, along with several dozen pieces of luggage, would be riding in a leased private sleeping car directly ahead of the *Silver Lining*. They would be on call and in attendance throughout the journey, ready and able to meet any demands made on them until the honeymooners returned home to *Lindo Vista*. Handpicked for their intelligence and loyalty, their task was to see to it that Mr. and Mrs. Burton J. Burnett had a wonderful and worry-free wedding trip.

Burt had hardly helped Sabella out of the carriage before they heard a train whistle blow in the near distance. Sabella looked up to see the fast-approaching locomotive.

"That's us, darlin'," Burt told her, grinning broadly, "the California Starlight."

Sabella was amazed at the speed and efficiency with which

the private Pullman car was hooked on to the rear of the train. Within minutes of the California Starlight's arrival, they were saying good-bye to Cappy.

Impulsively turning and hugging the big, brawny, gray-haired foreman, Sabella whispered against his leathery, freshly shaven cheek, "Thanks again for giving me away. I'll miss you while we're gone."

Cappy patted her back awkwardly. Swallowing down the beginning of a lump forming in his throat, he said, "Be happy, child."

Burt put out his hand to Cappy. "Watch the old place while we're gone. And watch after yourself as well."

"I'll do both, son," said Cappy.

Burt anxiously ushered Sabella aboard the *Silver Lining* and together they stood in the doorway waving to Cappy as the train moved slowly away.

Sabella was again amazed once she turned and stepped inside the plush private car. She wondered, as her eyes examined the lavishly furnished parlor, if she would ever become accustomed to the idea of one family having such immense wealth. It was mind-boggling to think that people actually lived the way the Burnetts lived. Just one of the fine pearl-gray velvet sofas she saw cost more than all the furniture the Rios family had ever had in their entire house.

Sabella felt her jaw tighten as her dark gaze swept slowly about the room. Her resentment, her deep and abiding hatred of the Burnetts suddenly surfaced with such passion it threatened to overwhelm her. These gray velvet sofas, the plush wine carpet, everything, including the sleek silver railcar containing all the fine furnishings—none of it really belonged to the Burnetts. They had . . .

"Sweetheart, what is it?" Burt asked, troubled by her strange expression. "You don't like the decor? We'll get rid of it. You can redo the whole car, fix it up any way you like."

Sabella made herself look up and smile sweetly at him. "I wouldn't change a thing. Really. It's the most handsomely . . ." She laughed then, put her arms around his trim waist, and admitted, "I was about to say it's the most handsomely appointed railcar I've ever been in, but that would be a bit silly since it's the *only* railcar I've ever been in."

"Stick with me, kid," Burt said, putting his hands on her

shoulders, and asking, a dark eyebrow lifted, "Would milady care to see the boudoir?"

"Only," she replied, "if milord promises not to try and keep me there."

"Sorry, Princess, I don't make promises I can't keep." Burt took her by the hand and led her back to the bedroom as the train picked up speed on the tracks.

The black velvet drapes were pulled against the midday sun. The only light was the soft mellow glow from the gray-shaded lamps on each side of the bed.

The pair stood holding hands, looking at the bed. Burt said, "Give you any ideas, sweetheart?"

"Yes," she was quick to reply, "it reminds me that I got almost no sleep last night."

He dropped her hand, turned about, and fell over flat on his back atop the bed. Folding his long arms under his head, he said, "I'm with you. Let's take a nap."

"Not on your life," she told him, moving to go back toward the parlor.

"Wait." He rolled into a sitting position. "I was teasing you, honey." He was up on his feet in a second. "In a few minutes we'll be stopping at the Capistrano depot and . . ."

"And I suppose several dozen of your closest friends will be at the station to say good-bye."

Burt looked properly sheepish. "I might have mentioned to one or two guests at last night's reception that we'd be coming through today." Head hung, he plucked at the shoulder gathers of her suit jacket's fashionable balloon sleeves. "You don't mind too much, do you?"

She shook her head. "I better see to repairing my hair. I must look a fright after that fast carriage ride."

Sabella's gleaming gold hair was neatly dressed atop her head when the train pulled into the depot. She and Burt were still in the railcar's bedroom when the locomotive's whistle blasted loudly.

"Come on," she said, lifting her long skirts and starting toward the parlor, "we'll stand in the door and wave."

"Wait, sweetheart," Burt stopped her. "Let me show you something."

He drew the heavy black drapes stretching across the compartment's back wall. Sabella gasped in astonishment. The car's rear wall was entirely of glass with a door on one side leading onto an open observation deck. A waist-high railing of hammered silver enclosed the deck, and overhead a black-and-gray-striped awning, rolled neatly up out of the way at the moment, shaded it, when necessary, from the California sun.

Before she could comment, Burt was handing her out the door to greet the gathered crowd. The newlyweds might have been visiting royalty, so many people had shown up. Many of last night's guests were present, some looking a bit tired and bleary eyed, but smiling and waving nonetheless. There were people Sabella didn't recognize, was sure she'd never seen before. But everyone knew Burt.

They cheered madly when he thanked them all for turning out. Graciously he accepted gifts of brandy and cigars while Sabella laughed gaily and leaned over the silver railing to receive a large satin-covered box of fancy chocolates from the spokesman for a group of wellwishers. Romantic young girls tossed flowers at the handsome, smiling couple, and shy young boys sidled up for a closer look at the beautiful, blond bride.

Showering the smiling, waving couple with kindness and good will, everyone in San Juan Capistrano was genuinely happy for them.

Well, almost everyone.

One pretty, dark-haired woman who happened to be in the village that day was not the least bit happy for them.

Gena de Temple, seated in a covered carriage which was parked across the tree-shaded street, watched the spectacle with cold fury. She wasn't sure whom she hated the most. Burt, for being such a fool he would fall in love with a Spanish peasant! Or Sabella Rios for spreading her legs and turning him into a brainless fool.

Did the scheming blond bitch really think she could steal something that belonged to Gena de Temple and get away with it?

Never! Gena silently promised the laughing, waving woman standing on the observation deck of the *Silver Lining* as if she belonged there. *Burt Burnett is a fool, but I am not. I will, if it takes forever, learn the truth about you!*

Chapter Twenty-four

Gena de Temple watched from inside the parked, closed carriage until the California Starlight pulled out of the San Juan Capistrano depot. She stayed where she was until Burt and Sabella, waving from the *Silver Lining*'s observation deck, became tiny specks in the distance. And then finally disappeared completely.

With the tip of her colorful silk parasol she tapped on the roof of the brougham. Dozing atop the box, old Julio jumped, startled, then put the matched bays in motion, turning the big rig about and heading out of the village.

Angry, upset, Gena de Temple went home to the haunting silence of a big empty mansion. Her father, the senator, was in Los Angeles. He had planned to be back by late evening, had invited his old friend, Don Miguel Andres Amaro, to come for dinner.

But a telegram, delivered while Gena was in the village, stated he was tied up and wouldn't be back until sometime tomorrow.

Reading, then rereading the wire, Gena de Temple swore under her breath. She had no way to get word to Don Miguel that her father was out of town. The stocky, silver-haired Spanish grandee would show up for dinner. And she would have no choice but to entertain him.

Gena shrieked so loudly a half dozen servants came run-

ning. She angrily waved them away, shouting at them to
"Leave me alone!"

She wanted to scream at the top of her lungs and keep
screaming until she could scream no more. She did *not* feel
like entertaining the don or anyone else. Her world had
fallen apart. *Her* man had married another woman, leaving
her to become a lonely, embittered old maid. How could she
be expected to receive callers? She couldn't and she
wouldn't! She was prostrate with grief. She would take to
her bed and stay there in seclusion for as long as she pleased!

Gena shook her head, sighed wearily, and squared her
slender shoulders determinedly.

She was, after all, a de Temple. The illustrious de Temple
name, her lofty station in life carried a certain degree of duty
and responsibility. Don Miguel Andres Amaro was a direct
descendent of Cortez, Mexico's famed Spanish conqueror,
and highly respected among California's elite. The polite,
charming, fifty-eight-year-old childless widower was one of
state's richest men, and one of the most powerful.

She could hardly snub such an influential gentleman.

Promptly at eight p.m. Don Miguel Andres Amaro showed
up at the de Temple mansion. The landed don arrived in a
fine black carriage drawn by a quartet of high-stepping, spirited blacks. The horses' trappings were heavy with gleaming
silver ornaments fashioned by the most talented silversmiths
in all of Mexico.

The portly don was dressed in his favorite Spanish grandee
attire. His formal black *charro* suit was trimmed in flashing
silver embroidery on the lapels and down the outside of each
tight-fitting trouser leg. His shirt was snowy-white silk and a
scarlet silk scarf was knotted at his stocky throat. His black
boots had been polished to such a high gleam they looked
like patent leather and their heels were very high, giving
the short don the appearance of being inches taller than he
actually was.

A full head of silver hair was clean and carefully brushed,
the nails of his square, brown hands neatly trimmed and
buffed. His dark, smoothly shaven face, heavily lined from
many years spent in the sun, still retained traces of his youthful handsomeness.

But the trim, well-proportioned body of which the don had

once been extremely proud now carried at least fifty pounds of excess weight, most of the girth centered around his thick waist.

Gena was informed that the don was waiting downstairs in the drawing room. Dressed and ready, she nodded, then made the don wait another twenty minutes before going down to join him.

When she swept into the lavish, lamp-lit drawing room, the short Spaniard came to his feet and smiled warmly, his teeth very white against his deep olive skin. Offering the don her father's heartfelt apologies for having been detained in the city, Gena extended her hand for him to kiss.

The don lifted her pale fingers to his thin lips and Gena noticed, with mild amusement, that his dark gaze was fastened on her bosom. She hadn't realized, until that moment, that the bodice of her new rose chiffon creation was cut so daringly low. His first look of undisguised interest was not to be his last. Gena was surprised. The don had never noticed her before, at least not to her knowledge. Now it seemed the gentlemanly, ever-polite grandee couldn't keep his eyes off her.

When dinner was announced, the don presented his arm to Gena. As he escorted her to the dining room, Gena was struck by what a comical-looking pair they made. The don was short, at least half a head shorter than she, and he was fat. His expensive, well-cut, black-and-silver *charro* suit might have looked spectacular on a tall, lean man, but on him the skin-tight trousers, the short bolero jacket only emphasized the spreading waist, the rounded belly.

It was all she could do to keep from laughing out loud.

Don Miguel devoted himself to being charming and entertaining throughout the lengthy, seven-course dinner in the candlelit dining room. Despite her despair, Gena found herself enjoying the meal and the company. Don Miguel never failed to have new, interesting tales to share and he was a talented storyteller.

Still, when the meal was finished and decorum dictated that she invite him to join her for brandy and coffee in the drawing room, she was hoping against hope that he would decline.

He didn't.

Not only did Don Miguel eagerly accept her invitation, he stayed much longer than was his habit. When finally he said good night and departed, Gena had consumed three glasses of cognac on top of the wine she'd drunk with dinner. She walked back into the drawing room after the don's departure, sighed with relief, and poured herself another.

Though the hour was growing late, she was neither tired nor sleepy. She was restless, bored, and unhappy. She roamed through the big lonely house, carrying her brandy snifter. In vain she searched for something to do to pass the time, some way to occupy herself until she was sleepy enough for bed.

She strolled unhurriedly into the library, moving along the tall mahogany shelves holding hundreds of first editions bound in blue and red Moroccan leather. She took a title off the shelf, flipped through the pages, then replaced it. She shook her head and exhaled loudly. She was in no mood for reading.

Feeling extremely sorry for herself, Gena moved listlessly across the library to a set of tall French doors that opened onto a stone side terrace. Brandy snifter cradled in the palm of her hand, she pushed the doors open and stepped outside. She stood for a moment looking about, then flung herself down on a padded chaise. She leaned her head back and studied the starry sky as a deep sense of melancholy enveloped her. She heard, from far off in the distance, a train whistle blow. The mournful sound brought back the painful sight of Burt and his bride standing on the observation deck of the *Silver Lining*.

Gena moaned, then ground her teeth viciously.

While she was here alone and unwanted, they were making love as the train sped down the tracks. The thought of it conjured up a mental image that made her physically ill. Damn them! Damn them both to eternal hell!

God, if only there was some way she could get even. If there was just something she could do . . . some evil deed, some awful act . . . that would hurt Burt half as much as he had hurt her.

Her brandy snifter empty, Gena impatiently rose. She didn't go back inside. Seething, she prowled along the terrace, moving toward the back of the house. Once she'd rounded the mansion's corner, she stopped and stared in the direction of the many outbuildings scattered about in a sprawling compound below the house. Her narrowed gaze moved over the bunkhouse and stables and barns to a small sand-colored adobe set apart and partially hidden in a copse of trees.

Gena's pulse leaped when she saw that a light burned inside. She was off the stone terrace, down the steps, and crossing the walled courtyard before she actually admitted to herself where she was going.

She paused at the tall black Spanish gates, told herself she was courting trouble, that she'd best go back inside and straight up to bed.

Gena pushed the heavy iron gate open and stepped out. She nervously looked about, terrified someone might see her. It was late. No one was around. The grounds were as quiet as a tomb.

Gena smiled as she yanked up the skirts of her rose chiffon gown and dashed headlong across the large, manicured lawns. Feeling the exhilaration that comes with doing something questionable, something daring and dangerous, she wondered why she hadn't thought of this sooner.

Gena didn't slow down until she stood before the heavy wooden door of the small, secluded adobe. Out of breath, a hand at her rapidly rising and falling breasts, Gena felt her knees tremble. She drew a deep, steadying breath. She smoothed down the folds of her flowing rose chiffon, then patted her upswept, elaborately dressed hair.

Licking her lips to wet them, she decisively raised a balled fist and knocked loudly on the door. It opened almost immediately and Santo stood before her.

He blinked in surprise and said, "*Señorita* Gena, something is wrong? The senator, he is sick, no?"

"No, no, everything's fine. I just ..." she faltered, shrugging slender shoulders.

From somewhere inside, Cisco's low voice said, "Please come in, Gena."

Santo began nodding. "Yes, come inside and—"

The gaunt, scar-faced Cisco stepped in front of his taller, younger brother. "Santo was just leaving," he said, looking into Gena's wide green eyes.

"No, I wasn't," Santo argued, "why I—"

"You heard me," said Cisco, as he reached out and drew Gena inside. His dark-eyed gaze never straying from her, Cisco took his younger brother's hat down from a peg by the front door, put it on Santo's head, and shoved him outside.

"Now, wait a minute here, Cisco," Santo complained. "I don't—"

The heavy door slammed in his face before he could complete his sentence. Santo stood there bewildered, staring at the closed door. Then he shrugged, turned and headed for the stables.

Inside the dimly lit *sala,* Cisco threw the bolt, locking the door. He leaned back against it, crossed his arms over his chest, and said, "Welcome to my *castillo, querida.*"

"Thank you, Cisco," Gena said, the wispy hair beginning to rise on the nape of her neck.

"Is there something special I can do for you?"

Already beginning to grow nervous, Gena shook her head. "No. No, I . . . I . . . was just . . ."

"Taking a nighttime stroll and happened to pass by my place?"

"Well, yes. Yes. I couldn't sleep, so I . . . I—"

His mocking laughter interrupted. She stopped speaking. His arms came uncrossed. Gena tensed as he moved quickly across the tile floor to a small eating table in the shadowy corner. Her eyes fell on a knife sticking up on the table, its blade's tip embedded in the rough wood.

She winced involuntarily when Cisco wrapped his hand around the knife's black handle and plucked it free.

"What do think you're doing?" Her tone became one of stern authority, although her green eyes widened in alarm as he slowly approached her.

"Why, *querida,* I am about to give you what you came here for." He grinned and idly scratched at the scar on his cheek with the knife blade's sharp tip.

"I have no idea you're talking about," Gena said, moving toward the door.

Quick as cat, Cisco slipped between her and the bolted door. "I think," he said, blocking her way, "you know exactly what I'm talking about."

She was half afraid of this strange, evil-looking man. He

was not behaving as she had expected. She had come here
expecting to be admired and adored, not frightened half to
death.

Her hands went to her hips. "My coming here was a mistake. Obviously, you have taken it the wrong way."

She shivered when the tip of his gleaming knife gently
touched her elbow and moved slowly, teasingly up her bare
arm. "Are you afraid of me, *querida?*"

"Certainly not," Gena haughtily responded, then laughed
as if the idea were absurd. She added nastily, "I was raised
never to fear the hired help."

Cisco chuckled, too, as his ropy arm slid around her. The
knife clutched firmly in his hand, he placed the long blade
perpendicular to the cleft of her buttocks. It pressed harm-
lessly through the swirling rose chiffon and lace petticoat.
Using only the slightest of pressure, he urged her to him.
Her gaze locked with his, she lifted her hands in a defensive
gesture. Her palms flattened on the smooth black fabric of
his shirtfront.

"Were you," he inquired, grinning, "taught to never make
love to the hired help as well?"

"As a matter of fact, I was," Gena said, her long red nails
like a cat's extended claws scratching, punishing his chest.

Sexual excitement and rising fear made for a heady mixture. Gena found she was suddenly tingling and over-warm
and very, very curious. She had wondered, more than once,
what this too-thin, dangerous-looking, scar-faced Mexican
did that made women swarm around him.

She knew she was about to find out.

Gena stiffened in real alarm when Cisco, wedging a knee
between her own, moved the knife from where it had lain
harmless against her buttocks. The long blade flashed in the
lamplight as he slowly raised it up to where she could see it.

She dared not move as the blade's tip went up to the
rope of pearls wound into the dark curls atop her head. The
shimmering ornamental rope was quickly severed. Gena
laughed with relief as precious pearls scattered and dark hair
spilled down around her shoulders.

When Gena left Cisco's adobe hours later, she wore only
her rose chiffon gown. Nothing remained of her expensive
French underwear except a few useless bits of lace and satin

lying about on the floor. Cisco had, with the sure deftness of a surgeon, cut away the full petticoats and lace-trimmed chemise and naughty satin drawers from her fevered body.

He hadn't stopped until she had lain totally naked and terrifically excited on his bed. The things he had done to her then, the unique ways he had made love to her as she lay bare and helpless while he remained fully clothed in his black shirt and trousers, were shocking, unspeakable, and incredibly thrilling.

Vowing she would never return to Cisco's adobe, Gena made her dazed way back to the mansion, sated, sore, and shamed.

Chapter Twenty-five

Burt sprawled lazily on one of the gray velvet sofas, his long legs stretched out before him, ankles crossed, feet propped up on a low table. His suit jacket long since cast aside, shirt collar open at the throat, and sleeves rolled up over tanned forearms, he held a silver bowl of muscat grapes balanced on his lap.

Sabella sat on the sofa beside him, her kid slippers kicked off and resting on the rug below, her stockinged feet tucked up under her. The tightly fitted bodice of her copper-hued traveling suit was unbuttoned down to the beginning swell of her breasts and her long skirts and petticoats were swirled up around her knees.

It was nearing sundown on that warm September Sunday afternoon.

The newly wedded Burnetts were cozy and relaxed in the *Silver Lining*'s comfortable parlor as the train rolled steadily northward. Popping grapes first into his bride's luscious mouth, then his own, Burt was speaking excitedly about his dreams and future plans for them and for *Lindo Vista*.

"I wish you could have been with me at the meetings last spring in Chicago," he said. "Honey, you'd be amazed at the technological advances being made in hydrology. I listened to those brilliant hydrologists speak and I got this wonderful vision of verdant, crop-producing fields where nothing grows now but cactus and chaparral."

Sabella chewed a grape, then swallowed. Skeptical, she said, "You actually believe there'll be water in the barren deserts someday?"

"Absolutely! No question about it. In the next few years we'll be able to irrigate all the lands of the *rancho*." He held a plump purple grape up between thumb and forefinger, studied it appreciatively. "Imagine, if you can, hundreds of acres of useless wasteland producing grapes like this one! Why, we'll start our own winery at ranch headquarters and bottle fine wines from grapes grown in our vineyards."

"Sounds a little farfetched to me. I mean, I—"

"Hard to grasp, isn't it?" Burt's gray eyes were alive with enthusiasm. "The scientists involved aren't just studying ways to better utilize the surface water. They're investigating methods of bringing water up from beneath the soil and from underlying rocks and the atmosphere itself."

"I'm sure they're experimenting," Sabella said, trying to comprehend such implausible wonders. "Still, I wouldn't count on having vineyards in the valley anytime soon."

"Not just vineyards"—Burt was not deterred—"besides grapes, we'll have all kinds of produce. Melons and vegetables and exotic fruits. I tell you, sweetheart, there's a big change coming and it's right around the corner. We're living in exciting times, you and I."

Nodding, Sabella said, "If you say so. If that were to happen . . . if you could get water to the far reaches of the ranch, you could run more cattle, couldn't you?"

"You bet, baby. As I told you, back before the terrible droughts, *Lindo Vista* supported thousands of head of cattle and horses. It could be like that again. And the profits are far greater now than in those days. As the population of California increases, there's a greater demand for beef. The old *Californios* made most of their money from hides; we make ours from beef."

Sabella shook her head no to another grape. "Until all this happens, you—"

"The best news of all," Burt eagerly interrupted, "is that I'm in on the beginning development of a new water system."

"Is that important?"

He lifted a dark eyebrow at her. "Honey, if we—the team I'm working with—make water plentiful in Southern California, we'll not only become unbelievably rich, we'll go down in the history books. You'll see the population of Los Angeles and San Diego explode. Why, with the mild climate and incredible beauty of the coast, anyone in his right mind will want to live here."

"Mmmmm," Sabella murmured. "That will be wonderful, but until it happens . . . until the technology is perfected and the complicated machinery is put in place, the creek that flows across the northern boundary of *Lindo Vista* is really the only substantial source of water on the entire ranch, isn't it?"

"Afraid so," Burt acknowledged, and set the bowl of grapes aside, raised his arms, and folded his hands behind his dark head. "Well, actually, that's not totally correct. It so happens that Coronado creek's not within our boundary line."

Sabella frowned. "The original creek bed is not on *Lindo Vista*?"

"Nope."

"Whose land is it on?"

"Senator Nelson de Temple's," Burt said. "They dammed and directed it from Dreamy Draw more than thirty years ago for our use."

Sabella's perfectly arched brows shot up. "Gena's father?"

"Gena's father," Burt confirmed. "For as long as I can remember we've been paying the senator a token annual fee for water rights."

"I see," Sabella said calmly. Then: "What would happen if the senator suddenly decided he would no longer allow you access to the water. What if—"

"Ah, darlin', darlin'," Burt interrupted again, laughing, taking his hands down from behind his head. Gray eyes merrily twinkling, he reached for her, gently drew her down into his arms. Carefully tucking her head beneath his chin, he wrapped his arms around her and teased, "leave it to a woman to come up with such an outlandish idea."

Sabella's head came up off his chest. She looked him in the eye and said, "Perhaps. But then Gena is a woman, too, remember."

The easy smile remaining on his handsome face, Burt reached up and casually began removing the pins from Sabella's upswept hair.

"That's true, she is. But then she's not half so clever as you." His smile widened with the pleasure of watching Sabella's heavy blond hair fall down around her shoulders.

Impatiently pushing a long strand of the loosened hair back behind her ear, Sabella said, "You think not? You're underestimating your former fiancée, Burt. She's just as smart as I."

"You're wrong, love," he said, his tanned fingers going to the tiny buttons of her copper suit jacket. "You're remarkably bright, by far the cleverest woman I've ever met."

"You think so?"

"Know so." Both his smile and his words were cocky. "After all, you were smart enough to trap me."

"*Trap* you?" She brushed his busy fingers from her bodice, stung by his choice of words, but determined to keep her ever-present guilt concealed. "Why, Burt Burnett, if you are not the most conceited man I ever—"

"True," he smilingly conceded, "but I'm also mighty lovable, don't you think?" She gave no reply, but she smiled at him. His fingers returned to her buttons. "Not nearly as lovable as you though." He pushed her opened jacket apart and fire instantly leapt into his smokey gray eyes. Tracing the lace-bordered top edge of her chemise with his forefinger, he asked, "Know what I want to do?"

"Tell me what you want to do."

"Hold you. Touch you. Taste you."

Sabella blushed. "Burt, the sun hasn't gone completely down."

"Does it matter?"

She lifted her shoulders in a shy little shrug. "It just seems indecent somehow to go to bed before sunset."

"I totally agree," Burt said. He winked at her and added, "Let's stay right here."

"I didn't mean—"

Burt's lips got in the way of any further protests. Sabella was surprised, as she always was, at the fierce sweetness of his kiss. Instantly her lips were open and ardent beneath his. Had she not wished it so, it still would have been that way.

This handsome man's kisses were incredibly stirring. No doubt about it, he possessed a power which excited her, caused her heart to beat faster.

Sabella melted, surrendering to the masterful mouth moving on hers, the deep-probing fire-lick of his tongue. She reasoned that it was a good thing he could draw a response from her, could make her pulses leap and her skin tingle.

Since the holy Virgin Mary was the only woman on record who had ever conceived without first being with a man, she *had* to let Burt make love to her.

Over and over again.

She couldn't conceive, couldn't give birth to his son without it, so she was thankful that he was an experienced, irresistible lover. Amazingly enough, after only a few savagely compelling kisses, passion and need swamped her and she made no effort to stop him when Burt began undressing her.

He was, she dreamily decided, surely the best of any man alive at undressing a woman. Moments after their first kiss, he had adroitly stripped her of every scrap of her clothing. And he had done it with such casual skill, his hands sweeping her clothes away while his mouth never left hers.

The two of them had not moved from the parlor, still sat there comfortably on the gray velvet sofa. Idly wondering if she were a shameless wanton at heart, Sabella smiled when finally Burt rose and carried her back to the bedroom. In seconds he was as naked as she and they were together in the big, soft bed.

Beneath her, the sheets of pale silver were cool and silky. Above her, flesh of deep bronze was hot and smooth. A marvelous sensation. The tickling, tantalizing texture of cool slippery silk against her bare back and buttocks and long legs. The pressing, pleasing feel of hot hard muscle against her breasts and stomach and thighs.

Her arms looped around Burt's neck, her legs apart, knees bent, bare feet flat on the mattress, Sabella lay in that comfortable bed languidly lifting her pelvis to meet the slow sexual roll and thrust of Burt's.

At some point in the languorous lovemaking, Sabella became vaguely aware that their warm, joined bodies were bathed a rosy gold hue. Curious, she turned her head slowly on the pillow and a foolish little smile immediately touched her lips.

The last bloodred rays of the dying September sun streamed in through the clear glass windows, washing over them and everything in the room.

At that moment in time it seemed the most natural thing in the world that they should be shamelessly lying here naked, intimately mating while the heavy black drapes, meant to ensure privacy, were completely open. Even the wide expanse of glass which served as the room's rear wall was undraped. Through it she could clearly see the silver-railed observation deck and the tracks and terrain beyond.

It seemed quite natural, as well, that as they moved together like perfectly fitted, well-oiled machines, the train moved. The slow, steady click-clacking of the wheels on the tracks, the gently swaying motion of the wide Pullman car somehow added to the rising sensual pleasure.

As the lovers moved together in a kind of lazy, flowing motion, the train struggled to slowly, doggedly climb a long, steep hill. The powerful locomotive's engine finally managed to reach the incline's summit.

And start down.

The rolling train swiftly began to pick up speed. So did the naked lovers. The constant clicking of the wheels on the tracks quickened to a lively, grinding rhythm. The cadence of the lovers' heartbeats speeded to match it. With the train's sudden acceleration, the cars shifted and swayed and danced crazily on the tracks. With the lovers' abrupt change of pace, their bodies ground and undulated and tossed savagely on the bed.

The marvelous machinery of the train worked perfectly. The powerful pistons sliding and pushing against pressure; the greased thrusting cylinder moving in and out of the cylindrical vessel. The equally marvelous mechanism of the mating humans worked on much the same principle. Burt's powerful erection sliding and pushing against pressure; the glistening, driving tumescence moving in and out of Sabella's tightly sheathing flesh.

Speed and pressure continuing to increase, both train and lovers raced out of control. It was a wild, exhilarating ride until . . .

At last the train reached a low, flat valley and the lovers reached a lofty, splendid peak. The train's whistle sounded a long, loud blast at the exact moment a scream of ecstacy escaped Sabella's parted lips. A deep, shuddering groan from Burt blended into the strange chorus.

Their mingled heartbeats slowing to the rhythm of the wheels turning on the track, the lovers lay spent, unmoving, their bodies still joined, little lingering shudders buffeting them.

Sabella's weak arms fell tiredly away from Burt's back. She sighed softly and with great effort turned her head slightly on the pillow.

The sun was completely gone. Twilight had cast the gently rolling bedroom into deep, concealing shadow. Recalling how the sun had shone on them when first they began making love, and how it had seemed so natural, so right, Sabella now felt her face grow warm with shame.

"Burt," she said softly.

"Hmmmm," he murmured, his mouth and nose buried in the pillow.

"The drapes are open. Do you suppose anyone saw us?"

A low, deep chuckle. Then tiredly, happily, "Baby, I don't much care."

Chapter Twenty-six

A bottle of amontillado, imported during George Washington's first administration, sat almost empty on one of the onyx night tables. Near it were two stemmed glasses, one carelessly turned over, a few drops of the precious wine spilled on the table's polished surface.

Beside the overturned glass was a bowl of ripe, red strawberries along with small silver vats of sour cream and powdered sugar for dipping. A large, succulent berry, generously dunked in the thick sour cream, then rolled in the confectioner's sugar, lay half eaten and forgotten beside the bowl.

A bonbon, carelessly plucked from a carefully constructed pyramid of the fine Belgian candies, had met with a similar fate. A couple of bites had been taken from the chocolate shell and nut-filled fondant center, then discarded.

Fragrant ivory rose petals from an enormous bouquet in a tall crystal vase, lay scattered about on the onyx table. Those delicate petals made a clearly defined path from the vase past the wineglasses, around the berry bowl, alongside the bonbon dish to table's edge.

Directly below lay a few petals on the deep plush carpet, their stark whiteness leaving a distinct trail across the rug's wine nap. A very short trail which led to the bed. There, dozens of the velvety white petals were sprinkled over the

large bed's gray silk sheets, matching comforter, and fluffy
pillows.

And on the naked pair lying amidst the petals.

A low-burning light from one of the gray-shaded lamps
cast the palest of illumination over the peacefully sleeping
Sabella and the equally peaceful, but wide-awake Burt.

Too happy to sleep, Burt lay on his side, head on his
folded arm, contentedly watching his beautiful wife slumber
in their bed.

It was nearing three a.m. and Burt was very tired, but the
day had been so memorable, he didn't want it to end. He
wanted to hold on to it, to stretch it out, to make the sweetness last and last. So he lay there looking at his bride, knowing that he was the luckiest man alive.

His gray eyes never leaving her lovely face, he smiled,
recalling the highlights of the day. The mad dash to the rail
spur. The lovemaking at sunset. The long bath together afterward. Dinner delayed until ten o'clock. Lingering at the table
until well past midnight.

Gravitating to the bedroom where the wine and berries
and chocolates awaited and the bed, as if by magic, had been
changed. Fresh sheets of silver-gray silk were inviting, the
top one folded back with the matching comforter.

After a couple of glasses of the vintage amontillado and a
couple of dozen kisses, he had been able to persuade his shy
bride to shed her robe. Promising not to make love to her
again, assuring her they would only relax together in their
big comfortable bed, he got her to agree.

But she hastily covered herself with the sheet, snatching it
up over her breasts and tucking it tightly under her arms.
Burt followed suit, pulling the sheet up to his waist. With
their backs supported against mounds of downy pillows resting against the tall headboard, they drank more wine, fed
each other berries and chocolates, and laughed and talked.

At his gentle urging, Sabella disclosed more about her
family and the hard times they had known.

". . . and when I was two years old, my father was in a
riding accident. The horse fell on him, crushing both his
legs."

"Jesus, baby, what an awful tragedy."

"He was left so badly crippled, he never rode again," Sabella continued. "But Carmelita and her husband, Victor, were such good friends—family really—they allowed us to stay on in our little adobe on their small ranch. But then those terrible droughts of the middle sixties came and the once profitable Rivera ranch became a debt-ridden wasteland. The Riveras had no choice, they were forced to sell."

"So you and your parents were . . . ?"

"Forced to move. My mother supported the three of us with a succession of low-paying, backbreaking jobs." Sabella paused, and shook her head sadly. "My father was a proud Spaniard. He loved my mother so much it broke his heart to see her have to work so hard. He felt useless, as if he were no longer a man. He withered away and died."

"I'm so sorry, Sabella."

"My mother struggled on for my sake, but she was a frail, delicate woman who hadn't been raised to work like a plow horse. Tired, beaten, she followed my father to the grave ten years after he died."

She fell silent then, closed her eyes, and leaned her head back against the stack of pillows.

"Sweetheart," Burt promised, touched by the sad tale, "I'll make it all up to you. You'll have all the things your poor mother never had. I swear it."

"I know," Sabella murmured, her eyes narrowing slightly in the shadows, "I know."

"Here, darlin', I've poured us another glass of wine."

Her eyes opened, she smiled at him, and they drank more of the amontillado.

And they must have, Burt reflected now, gotten a little looped because before long the covering sheet had fallen away and then was finally kicked to the foot of the bed and no one had objected.

He had plucked one of the long-stemmed ivory roses from its crystal vase and handed it to Sabella. She thanked him, lifted the blossom to her face, and inhaled deeply of its sweet fragrance.

Then she touched the rose to his chest and it tickled. He took it out of her hand and tickled her with it. She shrieked and scrambled away, moving to the far edge of the mattress. He followed. She leaped off the bed and circled it with him in hot pursuit. Laughing and teasing each other, they romped naked around the room until they were completely out of breath.

Squealing and kicking at him, Sabella tiredly collapsed on the bed. She fell over onto her back, her bare feet dangling over the mattress's edge, her arms as well as her unbound hair flung up around her head. Burt stood just above, his dark chest heaving, the half shattered rose poised and ready in his hand.

"No . . . don't . . . tickle . . . me anymore. . . ." she begged, giggling, her eyes tightly shut, her diaphragm jerking spasmodically.

The sight of her lying there below him, giggling and naked and beautiful, stole the laughter from him. He was tempted to toss the rose away, drop to his knees before her, push her legs apart, and show her another way of loving. Afraid it might shock her, he curbed his hunger.

"I won't tickle you anymore, sweetheart," he said, and plucking a petal from the rose, dropping it onto her quivering belly.

He pulled another petal from the rose, released it. It fluttered down and came to rest on her left thigh. Sabella opened her eyes, smiled, and lifted her hand to him. He took it. She pulled him down onto the bed beside her, pushed him over on his back, plucked a petal from the rose he still held, and dropped it onto his chest.

And that became a new game for them to play.

They sprinkled petals on each other and all across the bed. One by one the ivory petals were plucked and dropped on flesh and on silk. It took a long time for every last petal of the four dozen ivory roses to be scattered.

When finally the foolish game was finished, Sabella yawned sleepily and murmured truthfully, "I can no longer hold my eyes open, Burt."

"It's been a long day," he whispered, nodding. "Go to sleep, sweetheart."

"Mmmmm," she managed, sighed heavily, and was sound asleep.

That had been an hour ago.

For the past hour now he had lain and just stared at her, glad she was his. In slumber she looked much younger than her twenty-five years. Framed by an abundance of glorious golden hair, her beautiful face had the sweet innocence of a child. The dark sweeping lashes resting on high-boned cheeks. The small, perfectly shaped nose. The soft, luscious lips were slightly parted to reveal even white teeth.

Slowly his admiring gaze left the exquisite, childlike face, moved down, and he exhaled raggedly, slowly.

This was no child's body.

Stretched out like a lovely, tempting offering fashioned solely for his carnal pleasure, she was woman incarnate. Bare beautiful breasts with large satiny nipples were firm and full and rounded even with her lying on her back. Jutting proudly, they seemed to be silently inviting him to bend his head and kiss them.

Directly below the tempting breasts, delicate ribs shown one by one beneath the flawless golden-tan flesh. The waist was small, the stomach so flat it was almost concave. Flaring feminine hips met strong, perfectly sculpted thighs. And then those long, shapely legs with their slim ankles.

Even the feet were pretty. Small and narrow, the instep high, the heel soft, the toes cute, the second toe longer than the great toe.

Didn't that mean she was going to be the boss?

Everything about her was so exquisite Burt pensively wished that he could have her painted as she was now—naked, asleep, totally vulnerable and totally beautiful. He promptly dismissed the idea when he considered an artist seeing her exposed. Unless he learned to paint one day, this appealing picture would have to hang only inside his head.

Burt's foolish smile widened as he noted the rose petals tangled in his wife's golden hair and clinging to her golden-tan skin. His gaze touched a petal resting in the hollow just below her collarbone, moved on to another which was stuck to the undercurve of her left breast. A couple of the petals concealed the small indentation of her navel, and one rested at the top edge of the triangle of pale golden curls between her thighs.

His gaze stopping, resting there, Burt's wide smile widened even more. He scooped some loose petals off the silken sheet. Casting a quick glance at Sabella's sleeping face, he carefully turned onto his stomach and slid down the mattress until his torso was beside her hips.

Playing, entertaining himself, he very slowly, very carefully worked to cover the crisp blond curls and treasure they concealed with the white rose petals. As an artist at his canvas, he gave free rein to his imagination, placing each individual petal with a craftsman's keen eye, creating a veritable masterpiece with his talented hands and her beautiful body.

In no particular hurry to complete his rare work of living art, he was rigid in picking just the right petal for just the right spot. And like a true temperamental artist, he became frustrated and gritted his teeth in annoyance if a carefully chosen petal refused to lie just as he placed it.

His narrow-eyed focus never straying from his masterpiece in the making, Burt happily labored, lost in a world of his own making.

The sleeping woman upon whom he so painstakingly worked was deep in a dream. A mysterious dream. A shameful dream of erotic delight. So real was the dream she felt herself stirring with intense pleasure to the masterful touch of dark, lean hands on her bare, tingling flesh.

Her dark eyes slowly opening, Sabella was unsure if this were a dream or if it were real. She lay unmoving, groggy, neither fully awake nor fully asleep. Her gaze was drawn down to the dark head leaning over her. Her eyes widened as she watched the tanned hands placing rose petals on her flesh with the sure, gentle touch of a surgeon.

Surely she was still in a dream. And yet it seemed so real. She wondered at the strange ritual he was engaging in with her, was not sure what he was doing. All she knew was that it felt so good she didn't want him to stop. If she were awake, she wouldn't let him know.

While he played a secretive, solitary game, Sabella played one of her own. She pretended to be fast asleep in order to enjoy her own secret pleasure.

Forcing herself to continue to lie perfectly still, Sabella watched, fascinated, from barely slitted eyes as Burt unhurriedly positioned rose petals over her groin and between her slightly parted thighs. She told herself she should be shocked at his obvious pleasure in engaging in this strange clandestine exercise. But who was she to cast stones? If he were depraved, then so was she because she found the erotic game highly enjoyable.

It was both flattering and arousing for a man to be so enamored he would pay this kind of foolish, but strangely sweet homage to a sleeping woman. Sabella felt as if she were some kind of goddess he had placed on a pedestal and that he was worshipping her with the rose petals.

She desperately wanted to sigh and stretch, but she didn't dare spoil the delicious game. It was agony-ecstasy to lie there while his hands and the petals touched her tingling flesh. She stood it as long as possible, then softly spoke his name.

"Burt."

He looked up at her, and there was so much love and passion in his eyes, it took her breath away.

"Love me, Sabella," he whispered hoarsely. Quickly he shifted and was between her legs, the carefully placed rose petals crushed between their pressing bodies. "Please, sweetheart."

"Yes," she murmured. "Oh, yes."

Chapter Twenty-seven

The carefree journey on board the luxurious *Silver Lining* set the tone for the entire honeymoon trip. When the train arrived in San Francisco, a hired carriage was waiting to whisk the golden couple out of the depot and to their hotel.

Sabella had never been to a big city, so she was wide-eyed, craning her neck and turning her head this way and that as the carriage rolled down the wide, paved streets between towering buildings. The sidewalks were crowded with mobs of people, all hurrying as if anxious to reach their destinations.

At the fabled Palace Hotel, the carriage came to a stop beneath a high, glass-domed roof enclosing a courtyard. A distinguished doorman in full livery, and looking like a military general, stepped forward to greet them. Graciously, he ushered them into the hotel's grand lobby while a swarm of uniformed bellmen descended on the carriage to see to the luggage.

Sabella clung to Burt's arm as they were guided through the crowded lobby and shown upstairs to an opulent, sixth-floor corner suite. Burt smiled tolerantly as a curious Sabella dashed from room to room, shrieking like a delighted child at the ever-changing, always breathtaking views of the city and the bay from every tall, high window.

In the suite's main salon, she flung open the tall French

doors and stepped out onto the balcony. And drew in her breath at the spectacular view of the bay with the westering sun glinting on it. She grasped the balcony's decorative railing with both hands, threw back her head, and inhaled deeply of the cool, sea-scented air. In the distance, far from their rooftop suite, came the faint peal of a cable car bell.

Burt quietly stepped up behind her. He put his hands on either side of hers atop the railing, enclosing her inside his arms. She leaned back against him and for a long moment neither spoke.

Then Burt said in a low, masculine voice, "The city, the hotel, the suite, they all belong to you. Anything you want is yours. Any place you want to go, you're there. Anything you want to do, you will."

Sabella silently bristled at his words. Such supreme arrogance. At the moment her brain wasn't clouded from sipping too much wine, nor were her wits scattered from his heated kisses. She hadn't been herself on the journey north. He had kept her half tipsy and half aroused the entire trip.

She was thinking clearly now and her hatred burned as hot as the passion he'd awakened in her. She felt like shouting that there was only one thing she wanted from him.

His son and heir to *Lindo Vista!*

Her back pressed against the hardness of his broad chest, she laid her head on his shoulder and said, "You're awfully sure of yourself. Does the Burnett wealth and power reach even to San Francisco?"

"Try me," said Burt. "I challenge you. Do your dead-level best to think of something that will be impossible for me to give you."

"Mmmmm. A party invitation to the biggest mansion on Nob Hill."

"That's too easy, baby doll," Burt told her, his hands leaving the balcony railing, wrapping around her narrow waist. His lips against her golden hair, he said, "Try again."

"Give me some time to think about it?"

"As long as you need," he told her. "Just let me know when you've come up with something."

"I will," she said, her dark eyes narrowed, intent on thinking of something that even the vainly superior Burt Burnett could not manage to get.

Soon Sabella began to believe that her husband was indeed capable of fulfilling her every desire. If she but mentioned something, it became hers right there on the spot. Within days of their arrival in San Francisco she owned dozens of new dresses, and a quartet of elegant gowns for the opera, several pieces of exquisite jewelry, a long white ermine coat, scads of lacy French lingerie, and gloves and shoes and bonnets aplenty. Even a pair of navy suede British-style jodhpurs with a matching navy silk blouse, tall gleaming black boots, and braided quirt to complete the ensemble.

At the theater or the opera they were invariably seated in the most choice of private boxes. At the restaurants they commanded the best of tables. Sabella couldn't seem to trip her husband up; she couldn't ask for something he couldn't give her.

Still she tried.

"Know what I want to do tonight," she said one evening late as she lingered in her tub.

Burt stood across the spacious bathroom with his back to her, shaving. A towel around his neck, the lower half of his face lathered, he glanced at her in the mirror.

"Haven't a clue," he said, scraping the sharp straight-edged razor down his lean cheek in one quick, fluid motion. "Whatever it is, tell me and you'll do it."

"I want," she said, lifting a long leg up out of the suds, pointing it toward the ceiling, "to dine at the Cliffhouse."

"Is that all?" Burt shrugged bare shoulders.

"Just the two of us," she announced slyly, certain she had him. Surely even a Burnett didn't possess the clout to engage a famous restaurant at the very last minute for his own exclusive use. "No one else must be allowed in the restaurant."

An hour later they were alone in the elegant eatery, tended by a squadron of polite, smiling waiters. Crisp green salads on chilled china plates were set before them, along with glasses of frozen champagne punch. Hot French bread and sweet creamery butter came next. Then the tender fillet of beef, baked potato, and French green peas that Sabella had chosen from the menu. Vintage moselle accompanied the meal.

Dessert was rich plum pudding with brandy sauce.

Burt pushed his pudding away untouched, lighted a long

thin cigar, and leaned back in his chair to observe his gorgeous bride speculatively taste, then eagerly devour the rich custard. Studying her through a cloud of blue cigar smoke, he was again struck by how innocent she was, and not just in sex. She was unsophisticated, naive, unworldly.

And utterly enchanting.

"So, sweetheart," he said when she finally sighed and placed her spoon in the empty pudding dish. "What next?"

"You're too good at this game," she admitted, frowning. "I didn't really believe you could manage this."

Burt laughed and reached across the table to take her hand. "Sounds like you're half disappointed that I was successful."

Sabella forced herself to smile. "Not at all. Now, let me see. I would like to visit the lowest, liveliest dive on the Barbary Coast." Her smile widened triumphantly. She had him now. He wouldn't dare take her down to that dangerous, sinful playground.

"That would be the Golden Carousel," said Burt.

"Fine. Take me to the Golden Carousel immediately."

She lifted her chin defiantly and crossed her arms over her chest. And then blinked in surprise when Burt tossed his napkin on the table, pushed back his chair, and rose.

Within the hour they were walking through the black leather doors of the loud, noisy Pacific Street saloon known as the Golden Carousel.

When the honeymooners left the Bay city after a three-week stay, Sabella had been unsuccessful in her quest to ask for something Burt couldn't get her. She had seen all the sights, been all the places, done everything there was to do. Every far-fetched request she made had been granted. Every foolish desire fulfilled. Every hedonistic wish satisfied.

Far from being pleased, she was both angered and frightened. It infuriated her that the intangible magic wand Burt Burnett waved to get his way had been stolen long ago by his scheming thief of a father.

It scared her that Burt so effortlessly wielded such power. His total command and the depth of his love for her were but an indication of what a formidable foe he would be. She wondered fearfully what he might do to her if he learned her real reason for marrying him. She trembled at the prospect of stealing his only son from him.

As the California Starlight began its journey southward on a sunny Sunday morning, Sabella glanced warily at her husband. Engrossed in reading the *San Francisco Chronicle*, it was one of those extremely rare moments when Burt was paying her no attention.

Sabella thoughtfully studied him while he was unaware of her appraisal. A wayward lock of jet black hair tumbled forward over his high forehead, giving him a careless, boyish look. His hooded gray eyes with their incredibly long dark lashes could change color as well as expression. She'd seen them turn from pale silver to smokey gray to dark charcoal as his moods shifted. Those beautiful eyes could be playful, penetrating, or passionate.

His nose was straight and perfectly formed, as if carefully sculpted from smooth stone. The prominence of his high slanting cheekbones hinted at distant Indian ancestors. His mouth was sensuously full lipped but firmly masculine.

He was a strikingly handsome man, made even handsomer by his easy, devil-may-care, bad boy/good boy charm.

A funny little quiver shot through Sabella from just looking at him. She hadn't planned on feeling like this about Burt Burnett. Not that she loved him; she certainly did not, but there was no denying her fierce, almost helpless attraction to him.

Her face grew suddenly hot at the vivid recollection of the intimate things she had allowed this handsome man to do to her. And had done to him as well.

She was confused and disappointed in herself. She had known, of course, years before coming to San Juan Capistrano, that her plan would require the distasteful sacrifice of making love with a stranger, a man she despised.

But it *wasn't* distasteful. She almost wished that it were. It would be easier to remember, at all times, the only purpose of making love with him if it were not so enjoyable. Damn him, why did he have to be so darkly handsome, so potently masculine, so good at everything he did!

Burt abruptly tossed the newspaper aside, turned and scowled darkly at Sabella.

"God in Heaven!" he exclaimed loudly and slapped the heel of his hand against his forehead.

Alarm causing her pulse to leap, Sabella looked at him with wide, worried eyes. "What? What is it?"

"I haven't kissed you in an hour!" he said, grinning wickedly now as he reached for her. "You'll be charging me with neglect."

Releasing a caught breath, Sabella wished miserably she could make herself tell him not to kiss her now. That she didn't want to be kissed by him. She didn't like being kissed by him. Only problem was, she *loved* being kissed by him.

Burt kissed her. Sabella kissed him back. One kiss led to another and another and the heated kisses soon led to the bed. Overwhelmed by the depth of Burt's devotion and shocked, yet thrilled by his blazing ardor, Sabella knew he meant it when he murmured that he couldn't get enough of her.

Lying beneath him in their bedroom-on-wheels at midmorning, Sabella realized how wrong she had been in assuming that married couples made love only in the darkness of the night. Apparently, she had been misled.

It seemed a bit decadent and shameful to make love in the middle of the morning, but she and Burt were guilty of such behavior daily. One thing about it, surely as often as they made love, she would soon be carrying Burt's child.

And then she would never let him touch her again!

Chapter Twenty-eight

N ever! I will *never* let you touch me again!"
"Yes, you will."

"I most certainly will not!" Gena de Temple shrieked shrilly at the smiling, black-clad Cisco.

"Ah, *queirda*," murmured the scar-faced Latin, "you are being cruelly unfair, no? You ask the impossible."

The two were sequestered in Gena's upstairs peach-and-white salon that quiet September Sunday afternoon. Downstairs Senator de Temple labored in his office, having informed the staff he was not to be disturbed. Diligent in discharging his legislative duties, the preoccupied senator was blissfully unaware that his willful daughter was entertaining a visitor in her bedroom.

Senator Nelson de Temple was a stickler for propriety. He would have been outraged had he known that his pretty, patrician daughter would allow one of his hired *vaqueros* inside the mansion, much less inside her boudoir.

Gena de Temple wasn't the least concerned with her father finding out. She knew him well. When the conscientious senator went into his office and closed the door, he was oblivious to anything going on outside those four walls. She could have hired a circus troop to perform in the upstairs corridor and her father would never have guessed.

However, her overly protective maid was a different story

altogether. While Gena had always been able to feed her trusting father the most bizarre of tales and make him believe them, she could put little or nothing over on the ever-suspicious, keen-eyed Petra.

So Gena had sent Petra Gabriel into the village on an errand. An errand that would take most of the afternoon. Then as soon as the coast was clear, Gena had rushed downstairs and straight through the long corridor out to the back terrace. Encountering one of the house servant's young sons at play, she grabbed the child.

"Jose, do you know Cisco?" she asked hopefully. The little boy nodded, grinning. "Do you know where Cisco lives?"

"*Sí, señorita.*" The seven-year-old shook his dark head and pointed in the direction of Cisco and Santo's secluded adobe.

"Good." Gena produced a shiny silver coin, held it up before the child's big dark eyes. "The money is yours if you'll run down to Cisco's adobe and tell him Gena *must* see him immediately."

"When do I get the coin?" Jose asked shrewdly.

"Right now," Gena handed it over, but when the child turned to go, she stopped him. Smiling sweetly down at the boy, she said, "Just one thing more, Jose."

"*Sí, señorita?*"

"If you tell anybody about this, *el pingo,* I'll pinch your head off!"

"*Sí!*"

Back inside, Gena glanced down the corridor at her father's closed office door, then hurried back upstairs to wait. She was pacing anxiously when she heard Cisco's soft knock on the tall double doors leading from her bedroom to the balcony.

She counted to ten, took a deep breath, and called, "It's open."

The spare, mustachioed Mexican, dressed in his signature black, immediately slipped inside. Blinking, his dark eyes dilating from coming out of the bright sunshine into the dim, shadowy salon, Cisco stared at the pale-skinned beauty standing across the room before the cold peach marble fireplace.

He grinned as he stared at her.

She projected the image of a sedate, proper young lady in

her prim beige poplin afternoon dress. In the demure little dress with its high neck, girlish puffed sleeves, and long, full skirts, she was the epitome of propriety and feminine modesty. Her dark hair was pulled into a tight bun at the back of her head and her face was naked of powder, her mouth bare of lip rouge.

Miss Gena Lorraine de Temple was, as anyone who knew her was quick to point out, a regal, respectable lady in every sense of the word. Refined, cultured, educated, she was a charter member of the state's ruling hierarchy, envied and admired for her lofty position among the upper crust. She was, it was said, a genteel woman of high birth and unparalleled social standing whose behavior was exemplary, morals impeccable.

Cisco knew better.

For all her chaste and retiring demeanor, he saw her for what she really was and it made him smile evilly, causing the scar on his cheek to pull and pucker.

If her boring, blue-blooded crowd were here now, they would get an eye-opening glimpse of the real Gena de Temple. Her chilly green gaze was focused directly on him, pulling him closer, commanding him to come to her. She looked mean and cruel and deadly, like a beautiful, bloodthirsty vampire ready to devour him.

Cisco loved it.

This haughty, aristocratic senator's daughter might have everyone else fooled. Not him. He knew her kind. She might look ladylike and reserved, but she was as greedy, as treacherous, as common as he.

Cisco took off his black hat, tossed it on a table, ran a hand through his disheveled hair, and moved swiftly across the room.

"Don't touch me," Gena softly warned, raising her hands before her, palms open in a defensive gesture. "Sit down, please."

Cisco shrugged, nodded, and dropped down onto the peach brocade sofa. Patting the cushion beside him, he said, "Sit by me, *querida.*"

"Not yet." Gena shook her head. "I have something important to discuss with you."

"I am listening."

Gena crossed her arms over her chest. "I've been thinking a lot lately about what I could do to make Burt pay."

Cisco rolled his eyes. "Let it go. You cannot get even with a Burnett. No one can. No one ever has."

"I can and I will!" she snapped. Then she immediately softened, adding, "That is, with your help I can."

"There is nothing you or I can do to—"

"Maybe there is," Gena interrupted, her green eyes aglow. "What, I wonder, would happen if the dam on Coronado Creek were to suddenly disappear?"

Cisco thought about it for a moment. "The creek would immediately return to its natural path down Dreamy Draw to the Pacific. It would course across the de Temple strip, just as it did years ago before the creek was damned and the water diverted to ... to ..." Cisco stopped speaking, frowned, shook his head. "Gena, surely you are not considering—"

"Ah, but I am." She came to the peach sofa and sat down beside him. "Without the dam, *Lindo Vista* would have no water! The stock, the crops, everything on the Burnett *rancho* would die!"

"*Dios!*" Cisco muttered. "Only a woman would think of something so destructive!"

"Burt would be bankrupt within a year, maybe six months," Gena gleefully continued as if Cisco hadn't spoken. Her eyes alive with excitement, she declared, "He would lose everything he has. Including that avaricious Latin trollop, Sabella!"

Cisco roughly cupped Gena's face in his hands. "Forget about it, *querida*! The dam at Dreamy Draw is solid. It will be there long after you and I are gone."

Gena turned her face into his right palm and kissed it. She licked the long lifeline with the tip of her tongue, and murmured, "Not if we blow it up."

"*Pare! No tan aprisa.*" Cisco warned. "Stop. Not so fast." He took his hands from her face. "You can't just go around blowing up dams because—"

"Why? Why can't we?" she asked petulantly. "We get some dynamite and—"

"No, *querida*!" He rose to his feet, scowling. "You do not know what you are saying. You have gone *loco* in the head."

He frowned down at her. "Do not ask me to be a part of this madness."

Gena jumped up and wrapped her arms around his neck. Squeezing tightly, sounding as hurt as possible, she said, "And I thought you cared for me, Cisco." She looked up at him and murmured, "I guess I was wrong." She sighed sorrowfully and bent her head. She rubbed her cheek against the black fabric covering his chest.

A muscle worked furiously in Cisco's scarred jaw. He sighed as he cupped the crown of her head with his hand. "I am crazy mad for you, Gena. I think of nothing else but you."

Gena hid her triumphant smile against his shoulder. She bit him playfully through the black shirt and said, "Cisco, do you want to make love to me this afternoon?"

The Mexican swallowed hard. "*Sí, querida.* I will go now to my adobe. You come down when—"

"No, no. No need for that. You can love me right here. Right now."

"Your father?" Cisco's eyebrows shot up. "He is gone away?"

Gena unwrapped her arms from around Cisco's neck. She smiled seductively and her hands went to his belt buckle.

"My father is downstairs in his study."

"*Bruja,*" he said through clenched teeth. "You are a witch, a beautiful witch. What if we are caught?"

His black leather belt unbuckled, Gena started to work on the buttons of his fly. "What if we are? I like a bit of danger, don't you?"

"*Sí,* I do," he said. "I always have."

Her deft fingers paused. "Say you'll blow up the Dreamy Draw dam for me."

"Gena, *por favor!*"

"Then get out!" Her hands fell away from him and she stalked away in a huff. "I ask you to do one little thing for me and you refuse." She turned and glared angrily at him. "You will never touch me again!"

"Do not say that."

"I will say it! Never! I will never let you touch me again!" She added cruelly, "Furthermore, I'll have you thrown off this ranch if you ever so much as speak to me again."

Had any other woman said such threatening things to Cisco, he would have grabbed her by the hair and spent the next hour showing her exactly what she would and would not do.

For a long moment he said nothing. Then finally, "We would have to be very careful. It would take some time to plan and—"

"Of course," Gena purred, sensing his surrender. "It doesn't have to be done tomorrow so long as—"

"We'll bring the dynamite up out of Mexico. If we try buying it in Los Angeles, somebody might get suspicious."

Smiling now, Gena was back in his arms, her hands again at the buttons of his black trousers. "You're so smart, Cisco, so resourceful. I knew I could count on you."

"Always, *mi amor.*"

Chapter Twenty-nine

The California Starlight arrived in Los Angeles shortly before lunchtime on Monday. While the staff were left to bring the luggage, Burt and Sabella were driven to the harbor where the Burnett family's seagoing yacht, *California Cloud*, was moored. A smartly uniformed captain and a full crew were on board, ready to get underway.

The floating palace was even more extravagantly furnished than the *Silver Lining*. Below decks, Oriental rugs and silver-monogrammed velvets and expensive draperies and fine imported furniture filled the spacious cabins. The galley was overseen by a chief steward who made sure the boarding couple were served a sumptuous meal on deck.

Within the hour the sleek vessel had raised anchor and was plying the choppy channel waters en route to the tiny island of Catalina. Burt and Sabella remained at the luncheon table, relaxing in the sun and sipping chilled champagne as the luxurious *Cloud* ferried them toward the island.

The late September sun was still high in the sky when the enormous yacht reached the Catalina harbor. The couple were rowed ashore. Alone. All hands remained on board the *Cloud*.

A rig was waiting, a gray-bearded old man in a worn seaman's jacket standing beside it.

He nodded, introduced himself as Davey, and warned as

Burt handed Sabella up onto the high backseat, "Silver Peak Trail can be mighty tricky. Best hold on tight."

"We'll do that, Davey," Burt smilingly told the old man, and swung up into the seat beside Sabella.

A bell suspended from the rig's dashboard tinkled as Davey guided the big dappled gray along a narrow road ascending into the coastal hills of the island. Climbing past brushy hills and barren red badlands, they quickly gained elevation. The winding trail extended along the very backbone of the island's mountain range. The sun was beginning its slide into the sea by the time they neared the western tip of the island. They began an abrupt descent which took them in and out of oak-shaded canyons and down toward Starlight Beach. Sabella saw the pristine white cottage partially concealed in the trees well before they reached it. She saw no other houses, no signs of life. Nothing save a deserted beach stretching white and inviting below.

Old Davey pulled the rig to a stop fifty yards above the small cottage.

"End of the line, folks," Davey said.

Nodding, Burt eagerly stepped down, turned and reached for Sabella.

"Thanks a million, Davey." Burt warmly shook the old-timer's hand, leaving a bill in Davey's withered palm.

Davey's old eyes widened, then narrowed as he smiled brightly. "There's a flag pole on the porch of the cottage," he instructed, pointing. "You two need anything, you just run that red flag all the way up the pole and I'll be down here in exactly one hour. Otherwise, I won't be botherin' you."

"Sounds good," said Burt, his arm around Sabella's waist.

"When you hear the bell a-tinklin'," warned Davey, "you'd best stop what you're a doin', cause I'm comin' your way."

"We'll keep that in mind."

Pocketing the bill, the old driver turned the rig about and drove away, the bell tinkling as he disappeared over the rise.

Hurrying down toward the cottage, Sabella said, "Come on! Let's go in and look around."

His hand holding hers, Burt stopped, pulled her back. "No, wait. There's something we must do first thing."

"Oh? What?"

"Go for a swim!"

Laughing then, he drew her along with him down a narrow path over the vine-covered slope to the beach. Running to keep up, shouting for him to slow down, Sabella was out of breath when they reached the soft sugary sands of the beach now pinkened by the setting sun.

Burt dropped her hand, grinned, and unbuttoned his shirt halfway down. He reached up behind his head and impatiently yanked it off.

Dropping it to the sand, he said, "What are you waiting for?"

Sabella looked him, looked all around, then back at him. She said, "I have no bathing costume. Perhaps there's one in the cottage."

She turned away; he caught her arm. "You'll need no bathing costume other than your own beautiful hide. No one will see us here."

Skeptical, she raised her eyebrows. "You sure?"

"Darlin', this is your own private beach," he told her. "Now get undressed so we can enjoy the last of the light."

Wondering how anyone could possibly change as much as she had changed in such a short length of time, Sabella shook her head and began undressing.

"I can't believe I'm actually doing this. What have you done to me, Burt Burnett?"

"Made a woman of you, sweetheart," he said, his silver-gray eyes flashing with warmth as he watched her strip.

"A wanton woman," she accused.

"*My* wanton woman," he said happily.

Holding hands and laughing, the pair ran naked into the surf. Sabella had never swum in the ocean. She screamed when the first crashing wave hit her full in the face and knocked her down. Spitting salt water and pushing her soggy hair out of her eyes, she was relieved to feel Burt's powerful arms come around her.

He pulled her against him. Sabella anxiously threw her arms around his neck. He drew her legs up around his waist, clasped his hands beneath her bare bottom, kissed her wet lips, and said, "I've got you, sweetheart. I'll never let you go."

They played in the ocean until the sun had completely

disappeared, leaving only a lavender band of light on the distant horizon. When they ran dripping out of the sea, Burt pulled Sabella down onto the clothes he had left lying on the sand.

"No, Burt," she protested weakly.

"Shhh," he coaxed, kissing her wet lips, stroking her gleaming thigh. "We are already in paradise. Let's go on to heaven."

Sea birds circled above them. Night winds stirred the tall dune grass, setting it to swaying and undulating. The rising tide rolled in to shore, the rhythmic crashing of the waves pounding the sandy beach. Burt made love to Sabella slowly, sweetly, and with great care as twilight darkened into dusk.

The next week was spent in total privacy and seclusion in the cozy beach cottage overlooking the endless ocean. Those were, Sabella would one day realize, the most peaceful, perfect days of her entire life.

With not a single servant in sight, the pair had great fun cooking their own meals and pretending that they were the only two people on earth. The island, the cottage, the beach were so remote, so isolated it seemed as if they actually were alone on this island paradise.

They went native, wearing few if any clothes, enjoying being lazy, knowing there was nothing much to do, nowhere to go. They picnicked on the beach. They read dime novels. They hiked over the steep, foliaged hills. They took naps in the hammock that swung in the ocean breeze on the cottage's front porch. They swam naked in the ocean. They sunned themselves on the sand.

They again made love on Starlight beach. This time in the starlight.

And they talked for hours on end, each telling the other more and more about their lives before they met.

On their very last afternoon on the island, Sabella and Burt lay lazily in the gently swaying hammock on the front porch.

Burt listened fondly as Sabella spoke of learning to ride when she was barely four. She wanted to be like her father, the father she couldn't really remember. Her mother had told her that Tito Rios was a golden-haired god, so tall and lean and handsome she was jealous, afraid some other woman would steal his affections. Before the accident he had been an expert horseman, a daring *charro* admired and respected by everyone.

Laughing suddenly, Sabella said, "I guess I didn't realize I was a girl and would never be allowed to perform with the *charros.*" She shook her head. "Just a silly child's dreams. I don't know why I even brought it up."

"It wasn't silly at all," Burt said. "You looked up to your father, wanted to be like him. I think that's very sweet."

"And you?" She turned the conversation to him. "I suppose you wanted to be just like your father, too."

"Yes," Burt said without hesitation. "Like you, I learned to ride early. Had my own small pony when I was two years old. Been riding the range of *Lindo Vista* since I was seven or eight. I remember back when I was—"

The distinctive sound of a tinkling bell caused Burt to stop speaking in midsentence. Sabella heard it, too.

"Davey!" she exclaimed.

"Afraid so." Burt nodded, then laughed as he added, "I thought he told us it would take an hour. It hasn't been fifteen minutes since I raised the flag signaling him to come."

Anxiously leaping out of the hammock, Sabella warned as she crossed the porch, "Yes, well, if you don't want to get caught without your pants on, you'd better hurry."

"Hey, that's right," Burt said, "we're naked, aren't we?"

"As the day we were born," she said, disappearing inside.

"Damn!" Burt declared, following her. "It's going to be kinda' tough getting used to clothes again."

Chapter Thirty

Faintly illuminated by starlight, the *California Cloud* glided quietly through the coastal waters, a shadowy silhouette against a glistening sea.

Homeward bound, the sleek yacht had left the tiny Catalina harbor at dusk. The departure had been scheduled for three in the afternoon. But three o'clock had come and gone with no sign of Sabella and Burt.

Lingering until the last possible minute on the far side of the island, the suntanned honeymooners finally showed up at the landing as the sun was going down. Burt had purposely delayed their leaving the cottage after Sabella casually mentioned she thought it would be fun to cross back to the mainland at night.

And so it was fun.

Holding hands and looking up at the night sky where millions of stars twinkled brightly and a pale quarter moon sailed high in the heavens, the pair shared a padded lounge chair on deck as the *Cloud* cruised steadily eastward. It was cool, windless, a breathtakingly beautiful night on the ocean.

Sabella lay comfortably stretched out with her head resting on Burt's supporting shoulder, her hand enclosed in his. The warmth of his long, lean body pressed close gave her a sense of security, of being wonderfully safe. She caught herself feeling peaceful and content for the first time since childhood.

A little shiver of alarm rippled through her at the eye-opening realization. Quickly she reminded herself that the sweet tranquility had nothing whatsoever to do with Burt. It was a false serenity brought on by a slight sunburn, fatigue from too little sleep, and the romantic charm of the open sea at night. The erroneous mood would soon be gone and forgotten.

Nothing to be concerned about.

For a full week they had lived in a dream world of surf and sand and seclusion. Shut off from the real world and its worries and problems. Dependent on each other for everything.

That was over now. The return to normalcy had begun. She'd be herself again once they got back to *Lindo Vista*.

On Sunday afternoon, the third day of October, Cappy Ricks came bounding out of the sprawling white hacienda like an excited young boy. He had spotted the carriage as it turned in and rolled beneath the crossbars of the tall ranch gates. Hurrying down the walk, the big ranch foreman banged out the front gate, flicked his hand-rolled cigarette away, and started waving.

A big smile on his broad, sun-weathered face, light blue eyes crinkling at the corners, Cappy was yanking the carriage door open before it came to a complete stop on the gravel drive.

Arms open wide as if he were reaching for a small child, he yipped with joy when Sabella grabbed him and soundly hugged his neck. He plucked her out of the carriage and swung her around in a full circle before lowering her gently to her feet.

Keeping one big, work-roughened hand around her slim waist, he said, "Lordy, sugar, am I glad to have you home!"

"Good to be back," Sabella said.

Burt stepped lithely out of the carriage, clapped Cappy on the back, and said, "Hey, remember me? I live here, too."

Cappy's twinkling blue eyes shifted to Burt. "You do look kinda familiar." Laughing then, he released Sabella, turned and gave Burt a big bear hug. "God almighty, it's been quiet around here, son."

Embracing the older man, Burt said, "Well we'll see if we

can't liven things up a bit." He released Cappy, stepped back, and reached for Sabella. To her, he said, "What do you think? Should we tell him what we brought him from San Francisco?"

"Aw, now." Cappy briefly bowed his gray head, kicking at the gravel with the toe of his boot. "You kids shouldn't be buying me presents."

"Let's don't tell him." Sabella looked at Cappy, but addressed Burt, "Let's make him guess!" Then she smiled warmly at Cappy, took his arm, and said to both men, "First we'd better go say hello to the others."

The others to whom Sabella referred was the entire staff of house servants. Hearing the commotion, everyone had dropped what he was doing and hurried out to the shaded front gallery to welcome the honeymooners home. All smiles, the oldest to the youngest were lined up. Sabella won the hearts of each of them when she hurried forward to shake hands with the grownups and hug the youngsters.

Dazzled by her fresh beauty and genuine warmth, they were pleased that the easy-going Burt, of whom they were so fond, had married such a sweet, friendly young woman. And they were amazed and flattered that Sabella, having met some of them but once, remembered and addressed each one by name, and with kindness and respect.

They wholeheartedly approved of the new mistress of *Lindo Vista*. Sabella Rios Burnett was the perfect mate for their well-liked Burt. The opinion was unanimous.

Almost.

A sensitive young woman, Sabella noticed, if the others did not, that one of the servants was less than cordial. The chilly look in Annie Galager's light eyes spoke volumes. Sabella pretended not to notice. Her bright smile remained in place as she reached for the woman's hand and shook it warmly.

The evening was a special one. An extraordinary dinner had been prepared in honor of their homecoming, so Sabella wore one of her fashionable new frocks for the occasion and Burt donned a shirt of fine gray silk and a pair of impeccably tailored gray trousers. Cappy, scrubbed and starched and smiling, dined with the couple. The meal was laid out in the smaller of two dining rooms where the table was built from a solid plank of poplar. Elegant, antique, carved high-backed chairs were upholstered in wine-hued chenille tapestry. The table sat directly before a huge, Moorish-style window which was surrounded by beaten copper and looked out on the flower-filled southern courtyard.

After dinner, the entire household and a number of the cowhands assembled on the patio. The gifts Burt and Sabella had bought for everyone were passed out. Including the fancy hand-tooled, silver-embellished saddle for Cappy Ricks. Wine flowed freely and a big chocolate cake was served. Everyone enjoyed themselves.

Later that night, alone upstairs in their suite, Burt stood behind his wife helping her with the small stubborn hooks going down the back of her dress.

Standing perfectly still, Sabella said casually, "Burt, Annie Galager was missing tonight. She wasn't at the party."

"Annie wasn't there? I never noticed."

"I did."

"There," said Burt, the dress undone. He lowered it halfway down her arms, bent his head, and kissed her bare left shoulder. "Well, Annie's always got her butt on her shoulder about something, so I wouldn't worry about it."

"Annie doesn't like me, Burt."

"Honey, you're imagining things. I told you, she—"

"No, I'm not." She freed an arm from the dress sleeve. "That woman does not like me."

Burt ran the tip of his forefinger down her bared arm to her elbow. "Okay, I know what it is. Annie used to work for the de Temples. Five years ago she came to *Lindo Vista.*" He chuckled then and said, "I always figured Gena sent Annie over to keep an eye on me. No doubt Annie made regular reports to Gena."

"That explains it," Sabella said, nodding.

Burt turned Sabella to face him. "We'll get rid of her."

"No, that isn't necessary. What exactly are her duties?"

"Annie's in charge of the laundry detail."

"That's all she does?"

"That's it. She's rarely in the house. Spends most all her time down at the laundry."

"Then I won't be seeing much of her." Sabella smiled and

laid a hand on the soft gray silk of her husband's shirtfront.
"Let her stay."
"You sure?"
"Sure."

Sabella surprised everyone, including her husband, on their
very first morning back home. The October sun had not yet
risen on that early Monday when Burt awakened and slipped
silently out of bed. Naked he stood beside the bed, stretching
and yawning in the dim dawn light. He flinched, startled,
when Sabella softly said his name.

He turned to see her raised up in bed, weight supported
on her elbows. Her tangled blond hair fell around her sleepy
face and her dark eyes were half shuttered by heavily lashed,
lowered lids.

"Sweetheart," he said, coming back to the bed, sitting
down on the edge to face her, "I didn't mean to wake you."
Urging her back onto the pillow, he drew the covers up over
her bare shoulders. "It's very early. Go back to sleep."

"Where are you going?"

He smiled at her, brushing the hair from her eyes. "To
work, baby. I haven't turned a hand for a month. High time
I help out around here, don't you think?"

"Take me with you."

Burt blinked. "You're teasing me."

"Don't make me stay at the house all day. I want to ride
with you. Say I can."

Burt touched her cheek. "You don't need my permission,
Sabella. This is your home; you can do anything you please."

She threw back the covers and sat up. "I know. But would
it upset you if I were to—"

"Ride with me? Honey, I'd be tickled pink."

When Burt came down to breakfast a half hour later, Sabella was with him. She rode away from headquarters with Burt
and Cappy as the sun climbed over the eastern mountains.
A dozen of *Lindo Vista*'s regular hands also rode out that
morning. Forming groups of four, each contingent headed
for a separate location.

Autumn was just around the corner. Time to start checking
on and making counts of the herds that had been scattered
in the high mountain pastures all summer. A meeting would

take place at week's end. Burt, Cappy, and the regulars
would decide how many seasonal riders they needed to herd
the cattle down to the corrals for branding. This year, for
the first time in twenty-five years, *vaqueros* would be hired
along with the cowboys.

Burt had never had anything against the Mexicans and was
the first to admit that they were the best horsemen alive.

That sunny October day was the first, but it would not be
the last time Sabella rode the vast ranges of *Lindo Vista* at
her husband's side. Burt was pleased that this sweet, beautiful woman he married seized every opportunity to ride with
him across the valley meadows and up into the craggy mountains and out to the hot, bordering deserts. She was interested in every minute detail of the big ranch and the people
who worked it.

It was a dream come true for Burt.

He had spent years engaged to a woman who had never
been on a horse, cared nothing about the land he loved so
much. He realized more fully with every passing day what a
terrible mistake it would have been to have married Gena
de Temple. Not only had he never really been in love with
her, they'd had very little in common.

How incredibly fortunate he was that Sabella Rios had
come into his life. The dazzling beauty who filled his days
with joy, his nights with ecstasy, was not content to be just
the mistress of his house, the woman in his bed, the mother
of his children. She was his friend, his partner, his equal in
every way. He loved it. He would teach her everything there
was to know about *Lindo Vista*. He would keep nothing from
her, ever. He would show her and advise her and inform her
so well that if anything ever happened to him, she would be
prepared and capable of running the vast empire as well as
he ever had.

Burt Burnett was a happy man.

And since he was, his old Happy chair in their upstairs
suite got a real workout. Burt lolled often in the worn leather
chair, content, enjoying life as never before. Often he sat in
his Happy chair alone. More often he didn't. He coaxed Sabella into sharing the Happy chair. He held her on his lap
while he sprawled there, being happy.

Burt never, while seated in the Happy chair, discussed

business or the ranch or spoke of anything of a serious nature. Anytime he sank down into the comfortable leather cushions of the Happy chair, it meant playtime. Pleasure, peace, or a combination of both ensued.

Together in that big Happy chair, Burt and Sabella shared late suppers and midnight snacks. They read there. They sang songs there. They laughed and tickled each other there. They took naps there. They undressed there.

They made love there.

The big comfortable Happy chair proved to be such a perfect place for it, they made love there almost as often as they made love in their big soft bed. Either place, chair or bed, Sabella occasionally forgot—in her ecstasy—the reason she had married Burt.

Sometimes when they were lying close in the darkness, so close she could feel each beat of his heart, she experienced painful twinges of guilt and regret. This man loved her. *So much.* More, much more than she'd ever dreamed anyone would love her.

She was almost sorry that she had to hurt him.

Chapter Thirty-one

Autumn in Southern California.
In that golden land of perpetual sunshine the fall weather was as near perfect as could be found anywhere on earth. Mornings were wonderfully clear and bright. The afternoons, warm, still, and hazy. And the nights? Sharp, cool, chilled by gentle ocean breezes. Ideal for sleeping.

Or for making love.

Life on *Lindo Vista* that autumn matched the perfection of the exemplary weather. The splendid season brought a whirl of exciting activity. Nobody's days were idle. Everyone on the big coastal spread kept busy. Including Sabella.

Often she rose with the cool, gray dawn to ride the range at her husband's side. After their initial surprise, the *rancho*'s tough, seasoned cowboys thought nothing of seeing Burt's blond bride out on the distant stretches, riding and working as if she were a man.

On the first such occasion, Sabella caught the gritty cow-hands exchanging covert glances. They were, she knew, more than a little skeptical. They soon changed their tune. Early doubts were quickly dispelled as she went out of her way to prove herself.

Grudgingly at first, then with open admiration and respect, the cowboys came around. She had shown that she was no foolish, spoiled female out on a lark. They wouldn't be hampered by a weak woman suffering from vapors the first time dust blew into her eyes or a prickly pear's stickers snagged her trouser legs.

Quickly they learned that the slim blond female astride the big chestnut stallion was resilient, capable, and as expert a horseman as any of them—even better than most. Furthermore, she asked no quarter and gave none. She pulled her own weight, but didn't throw that weight around. Never once did she remind anyone, either by word or deed, that she was the boss's wife.

She didn't complain when the heat caused her white shirt to stick to her slender back just as their sweat-soaked shirts stuck to theirs. She never hesitated to drink from a canteen when she was thirsty, never griped about eating from a tin plate at noontime. Nor did she whimper and moan at the end of a long hard day when she was so tired she could hardly stay in the saddle.

Above all, Sabella proved to the hands that she was a good sport.

She showed up at the stables one morning in the navy suede jodhpurs and knee-high boots she'd bought in San Francisco. Cappy Ricks was the first one to burst out laughing. He wasn't the last. The hardened, leathery-faced cowboys teased her unmercifully about being out in her "bloomers." Sabella took it all in stride and laughed harder than anyone.

On the days she didn't ride with Burt, she occupied herself by eagerly examining the many rooms of the big white hacienda, or by taking long walks around the sprawling estate. *Lindo Vista* was, she decided, the most beautiful place on the entire earth. An exotic coastal paradise with grape arbors and groves of lemon and orange trees beyond the terraced, manicured yard. Orchards of olive and guava trees stretched into the distance on the south side of the house.

The pleasing scent of the sea was constant, and on more than one warm, lazy autumn afternoon, Sabella burst out of the mansion's back door, crossed the flagstone patio, dashed through the large, flower-bordered yard, and eagerly descended the eighty-eight steps to the beach below.

Changing into a bathing dress and hauling one of the folding beach chairs out of the bathhouse onto the sand, she'd lie in the sun and watch the sea stretching endlessly blue and beckoning to the west. She'd read and doze and daydream. And sometimes she'd catch herself smiling foolishly and sighing softly with the sudden recollection of the passionate love words Burt had whispered last night in the darkness. The hot kisses. The intimate caresses.

Stop it! she'd furiously warn herself, leaping up from the beach chair to race across the sand and plunge into the sea. Diving into an oncoming wave, she lectured herself. *Do not allow yourself to weaken! You cannot care for this man! Never, ever!*

But, oh, dear God, it was hard not to care.

In those golden sun-warmed days of that glorious California autumn, Sabella and Cappy Ricks became the closest of friends. In an unspoken agreement between Burt and Cappy, Cappy was appointed Sabella's chief protector. He stepped quite naturally into the role of bodyguard to the energetic young mistress of *Lindo Vista.*

If Sabella decided to go for a ride when Burt was not at home, Cappy Ricks rode with her. Sabella didn't mind. She was fond of Cappy. She grew fonder still of the rugged, gray-haired ranch foreman when one day he confided that his life would have been a lonely, empty one if not for the Burnetts.

The two of them had ridden all the way up to the Dreamy Draw dam on a warm, sunny afternoon. There they dismounted and Cappy ground tethered the horses. Sabella wandered down a few steps nearer to the man-made concrete barrier holding back the rushing waters of Coronado Creek.

She dropped down onto the soft green grass and stretched out on her back, folding her hands beneath her head. "Let's take a nap, Cappy," she said, sighing, stretching, and squinting up at him.

Cappy smiled indulgently and dropped down to sit cross-legged beside her. "You sleep if you're tired, sugar. I'll relax and enjoy a smoke."

While he built and smoked a less-than-perfectly shaped cigarette, Cappy talked, at Sabella's gentle urging.

"I've been at *Lindo Vista* for the past thirty years," he said, the cigarette dangling from his lips. "It's home to me, the only one I've ever really had. When I was a young man, I ..."

He began to talk freely, to open up. Sabella listened attentively as Cappy told her things she'd never known. About himself. And about the Burnetts. He had, he revealed, been pretty much just a worthless, rum-soaked loner until Raleigh Burnett had dragged him out of a San Diego saloon one gray rainy day in 1850 and brought him down to *Lindo Vista.*

"You see," Cappy said wistfully, "back then I didn't care if I lived or died. One way or the other, it didn't matter to me. I didn't think I would ever care again."

In a low, whiskey-and-cigarette-roughened voice, Cappy Ricks told Sabella that when he was a young man he worked for the Bixby family at the old *Rancho Alamitos* outside Los Angeles.

"Some cousins from Philadelphia visited the Bixbys in the summer of '35. One was a pretty seventeen-year-old girl with dark hair. Miss Geneva Ruth Darling." His blue eyes twinkled when he said her name. "She was that all right ... a real darling. I was twenty-one and not half bad looking if I do say so myself. 'Course her family was horrified. They didn't want their little Geneva fooling around with a common cowhand, much less marrying one." He chuckled and took a long drag on his cigarette.

Smiling, fascinated, Sabella raised up onto an elbow. "But Geneva defied her family and married you?"

Nodding, Cappy said, "She didn't go back to Philadelphia. I wouldn't let her. She married me and a couple of years later we had a baby girl."

"Cappy Ricks! You have a daughter?"

"Had. Had a daughter." A cloud passed over his eyes. "In '45 when the baby—Beth we called her, her name was Elizabeth May—was eight years old, Geneva took her to Santa Fe. I couldn't go with them; I tried to talk Geneva out of going. But her only sister had moved to Santa Fe the year before and Geneva wanted to see her." He flicked the ashes from his cigarette. "I knew it wasn't safe. The 'Paches had been acting up all that summer and ... and ...." he exhaled loudly. "A renegade band attacked the stage just the other side of Strawberry Crater in northern Arizona."

"Oh, Cappy, no . . ." Sabella sat up fully, laid a hand his forearm.

For a long moment he said nothing. Then: "I was always grateful that the savages didn't scalp Beth." A mist of tears glistened in his eyes. "She had the prettiest pale white hair I ever saw. Felt just like fine silk. I used to brush it for her at bedtime; then I'd brush her momma's."

"I'm so sorry," Sabella said, her hand tightening on his arm.

Cappy patted her comforting hand. He shook his gray head. "I shouldn't be burdening you, child. You've had more than your share of misery." He blinked away his tears, smiled, and said, "Anyway, after I lost my girls, I didn't care if molasses went up to a dollar a sop or if the old world stopped turning on its axis."

He squeezed Sabella's hand, released it. She moved it from his arm.

Wrapping her arms around her knees, she said, "I don't blame you. Not one bit."

"I started drinking to blot it all out. I guess I fell in the bottle pretty good. Lost my job at *Rancho Alamitos* and they kicked me off the place. I didn't care. Didn't give a damn. Drifted for several years, down to Mexico, then up to Texas, over to Louisiana. Eventually, back to Southern California."

"And Raleigh Burnett found you."

Cappy grinned and nodded. "Raleigh and Dana, his pretty red-haired wife, had a baby son. Now Burt was a year old and the cutest little rascal you ever did see. Walkin' and talkin' and into everything. Anyway, Raleigh said he didn't know a lot about ranching and he was looking for a good foreman. Told me he'd heard about me back when I was helping run things at *Rancho Alamitos*."

"So he hired you even though—"

"Told me he wanted me to be his foreman, but if he ever caught me drunk, he'd boot me right off the property. Since I didn't have enough money that day to buy another drink, I took him up on his offer." He laughed then.

Sabella laughed, too. "And you've been there ever since."

"Yep." Cappy paused, his gray head swung around, and he looked straight into her eyes. "Raleigh Burnett saved my life. He was the best friend I ever had. And Burton . . . well, he's been a son to me." Sabella said nothing. She remained completely composed, purposely keeping her expression placid. But she couldn't keep from swallowing convulsively when Cappy added meaningfully, "Anybody hurts my boy answers to me."

She forced herself to smile. She said, "Burt's fortunate to have you, Cappy."

Cappy smiled back at her. He said, "Burt's even more fortunate to have you, sugar."

Chapter Thirty-two

"Okay, okay . . . I'll get up . . . but I'm not going to school," Sabella teased.

And she stayed in bed on this cool Friday morning in mid-November. Instead of rising early with Burt as was her custom, she had, in fact, lingered in bed all week. The first couple of mornings Burt supposed she was just unusually sleepy. He'd said nothing, just kissed her sleepy face, carefully covered her, and left her to slumber peacefully.

But after five days of this new drowsiness, he was beginning to worry. When he awakened this Friday morning, he slowly turned his head on the pillow and gazed lovingly at the beautiful woman sleeping beside him. His heartbeat quickened from just looking at her and he realized how much he missed having her rise with him each morning. He missed dressing with her. Having breakfast with her. Making plans for the day with her.

He wanted her to smile at him. To talk to him. To kiss him good morning.

He wanted her to wake up!

Burt grinned mischievously. He reached over and carefully curled his lean fingers around the top edge of the silky sheet and matching comforter. Then he swiftly yanked all the bed covers off Sabella, kicking them to the foot of the bed.

The chill of the early morning sea air touched Sabella's

naked flesh. Her eyes didn't open, but she shivered involuntarily, squirmed and turned onto her side, facing away from him. She pulled her knees up and put her spread hands between them.

One dark eyebrow raised, Burt continued to watch her, wondering how long it would take before the cold penetrated her sleep and she awakened. His grin broadened when—still sleeping soundly—she began to gravitate toward him. Seeking his body heat, she was pulled like a magnet toward his warmth.

Her lips fell open and she sighed softly in her sleep when her slender back and soft, rounded bottom came in contact with his chest and belly. Burt laughed softly. She was adorable as she wiggled and twisted, getting as close to him as possible.

She expelled a long, deep sigh of satisfaction when he put his arms around her, gently drew her closer, and curved his body around hers in spoonlike fashion. Lifting his legs and bending his knees to press them warmly under hers, he placed a spread hand on her flat stomach, cradled her close against him, and let her sleep a few more minutes.

As the big bedroom grew steadily lighter and warmer, Burt knew he could put it off no longer. It was time to get up. He had to go into the village. Much as he hated to leave Sabella, he had to ... to ... He'd take her with him! He'd take the gig up the coast to Capistrano instead of riding Sam, so she could go with him. Just the two of them. She could shop and visit her young girlfriends, Cynthia Douglas and Janie Desmond.

"Sabella," he said softly, raising a hand to sweep her heavy blond hair off her face. "Honey, wake up."

"Mmmmm," she murmured and squirmed against him.

"Baby, it's after seven. Time to get up."

Her eyes remaining closed, Sabella slowly turned in his embrace.

"I don't think so." She snuggled close, her warm, soft breasts pressed against his chest.

Burt chuckled. "What does that mean? You don't think so."

Softly spoken words muffled against his throat. "I don't think I'll get up this morning."

"I'm going into town today, remember. Be gone all day. How would you like to come along with me?"

Flatly: "I'm not going."

The smile left Burt's face. He pulled back a little, so he could look at her. Her dark eyes opened and met his gaze.

"Honey, are you sick? You've stayed in bed late all this week and I'm getting worried."

Sabella smiled mysteriously at him. "I feel wonderful." She slid her hand up his chest, over his throat to his face. She touched the cleft in his chin with her fingertip and said, "Don't look so worried. I am fine. Honest I am."

"Then why don't you want to come with me?"

"Things to do here," she said, running her foot up his calf. "And one of those things is getting another hour of sleep."

"You sure you're feeling well?" Burt wasn't convinced.

"I'm sure. Very sure." Again, that enigmatic smile.

"Okay, then," he said finally, puzzled. "Be a lazy bones, but I have to get up."

He kissed her quickly, rolled away, swung his long legs over the mattress's edge, and stood up. He turned back and looked down at her. She was attempting to snag the lowered bedcovers with her toes, too sleepy and lazy to sit up and reach for them. Enchanted, Burt leaned over and brushed a kiss to her pale bare belly. Then he carefully drew the covers up over her.

"Sleep well, sweetheart. And do me a big favor."

Her eyes closing again, Sabella mumbled, "Mmmmm ... what?"

"Since you like staying in bed so well, how about being here when I get home this evening? Right where you are and just as you are. Naked in bed. Think you can manage that?"

"Try me," she murmured, rolled over, and was at once asleep.

When Sabella again awakened, the November sun was high in the sky and the bedroom was flooded with bright light. With a burst of energy and cautious hope, she sat up and threw off the covers. Anxiously, she carefully examined herself, checking the insides of her bare thighs, searching for any signs of the damning evidence which would so sorely disappoint her.

Seeing nothing, she got up, snatched the bedcovers completely off and examined the bed with the same careful scrutiny she had given her body. The sleep-tumbled gray silk sheets were spotless.

Sabella clapped her hands with glee and spun around in a circle. She was almost sure now. Almost positive. Another couple of days and she would be absolutely certain that she was carrying Burt's child.

Sabella excitedly skipped into the dressing room. She stood before the full-length mirror and studied her naked body. She placed her hands on her flat stomach and pressed gently, awed suddenly by the miracle of conception.

The hours she had lain in Burt's arms, the heated love they had made, had started a new life inside her. The thought was overwhelming. She, Sabella Rios Burnett, was going to have a baby. By this time next year she would be a mother. She would have a son.

Burt's son.

Sabella suddenly felt weak and dizzy. All at once the weight of this shocking new knowledge of which she alone was aware, was almost too much to comprehend. To believe.

She left the dressing room without dressing. It was ridiculous, she knew, but for some senseless reason she wanted to stay naked. It all seemed more real if she didn't put on her clothes. She felt more like a woman, more like a mother-to-be, if she was totally nude.

Congratulating herself on attaining the all-important goal, Sabella decided she'd spend the entire morning naked. Stay in the privacy of her bedroom and secretly enjoy being nude, natural, and newly pregnant.

She laughed at her foolishness, hugged herself, and danced dizzily about the sun-filled room, humming a lullaby. Finally she breathlessly dropped down into the deep cushions of an old, worn leather chair with a matching ottoman. She swung her long slender legs up onto the ottoman and crossed her bare ankles. She pressed her head against the chair's high back and giggled foolishly.

Naked, swinging her feet off the edge of the ottoman and twisting a lock of tangled blond hair around her finger, Sabella sat in the comfortable brown leather chair, laughing giddily for several long minutes before all at once it dawned on her where she was sitting.

Again.

In the past few weeks she had caught herself—more than once when she was alone—instinctively choosing this chair. The Happy chair.

The smile left Sabella's face. Her heart pounded against her ribs. She drew her legs up and curled herself into a tight defensive ball. Hot tears sprang to her eyes and she wasn't sure what they meant.

Sabella began to weep. She sat there in the Happy chair and wept, suddenly bitterly unhappy. She faced, for the first time, the reason for her misery.

She had fallen in love with Burt Burnett.

Crying—heartbroken—Sabella jumped, startled, when she heard a knock on the bedroom door, followed immediately by Carmelita calling out, "Sabella, let me in. Open the door, *por favor!*"

Sniffing and rubbing her puffy, red-rimmed eyes, Sabella managed, "Ju-just . . . a . . . a . . . minute."

She rose from the Happy chair and looked frantically about. She saw no sign of the robe she'd worn last night. But a black silk one belonging to Burt was tossed carelessly over the velvet-padded bench at the foot of their bed.

She drew it on as she crossed to the door, tying the long streamers in a knot at her waist. When she reached the door, she attempted to draw a deep breath, couldn't, gulped for air, and opened the door a crack.

"Madre de Dios!" the worried Carmelita exclaimed upon seeing her swollen eyes. "You are sick, *sí?*"

Sabella's reply was a shake of the head and a fresh burst of tears. Carmelita hurried anxiously inside to take the unhappy young woman in her comforting arms. Thoughtlessly, she left the door ajar behind her.

"La tristeza," Carmelita exclaimed. "The sadness! Why, the sadness? What it is, *nena?*"

"Oh, Carmelita," Sabella sobbed, "I'm going to have a baby."

"No! But that is what you wish for, *sí?*"

"Yes, but I . . . I . . . oh, what have I done?"

"Shhh, shhh," soothed the stocky Mexican woman. "We wash your face, then we talk."

They did talk, the two old friends, speaking freely, knowing their privacy was total. No one else was upstairs except the two of them. So they talked. Sabella told Carmelita that she was almost certain she was pregnant. But she wasn't happy. Far from it. For weeks an unexpected affection for her husband had been steadily growing, plaguing her. She had begun to wonder: Could Burt be innocent? Surely it was possible. Maybe he really wasn't aware that his father had stolen *Lindo Vista*. And if that were so, then it was very wrong to punish him.

Neither woman heard Annie Galager coming down the long silent corridor. Her arms filled with freshly washed linens, *Lindo Vista*'s head laundress was unaware anyone was still upstairs at this late hour of the morning. Her footfalls making no sound on the corridor's deep carpet, Annie was heading for the big upstairs linen closet when she heard voices.

She paused, turned her head, and listened. She recognized Sabella's voice. Curious, she moved a few steps closer to the door at the end of the hall. A door that was evidently wide open. When Annie heard Burt's name, she began to pay very close attention. And when she heard the shocking things his bride was saying about him, about herself, about their marriage, Annie sneaked silently down the hall to the linen closet. She crept inside the big storage closet, pulled the door almost shut, and continued to listen.

Annie Galager, hiding there in the closet, learned the whole shocking story. Everything. Including the fact there was a journal. A journal belonging to Carmelita's deceased husband, Victor Rivera, which documented that Raleigh Burnett swindled Teresa Carrillo Rios out of her rightful inheritance, *Lindo Vista*. The Rivera journal meticulously tracked Attorney Raleigh Burnett's crafty theft of *Lindo Vista* from its rightful owner. The damning journal was now in the possession of Sabella Rios, the daughter of the cheated Teresa Carrillo Rios.

Blinking in disbelief and delight, Annie Galager smiled in the dimness of the linen closet. Sabella and Carmelita recounted the whole story. They talked of learning all they

could about the Burnett family; of clipping and keeping
newspaper articles for the past decade. Of coldly planning,
from the time Sabella was just fifteen years old, to come to
San Juan Capistrano, the two of them, Carmelita and herself,
to reside there for six months. And in that six months, Sabella would make Burt Burnett fall in love with her, marry
her.

Then, she would have her revenge on the Burnetts.

She would have Burt's son—the future heir to *Lindo
Vista*—and take the child away from him.

But now, apparently, Sabella had changed her mind.

"Carmelita, Burt is the kindest, most caring man I've ever
known," Annie heard Sabella say. "It's almost impossible to
imagine him stealing anything." Sabella sighed wearily, her
slender shoulders lifting and lowering beneath the slick silk
of Burt's too-large black robe.

Nodding, Carmelita agreed, "*Señor* Burnett is good man
in many ways."

"He is and even if . . . even if Burt was in on the swindle,
I wish we had never come here. I wish I had never sought
retribution. I didn't plan on something like this happening,
never dreamed that I would . . . would . . . I can't help myself,
I'm in love with Burt." She closed her tear-reddened eyes
and sadly shook her head. "Dear God, how could this be? I
love the man I should hate above all others." Her eyes
opened and she admitted, "I never knew life could be so
sweet. The weeks . . . the months I've spent with Burt have
been the happiest of my whole life."

Carmelita sympathized, smiled, and wisely advised, "Then
forget about seeking revenge. You have the land now. It is
yours. Yours and your husband's. He loves you very much
and now you are going to have his child. Let go of the past."

Sabella's scratchy eyes, narrowed with hopelessness, began
to widen slightly. Her aching heart skipped a couple of beats.
Her mind raced as she seriously considered what Carmelita
proposed. How simple it would be. How wonderful to put
aside all the bitterness and hatred and spend the rest of her
life on *Lindo Vista* with the man she loved.

"Yes!" she exclaimed excitedly. "That's exactly what I'll
do. Burt doesn't know who I am, why I came here. He'll
never have to know. I love him, I'll be a good wife to him.

I'll spend the rest of my life making up for what I've done. Oh, it's the answer, Carmelita, I know it. He does love me and I love him. We can be happy together. He need never know the truth!"

Smiling, Carmelita nodded agreeably and walked out into the silent hall. Sabella waited a minute, then anxiously followed. Pausing in her newfound hope and excitement, she frowned worriedly, and called after Carmelita, "He won't find out, will he?"

Carmelita noticed the door of the linen closet was open a crack. She shut it, leaned back against it, and crossed her fingers when she said, "No, child, he will never know."

Chapter Thirty-three

"D id you get it? Did you buy the dynamite?"
      "No. Not yet."
Gena whirled about and glared angrily at Cisco. "I send you down to Baja to buy dynamite. You spend three days and come back empty-handed?" Hands on her hips, chin jutting, she stepped closer to the tall, spare Mexican. "What did you do while you were down there? Squander my money on some cheap whore?"

"No, *querida.*" Cicso grinned evilly, shaking his head. "I only enjoy expensive *putas.*" He grabbed her arm, roughly pulled her to him. "Rich beautiful whores like you, *mi amor.*"

"You filthy bastard!" she hissed loudly. "You can't speak to me like that! I am Gena de Temple, Senator Nelson de Temple's daughter while you"—she made a sour face—"you are nothing. A lowly *vaquero.* A hired hand to be bossed about. I can fire you anytime I choose."

"Then do it," Cisco said, the evil grin never leaving his dark, gaunt face. "What are you waiting for? Fire me."

"Fine!" she shouted, her chin lifting a half inch higher. "You're fired! Get out of this house and off my—"

His hands were rough and his mouth hot and eager as he hushed her. When finally he released her, Gena was weak in the knees and breathless. She swayed dizzily on her feet and clung helplessly to him.

"Now, *querida*," Cisco said, the nasty smile pulling the long slashing scar on his cheek, "tell me I am fired."

Her hands gripping his ropey upper arms, Gena's forehead sagged against his chest. "Cisco," she whined, scolding him, "you are mean and cruel. I despise you. You are a monster."

"A monster is what you need, *querida*," he said coldly. Then he pushed her from him so forcefully, Gena lost her balance, stumbled, and fell to the floor. He looked down on her and said, "I will get the dynamite, but these things take time. Now, are you going to straighten up and behave yourself?" His fingers settled atop her head; he gathered a handful of dark hair and pulled painfully. "Or must I punish you for being a bad girl?"

"No, please, Cisco, you're hurting me." She grabbed his bony wrist. "Stop. I'll behave."

His hand loosened its grip on the dark lustrous locks, and began to stroke soothingly. "Then I reward you. Make love to you here in your father's house. In your own bed."

Gena sighed, wrapped her arms around his black-trousered right leg, and nodding, said, "Yes. That sounds delightful. What time is it?"

Cisco's glance shifted to the clock on the peach marble mantel. "Is five minutes to five."

"We have an hour, no more. I expect Father and Don Miguel Amaro about six." Gena released her hold on Cisco's leg, sat back on her heels, and smiled coyly up at him. "Do what you will with me, but you must be gone before—"

A loud intrusive knock caused them both to turn and look at the locked door. Gena, laying her forefinger perpendicular to her lips signaling Cisco to be quiet, called out, "Yes? What is it?"

"You have a visitor, *Señorita* Gena," came the reply from a servant. "Annie Galager is downstairs. She says she must see you at once."

Gena sighed with irritation. "Tell her I'll be right down." To Cisco, she whispered, "I'll be back in five minutes, no longer." She rose before him, stepped very close, put a bold hand on his groin, and slid her fingers slowly between his legs, cupping him. "Don't undress. Allow me the pleasure of

unwrapping all the goodies when I get back." She gave him
a naughty little smile, squeezed him gently, and left.

Impatiently, Gena hurried downstairs and into the east
drawing room where Annie Galager waited.

"Annie, I hope this is important," Gena said by way of
greeting. "I'm a very busy woman and I—"

"I'm sure you have time to hear what I've come here to
tell you," the *Lindo Vista* laundress interrupted, smiling like
the cat who'd swallowed the canary.

Her interest immediately piqued, Gena sat down beside
the smiling woman.

Excitement starting to build, Gena asked hopefully, "It's
about Sabella Rios . . . ?" She couldn't bring herself to say
Burnett. "You've discovered something that will—?"

"Yes!" Shaking her head, Annie said, "Miss Gena, you
are not going to believe what I overheard this morning!"

Gena smiled with eager anticipation. "What? Tell me! Tell
me everything!"

Annie Galager took a deep breath. Speaking rapidly, excitedly, she told Gena that she had accidentally overheard Sabella Rios Burnett talking confidentially with Carmelita
Rivera.

The longer Annie spoke, the more she told, the wider
Gena's green eyes became. Her mouth rounded in an O, she
listened, enraptured, feeling the blood zinging through her
veins, her heart hammering in her breast.

When at last Annie Galager finished speaking, she beamed
proudly, and waited for Gena's praise.

"Burt," Gena murmured, "I must tell Burt. I must—"

"I happen to know," Annie said, "that Mr. Burnett is in
Capistrano today. He had a board meeting at the bank this
morning."

"This morning? But it's five o'clock!"

"This afternoon," Annie continued, "he was to meet—at
the Mission Inn—with a gentleman from Los Angeles for a
lengthy business session of some sort. A hydro . . . a hydrol
. . . Well, anyway something to do with water."

"Then Burt is still in town?"

"I'm almost sure he is. I overheard at breakfast him tell
Cappy Ricks that he wouldn't be home until around seven
this evening so—"

"Julio!" Gena leaped up and ran into the corridor shouting for the old servant. "Julio, get in here this instant!"

The aging servant, leaving his freshly poured cup of coffee behind at the kitchen table, shuffled into the hall. *"Sí, Señorita?"*

"Julio, go to the Mission Inn. Find Burt Burnett. Tell him he must come here at once! It is a matter of life or death!"

"Is matter of life or death!" repeated Julio, his dark eyes blinking.

"Yes! If you let him get out of town before coming here, I'll ship you off to furthest Mexico! You'll spend the rest of your life in the fields picking vegetables in the hot sun. Now go!"

"Sí, sí," murmured the frightened old man and lumbered down the hall toward the back of the house.

Annie Galager had come into the corridor. "I hope I've been of some help, Miss de Temple." She was expecting a reward, perhaps an offer to return to the de Temple mansion at a handsome pay raise.

"Let yourself out," Gena said distractedly. "I must change before Burt arrives." Gena laughed then, almost hysterically, and murmured to herself, "He will, after all, need a great deal of comforting!"

Gena raced up the stairs and down the hall to her suite, eagerly planning the evening ahead. When they were alone, she would tell Burt how his scheming bitch of a wife had duped him. She would first make sure there was plenty of liquor on hand to ease his pain. And, of course, she would do a little easing of his pain herself. To hell with her father and Don Miguel Andres Amaro. They could dine without her. She would, she hoped, be occupied all night!

Gena burst into her suite, slammed the door behind her, and saw Cisco sprawled on the peach brocade sofa, a long leg hooked over the arm. Having forgotten all about him, she was suddenly furious at seeing him there.

"What do you think you're doing? You shouldn't be here! Someone might see you."

"Querida," he said in a low voice, "come here and undress me."

"Undress you? Are you out of your mind? You must go.

Leave right now," she commanded. "I'm expecting a guest shortly."

"Gena, my sweet, you just had a guest. Now it is *our* turn."

"No, Cisco, now it is *my* turn." She smiled triumphantly. "Will you leave or must I have you thrown out?"

Cisco's smile was just as triumphant as hers. "There is," he said meaningfully, "only one way you can get me to leave." With that his hands went to the buttons of his fly.

"Oh, for heaven's sake!" she snapped, desperate to get him out of the house.

Irritably, she dropped to her knees between his spread legs, brushed his hands aside, deftly unbuttoned his black trousers, and freed him. When she bent to him, Cisco's hands went to her head, his fingers entwined in her hair.

He grinned.

She was in a big hurry. So of course, he was not. He purposely held back, resisting the climax she was working so diligently to bring on. Grinning evilly, Cisco sat there watching her, wondering how long he could last. How long she could last. He began timing them. His amused gaze lifted to the clock on the peach marble fireplace mantel.

Five minutes. Six. Seven.

He silently recited the words to his favorite Spanish ballads, determinedly distracting himself.

Ten minutes. Twelve. Fifteen.

Twenty-one minutes passed before he finally took pity on her and gave in to ecstasy. Focusing fully on her and what she was doing to him, he was soon groaning and shuddering with satisfaction.

Gena raised her head. Eyes snapping with anger, she wiped her gleaming mouth on her dress sleeve. "You son of a bitch! You did that on purpose!"

"Did what, *querida*?" he asked innocently, shrugging. "*No comprendé.* I do not understand."

She shot to her feet. "Will you please go!" She pointed anxiously toward the balcony doors. "Go and stay away from ... and, oh yes, you can forget about the dynamite."

"No dynamite?" Cisco rose, leisurely buttoning his black trousers. "Why? What has changed, *querida*?"

"Everything," she said happily. Then she smugly told him, "I'm getting my man back!"

"Who? Burt Burnett?" Cisco laughed cynically. "And just how do you plan on getting rid of the beautiful Sabella Burnett?"

Shoving him anxiously toward the door, a confident Gena licked the corner of her mouth with a pink tongue, and said, "Piece of cake."

Chapter Thirty-four

Sabella Rios Burnett was, at five o'clock that same afternoon, happy as only the young, healthy, and madly in love can be. Happy beyond belief. Never in her most longed for, girlish dreams had she imagined such complete happiness as was now hers.

This warm, clear autumn day was, she decided, the best one yet. Better by far than her September wedding day. Better than the exciting days in San Francisco. Better even than those lazy idyllic days on remote Catalina Island.

This was the day she would remember all her life. An historic, not-to-be-forgotten day when she would, for the first time, put her arms around her husband's neck, tell him how much she loved him, and mean it with all her heart.

Sweet anticipation built as the crisp, sunny afternoon waned. Looking forward eagerly to the nippy November night stretching before her, Sabella went about smiling.

She planned a very special evening.

She had dashed breathlessly about the mansion throughout the afternoon making sure everything was done. Martha, the head cook, and her assistants had quickly caught the spirit and busied themselves in the kitchen preparing Burt's favorite foods.

Blanton, who was head butler as well as Burt's personal manservant, coolly issued a myriad of orders to the staff.

Then checked periodically on their progress. Had the correct wine been brought up from the cellar? Had every inch of redwood paneling and grand staircase been thoroughly polished? Had a table, complete with spotless damask cloth, matching serviettes, and tall white tapers in silver candelabra been set up in the master suite? Was the table properly situated so that the dining couple could see from the tall windows which looked out on the Pacific bluffs across the long, rolling lawn?

While Blanton and Martha worked their magic, Sabella worked a little of her own. She languished in the bubble-filled marble tub longer than usual, then carefully shampooed her long blond hair. Carmelita joined her after her bath and the two of them, giggling like a couple of young girls, readied Sabella for the special evening.

The dress they agreed on for the occasion was picked after considering, discussing the merits of, then discarding at least a dozen possible selections.

Sabella wanted to look just right. Not too sophisticated. But not too naive either. Not too old. But not too young. Not too glamorous. But not too plain.

She wanted to look like exactly what she was. The healthy, happy young wife of a handsome, prosperous rancher who had just learned that she was expecting their first child.

It was Carmelita who struck on the perfect dress. When she held it up for Sabella to inspect, Sabella clapped her hands and nodded.

Carmelita assured her she looked both earthy and angelic in the simple, but beautiful gown of lush rose-pink velvet. Long-sleeved and high-throated, the tight-fitting bodice molded Sabella's full breasts and hugged her narrow waist before angling to a center point low on her flat stomach. The long skirt was very full, falling in soft gathers to the floor. Not one inch of flesh showed from the front.

But when she turned about, Sabella's delicate, golden-skinned back was bare to the waist, the cut of the gown both daring and demure.

Just right.

Knowing her husband preferred her hair to be worn loose and flowing, Sabella stood perfectly still while Carmelita brushed the heavy locks back off her face and down her bare back. For a finishing touch, Carmelita plucked a delicate pink Castillian rose from a nearby vase, broke off the long stem, and tucked the velvet-petaled blossom into Sabella's gleaming gold hair.

By sunset everything was ready.

Lights shone brightly from every window in the whitewashed adobe hacienda. In the master suite upstairs, where a fire blazed in the stone fireplace, heavy Georgian silver and fragile china adorned a damask-draped table for two. An exquisite meal was ready and waiting in the kitchen.

And downstairs in the spacious drawing room, Sabella, stunning in the long, rose velvet gown, eagerly waited for Burt to get home.

Any minute now she would hear the drum of hoofbeats on the palm-lined gravel avenue. Too nervous to sit, she swept about the lamplit room, touching objects, rehearsing what she would say to him. Going over in her mind exactly how she would tell him about the baby. Sabella jumped when the tall cased clock out in the corridor struck seven p.m.

It wouldn't be much longer now.

Sabella moved to a front window, drew back the heavy curtain, and peered out. The early November dusk had turned into enveloping darkness. She could see nothing. She dropped the drapery back in place and rubbed her hands together.

Any minute now.

When the clock chimed eight, Sabella was pacing back and forth, battling a nagging feeling of rising uneasiness. She checked with the kitchen and was assured everything was fine, the carefully prepared meal was warming, it would be edible even if Burt was a little late.

By nine o'clock Sabella was genuinely concerned.

By ten she was beside herself with worry.

At eleven Sabella insisted the kitchen crew give up and go to bed. Her nerves raw, she paced and worried and tried to hide her anxiety when Cappy, Blanton, and Carmelita periodically came and checked on her. Each, in an effort to reassure her, suggested that Burt's business meeting had probably run long and he had decided to stay in town, to spend the night at the Mission Inn.

"Yes, of course. I'm sure that's it," Sabella agreed with them. "Please, go to bed. I'll go up in a few minutes myself."

One by one they retired to their respective quarters, leaving her to pace and worry alone. It was after midnight when at last she heard the distinctive sound that made her immediately sigh with relief.

"Thank God," she said aloud, and hurriedly checked her appearance in the mirror mounted over the mantel.

She raced to the window again—for at least the hundredth time—yanked back the curtain and saw the dark horseman galloping up the palm-bordered avenue in the moonlight. Heart racing with excitement, she watched as Burt pulled the lathered Sam to a gravel-slinging stop in the circle drive just beyond the yard. He swung to the ground and tossed the reins to a yawning stable boy.

Dropping the curtains back in place, Sabella whirled away, lifted the long full skirts of her rose velvet gown and rushed out into the wide silent corridor. Smoothing her hair and flipping it back over her shoulders, she stood smiling, waiting for him to open the front door and eagerly take her in his arms.

It never happened.

The front door suddenly exploded inward and Burt filled the doorway. IIis hair and his clothes badly disheveled, he looked angry and menacing.

And drunk.

His dark face set, his silver eyes opaque, he started toward her and a chill skipped up Sabella's spine. Instinctively she cowered as he aggressively advanced on her, leaving the front door ajar behind him.

"I ... I ... was getting worried, Burt," she said, a hand pressed to her racing heart. "It's so late and ..." She tried to smile, but failed. She continued to back away toward the grand staircase, watching him warily. "Are you all right?"

"As if you cared," he spoke at last, his words slurred and thick. His eyes were pale as ice in his dark, sullen face and the lean muscles along his jaw pulled tight. He bore steadily down on her.

"Of course, I care, darling." She swallowed hard, her heart thumping against her ribs. Anxiously continuing her retreat, she asked, "What is it, my love? What has happened? Why ..."

Her throat closed.

She could no longer speak. Burt reached her. He stood towering over her, the expression in his pale silver eyes one of contempt, hatred.

Abruptly he turned away, went into the lamplit drawing room.

Half panicky, knowing something was very wrong, Sabella anxiously followed. Softly she said his name, looked questioningly at him. He stopped, turned back. He had a dangerous look in his eyes, a look that made her shiver. He didn't speak, but gazed at her strangely, his cold silver eyes boring into hers. She stared at him, perplexed and more than a little frightened.

"You ... you have been drinking," she finally managed as he started toward her.

He went directly for the whiskey decanter. He splashed three fingers of bourbon into a glass, turned it up, and drained it.

"How perceptive you are, my dear," he said sarcastically. "I have indeed been drinking. I will continue to do so if you've no objection." He gave her a sneering smile. "As a matter of fact," he said, his voice devoid of inflection, "I will continue if you *do* object." He poured another.

"Burt, what is it? Tell me what's wrong?" Sabella said, her throat tight, heart pounding.

Burt slowly turned, held up his glass to her in salute. "To you, my dear. I have to hand it to you. You're the best I have ever seen."

Fear steadily rising, Sabella murmured, "I ... I don't know what you mean."

Burt tossed off his drink, slammed the glass down, and wiped his mouth on the back of his hand.

Advancing on her, he muttered blackly, "Drop the act, Sabella. I know everything. That lying Rivera journal. Everything."

Stunned, Sabella was speechless.

Burt stepped around her and drunkenly weaved from the room. He climbed the stairs, walked down the long upstairs hall to their suite, and fell into a deep, drunken slumber.

Chapter Thirty-five

S abella was indecisive for only a few short minutes. After Burt left her, she moved trancelike into the corridor and stood at the base of the redwood staircase, trembling with anger and despair, wondering what to do. Her eyes swimming in tears, her heart squeezing painfully in her chest, she was so miserable she felt like giving up on everything. It was over. She was beaten. And she was tired, so very tired. She wanted nothing more than to slump down onto the stairs and cry until she could cry no more.

Sabella blinked away her tears, squared her shoulders, lifted the long skirts of her rose velvet gown, and determinedly climbed the stairs. Jaw set, tear-bright eyes flashing, she reached the upstairs landing, drew a deep breath, and marched down the long corridor directly to the master suite.

The door stood open.

She went inside, glanced at the bed, and saw Burt sprawled there on his back, fully clothed. Sound asleep. She immediately flew into action. She was wriggling out of the rose velvet gown before she reached the dressing room. Once inside, she stepped out of the dress, leaving it where it lay in a colorful rose heap on the carpet. She kicked off her slippers and peeled the silk stockings down her long legs.

Wearing only her lace-trimmed underwear, Sabella passed up all the fine dresses, luxurious gowns, and fancy riding habits Burt had bought for her. She rummaged until she found, at the very back of the dressing room, her old leather trousers, white blouse, and scuffed boots. She hurriedly dressed in the well-worn outfit, leaving everything else behind.

Twisting her long blond hair into a rope and pinning it atop her head, she snatched her old sombrero down from a high shelf. She exited the dressing room, glanced again at Burt, and headed for the door. She paused when she reached it. She closed her eyes, opened them. Slowly she turned and glanced across the room. She couldn't help herself.

Tiptoeing softly, Sabella slipped silently toward the bed. She reached it, and hardly daring to breathe, looked down at the dark sleeping man. She winced soundlessly as she looked—one last time—at the dear face so boyishly handsome and youthful-looking in repose. Clamping a hand over her mouth to stifle the sobs building in her aching throat, Sabella backed away.

Out in the corridor, she sagged against the wall, fighting the knifelike pain in her chest, the waves of weakness washing over her. In seconds she straightened, rushed down the hall, opened the linen closet, and withdrew a couple of blankets and some towels. She descended the stairs, stopped off in the kitchen, and hurriedly filled a picnic hamper with food left from the special dinner that was never served.

She didn't dare knock at Carmelita's door; instead she slipped quietly inside. Dropping her gear, Sabella gently shook Carmelita awake, signaling her to remain silent. Whispering, she explained what had happened. Burt had found out, he knew everything.

Frowning, shaking her head, Carmelita murmured, "No! *Madre de Dios!*"

"Get dressed," Sabella ordered. "We're leaving. Right now, tonight."

"But what about—"

"It's all right. I have what I want. I'm carrying Burt's child. The California laws of inheritance are very firm. The heir to *Lindo Vista* is already growing in my womb. Nothing else matters. Now hurry!"

Under the cover of darkness, the two old friends managed to leave the house without awakening anyone. At the stables they crept into a shadowy barn and past a young boy asleep in the tack room. Sabella's big chestnut stallion immediately recognized her and began neighing loudly.

"Shhhh!" she warned him, shaking a finger in his face, then hugged his head to her breasts.

Sabella knew the black gelding in the next stall was a good, gentle saddle pony, capable of great speed. Pointing, she signaled Carmelita she was to ride the black. The young boy slept on soundly when Sabella took bridles and saddles from the tack room.

While Sabella saddled the mounts, Carmelita wrapped the blankets and towels into bedrolls to be strapped behind the saddle cantles. She transferred all the food to a couple of saddlebags.

Fifteen minutes after reaching the stables, the two women rode out into the darkness.

"The guard on the gate would stop us," Sabella whispered to Carmelita. "We'll have to slip out the back way. Ready? Follow me."

They walked their mounts until they were a couple of hundred yards away from the *rancho*'s many outbuildings. Sabella pulled up on her chestnut, stood in the stirrups, and cast a longing look at the big whitewashed adobe on the cliffs.

Turning to Carmelita, she said, "We must put as much distance as possible between us and *Lindo Vista* while it's still dark. Can you ride hard for two or three miles?"

"*Sí*, I can, more if necessary. But where are we going?" Carmelita asked worriedly. "What are we going to do?"

"I don't know," Sabella admitted. "We'll head east—head over the mountains and into the desert—ride as far as we can, and think about it later. Let's go!"

She kicked the chestnut into a gallop and streaked headlong toward the coastal mountains rising tall and black against the moonlit eastern horizon.

Burt struggled to open his eyes.

When finally he was successful, he quickly closed them again, the brightness of the morning sun momentarily blinding him.

Muttering oaths under his breath, he lay there for a while

with his eyes tightly shut, wondering why he had such a terrible headache, why his right arm was numb.

Then he remembered.

Burt's eyes flew open and he lunged up so swiftly he almost blacked out. Dizzy, nauseated, he swung his feet to the floor and sat up.

"Jesus Christ," he moaned in agony and put his elbows on his knees, dropped his aching head into his hands.

When the room stopped spinning, he slowly raised his head, looked cautiously about, and muttered, "God. Oh, God!"

The terrible events of last night came flooding back with vivid clarity as Burt rose on shaky legs. His eyes bloodshot, his face covered with a black stubble of beard, he looked as bad as he felt. Heart fluttering erratically, he left the room.

As he walked down the hall, Burt irritably shrugged out of his sleep-wrinkled suit jacket and dropped it to the carpet. His silver eyes narrowed, his mood as black as his badly disheveled hair, he muttered to himself as he descended the grand staircase.

Halfway down, he saw something lying on a carpeted step. Frowning, he stopped and stared.

He slowly bent, picked up the wilted pink Castillian rose, and instantly recalled seeing the blossom tucked in Sabella's long golden hair last night. An involuntary groan of despair passed Burt's lips and he hung his head in sorrow.

But only for a moment.

Burt lifted his aching head, straightened his broad shoulders, stood up, gritted his teeth, and went downstairs.

The wilted rose stuck inside a pocket of his wrinkled white shirt, Burt decisively moved into the library and rang for Blanton. The servant immediately appeared.

"Good morning, sir," Blanton said to attract the attention of the tall man standing across the library, hands in his trouser pockets, looking out the windows.

Burt slowly pivoted. "Have you seen Mrs. Burnett this morning, Blanton?"

"No. Nor Carmelita either."

Burt nodded. "I thought as much. She's gone," he said flatly.

"Yes, sir," said the servant.

"Get Cappy."

Cappy Ricks, looking pale and shaken, came into the library. Before Burt could speak, Cappy said anxiously, "Burt, there's something I have to tell you.... your father—"

"Later, Cappy." Burt shook his head dismissively. "Sabella's gone. I want her back. Organize the best riders. Send them out now, this morning, as soon as they're ready to ride. Three contingents. North and south must be covered, but she'll probably head due east. The majority of the men ride east."

"You going?" Cappy asked.

"No."

"All right. But before I leave, I wanted to tell—"

"Time's wasting, Cappy. You ride with the bunch going east. I'm sure that's where she's headed."

"Okay, son."

"When you find her, have her sent in here to me," Burt said, dropping down into the tall-backed swivel chair behind the desk. His tone was tinged with bitterness when he added softly, "I'll be right here. Waiting."

Sabella and Carmelita were well up into the higher elevations of the coastal ranges before they finally stopped. The sun was up, warm and bright, and the horses were lathered and thirsty. Carmelita was totally exhausted. Sabella wasn't particularly tired, but she was suffering from a nagging backache which she prayed was nothing more than too many hours in the saddle.

The campsite she carefully chose was in a steep-sided, twisting canyon whose narrow mouth could be easily guarded. The level floor of the upland valley offered spotty grasses for grazing and around a conical curve, two hundred yards back inside the winding canyon, a trickling mountain stream splashed over fallen boulders at the base of a sheer rock wall.

"This is perfect," she said to the weary, nodding Carmelita, threw her leg over and dropped to the ground just inside the canyon's mouth.

Stepping up to the side of the winded chestnut, Sabella untied the bedroll and dropped it to the ground. The loaded saddlebags followed. She unbuckled the cinch and swept the heavy saddle and blanket to the ground near the gear.

She cast a glance at Carmelita. The tired woman was still mounted, slumped over in the saddle. Sabella helped her down, and supporting her, said, "I'll take care of the horses. You spread out the bedrolls, eat something, then get some rest."

Patting Sabella's hand, Carmelita said, "But you are tired and sleepy, too, and—"

"No," Sabella said truthfully, "I'm not sleepy. I'll water the horses, unbit them, and let them graze while I clean up a little."

Carmelita nodded sleepily. "I am too tired even to wash."

"When you wake up," Sabella said. "Sleep now."

Sabella left Carmelita asleep in the shade of a rocky over-hang. Leading both mounts, a couple of towels tucked underneath her arm, she wound her way back inside the canyon to the cold mountain stream. Sabella removed the horses' bridles, speaking aloud to her chestnut, warned him, "Don't even think about running away. And tell the black I said so."

The chestnut blew and whinnied and nudged her affectionately and she knew she could trust him. The horses drank thirstily for several long minutes then turned away to crop at the grass fringing the stream.

Sabella put a hand to her aching back and, frowning, moaned softly. Maybe a bath would help. The water was cold, of course, but perhaps if she swam about for a while, she would work the kinks out and her back would stop hurting.

She dropped down onto a big slanting boulder which pro-truded up out of the water. She drew off her boots and wiggled her toes. She rose, unlaced the fly of her worn leather trousers, and putting her thumbs into the waistband at each side, pushed the pants down over her hips as she wriggled and twisted free.

She stepped out of the trousers, sat back down, knees bent, bare feet flat on the huge rock, and began unbuttoning her white blouse.

She stopped abruptly.

Her dark eyes grew round as she stared down at her lap.

She anxiously spread her legs apart and stretched them out before her.

"No!" she groaned, staring in horror at the bright red blood staining her white silk underwear. "No! No! No!" she wailed in despair, defeat crushing her.

Now all was lost.

She was *not* pregnant with Burt's child!

Heartsick, Sabella put her face in her hands and wept.

Seventy-two hours after her disappearance from *Lindo Vista*, Burt's men, with Cappy leading them, caught up with her. Camped in the Coachella Valley five miles west of the Salton Sea, Sabella was awakened in the middle of the night by the sound of drumming hooves.

She bolted upright, but before she could fully rise, a firm hand was on her arm and Cappy's low voice said, "Just relax, Mrs. Burnett. We're not going to hurt you. We're here to take you home."

It was late afternoon, three days later, when Sabella saw the big white hacienda rising in the near distance. The November sun was setting behind the imposing adobe, lights were coming on, one by one, inside the mansion.

At the stables Sabella was lifted down off her chestnut stallion as if she were helpless. Flanked by a pair of big, unsmiling cowhands, she was ushered directly up to the hacienda. Inside she was marched through the silent downstairs corridor to the closed door of the library.

One of her escorts reached out and opened the door. The other handed her inside and closed the door behind her.

It was dark in the library. Sabella blinked, unable to see much of anything. Only one light burned and it was a small, shaded lamp casting a concentrated circle of illumination on the redwood desk it sat atop. A half full decanter of bourbon sat beneath the lamp. A shot glass half full of the amber liquid was beside the decanter.

Sabella flinched when a dark, lean hand moved slowly out of the deep shadow and curled around the shot glass. The hand, the glass, left the light momentarily. Then returned.

The glass was empty.

A faceless voice in the deep shadow said, "Welcome home."

Sabella swallowed nervously, and said nothing.
A long silence.
Finally Burt leaned up into the light and Sabella shuddered. He was unshaven, the lower half of his face covered with a growth of thick black whiskers. His raven hair was uncombed and falling into his half-shuttered eyes. His shirt was badly wrinkled and half open down his dark, perspiring chest. Unkempt, unsmiling, he looked sinister, dangerous.

Sabella kept waiting for him to speak again. But he said nothing. Nor did he rise. Just sat there staring coldly at her.

Finally she asked, "Why? Why did you come for me? Why did you bring me back?"

Calmly Burt said, "Because you're mine."

PART
3

PART
3

Chapter Thirty-six

Sabella unconsciously trembled when he rose, circled the desk, and slowly advanced on her. It took every ounce of her determined will not to cowardly back away from him.

Burt reached her, stood towering over her.

He looked down at her with the coldest, meanest eyes she had ever seen. He wrapped a hand around her upper arm and ushered her out of the library. Heart racing, Sabella struggled in vain to free herself as he calmly took her up the stairs and down the long corridor to their suite.

She screamed at him, she threatened him, she hit at him. She hotly ordered him to let her go or else.

Deaf to her threats, Burt handed her inside their suite, followed her in, and threw the heavy bolt in the lock behind them.

"You bullying bastard!" she hissed, her dark Latin temper fueled by rising fear, "you can't—"

"I can," he cut in flatly, turning to face her. "Anything I want."

"No, you cannot! I refuse to let you—"

"Quiet," he commanded without raising his voice, his tone low and deadly. His silver eyes impaling her, he leaned back against the solid door, crossed his arms over his chest, and said, "I never knew you, did I, sweetheart? Didn't know you at all." He smiled then, but it was a cold, rueful smile. "But

then, you don't know me either. Did you really suppose I
would let you walk in here and take *Lindo Vista* away from
me? That is your plan, isn't it?"

Anger, hatred, and pride stiffening her spine, Sabella
glared at him, lifted her chin defiantly, and said, "I don't
want a damn thing that belongs to you! I only want what is
rightfully mine. And this *rancho* is mine!"

"You're mistaken, my love. This land belongs to me and
no woman in tight leather pants is going to ride onto this
property with some trumped up claim and expect me to hand
it over."

Burt's long arms unfolded. He ran tanned fingers through
his disheveled black hair and moved lithely toward her. His
dark hand shot out, cupped her chin, and he turned her face
up to his. "Congratulations, sweetheart," he said softly. "You
made a fool of me and in record time."

"No! No, it isn't like that and—"

"Shut up." A vein stood out on his neck and he flushed
suddenly. A muscle clenched in his jaw and he ground his
teeth savagely, then drew a breath. "Spare me any more of
your honeyed lies. You are a very beautiful, very convincing
little liar and thief. You cleverly stole my heart solely to—"

"I am not a thief!" Sabella passionately interrupted, her
pride intact, her temper white hot. Wrenching her chin out
of his grasp, she said accusingly, "You're the thief! You and
your father. You stole *Lindo Vista!*"

His silver eyes narrowing with controlled fury, Burt said,
"I never stole anything in my life and neither has my father.
The Burnett name is an old and respected one in this state.
My uncle—a Burnett—was the first governor of California.
I'm very proud to be a Burnett."

"Be as proud as you like," she hissed acidly, "but you're
a thief all the same. You and your shrewd attorney father
before you."

Burt opened his mouth to speak, clamped it shut without
uttering a sound. Sabella thought for a moment that he was
going to strike her. Blood rushed to his tanned face and
another vein pulsed fiercely on his forehead. The tendons
stood out in bold relief on his bared brown forearms as his
hands balled into tight fists at his sides. His pale silver eyes
flashed with naked rage.

Then suddenly the faintest smile came into his intelligent eyes and that unnerved her even more.

Calmly, in a low modulated voice, he said, "If what you contend were actually true—which it is not—why didn't you come to me? Give me a chance to make it right?" He shrugged his wide shoulders. "Who knows? Had you been able to prove your claim, I might have handed *Lindo Vista* over. I might have wanted to make amends, to set things straight. But you didn't. And I didn't." His frigid silver eyes pinning her, he said, "Now you will not get—or take—anything from me."

"Fine! All I want is you out of my sight!" she loudly declared and started past him. He stood blocking her way, tall and threatening. She stopped.

He said, "I am fully aware, my dear, that you have but one use for me. To father your child. Your reason for wanting my child, I am told, is twofold. To produce the heir to *Lindo Vista.* And to break my heart by taking my son away from me. Have I stated it correctly?"

"Absolutely!" Sabella angrily confirmed, all the old burning hatred welling up in her. "Why else would I sleep with a thief!"

"Why indeed? And have you been successful? Are you, even as we speak, carrying my child?"

"No! No, I am not!"

"That's a shame," he said, running a hand over his bearded chin. "Tell you what I'm going to do, sweetheart. I am going to honor your wishes. We Burnetts are honorable men and a deal is a deal." Sabella blinked at him, confused, wary. He continued, "I will see to it that you have a son. My son."

"No! Not in a million years! I do not want—"

"I will make you pregnant," he smoothly cut in, "if it takes months, even years to do so. And when finally you are carrying my child, I'll make sure that you have the best of care. I'll see to it you are constantly pampered and tended so that nothing endangers the life of our unborn baby."

Burt reached out then, grabbed the open collar of her dirty white shirt, and roughly pulled her to him. His black-bearded face only inches from hers, his hooded silver eyes looking directly into her startled dark ones, he told her coldly, "And when you have

delivered a healthy baby boy, I will banish you from this house
and this ranch empty-handed. I will keep the land and the
child." He released her. "You will never see either again."

Without another word he left her. Livid, shaking with emo-
tion, Sabella shot forward and slammed the door after him.
Anxiously locking it, she turned about, sagged back against
it, and silently vowed it would be a bitter cold day down in
Hades before she allowed Mister Burton J. God Almighty
Burnett to lay a hand on her again!

Stripping off her dirty, grimy clothes as she went, Sabella
headed straight for the big marble tub and a much needed
bath. Sinking gratefully down into the depths of the suds and
hot water, she stayed there for the next half hour, plotting
how she would get away again.

The door to the suite stayed locked all day.

Sabella refused to open it. She refused the supper a servant brought up on a tray. She refused to even open the
door to a worried Carmelita. She would open it to no one.

Later that night, when the big house was sleeping and
silent, Sabella took another refreshing bath, drew on a shimmering nightgown of sky blue satin and got into bed. Exhausted from the week-long ordeal, she was soon asleep.

Long past midnight, she sprang up in alarm when Burt
knocked loudly on the door and ordered her to open it.

Sabella leaped from the bed, flew across the darkened
room, and shouted through the locked door, "Go away!
Leave me alone! I hate you. I have no intention of allowing
you inside this room tonight or any other night!"

She screamed and retreated in horror when she heard the
loud forceful whacking of Burt's booted foot against the heavy
door. Eyes round, hand at her throat, Sabella stood there
trembling, telling herself the door was solid. It would not give.

A loud boom like a great explosion.

The door flew open and an angry, dangerous-looking Burt
stood framed in the portal. He banged the battered door
shut behind him and started toward her.

Truly frightened, Sabella warily backed away as the tall,
angry, black-bearded man bore steadily down on her. A chair
stopped her flight. Burt grabbed her wrist, yanked her to
him, and said, "This is *my* house and *my* bed and you are
my wife."

With that he swept her up into his arms, carried her to bed, dumped her on it. He began unbuttoning his shirt. Sabella was up in a flash and off the bed, fighting him, pounding on his chest with her fists and telling him she'd kill him before she let him touch her.

"I don't belong to you," she shouted at him, "I never have! I never will! Never, never, never," she screamed, tears starting to stream down her hot cheeks.

Burt paid no attention to her tirade. He never lifted a hand to defend himself. He continued to calmly undress as she rained blow after blow on his bearded face, shoulders, chest, and ribs.

Finally Sabella was out of breath and too weak to stand, much less fight any longer. Hiccoughing with sobs, she sagged tiredly against him, her hands clasping his hard biceps. Her anguished tears wetting his bared chest, she jerked spasmodically against his lean naked frame.

Burt turned her about so that she was leaning back against him. He commandingly peeled the blue satin night gown off her shaking shoulders and down her arms. The gown snagged on her flaring hips. Burt gave it a yank and it slithered to the floor at their feet, leaving her as naked as he.

Sabella winced when an arm of steel came round her waist and pressed her to the hard, hot length of his tall muscular body. Her head fell back onto his supporting shoulder and Burt's lean fingers curved around her arched throat.

He bent his head forward and put his lips against her cheek. The thick black whiskers of his beard tickled her when he said, "How do you want it? Standing up or lying down?"

"You vile, vulgar bastard, I don't want it! I don't want you! I never did," Sabella lashed out, hoping to hurt him.

But even as she spoke the words, she was vitally aware of the length of his body against her back. His hands began to caress her skin, sending unwanted shivers of delight through her. A pounding started in her blood and in a matter of minutes she was no longer in control of her own flesh.

"It should be no more disagreeable than usual," Burt said casually, "since you *never* wanted me."

His possessive hands swept over her, fondling her, caressing until she was instinctively arching and straining against him, little gasps of pleasure escaping her lips. Hardly realiz-

ing she was doing it, Sabella's hands moved back to clutch
at Burt's hard thighs. Her sharp nails dug into the tanned,
hair-dusted flesh, and reflexively drew him closer.

She shuddered deeply when his rock-hard tumescence
pulsed against the cleft in her buttocks and she immediately
tried to pull away. But he held her fast, pressed her even
closer to his heat and hardness, and continued to excite her
with his intimately stroking hands.

Sabella felt herself slipping away, losing control, falling
under his erotic spell. She desperately wanted to be repulsed
by his touch, to hate what he was doing to her. But she
wasn't and she didn't. The more he excited her, the more
she tried to deny his sexual power over her.

"I . . . don't want . . . I . . . hate . . . you. . . ." she whispered
as he touched her in ways that flooded her entire body with
fiery heat and incredible yearning.

"Yes, I know," he said, his voice low, emotionless. "But
you want me to touch you like this. Don't you?"

"No," she breathed. "No, I . . . ahhhh . . ."

Tingling all over, she didn't, couldn't find the will to object
when Burt abruptly sat down on the edge of the bed, and
drew her to stand between his spread knees. He allowed her
to face him for only a moment, then turned her so that her
side was to him, explaining as he did so that he would be
better able to touch her all over.

It made perfectly good sense to her.

Thrumming to the fiery touch of his dark stroking hands
on her bare, sensitive flesh, Sabella began to sigh and moan
and feel as if she were a priceless instrument upon which his
talented fingers were composing a beautiful symphony. With
both his gifted hands on her, his fingertips played magnifi-
cently along the column of her throat and the sensitive nape
of her neck underneath her unbound hair. Then those lean,
dexterous fingers moved on to her swelling breasts and the
small of her back. Her flat belly and dimpled buttocks.

Sabella breathed through her mouth when those accom-
plished hands moved lower still, one stroking, touching, sliding over and through the blond triangle between her
quivering thighs. The other boldly touching, tracing, spreading the rounded cheeks of her buttocks.

Burt's hands slipped between her legs and met, and Sabella caught her breath. His bold, masterful fingers did wonderfully forbidden things to her that swiftly ignited a raging firestorm of voracious passion.

"No," she protested feebly, knowing he wouldn't listen, not really wanting him to, "don't . . . do . . . that. . . ."

His skilled fingertips playing upon the slick, burning hot, highly sensitive feminine flesh, Burt didn't heed her weak demands for him to stop. He knew she didn't really mean it. He could tell by the powerful pulsing and the silky wetness drenching his intimately exploring hands. He was shocking her, exciting her, arousing her.

And she loved it.

Sabella *did* love it.

So much she surrendered completely to the exquisite joy rippling through her. She stood naked in that darkened room between Burt's spread knees and writhed and squirmed and shamelessly rocked and rubbed her throbbing flesh against Burt's practiced probing fingers.

"Please, oh . . . please," she was soon whispering breathlessly as he teased and toyed and purposely withheld what she was striving and begging him for. The fiery tip of his middle finger adroitly circling her tiny swollen pleasure point of sensation, Burt caressed her that way until she was just about to reach a climax.

Then he stopped abruptly.

He withdrew both hands from her and Sabella's glazed eyes came open in shocked disappointment.

"What are you . . . why . . . ?"

"You want it, sweetheart." It was statement, not a question. Burt's silver eyes flashed in the dimness of the room. "You want me to make love to you. Don't you?"

Burning up, suspended in sweet agony, feeling as if she would surely die if he didn't take her all the way, Sabella murmured, "Yes, yes."

"Then say it. Tell me you want me to make love to you."

"You cruel bastard," Sabella said, her breath shallow, her heart pounding with a mixture of desire and anger.

"Not half so cruel as you, my love," Burt coolly replied. He lifted a hand up before her and showed her his lean fingers, glistening from the hot wetness flowing freely from her. "See how much you want me. You're wet and hot. Say it. You want me to make love to you. Tell me."

"Damn you to eternal hell," Sabella muttered, thrust her hands into his hair and roughly pushed his head back. She bent and aggressively kissed him, thrusting her tongue into his mouth, kissing him deeply, erotically, determined to make him want her as much as she wanted him.

When at last she tore her burning lips from his, she raised her head, looked into his silver eyes, and gritted her teeth in frustration when she saw that they still held a calm icy expression.

"Give up?" he asked, his hands settling on her flared hips. "All you have to do is ask for it."

Sabella gave no reply. Instead she smiled seductively at him, raised a hand to her mouth, put out her tongue, and licked the tips of her fingers until they were shiny wet.

"Watch," she commanded, lowering her eyes and her hand to him. "Feel good?" she asked softly as she ran her dampened fingers over the pulsing tip of his thrusting tumescence, teasing him, toying with him.

She expertly tormented him until, unable to stand it any longer, Burt, trembling with passion and anger, seized her wrists, tore her hands away from him. Sabella laughed triumphantly and her arms swiftly went around his dark handsome head. Fiercely she hugged him to her.

Burt shuddered.

His hot, bearded face was buried against her soft warm breasts. He could feel the racing of her heart against his whiskered cheek.

He wanted her so badly he was almost ill with desire.

But he said nothing, did nothing, stubbornly willing to suffer in silence, staunchly refusing to surrender to the blazing desire she aroused in him.

Unless she said the words aloud. Unless she admitted she wanted him. Unless she asked him to make love to her.

Sabella fought a similar battle. She knew exactly what he was doing. Knew that he had purposely so aroused her that she felt as if she would die if he didn't make love to her. She wanted him so badly she was ready to get down on her knees and beg him.

Hating him, loving him, Sabella finally murmured miserably, "I want you. Make love to me, Burt."

Chapter Thirty-seven

From that long, unsettling night—the eighteenth of November—a night of intensely tempestuous lovemaking, the pair lived together in the most unconventional of marriages.

Polite, distant strangers in the cold light of day, they were insulting, insatiable lovers in the hot darkness of night.

Burt rarely spoke to Sabella, hardly acknowledged her presence. She might have been a piece of the furniture for all the attention he paid her.

When she walked into the room, not a flicker of emotion was evident on his dark, handsome face or in his icy silver eyes. His strong masculine features were constantly set in an unreadable mask. His expression, or lack thereof, was inscrutable.

Except at night in their bedroom upstairs.

There his silver eyes glinted with unleashed desire and his unsmiling, sensuous mouth took hers again and again in ravenous, savage kisses. He made love to her with a passion so fierce it almost equaled his burning hatred.

Sabella hated him as well, but she felt a dark, dangerous pleasure rising every time he took her in his arms. That certain chemistry, that special erotic spark had not died even if affection and respect were not a part of their relationship.

Sabella was as perplexed as she was miserable.

She couldn't escape this dark, powerful man who openly despised her. Guarded round the clock, she could not leave. She was no longer allowed to ride or to go into the village. She was kept inside the hacienda, constantly watched as if she were a criminal.

While she was held captive in the big whitewashed adobe, Burt was rarely at the mansion. When he was, he was withdrawn, sullen, cold. Burt was not the charming, entertaining, smitten husband anymore. Sabella was not the laughing, adventurous, outgoing bride.

The two of them no longer did things together. Sabella didn't ride the rugged range at her husband's side or skinny-dip with him in the cold mountain streams or sing for him while he strummed a guitar. Or sit with him in the Happy chair.

Winter had come early this year, both inside and out.

Burt and Sabella were not the only ones who suffered from the climate of deep, foreboding chill that had permanently settled over *Lindo Vista.*

Cappy Ricks blamed himself for all their unhappiness. Guilt and regret were his constant companions. He wished he could go back in time to that day last June when the dying Raleigh Burnett made him promise to tell Burt the truth about everything. To warn Burt that Sabella Rios wanted justice—and revenge, would surely break his heart.

Sabella *had* indeed broken Burt's heart. Burt had changed so much, Cappy hardly recognized him. That big, wide Burnett smile for which Burt had been famous since he was a chubby toddler was now missing. The warm gray eyes that once sparkled with merriment were lifeless in his handsome, somber face. There was nothing of the playful, boyish Burt in the brooding, taciturn man who now moved silently about like a dark, sinister specter. The big, gregarious fellow who had once been friendly to a fault was now aloof, forbidding, unapproachable.

More than once Cappy had told Burt that he badly needed to talk to him. But each time the apathetic Burt had dismissed him with a shake of his dark head, the silent refusal demonstrating his total indifference.

Cappy worried about Sabella as well. He couldn't help it. From the first time he had met her, she'd gotten a firm hold on his soft heart. He had found her to be one of the prettiest, sweetest, most likeable young women he had ever met. The sun had shone a little brighter when she was around and it was impossible for him not to feel protective and fatherly toward her.

Cappy supposed that he should now dislike her intensely for what she had done to Burt. But the truth was, he could understand why she had done it. Sabella Rios had been cheated out of a vast inheritance. She'd seen her mother work herself to death when the poor woman should have been the wealthy, idle mistress of *Lindo Vista*. It wasn't right, what Raleigh Burnett had done. Not right at all.

Sabella's only mistake, as far as Cappy was concerned, was that she had made the wrong Burnett pay. Raleigh Burnett was the one who had wronged her mother. Sabella should have meted out her revenge on him, not on Burt.

But then, maybe she had no idea that Burt was innocent of the terrible misdeeds his father had committed.

Cappy agonized over telling her the truth. But he was never afforded the opportunity. She didn't ride with him anymore. Didn't sit with him out on the south patio in the sun. Didn't play checkers or double solitaire with him the way she used to.

Sabella hardly left her room and when she did, she was not alone. Blanton or one of the servants was always at her elbow, keeping a close eye on her.

With no chance to talk with either of them, Cappy reasoned sadly that neither Burt nor Sabella knew the whole truth about each other. Burt didn't know that *Lindo Vista* was stolen from Sabella's mother. Sabella didn't know that Burt had no idea the land had been stolen.

Only Cappy knew.

And that knowledge weighed heavy on his heart. He lay awake nights worrying about the unhappy pair.

And blaming himself for all their misery.

Sabella was both surprised and incensed one chilly dawn in early December when Burt shook her awake and said, "Have Carmelita pack a valise for you. We're going into Capistrano this afternoon."

"Who's going into Capistrano this afternoon?" she asked

irritably, clutching the sheet to her breasts, pushing her hair from her sleepy eyes.

"The two of us. You and me." Burt rose, uncoiling his tall, lean body, and stretched the kinks from his muscular legs. "Tell Carmelita you'll need a gown suitable for dining out this evening. We'll be spending the night at the Mission Inn." He walked away.

Her dark eyes, venomous with hate, followed Burt's tall naked figure as he strode toward the dressing room. "I don't want to go into the village," she announced firmly.

"I don't particularly care what you want, my dear."

"I am *not* going!"

Over his shoulder: "You're wrong, sweetheart. You most definitely are going."

"Why?" Sabella angrily sat up, shouting at him now. "Why on earth would *we* go to the village together?"

Burt turned and smiled at her. A cynical smile that lifted one corner of his mouth did not reach his pale silver eyes.

His tone mocking, he said, "To show the world how much in love we are." He was at the open archway to the dressing room. He raised a long arm, braced it against the polished woodwork. "People are prone to talk. We'll prove that the nasty gossip going about is groundless. That happiness is ours."

"But it isn't. You aren't happy and I—"

"Happiness is a vague term," he interrupted and suddenly there were traces of sadness etched in his carved features. "We've had a few happy moments. . . . Perhaps that's all anyone can hope for."

Sabella experienced a sudden rush of tenderness and her voice was soft and warm when she said, "We did have some happy moments together, didn't we?"

The brief flood of empathy dissipated when Burt cruelly said, "There were times when I was incredibly happy—but who knows what lies behind a liar's smiles and kisses."

Hurt, she swiftly lashed out at him. "How right you are! And now the pretense bores me. So I can hardly go into San Juan Capistrano with you and pretend I'm happy!"

His expression totally impassive, silver-gray eyes half shuttered, Burt released his hold on the arched doorway and came toward her, his tall, bronze body moving with the supple litheness of a forest animal.

He reached the bed, stood looking down at her. "*You* can't pretend? Surely you jest." He reached for her. She drew away. He shrugged and smiled. "You're an expert actress, my dear. The best I have ever seen. You definitely belong on the stage." He took hold of the covering sheet, gathered it up in his fist, and forcefully yanked it off the bed, leaving Sabella naked and blinking at him in anger and fear. Burt dropped the silk sheet to the floor. He put a knee on the mattress, reached out, gripped Sabella's upper arms, and swiftly drew her up to kneel before him.

He looked into her dark eyes for a long moment, then told her, "I'm not much of an actor myself. Too honest I suppose." His hands tightened their grip. "But I'm amazingly adept at getting a good performance out of others. You are going into the village with me this afternoon. We will do a bit of Christmas shopping, enjoy a late dinner at the Mission Inn, and spend the night in our suite at the hotel." He drew her closer, so close her breasts were touching his broad, hair-covered chest and her face was mere inches from his. "At the shops, in the hotel dining room, and upstairs in our suite, you will perform beautifully, I know. Like the professional you are."

"And if I don't?" she asked rebelliously, her chin lifting in defiance, dark eyes flashing.

"Don't go?" he said. "You're going. Count on it."

"No. I mean what if I don't perform?"

His voice was flat and unemotional when he replied, "Try it and find out."

Chapter Thirty-eight

Burt regarded Sabella with a certain cold curiosity as she descended the stairs shortly after two o'clock that afternoon. Sabella glanced at him and her jaw immediately tightened.

His was an attitude of dominance. He stood at the base of the grand staircase, booted feet planted firmly apart, arms crossed over his chest. Arrogant and intimidating, like the mighty lord of his fiefdom.

He was also, Sabella grudgingly noted, exquisitely handsome, almost beautiful. Strong, flawless features, his hair jet black, his skin smooth and healthily suntanned. His open shirt and rolled-up sleeves exposed the ripple of muscles on his chest and arms.

Sabella very nearly made a misstep, caught herself, and looked him straight in the eye with a kind of fearless self-assurance.

Unmoving, but not unmoved, Burt watched Sabella slowly descend the stairs and was struck with the thought that she had surely concocted a thousand different ways to punish and torment him. When she but walked into a room, there was a change in his heartbeat. When she said his name, his stomach muscles tightened.

Today was no exception.

She was breathtakingly beautiful, almost perfect. Flawless

features, her hair a pale blond, her skin baby soft with a hint of golden tan. The open throat and tight bodice of her fashionable beige wool suit exposed her delicate throat and the beginning swell of her breasts.

A muscle leaped in Burt's tight jaw.

How, he wondered angrily, could a woman so angelically beautiful be so devilishly evil? And how, he wondered even more angrily, could she still possess the power to tempt and to hurt him?

Sabella reached the foot of the stairs.

Without so much as a nod of greeting she said, "I really can't see that this trip is necessary."

Burt's arms came unfolded, but he didn't step forward. Nor did he reply. He merely inclined his dark head toward the front door where Blanton waited, ready to open it for them. Outside, Burt fell into step beside Sabella.

"Never," he warned softly, as they moved down the front walk, "discuss our personal life in front of a servant."

Sabella looked at him sharply. "I have no idea what you're talking about? I would never—"

"You said, before Blanton, that you didn't think this little journey was necessary."

"Oh, that. Well, I meant it. I don't see why I have to—"

"A piece of good news gets out to one person," Burt cut in. "A piece of bad news gets out to ten."

"Sorry, I don't follow you," she said flippantly.

"Yes, you do." He took her arm, stopping her. "You have been given an assignment. By me. Do it and be glad I ask no more of you."

Sabella jerked her arm free. She stormed on down the walk and out to the shiny black covered carriage waiting in the circular drive. Her anger subsided and she smiled with genuine pleasure when she saw Cappy Ricks leaning against it. Maybe the overnight stay in Capistrano wouldn't be so awful after all, not if the likeable ranch foreman was going with them.

"Cappy!" she said and hurried to greet him.

"How you doin', sugar?" Cappy didn't hug her. He put out his hand for her to shake as he glanced nervously at Burt.

Sabella took his big, work-roughened hand in both of hers,

and ignoring the scowling Burt, said, "I'm so glad you're coming to town with us, I was—"

"He isn't," Burt interrupted.

Still clinging to Cappy's hand, Sabella looked angrily up at Burt. "Well, he *is* driving us to town." She turned her attention quickly back to Cappy. "Aren't you?"

"Not today," said Cappy, shaking his gray head as if in apology.

Sabella quickly looked about, saw no one else. "Then who is?"

"I am," Burt said.

Releasing Cappy's hand, Sabella whirled on Burt. The prospect of being alone with him all the way into San Juan Capistrano filled her with dread. "But why ... ?"

"Because I said so."

With that, Burt opened the carriage door and lifted her up inside. As she haughtily settled herself on the comfortable leather seat, Burt tucked the skirts of her beige wool suit around her feet, and carefully closed the door.

He turned to Cappy, put a hand on the foreman's shoulder, and said, "We'll be back sometime tomorrow afternoon."

"Good enough," said Cappy.

Lowering his voice, Burt said, "Why are you looking so worried? I know the way."

Cappy gave no reply, just nodded, turned, and ambled away. Burt shrugged, circled the carriage, yanked the door open, and swung up onto the seat beside the bristling Sabella. He never even glanced at her. He took up the reins and put the matched steeds into motion.

As they rolled down the palm-lined avenue toward the tall, ranch gates, Sabella made up her mind that she would not speak to Burt all the way into the village. Even if he decided to be civil, she was not going to say one word to him!

She needn't have worried. Burt made no attempt to engage her in conversation. He treated her exactly as he treated her each day at the hacienda.

As if she did not exist.

That changed when they reached the village. After having accused her of being an actress, he put on quite a show himself. It was Saturday and San Juan Capistrano was crowded with ladies busily shopping and gentlemen loafing on the streets.

Her hand firmly enclosed in his, Burt and Sabella strolled up and down the wooden sidewalks and in and out of shops. They bumped into scores of Burt's old friends and Sabella could tell that they had heard what had happened. Gena had told them. It was written all over their worried faces.

But Burt Burnett, when he turned on the charm, was as powerful as ever. He had this gift, this presence, this unique ability to command and seduce. And to make doubters believe that all was well. That everything they had heard was nothing more than the petty lies and wishful thinking of an incensed ex-lover.

Without a single question asked or a word of explanation offered, everyone was soon satisfied that the handsome young newlyweds were the happiest of couples. No one saw a clue to the contrary. Nobody detected a hint of trouble. The famous Burnett smile was broader than ever, and it was easy to see that Burt adored his beautiful bride and she him.

Sabella heard someone excitedly call her name, turned, and saw hurrying toward them her two young friends, Cynthia Douglas and Janie Desmond. There were hugs all around and Sabella marveled at her own hypocrisy as, eagerly embracing them both, she heard herself say that they "really must marry because marriage is truly a grand state."

By the time Burt and Sabella retired to the Mission Inn, the gentry of Capistrano was convinced that all was well between them. That the nasty rumors circulating were totally without merit. Thank goodness.

Once inside the luxurious corner suite on the top floor of the inn, Burt dropped the pose. The swiftness of the transformation was amazing. The laughing, smiling man Sabella had seen throughout the afternoon was, in the blinking of an eye, again cold and unreachable.

No sooner were they inside than his smile disappeared completely, his warm gray eyes became cool silver, and his tone of voice was low and impersonal when he said, "I'm going out for a while and—"

"Where to?" she turned, and gave him a questioning look.

"We will dine at nine o'clock," he continued, leaving her question unanswered. "At the appointed hour, I will be wait-

ing downstairs in the bar. You can find me there." He turned
to leave.

"What if I grow hungry before the hour of nine?" Her
hands went to her hips.

His silver gaze touched her, dismissing her. "That, my
dear, will be your misfortune."

"Wait just a damn minute," she said, her voice lifting. "I
have come to the conclusion that—"

"Come to any conclusion you like. I really don't care."

Furious, Sabella shouted, "Nine is too late! We will dine
at eight o'clock!"

"No," he said, his voice devoid of inflection. "We will dine
at nine."

"Eight!" she shrieked.

In the same flat tone of voice he told her, "It is I who will
give the orders. And you who will obey. Nine, downstairs."

He left her to seethe and storm about and call him names.
And to promise herself that she would again run away, that
she would be free of him soon.

When her temper had cooled a little, Sabella looked
around the opulent suite. Her gaze sweeping about the elegantly appointed drawing room, she crossed to the double
doors opening into the sunny corner bedroom. She was taken
aback when she stepped inside.

A huge mahogany bed with a gold velvet spread sat
squarely in the middle of the room. Brow puckered, Sabella
went to the bed, and sat gingerly down on it. Her hand
gliding across the smooth gold velvet of the spread, she immediately knew why the bed sat where it did. And at whose
direction it had been placed there.

Rows of floor-to-ceiling glass windows across the front and
north side of the room afforded the bed's occupant—or occupants—an unobstructed view of the Pacific Ocean.

Sabella abruptly jumped up.

Frowning, she wondered how many women had been in
this bed with the ardent Burt Burnett. That unpleasant
thought had no more than occurred than she told herself she
didn't care. Didn't give a tinker's damn. A dozen. A hundred. It made no difference to her.

She decided then and there not to let him touch *her* in
this bed. She'd be damned if she'd allow him to make love

to her in a bed where he'd held other women. She hadn't wanted to come here in the first place. He had made her come in to Capistrano so everyone would see them together. He had pulled the strings as though she were a puppet!

She would be no puppet tonight.

Wanting to punish him for putting her on display and disgusted with herself for her own hypocrisy, Sabella firmly made up her mind.

She would *not* yield to him this night!

Despite that fact that she was starving, Sabella pointedly waited until twenty minutes past the hour of nine o'clock before she left the suite, and went downstairs to meet Burt.

She was, she realized without a trace of conceit or joy, quite stunning in a daringly cut gown of lush black velvet. Her golden hair was upswept and coiled tightly atop her head. She never wore it down anymore because that's the way Burt liked it.

A large black pearl, suspended from a black velvet band, rested in the hollow of her throat. Her black gown's square neckline plunged so low and her waist-cinching black corset pushed her breasts so high, she was in danger of spilling out of the snug bodice.

Sabella frowned as she studied her reflection in the free-standing mirror. The gown was one of several purchased on their honeymoon stay in San Francisco. She had never, until tonight, worn the dress. She had forgotten it was cut so severely low. Wishing she had packed something more suitable, Sabella made a face at herself.

Then she laughed bitterly. She was being foolish. It made no difference what she wore—Burt wouldn't notice. He never noticed her anymore.

Sabella left the suite, moved down the silent corridor, and descended the wide marble stairs. The long black gown trailing behind her, whispering on the gleaming marble floor of the gigantic lobby, she moved regally toward the dining room.

Sabella stopped when a deep, familiar voice said her name. Turning, she saw Burt at a long, polished bar inside the dimly lit, paneled tavern. A glass in his hand, he stood with a knee slightly bent, his leather-shod toes resting on the shiny brass foot railing.

He was strikingly good looking in a beautifully cut dinner jacket with a white carnation in his buttonhole. His jet hair had been freshly cut and carefully brushed. His tanned face was smoothly shaven.

Sabella looked at him and for an instant the smokey gray eyes that met hers smoldered with hot feeling. She felt the warmth burn into her. The look and the warmth were gone immediately and his eyes became almost frightening. They were as splinters of ice, cold and unwavering.

Asking nothing, telling nothing.

Boring right through her as if she didn't exist.

Sabella swallowed hard, gave him a frosty stare, and stayed where she was as he drained his liquor glass, set it atop the polished bar, tossed a bill down beside it.

Finally he came out to meet her. He said nothing. He took her arm and ushered her into the dining hall. They were led up some steps and to a choice table overlooking the ocean.

Burt ordered for them both, choosing dishes that required a great deal of time to prepare. While they waited, he made polite table conversation, but Sabella knew it was for the sake of the other diners. Not her. He refilled her wine glass the moment it was empty, but drank very little himself.

The meal turned out to be a long, leisurely one. And even after they had finished their rich desserts, it seemed to Sabella that Burt was in no particular hurry to leave.

That suited her fine. She was glad that he lingered over his coffee and cognac despite the fact that it was very late and they were the only two diners left in the room. She assumed it meant he had no intention of making love to her. That simplified things.

Sabella was yawning sleepily when finally they climbed the stairs to the suite. Once inside, Burt stopped in the lamp-lit drawing room directly before the teakwood liquor cabinet. As he poured himself another brandy, Sabella went straight into the bedroom, not even bothering to say good night.

Convinced she had been let off the hook for tonight, she headed for the dressing room, kicking her slippers off as she went. She quickly peeled off the revealing black dress, black corset, black underwear, black sheer stockings, everything.

She was pulling on a soft white nightgown when Burt stepped up behind her, caught the gown before it could fall down over her hips, lifted it back up over her head, and dropped it to the carpeted floor.

Sabella stiffened.

Burt leaned down, kissed the nape of her neck, and drew her back against him.

He was still fully clothed. The fine fabric of his dinner jacket brushed against Sabella's bare back. She drew a shallow breath, closed her eyes, and silently begged him to leave her alone. To stop before he started. To amuse himself someplace else with someone else.

And she ordered herself not to surrender, no matter what he did to her. Not to give him the satisfaction of thinking she couldn't resist him. Teeth gritted, she recited a silent litany: *I will not respond. I will not respond. I will not respond.*

"Yes, you will," Burt said in low, cool voice as if he had read her mind.

He began to touch her, to kiss her, to arouse her until she was lost. And so was he.

Naked, they came eagerly together in the center of the bed in the center of the room. Kneeling there, Burt sank back on his heels, spread his knees wide. His hands on Sabella's flaring hips, lips on her throat, he held her astride, her legs and arms wrapped around him.

He ordered her to look into his gleaming eyes as they moved slowly, erotically together, their bodies if not their hearts in sync. Bathed in silvery moonlight, they welcomed the chill autumn breeze blowing in through the open windows. The strong sea-scented winds ruffled the heavy velvet curtains, swept loose leaves in to drift across the carpet, and tossed about the long golden hair that Burt's hands had freed.

And cooled their heated flesh.

For the moment, at least.

Chapter Thirty-nine

But as they drove home the next afternoon, Sabella ashamedly recalled the events of the previous night. She blushed remembering how many ways and how many times she had allowed Burt to make love to her. Images of herself, naked save for the black pearl at her throat, tumbling about on the bed with this cold, uncaring man kept plaguing her.

Sabella ventured a covert glance at Burt. Seated beside her, he held the long leather reins loosely in one hand. A thin brown cigar was stuck in the side of his mouth and a faint cloud of tobacco smoke drifted up into his heavy-lidded gray eyes. He was hatless and a shock of wavy jet hair fell over his forehead.

Sabella's pulse leaped. An unbidden warmth rushed through her and she felt her cheeks flush. She immediately looked away in annoyance. Her lips tightened into a stern line.

His physical prowess and animal magnetism were potent. Too potent. She resented it. She resented him. She resented him for having the power to excite her with just a touch or a look. Her resentment grew with each occasion he so easily, masterfully possessed her.

The thoughts running through Burt's mind were almost identical to Sabella's. He, too, was recalling last night's fiery lovemaking and the recollection caused his heart to pound, his groin to ache. He kept his eyes off her. His jaw was rigid. Her blond good looks and feminine allure were potent. Too potent. He resented it. He resented her. He resented her for having the power to arouse him with just a touch or a look. His resentment grew each time she so effortlessly made him want to possess her.

As they rode along in the November sunshine, they did not look at each other. They did not talk. They did not touch. Yet both, much to their annoyance, were stirred by a rapidly growing desire. An undeniable yearning. A sexual longing which—although unspoken—was almost tangible.

The emotion was so strong, the hunger so great, Sabella didn't question it when Burt abruptly turned the big vehicle off the road. Holding on to the seat, silently urging him to hurry, to go faster, Sabella's heart began to pound with anticipation.

She looked at Burt as he anxiously guided the matched pair over the uneven ground toward a dense grove of tall eucalyptus trees. His lean face was granite hard, his eyes focused solely on the copse of trees ahead. He looked both sinister and sexy, and it thrilled her to no end. She could hardly wait to kiss away the tension from his mouth, to run her eager hands over his broad, bare chest.

They reached the dense grove of eucalyptus. Burt swiftly located a narrow opening in the impenetrable-looking thicket and sent the big carriage crashing through. Tree limbs struck the startled horses and slapped the sides of the carriage. Dust and birds and leaves flew.

As quickly as he could, Burt wrestled the frightened steeds to a plunging stop. The black brougham was parked in deep shade, completely hidden from the road a hundred yards below. Not bothering to wrap the reins around the brake handle, Burt dropped them and reached for Sabella.

She came into his arms in a shot, as eager as he for the loving. They kissed as though they were starved for each other, their mouths open wide, their tongues tasting, stroking, fighting for domination. This was no slow, sweet buildup to burning passion. It was an eruption of pent-up desire. Her arms wrapped tightly around Burt's neck, Sabella's fingers captured a handful of his jet hair at the back of his head.

Her eager lips refusing to release his, she sighed and moaned into his mouth as his tanned hand found its sure way up under her billowing skirts.

After the extraordinary long, searing kiss, their lips finally separated. They gasped for breath. They looked into each other's eyes. Sabella anxiously unbuttoned Burt's shirt and Burt's seeking hand moved underneath her frilly petticoat and slid caressingly across her stomach.

Then his lips were back on hers, hot and commanding, as he impatiently tugged at the waistband of her lacy, Paris-designed underwear.

Sabella was pressed back against the carriage seat, her hands stroking his shoulders, his bared chest, nails raking through the crisp dense hair. His mouth moved masterfully on hers. She'd never know quite how he did it, but he managed to effortlessly peel her wispy lingerie off. She felt the frothy underwear slip down over her stomach and hips. Felt Burt's hand wrap around the lacy fabric and tug until it slipped down and snagged beneath her buttocks.

As if obeying some silent command from him, Sabella raised up just enough to free the caught underwear and was immediately rewarded with the fiery touch of Burt's hands cupping the rounded cheeks of her bottom. He slid the freed underpants down her golden-skinned thighs.

His flaming lips left hers and Burt lifted his dark head when the lacy underwear reached her knees. His gray eyes were hot, molten lead as they gazed into hers and she could see that his patience was gone. He recklessly tore the wispy underwear away. She heard it rip and was overjoyed to be totally free of the encumbrance.

She gasped in excited pleasure when Burt flipped her dress and petticoats up around her waist, leaving her bare to his burning eyes, his magic touch. Her heart pounding, her breath shallow, Sabella made a funny little sound of shock and pleasure when Burt slid down off the leather seat to the floor of the carriage.

Instinctively, she modestly pressed her bare legs tightly together, but found it difficult to hold them that way because the muscles in her thighs were jumping involuntarily.

Burt's hand wrapped itself around the back of her shapely

calf. He sat down on the floor, bent his dark head, and kissed her dimpled knees.

Sabella squirmed and sighed as Burt, brushing kisses to the tingling flesh of her clenched thighs, gently, skillfully urged them apart. Vulnerable, completely exposed, Sabella felt no embarrassment or shame. Only white-hot passion. Looking straight into her eyes, Burt eased her bent knee up, ducked under, and repositioned her legs so that he was between.

He again lowered his dark head and kissed her trembling thighs, now open to him. His dark face moved higher and higher and Sabella felt the white-hot fire of his lips on her skin.

Her breath grew rapid and shallow. She felt as if her entire body was rigidly taut, so tense it was almost painful. At the same time it was as though her body was entirely without bones, so limber and pliable that this bold fiery lover could surely move and mold her with the greatest of ease.

The silky hair of Burt's dark head tickled Sabella's bare stomach and she shuddered deeply. Her dark eyes glazed, she timidly swept the bunched skirts a little higher and glanced down. She found the shockingly pleasing sight of Burt between her legs, kissing her, to be so erotically pleasurable she couldn't look away.

She anxiously pulled the dress and petticoats higher, pushing them back out of the way with her elbows so she could better see what he was doing to her.

Then, of their own volition, her stockinged legs fell farther apart and her bared bottom slid nearer to the edge of the leather carriage seat. Nearer to the hot, hungry mouth and tickling tongue spreading lovely heat up along the insides of her thighs. That marvelous mouth moved higher. The white heat blazed hotter. The flames licked closer.

Sabella felt strangely as if she were poised before a dangerous abyss, about to fall in and be lost. Unsure what form of heaven or hell awaited her in the dark, mysterious depths below, she felt herself helplessly going over the edge.

And then at last, his face was buried in her. He was kissing her where she had never been kissed before. Where she most wanted and needed to be kissed. The fire his lips ignited swiftly spread, radiating outward from the place where it began.

But oddly, blessedly, the flames did not scorch her. They lapped at her throbbing flesh, oh, so soothingly, like the ripples in a cooling stream. Gently splashing her. Consolingly washing over her.

Sabella arched to meet the hot, handsome face, the delicious, dazzling mouth. Her neck would no longer support her head. It fell back. Her lids were heavy, would not stay open. Her eyes slipped closed. She breathed slowly through her mouth, gliding happily on wave after wave of slow incredible pleasure, hoping against hope that this languid, fiery pool which was lapping at her would never go dry. Without its cooling balm, she would surely burn up.

Sabella finally opened her eyes, looked curiously down, and met the smokey hot gaze of Burt's boldly staring, mesmerizing gray eyes. Their gazes locked. Her dark eyes pleaded. His silver eyes promised.

Her dark flashing eyes asked only this. That his dazzling mouth would give her more, more, and still more. Deeper, deeper, ever deeper. His gleaming eyes answered reassuringly. They vowed to give her more, more, and still more. Deeper, deeper, ever deeper.

His thick, dark lashes fluttering, then lowering over his silver gaze, Burt gave her more. He buried his face more deeply in her. He wrapped long fingers around the slim ankle of her left leg and urged her bent knee up, positioned her slippered foot on the carriage seat's edge.

Sabella's incredible pleasure instantly intensified.

A nervous hand went to his dark head, tangled in his luxuriant hair, and pressed his face yet closer still. She smiled foolishly, sighed softly, and sat there in a haze of happiness, slowly, rhythmically rocking her pelvis forward.

All at once the soothing, lapping pool changed into a licking liquid fire whirling around and around the swollen, throbbing point of sensation which she was frantically pressing against his mouth. Jolts of pleasure she couldn't control surged over and through her. Joy of a kind she had never experienced hurled her rapidly toward total liberation.

When finally it fully began, her deep, wrenching climax was so powerful it was both wonderful and frightening. Sabella cried out in a mixture of ecstasy and fear. Gripping Burt's dark head with one hand, his opened shirt collar with the other, she felt herself erupting in a volcanic seizure of blinding, shuddering rapture.

"Burt! Burt!" she screamed as her passion-glazed eyes opened and closed and her body jerked spasmodically.

So intense was the great explosion of heat and ecstasy claiming her, Sabella could hear as well as feel it. A deafeningly loud explosion literally rocked the carriage beneath her, the echoing sound reverberating in her ears.

It was with the last of the little aftershocks of elation still buffeting her that Sabella began to faintly realize there really had been—simultaneously with her own—an actual great explosion somewhere close.

Staying with her through both rocking explosions, his mouth warmly enclosing her throbbing flesh, Burt waited until he was sure Sabella had attained total release. He kissed her, he licked her, he loved her until the final instant when her scream drowned out all else and she frantically pushed his face from her, unable to stand another second of contact.

Burt immediately lifted his dark head, slid up onto the leather seat, and reached for the reins, saying, "Jesus Christ! The Dreamy Draw dam!"

Chapter Forty

The loud, earsplitting explosion abruptly shattered the afternoon stillness, the powerful boom rattling the leaded windows of the old solidly built hacienda.

"God Almighty! The Dreamy Draw dam!" Cappy Ricks swore, slammed his mug down on the kitchen table, and shot to his feet.

"*Dios!*" murmured Carmelita Rivera fearfully. "What is it? What has happened?" She, too, leaped up from the table.

The two of them were sharing a midafternoon cup of coffee and an amicable conversation.

"Broken rock dam up at Dreamy Draw," Cappy told her, looking frantically about for his misplaced hat. "It's for sure broke now."

"Broke? How could the dam break?"

"Somebody's blown it up!"

"No!" Carmelita exclaimed, plucked his old Stetson off an empty chair and anxiously followed him to the back door. "Who would do such a terrible thing?"

"God only knows!" Cappy grabbed the hat from her, slammed it on his head. "Some rotten, troublemaking, no good bastard . . . begging your pardon, Carmelita."

"What does this mean, Cappy?" Carmelita followed the worried foreman outside. Impulsively she placed a hand on Cappy's arm. "If the dam is gone, then this is very bad, no?"

"Downright devastating!" he admitted, absently patting the plump fingers clutching at his arm, and hurried away.

Carmelita stood in the sun, a hand raised to shade her worried face, and watched the robust Cappy Ricks run toward the stables with the swiftness of a much younger man.

"Get me the dynamite!" Gena said.

Those were her orders.

Well, this ought to satisfy the bitch, Cisco thought as the thunderous explosion echoed across the valley. A pair of powerful field glasses raised to his narrowed, squinting eyes, the scar-faced Mexican watched the fun from a well-concealed vantage point a half mile above the dam.

The corners of his thin, mustachioed mouth lifted into a satisfied grin. Cisco had waited there alone, tense, counting the seconds, until the mighty blast was scheduled to go off. The discharge of dynamite had occurred precisely at three o'clock.

Just as planned.

Cisco watched the broken rock dam disintegrate before his very eyes. It had taken months of hard, backbreaking labor by dozens of Indian slaves years ago to construct the sturdy rock dam.

Alone, he had destroyed it in a matter of seconds.

Well, not completely alone. He'd had Santo do the dirty work—place the sticks of dynamite, etc. But he, Cisco, was the one who'd masterminded the caper and detonated the dynamite.

He chuckled gleefully as the powerful blast sent huge boulders raining down over a wide radius of ground and a thick cloud of dirt rose high into the air. He laughed out loud when a great surge of rushing water roared through the gaping crater left by the destructive explosion. Carrying tree limbs and rocks and a myriad of debris along with the swirling tide, Coronado Creek immediately returned to its original path, roaring rapidly down toward the Pacific.

Not so much as a dipper full of its rushing water would ever again flow onto the vast acreage of *Lindo Vista*.

Booooooooommmmmm!

The force of the blast was so strong, the sound of the

explosion so deafeningly loud, Gena jumped, startled, even though she was expecting it. Had been waiting on pins and needles to hear it all afternoon.

Three o'clock.

Right on time.

Heart in her throat, she leaped up from the peach sofa and her hands went to her cheeks. She trembled, feeling suddenly short of breath and faint. She hadn't actually considered the magnitude of destruction which would be caused by such an explosion. Afraid to go out and look, momentarily sorry for her rash decision to have the Dreamy Draw dam blown up, Gena worriedly shook her head and asked herself miserably, "What have I done? My God, what have I done?"

Shaking, she buried her face in her hands. She waited for the tears of shame and regret to come.

Her eyes remained totally dry.

The moment passed.

The weakness and the worry vanished. She lifted her head, threw back her shoulders. She knew exactly what she had done! And she was damn sure glad she had done it!

Gena began to smile. Then to laugh. Then to dance. She danced giddily about her bedroom, laughing merrily. She felt wonderful. Wonderful! Happier than she'd felt in weeks, months. And why not? Why should she be sorry for what had happened when she was not the one to blame.

The fault was not hers, it was Burt Burnett's.

The bastard was getting exactly what he deserved and she was *soooo* glad she was able to give it to him!

Things could have, should have been very different. She had given Burt a second chance, but he hadn't taken it. She had been certain that once she told him the terrible truth about his conniving Spanish wife—when he fully realized that Sabella Rios had married him only to get her hands on *Lindo Vista*—he would immediately seek a quick divorce and come back to Gena on his knees.

But he hadn't done it.

Well, okay! Fine. Now it was too late! He wouldn't be getting any more chances. For far too long she had been patient, understanding, forgiving, but no more. It was high time she thought of herself for a change.

Gena continued to dance dizzily around the room, stripping as she danced.

She was expecting Cisco within the hour.

She had promised him that if the explosion proved successful—when Coronado Creek no longer flowed onto Burnett land—she would show him her heartfelt gratitude. And he would thoroughly enjoy every second of her thanks.

Gena swayed across the room toward the bed.

"Boom. Boom. Boom," she said in a sing-song voice, swinging her derriere from one side to the other in tempo with the booms. "Boom. Boom. Boom," she repeated as she raised her dress high and did a few spirited kicks. "Boom. Boom. Boom," she continued as she reached the bed, spun about, and sat down.

Her dress raised, she kicked a leg into the air, took off a blue satin garter, swung it around on her thumb for a while, then pulled it back like a slingshot and let it fly, laughing as it sailed across the room.

She peeled the sheer stocking down her leg and dropped it carelessly to the carpet.

"Boom. Boom. Boom," she said again, falling over onto her back, flinging her arms up above her head. "Did you hear it, Burt?" she asked the silent room. "Did you hear the boom that will turn your precious *Lindo Vista* into a worthless wasteland?"

Chapter Forty-one

The bastards have blown up the dam," Cappy shouted loudly, running to meet the black brougham as it rolled to stop on a hill directly above the demolished dam. "Damn that Cisco and Santo! I'll—"

"You'll do nothing," Burt said with sad resignation, climbing down out of the carriage. Squinting at the destroyed rock barricade, he said flatly, "It's their dam, their draw, and their dynamite."

Sabella remained in the carriage, her horrified gaze focused on the demolished rock dam. Disbelieving what she was seeing with her own eyes, she overheard the conversation between Burt and Cappy. She heard Burt tell his ranch foreman in a flat, emotionless tone that they couldn't blame Cisco and Santo for blowing up the dam.

She heard Cappy say, "Jesus, son, surely you don't think Senator de Temple is responsible. Why the senator is as fine a man as I've ever known. He'd never do such an insane thing."

"No, of course not," was Burt's low, dispassionate reply. "This was solely Gena's show." A cheerless smile touched his full lips and he added softly, "Guess she figured since apprising me of the truth about my wife didn't finish me off, she'd have another whack at me."

"God in Heaven, you actually believe—"

"Sure I do," Burt said with a bitter, self-deprecating grin.

"I'm one lucky son of a gun, huh, Cappy? I don't have just one, but two clever, castrating women bent on ruining me." He turned back toward the carriage.

"Well, wait a minute," Cappy said, frowning. "Where you going?"

"To hell it looks like," said Burt with shrug and a shake of his dark head.

He returned to the brougham. When he climbed up onto the seat beside her, Sabella saw, for one unguarded moment, the defeat in his hooded gray eyes. She was aware of the tension in his tall, lean body. She felt terrible for him; wished there was something she could do, some way she could help.

Impulsively she slid closer, laid a hand on his muscular forearm. "Burt, I just want you to know that—"

"Will you shut up," he said coldly, pinning her with icy silver eyes. "Can you do that? Can you just leave me the hell alone?"

"Yes," she said, her anger flaring instantly, "I sure as hell can!"

Sabella left Burt alone.

Once they arrived back at *Lindo Vista,* she retired to their upstairs suite and didn't see him again for the remainder of the day. At shortly after eleven she went to bed. Alone. After tossing and turning for half an hour, she fell tiredly to sleep.

At sometime past two in the morning, she was awakened by a hot persistent mouth pressing soft, stirring kisses to her parted lips and a pair of warm, caressing hands touching her in all the instantly responsive places.

Then kissing her *there.*

When Burt's fiery lips returned to her mouth, his tongue searched for and found a fervent answer, a wild response that shook him to the bottom of his bare brown heels.

He quickly moved between Sabella's long slender legs and sank into her soft, hot flesh. Rolling his hips, thrusting his pelvis, he felt her take him deep inside and trap him there. Her arms came around his neck, her silken-skinned legs around his back.

His hands sought the rounded cheeks of her buttocks; he lifted her to him, drove desperately into her as she clung to him and twisted and bucked against him.

After only a few brief, wildly physical moments, the magical feeling began. Their mutual orgasm came with a sudden powerful eruption of ecstasy that left them perspiring, limp, and panting for breath.

But when it had passed, Burt quickly rolled away, callously turning his back on Sabella. Tears stinging her eyes, she lay awake for long time in the darkness, wondering how the beautiful naked body of the man stretched out beside her could radiate such intense heat when the heart inside his splendid chest was as cold as ice.

A pall settled over *Lindo Vista*.

Everyone was worried. And with good reason. In this dry, sunny land nothing could live without water. Not man. Not animal. Not vegetation.

Nothing.

No appreciable amount of rain had fallen in Southern California since the last of the late afternoon thundershowers back in August. Without the dam at Dreamy Draw, Coronado Creek no longer flowed onto *Lindo Vista* to constantly replenish the shallow irrigation ditches. The network of ditches would go dry quickly without the roaring creek.

A good rain would help temporarily, but would not solve the longterm problem. Unless a new water source could be found to supply the ranch, the mighty empire that was *Lindo Vista* would be no more. The cattle and horses would have to be sold early and at a heavy loss. The fruit and almond orchards would wither and die. Grapes would fall from the brittle vines, scorched and shriveled by the sun. The high dry desert would start to reclaim the verdant valley, turning it into a parched, barren wasteland.

Thanksgiving came and went with very little for which to be thankful. The gloom pervading the big hacienda did not lift for the holiday. Martha and her kitchen staff cooked a meal fit for royalty, but nobody was really hungry.

A brooding Burt left the noontime feast mostly untouched. Pushing his plate away, he reached for the bottle of wine which was chilling in a silver bucket on a stand at his elbow. Snagging it between two fingers, he rose to his feet, excused himself, and went to the library.

There he stayed the rest of the day.

But he came to Sabella's bed on that cool Thanksgiving night just as usual. His kisses tasting not unpleasantly of wine, he made slow, exquisite love to her. Satisfying her to the point of sweet exhaustion, he allowed her to fall asleep in his arms. She had no idea how long she slumbered, but when—deep in the dead of night—she abruptly awakened, she found that his arms still warmly encircled her, that her body was pressed against his.

Slowly, sleepily, she raised her head to look at him and shivered when she saw his silver eyes flashing in the darkness.

He was still wide awake.

He quickly drew her closer, pressing the length of her sleep-warm nakedness against his long, lean body, his hands stroking freely over her back, her hips, the twin cheeks of her bottom. Sabella felt her breasts crushed against his chest and an awakening tremble as passion swiftly rose.

In seconds she found herself astride him, his throbbing flesh buried inside her. She met his sudden lust with her own, taking him into her squeezing depths and holding him prisoner there. Rolling her hips and pummeling him with her pelvis, she leaned down and nipped at his heaving chest, running her tongue over his ribs, letting her unbound hair swish across his face and broad shoulders.

The nightly loving continued and by Christmastime, Sabella suspected she was pregnant. Still she waited until year's end to summon Doctor Ledet to *Lindo Vista*. The doctor arrived on a cool, cloudy Friday afternoon, the very last day of December, 1880.

After conducting a short, but thorough examination, he confirmed Sabella's suspicions. She was indeed going to have a baby. He couldn't be certain, but he would estimate that the birth of the child would occur sometime around the first week of September.

Smiling, starting downstairs, the silver-haired physician said, "So where's Burt? Waiting in the library? Shall I tell him, or do you want—"

"Burt isn't home at the moment," Sabella said, not adding that she wasn't sure where he was. Or when he might be back. "I'll tell him," she said, forcing herself to smile, to appear happy.

"Don't blame you a bit," said the beaming doctor. He laughed then, a hearty, deep-chested laugh, and said, "It's New Year's Eve. You might want to wait until midnight." He winked at

her. "Hand him a cup of eggnog and get him under the mistletoe for a kiss and then give him the joyous news. A romantic
way to begin a New Year, hmmmm, Mrs. Burnett?"

"Yes," replied Sabella, wishing it could be that way, half
hoping that it might.

It wasn't.

Midnight came. The old year died and the New Year was
born with no sign of Burt. Feeling foolish and angry and
sorry for herself, Sabella was all alone in their suite. She
looked from the blazing cedar logs in the fireplace to the big
silver bowl of rich frothy eggnog by the bed to the large
bough of green leafy mistletoe above the door.

Tears stinging her eyes, she stood before the fire and undressed, letting her clothes slide to the carpet at her feet.
Naked she stood staring into the leaping flames, feeling the
heat on her bare flesh, the pleasing warmth counterbalanced
by the cold ocean winds blowing in through the open balcony doors.

Shaking her head sadly, she wondered at her sanity.

Had she really supposed—simply because she was pregnant—that it would change anything between Burt and herself? Had she actually believed that the two of them would
spend a romantic evening here together in their suite, toasting each other with eggnog and kissing under the mistletoe?

Gritting her teeth and clenching her fists, Sabella whirled
away so swiftly to march to the bed that she stumbled against
a foot stool which rested before an old worn leather chair.
A chair in which she had experienced some of the most
thrilling moments of her life. A chair in which no one ever
sat now.

The Happy chair.

No one was happy in this room anymore. Not Burt. Not
her.

Dispirited, Sabella sighed heavily, stepped around the
empty, lonely looking chair, and trudged to the bed. She
didn't bother with a nightgown. After four months of being
married to Burt Burnett, she was just about out of the habit
of wearing nightclothes.

Naked, she slipped between the cool silky sheets, turned
onto her side, and closed her eyes. She thought about all

that had happened in the year just past. She considered all that might happen in the one ahead.

A little sob of despair passed her lips and Sabella placed a spread hand on her bare flat stomach. It had been but a few short hours since she'd learned she was carrying a child, but already she felt protective toward the new life beginning inside her.

A child. A son. *My* son.

Sabella knew in that moment, as she lay there in the cold firelit room alone, that she would *never* allow Burt Burnett or anyone else to take her son away from her!

Her eyelids growing heavy, she began to consider names for her son, putting herself to sleep with the pleasant exercise. Just when she was about to drop off, she heard the door open.

Clutching the sheet to her breasts, she slowly, quietly turned over, and saw Burt walk inside, ducking his dark head to avoid the bough of fragrant mistletoe. She started to speak, to say his name, but decided against it.

Since he hardly glanced at the bed, he obviously didn't know or care if she were asleep or awake. In silence she watched as he undressed. She continued to watch as he did what she had done earlier; stood naked before the fireplace, staring into the fire. He was, she realized, enjoying the warmth of the flames as well as the chill night winds stroking his nakedness. Slowly, he turned about so that his backside was to the fire.

Sabella took a sharp, shallow intake of breath.

He was awesomely beautiful. With the firelight flickering on the bare bronze skin revealing various scars marring the smooth flesh, he might have been a brave Roman gladiator. A tall, powerful specimen who had thrilled the bloodthirsty throngs crowding the Coliseum with his heart-stopping victories over man and beast. A triumphant conqueror who would live to see another day.

And now he had been sent to the bed of a lusty, willing pagan wench who had watched him in battle and had been given to him for the night. She was his reward.

Burt's burnished naked beauty and the foolish sexual fantasy it inspired made Sabella tingle with sweet anticipation. Her heartbeat quickened when Burt came to the bed, pulled the covering sheet away, and stretched out beside her. For a long tense moment he didn't touch her.

He just lay on his side, head resting on a folded arm, looking at her.

Sabella's caught breath came out in a rush when finally his tanned hand reached out, his lean fingers touched her face, her lips, her chin. Those fingers fanned over her bare shoulder and moved down her slender arm to her elbow. Then he was looming over her, looking at her, the firelight reflected in the depths of his hot silver eyes.

He bent his head, kissed the hollow of her throat. His dark silky hair ruffling against her chin, he stroked her hip, her thigh.

Sighing with pleasure, Sabella whispered breathlessly, "Burt, I . . . I have something to tell you."

"Mmmmm," he murmured, his mouth beginning its slow slide downward.

"It's . . . happened," Sabella said softly. "Doctor Ledet was here this afternoon. He said that I am—"

Burt's lips left her throat, his hand moved from her hip. "You're positive?" His head raised, his eyes were boring into hers. "The doctor couldn't make a mistake? You're absolutely sure?"

Nodding, she said, "I'm absolutely sure. Doctor Ledet said I will be having the baby sometime around the first of September."

She waited for him to react, to say something. Burt didn't say a word. Instead he promptly got out of bed, walked across the room, and retrieved his discarded trousers. Standing before the fire, he pulled on the pants and buttoned them up over his brown belly.

Returning to the bed, he stood looking down at her. He said, "I won't be bothering you again, my dear. I've stood stud for my last time. I need some rest and so do you. Sleep well."

He turned, crossed to the door, opened it. He started through it; the mistletoe brushed the top of his head, startling him. He glanced up, smoothed his hair down, and turned to look at Sabella.

"Oh, by the way," he said, smiling coldly, "Happy New Year."

Chapter Forty-two

"My dear friends," said Senator Nelson de Temple, an arm around Gena, a champagne glass raised in his hand, "my daughter, Gena, and I wish you one and all a Happy New Year!"

"Happy New Year! Happy New Year!" rose shouts above the music and laughter as the glittering crowd drank toasts to 1881.

The senator downed his champagne, then kissed his daughter's cheek lightly, and was about to step down off the flower-draped podium when Gena caught him, drew him back.

"Wait, Father," Gena said, smiling mysteriously, "I have an important announcement for you to make."

Senator de Temple immediately frowned, worried. What next? He still was not satisfied that she had had nothing to do with the destruction of the Dreamy Draw dam. He was afraid to hear what she was up to now. He should, he realized sadly, have disciplined her more severely when she was growing up.

Inwardly cringing, the senator nodded, and raised his hands for silence. It was several minutes before some of the tipsy merrymakers in the de Temple ballroom could be quieted down. When at last the senator had everyone's attention, Gena whispered in her father's ear.

His mouth fell open in shock and disbelief. Before he could say a word, the portly, smiling Don Miguel Andres Amaro had made his way through the crowd and was stepping up on the platform to join father and daughter. The beaming middle-aged don proudly took his place beside Gena, wrapping a short arm around her waist.

The stunned senator finally found his tongue. Relieved, pleased beyond words, he cleared his throat, then happily announced to the curious guests, "My friends, this is *indeed* a Happy New Year! My beautiful daughter has just informed me that she has—this very night—agreed to become the bride of my dearest friend, Don Miguel Andres Amaro!"

Gasps and shrieks and shouts and whistles followed the astounding announcement. Then loud applause as Gena smiled charmingly, turned, and took the short, stocky Mexican grandee's fleshy face in her hands and kissed him soundly.

An hour later Gena kissed the don again as they stood alone in the winter moonlight on the balcony outside the still-crowded ballroom. This kiss was his reward for promising to give her what she wanted most. She wanted, she beseechingly told him, to get away from the cloying boredom and smothering small-mindedness of San Juan Capistrano! She wanted to have some fun. She wanted to meet interesting new people and have something of a social life. She wanted to move to Los Angeles!

The don quickly agreed.

He would, he assured his bride-to-be, build for her the most magnificent mansion on Seaside Avenue and staff it with squadrons of servants to tend to the every need and wish of their beautiful mistress.

"Miguel, my dearest Miguel," Gena said in a soft, little-girl voice, running her fingers up and down the wide lapels of his black evening jacket, "there's one more little thing. . . ." She let her words trail away, acting as if she were too shy to continue.

His pudgy hands anxiously squeezing her waist, the troubled don said, "What is it, *querida*? You must tell me. I will give you anything you desire."

"There are, I'm told, many dangers in the city," she said.

"You will be in no danger! I would not—"

"How can you be sure? Have you forgotten that brazen bandits rode on this ranch in broad daylight and blew up Dreamy Draw dam?"

"Ah, *sí, sí,*" the don murmured, nodding.

"I want to take my trusted Cisco and Santo with us to Los Angeles. I'd feel so much safer with them there to guard me when I'm alone."

"Gena, my precious little dove, you will never be alone! I will be at your side always."

Her hands slipped up around the don's thick neck, and she locked her fingers behind his head. "I know, but . . . on those rare, dreadful occasions when you cannot be with me."

"Oh, *mi amor.* But, of course! You *must* bring them with us, I insist! And anyone else you wish to take."

"No one else," Gena said, smiling sweetly at him. "You are so good to me, Miguel. Kiss me, my darling don."

When the tall, cased clock struck three, Gena was again kissing the don. Impatiently kissing him good night in the empty, silent foyer. When his lips tried to cling to hers a moment longer, she drew away, giggling softly as if shocked and embarrassed.

The don immediately apologized. "*Querida,*" he murmured, "forgive me. You are so beautiful, I forget myself." He raised her hand to his lips, kissed the palm, and never saw the look of annoyance and boredom in Gena's eyes. He said, "I count the days, the nights. I cannot wait until you are my bride."

"Nor can I," she said, smoothly maneuvering him to the front door.

The stocky, starry-eyed grandee hadn't reached his waiting, crested carriage before Gena was rushing up the stairs to her suite. She slipped inside the dim, firelit room, looked eagerly about, and saw no sign of Cisco. She was immediately angry and disappointed. Then she heard the splashing of water. Starting to smile again, she moved through the shadows to the spacious bathroom.

Her smile broadened.

A silver candelabra containing six lighted candles sat on the floor beside the peach marble tub. The flickering candlelight fell on the gaunt, scarred face and wet hair-covered chest of the dark man lolling in the suds-filled tub.

A cigar clamped firmly between his white teeth, Cisco held up a soapy sponge and said by way of greeting, "Bathe me."

Gena laughingly obliged. She was on her knees running the sponge caressingly over his back when she heard Cisco say in a surprisingly gentle voice, "Marry me, Gena, so I can move in here with you. Marry me."

"Marry you?" She was incredulous.

"Yes. Why, not? What have you got to lose? Burt Burnett's never coming back. Besides, we're two of a kind. Marry me, *querida*."

Gena reached up, grabbed a handful of his dark wet hair, and pulled his head back to rest on her breasts. "Are you insane? I can't marry you."

"Why not?"

"Because you have no position—no money."

"No, but you do."

"Not nearly enough," she said, then told him, "I've agreed to marry Don Miguel Andres Amaro."

"*Dios!* You would leave me for that fat old grandee?"

"That fat, *rich*, and *powerful* old grandee," she laughingly corrected. Then she said, "But I'm not about to leave you. Never! I'm taking you with me, you foolish man. Nothing need change between us. I will have my own suite." She released his hair, dropped the sponge into the tub, and rose to her feet.

Hands on her hips, she ordered, "Now get out of that tub and into my bed before I change my mind."

Chapter Forty-three

Storms—one after another—blew in off the ocean throughout the month of January, bringing high, punishing winds that stripped the branches from the trees and rattled the leaded-glass windows of the adobe hacienda. The bleak gray skies seemed permanently leaden, the chill air heavy with dampness.

Yet no rain fell.

Upstairs in her suite one interminably long Saturday afternoon, a bored, lonely Sabella nudged back the heavy curtains and stared out at the boiling black sea. Then up at the dark, threatening sky. Maybe tonight it would rain. Or tomorrow. It *had* to rain soon. It had to!

Dear God, please make it rain and put an end to this damnable drought, she prayed.

Sighing heavily, Sabella's sad dark gaze lowered to the big windswept backyard. A solitary figure on the solitary bench quickly caught her attention. Her hand went to her throat as her eyes widened and stared unblinkingly.

Burt sat alone in the gloom, gazing wistfully out to sea. The strong chill winds tossed locks of his raven hair about his handsome head and pressed the soft cream fabric of his loosely laced pullover chamois shirt against the flat muscles of his chest. He seemed not to notice the wind, the cold.

He sat unmoving, as still as a statue. He looked so troubled, so terribly hurt and vulnerable, Sabella bit her lip, wishing she could help him, knowing she could not.

She was his problem, she thought sadly. At least the biggest part of it.

Burt continued to sit on the hard cement bench until the early winter dusk gathered around him. Finally he rose and glanced up at the house—a slow, brooding stare—then back out to sea.

Sabella's heart beat in her throat as he walked unhurriedly toward the high, rugged cliffs overlooking the churning, restless ocean. Genuinely worried, she stayed where she was, anxiously squinting into the deepening darkness, until at last she saw Burt return safely to the house.

Only then did she sigh with relief and turn away.

Sabella had come to hate herself for all the unhappiness she had caused. But when she felt as if she could bear it no longer, she reminded herself that the Burnett family was not blameless.

Lindo Vista was stolen from her mother.

But that knowledge no longer soothed her the way it once had. She wished with all her heart that she had never heard of *Lindo Vista* or Burt Burnett. This purgatory in which she now dwelled was far worse than any hell she could have ever imagined.

The cold starry nights brought pain and despair as time after time Sabella reached out in her lonely bed, seeking the warmth of the lean, hard body that was no longer there. That would never be there again.

She missed her Burt.

She missed hearing his low, familiar voice whispering her name in the darkness. Missed having his strong arms around her, holding her as if he would never let her go. Missed hearing the steady, reassuring beat of his heart beneath her cheek. Missed the sweet ecstasy he had taught her to enjoy, a kind of rapture she would never know again.

While she was alone in the night, she wondered miserably where Burt was. She wondered where he went each evening. She saw him ride out almost nightly, cantering Sam down the palm-lined avenue and underneath the tall crossbars. She never heard him come in, had no idea when or if he returned. Tortured, she imagined him going to Gena de Temple or to a brothel. She envisioned all sorts of things, none of them pleasant. The thought of Burt with another woman—making love with someone else—sickened her.

Mornings brought their own special brand of misery.

The rising of each new sun found Sabella unable to get out of bed. She forced herself to sit up, only to be overcome with waves of nausea so violent, she sagged back on the pillows, groaning with agony. The smell of breakfast made her retch with such dry, racking heaves, Carmelita soon gave up on trying to get her to take a few bites of food.

Dark circles appeared under Sabella's eyes and she began to lose weight, instead of gaining. Carmelita was worried. She expressed her concern to Cappy Ricks, and Cappy immediately sent for Doctor Ledet.

The doctor arrived that very afternoon. Cappy and Carmelita paced the quiet corridor outside Sabella's door, each assuring the other that she was going to be "fine, just fine."

They pounced anxiously on the doctor when he came out. Worried and talking at once, each shushed the other warningly. The doctor laughed and told them both to calm down. Mrs. Burnett, he assured them, was only suffering what many young, healthy women suffered in the beginning weeks or months of pregnancy. It was most unpleasant for the mother-to-be, but not dangerous. Any day Sabella's nausea would cease and then she would likely be healthier and happier than she'd ever been in her life.

Relieved, Cappy and Carmelita exchanged I-told-you-so's and then thanked the doctor for coming. Neither mentioned to Burt that the doctor had been there, so Cappy was taken aback when, well after ten that night Burt knocked on his door, stuck his head in, and asked, "What did Doc Ledet say? Is Sa ... is Mrs. Burnett ill?"

"Naw, Sabella's fine. Just a little morning sickness. Lot of women go through that. My Geneva was the same way when she first got pregnant with Elizabeth May."

Burt nodded and said quietly, "Tell Doc Ledet he's to come out once a week until the baby is born."

"I'll do it."

Cappy didn't care if Burt liked it or not, he took to going upstairs every morning to check on Sabella himself. Seeing her so sick and miserable couldn't have hurt him more if she'd been his own daughter.

"Sugar, I'm so sorry, so sorry," he'd murmur sympathetically, shaking his gray head. "It's not fair for you women to have to do all the suffering. I don't know what the Almighty was thinking of."

Cappy's concern was not just idle conversation. He sat at Sabella's bedside and soothingly pressed damp cloths to her perspiring forehead and pale cheeks. He supported her with his work-roughened hands when her weak, slender body was racked with fierce, uncontrollable retching. When the wrenching upheavals had passed, he'd rock her in his big, powerful arms as if she herself were a helpless baby.

The unflagging caring and tenderness Cappy showed Sabella were not lost on Carmelita. She had liked the big ranch foreman from the beginning. She had come to admire and respect him as well. And for the first time since losing her dear husband, Victor, she was attracted to a man. She said nothing about it to anyone. Cappy liked her, she was sure, but he'd given no indication that he thought of her as a woman.

But then why should he? Long ago she had lost her slender, girlish figure and her dark hair was now streaked with wide bands of silver. She was, she realized glumly, a plump, middle-aged Mexican woman whose place in life was solely tending the young, beautiful—and now pregnant—Sabella Rios Burnett.

Carmelita and Cappy were not the only ones who took good care of Sabella. Just as promised, she was coddled and humored by the entire staff. Doctor Ledet came to call once a week, although Sabella insisted it wasn't necessary. When the morning sickness passed, Martha cooked huge, tempting breakfasts which were served to Sabella on a bed tray.

Anytime she left her room, Blanton immediately appeared to escort her downstairs. If she wanted to sit in the sun on the south patio, he saw to it she was covered warmly with a lap robe. If she wanted to go to the beach, he insisted on helping her down the steep steps. Everyone babied her as if she were an invalid.

Everyone but Burt.

He paid her no attention whatsoever.

Whole days went by without her even seeing him. Then several. Sleepless in her big lonely bed on a cold night in early February, Sabella counted the days that had passed since she'd last seen Burt Burnett. Four. Four whole days. And nights. And then she'd only caught a fleeting glance of him as he rode Sam out alone one morning at dawn.

Sighing, Sabella turned onto her stomach and told herself she hoped it was four more before she saw him again. Or twice that long. Or never.

She closed her eyes and waited for sleep. It didn't come. She flopped over onto her back. She wasn't comfortable. She turned onto her left side. Then her right.

Frustrated, she finally threw off the covers and got out of bed. Slipping a blue silk wrapper over her nightgown, she headed downstairs to the library. She'd choose a book, bring it back up, and read until she fell asleep.

She moved down the dim, silent corridor, descended the redwood staircase, and started down the lower hallway toward the library. She jumped when the tall, cased clock struck two. And she frowned, puzzled, when she saw a rectangle of light spilling out of the open library door.

She paused, turned to go back upstairs without a book, then changed her mind. The servants had likely forgotten to extinguish the lamp after someone had used the library earlier in the evening.

Sabella moved on.

She reached the open door, peered cautiously inside, and her heart constricted in her chest. Sound asleep, Burt sat beneath the one lighted lamp in a high-backed burgundy wing chair. On his lap were a couple of open books, and scattered about on the floor at his feet were several more. The books were spread out and all were open.

Curious, Sabella silently tiptoed closer, glanced at his sleeping face, then knelt down to one of the open books to see what he was reading.

"The Appurtenancy Rule is that law which states a water right to surface or groundwater must be . . ."

Hydrology.

He was searching through the many tomes housed in this extensive library for a solution to the *rancho*'s water shortage. He had excitedly told her, on their honeymoon, about the water system being researched and developed by the hydrologists—desalinization of ocean water—which would change everything.

But that was still several years away.

Slowly rising to her feet, Sabella cast a sympathetic glance at Burt. She was not afraid of his waking up. He was sleeping soundly, obviously exhausted. It was chilly in the room and she worried that he might be cold. She longed to spread a warm comforter over him, but didn't dare.

Her gaze moved from the handsome sleeping face down over his chest, rising and falling evenly, then to the lean hands in his lap. One was spread on the face of an open book. The other was tightly clenching something. Sabella leaned closer.

Her lips fell open. Long, lean fingers were gripping a dried blossom as though it were priceless. Why on earth would he be holding a worthless wilted flower? What would he want with . . . with . . .

The entire scene instantly flashed through her mind—the terrible night when Burt had found out the truth. She had worn a rose velvet gown, and in her hair Carmelita had tucked a pink Castillian rose. The rose had fallen to the stairs as she ran to their room.

Burt had found the rose. He had saved it. He was holding it in his hand.

Overcome with emotion, Sabella slowly backed away, staring fondly at the sleeping man clutching the wilted pink rose. Tears were beginning to clog her throat. Her heart was aching with compassion, love, and a small degree of hope.

She reached the door and paused. It was then she recognized the chair in which Burt had chosen to sit. Winged, high-backed, supple leather of a rich burgundy hue, so little used it appeared to be brand new.

The Worry Chair.

Chapter Forty-four

The winter rains finally began, but they consisted of only light, sporadic drizzle peppering the dry, hard ground. Knowing every single drop of water had to be preserved, the *rancho*'s many cowhands labored long hours in the cold misting rain.

Some of the hands cleared the shallow irrigation ditches of debris and built temporary cistern tanks of anything that would hold water. Others monitored and moved the great herds of listless cattle about, driving them to the few remaining grassy upland meadows.

More than one cold drizzly morning, Sabella stood at a rain-streaked window and watched a squadron of slicker-garbed cowboys ride out to relieve those who had worked through the night. She stayed at the window until the exhausted night crew came riding in.

Knowing Burt and Cappy worked alongside the weary men through the long dark hours of night, Sabella couldn't relax until she caught sight of Burt's big paint stallion, Sam, followed closely by the rangy sorrel Cappy rode. When the pair were in sight, when she could see for herself that both men were upright in the saddle, she breathed a little easier.

They were safe. They were home. They were all right.

Burt *was* all right. But on the fourth night out, Cappy caught a slight cold.

Sabella noticed it that evening when Cappy came up to look in on her. She warned him that he'd best stay indoors until he had conquered the sniffles. Cappy laughed away her concern. The stubborn, loyal ranch foreman rode out again that very night, refusing to stay behind, insisting he felt as fit as a fiddle.

"Jesus, it's my fault," lamented Burt, his gray eyes clouded with worry. "I should have ordered him to stay behind. I should have—"

"Don't blame yourself," said Doctor Ledet. "Nothing could have kept this old cowboy inside when there was serious work to be done on the range."

More than a month had passed since Cappy had contracted the cold. Had he taken care of himself the way he should, he might have gotten well in two or three days. But he didn't. And he hadn't.

What had begun as nothing more serious than a bothersome head cold had tenaciously lingered and finally had turned into a dangerous, life-threatening case of double pneumonia.

The big, ruddy-faced foreman, who had never been sick a day in his life, now lay pale and lifeless in his bed. His lungs badly inflamed and filled with vile fluid, he struggled to breathe. He could barely swallow. He could hardly speak, his vocal chords failing along with his respiratory system.

For the past twenty-four hours, Cappy had begun drifting into and out of consciousness. Doctor Ledet didn't mince words. He said flatly that Cappy Ricks was slipping slowly, and dangerously close to death.

The doctor put a comforting hand on Burt's shoulder. "Better get some rest now while you can, Burt. He'll need you. I think he'll make it."

"I will," Burt said.

Dropping wearily into a chair pulled up to the bed, Burt sat there with Cappy as the March sun went down and the room filled with shadows. Blanton came in quietly, lighted a lamp, and asked Burt if it would be all right for Carmelita Rivera to look in on Cappy.

"She's awfully worried about him." Blanton's voice was

low, soft. "The two have become good friends in the weeks he has been laid up here."

Burt rose to his feet. "Of course. Maybe she'd like to sit with him until bedtime."

"I'm sure she would."

Carmelita was so worried about Cappy, she didn't sit in the chair beside his bed, she stood over him. Watchful for any sign of change, she was elated when his pale blue eyes opened and he recognized her.

Her heart felt as if it might explode when he tried to smile and rasped hoarsely, "Dear, sweet Lita." No one else called her Lita. No one else ever had. Only Cappy. It was music to her ears.

Tears flooding her dark eyes, Carmelita took his calloused hand in hers, and whispered, "Can I get you anything, Cappy? Some broth? Hot tea?"

"Burt," he murmured, as if it were a matter of life and death. "I *must* speak to Burt." His words were barely audible.

"Right away," she told him, pressed his hand to her cheek, and left.

Down the hall in the library, Burt was asleep in the winged-back burgundy Worry chair. Blanton gently shook him awake and informed him that Cappy was conscious and had asked to see him.

Burt hurried to Cappy's side. "What is it, my friend? What can I do for you?"

Cappy croaked anxiously, "Son, there's something I have to tell you before I go and—"

"You're not going anywhere," Burt told him, trying to smile.

"Don't count on it," rasped Cappy. Then quickly; "I know you think Sabella is—"

"I don't want to talk about my wife," Burt interrupted.

"But I do. I have to." Cappy weakly clasped Burt's forearm. "I have to talk about both your wife and your father."

A muscle flexed in Burt's lean jaw and his dark eyebrows lifted. "What does Dad have to do with Sabella Rios?"

Tears filling his eyes, his voice faint, Cappy finally told Burt the secret that had been plaguing him all these months. He admitted that Raleigh Burnett, shortly before he died, had confessed to stealing *Lindo Vista* from young Teresa Carrillo—Sabella's mother.

Burt listened, speechless and horrified, as Cappy sadly explained that long ago Raleigh had promised his dying friend, General Norman Patch, to hold *Lindo Vista* in trust for the general's ten-year-old sister-in-law, Teresa Carrillo. When Teresa turned eighteen, she was to take possession of her inheritance. Cappy told Burt the entire story just as it had been told to him.

"Don't think too harshly of your father, Burt," Cappy, tiring, said in conclusion. "He was good man. . . . He saved General Patch's life in the Mexican War and . . . and . . . what with taxes and all saved *Lindo Vista.*" He paused, fought for a breath, and added, "I should have told you . . . should have told you before you. . . ."

"Doesn't matter," Burt said, patting the sick foreman's night-shirted shoulder. "Wasn't your place to tell me; it was Dad's. You had nothing to do with any of it."

"Now you can understand why Sabella . . . why she would . . ." Cappy again paused, resting, then added in low, soft tones hardly above a whisper, "See, she thinks you were in on it. She believes you knew everything. You're being too hard on her, Burt, and she—"

"Get some rest, Cappy," Burt cut him off. "You're tiring yourself."

And finally at four a.m. Burt retired to a guest room for a few hours needed sleep.

At shortly before six a.m., Blanton knocked on Sabella's door.

"Sorry to disturb you so early," Blanton said when she opened the door. "Cappy wants to see you."

"I'll be right there!" she said. "Five minutes!"

Her hair in wild disarray, her hastily donned dress uncomfortably tight around her thickening waist, Sabella flew down the stairs and into Cappy's room. His eyes lighted slightly when he saw her lean over him.

"Hi, sugar," he said weakly.

"Hi, yourself," she said, giving him a quick kiss on his fevered cheek. She took his hand. "Sorry I look such a fright."

"You look pretty as a picture to me," he managed.

"No such thing! My hair hasn't been combed and I'm getting so big and fat, my clothes are too tight." She smiled then and said, "You know what I'm going to do, Cappy? I'm going to name my son after you."

"*Your* son? It's Burt's son, too," he wheezed, holding her hand. "Listen to me, Sabella, I know that there's bad trouble between you and Burt. You're right. Your land was stolen— but young Burt knew nothing about it. Honest to God, he didn't know anything about it."

Sabella's dark eyes widened, but she said, "You're wrong, Cappy. *Lindo Vista* belonged to my mother and—"

"I know, I know. But Burt didn't know. Never knew. He knew nothing about any of it. He had no idea that his father had stolen the land from your mother. Nor did I, until Raleigh finally told me the whole thing when he was dying. He asked me to tell Burt." Cappy's sick eyes closed for a second, he drew a painful breath. "I didn't do it. I knew how much Burt loved you both. Knew it would hurt Burt real bad and I foolishly hoped that . . . that . . ." Cappy's eyes fluttered weakly open. "He's a good man, Burt is. One of the best. It's not right for the sins of the father to be visited on the son. Burt is innocent. Let me leave you with that, child. You think about it."

"I will," Sabella said.

Chapter Forty-five

Sabella exited Cappy's room to find Burt leaning negligently against the wall. His dark head was bowed, his beautiful silver eyes were closed. The dim, early morning light made his cheekbones stand out and his eyes sink back in shadow. He looked ruggedly handsome in a frayed denim shirt, dirty blue jeans, and a three-day beard. He also looked tired, worried, and haggard.

Sabella's heart began beating so she couldn't trust herself to speak. A small smile came to her lips as she stared adoringly at the dark, brooding man. She was instantly filled to overflowing with love and compassion for him. Absurdly, she half expected Burt to open his eyes, see her, and anxiously sweep her up into his arms.

Burt sensed Sabella's presence, looked up, and his eyes, when they met hers, were cold, indifferent, uncaring.

Her hopes dissolved completely as his expression became glassy, without life or recognition.

"How is he?" he finally said and his voice was rough and dry and expressionless.

"About the same," she managed coolly and swept haughtily past him as if the last thing in the world she wanted to do was talk to him. Sabella hurried down the hall, holding back tears of bitter disappointment and regret.

How foolish of her to suppose things would be any different between them. She saw everything in a new light now since learning Burt was totally innocent and ignorant of his father's terrible duplicity. But for Burt, nothing had changed. Nothing would change. He would never find it in his heart to forgive her.

Burt continued to stand there, leaning against the wall. His dark head never turned. His gray gaze didn't follow her. But when she was completely out of sight and several long minutes had passed, he slowly turned. He placed his forehead against the wall. His haggard face twisted in pain. With a clenched fist he slowly beat against the wall.

How ridiculous of him to suppose things would be any different between them. Sure, he saw things in a new light now that he'd learned the terrible truth, that his father had actually stolen *Lindo Vista* from her mother. But for Sabella, nothing had changed. Nothing would change. She would never find it in her heart to forgive him.

In the desperate days that followed, Burt and Sabella shared only one thing: their deep concern for the gravely ill Cappy Ricks.

Cappy had slipped back into unconsciousness, so he was not left alone for a minute. Burt, Sabella, and Carmelita practically fought for the privilege of sitting at his bedside.

When it was Sabella's turn to sit with him, she talked as if he could hear and understand every word. She told him repeatedly that he was going to get well. They needed him, couldn't get along without him.

And in those long, silent hours, she also talked wistfully about Burt. She was, she said, sad and sorry for all the pain she had caused.

"If I had to do it all over again, I'd never have come to *Lindo Vista* and caused all this trouble. What I did was abominable, unforgivable. But, Cappy, you have to understand that I was raised on a deep, abiding hatred of the Burnetts. I hated Burt before I ever laid eyes on him. I really did."

Sabella sighed, then sadly smiled.

"I'll never forget the first time I actually saw him. It was at his engagement party and he arrived late. I remember everyone was talking and laughing, then all of a sudden there was some kind of disturbance at the arched entrance to the ballroom. Conversations lowered and died away. A low buzz of twittering excitement rippled through the room.

"Well, naturally I was curious. I quickly maneuvered myself in front of some guests just as a tall, broad-shouldered man stepped into view. He paused directly beneath a big chandelier and my knees began to shake. He was wearing a tuxedo that was as black as his hair, and a snowy white shirt that contrasted beautifully with his smooth, suntanned face. I knew in that instant it was Burt Burnett."

Sabella fell silent, remembering.

When finally she spoke again, she said, "I never dreamed I would fall in love with him. I have and there's nothing I can do about it. Nothing." She exhaled slowly, and shook her head sadly. "But you know something, Cappy? When I'm an old woman and my eyesight is failing and so is my memory, I'll still remember that night. And many nights that followed. For a brief, beautiful time Burt gave me more love and happiness than I'd ever dreamed existed. And even if it didn't—couldn't possibly last, I'll always have those memories to hold here in my heart."

Softly, barely above a whisper, she said, "I love Burt and I would give anything if I could make it all up to him. But I know he will never forgive me."

When Burt took his shift at Cappy's bedside, he talked just as Sabella did. He assured the unconscious ranch foreman that he would regain his health. In no time he'd be back out on the range where he belonged. No doubt about it.

And in the quiet, slow hours, Burt also talked about Sabella. He had been, he admitted, the world's biggest fool. She had stepped into his life and wrapped him around her little finger in record time.

"Trouble is, if I had to do it all over again . . . if I'd known exactly what she was up to from the very beginning . . . I'm not sure I wouldn't have done the same thing."

Burt sighed loudly, then began to smile sadly.

"Jesus, I'll never forget the first time I saw her. I was late to my own engagement party. When I got there, the ballroom was packed, but when I walked through the archway, I stopped and for some reason I looked across the room and saw her. And then I saw no one else.

"She was stunningly beautiful. A breathing, living golden goddess with silky blond hair and lightly tanned skin and a slender body all wrapped up in shimmering white silk. The largest, darkest eyes I've ever seen were looking straight into mine."

Burt whistled low under his breath, and fell silent, remembering.

When finally he spoke, he said, "I knew then and there I had to have her no matter what the cost. Hell couldn't have held me." He chuckled mirthlessly at himself then and added, "God, I fell so much in love with her I didn't just hand her my heart, I gave her my soul as well." Burt inhaled, shook his dark head. "But you know what, Cappy. I don't regret it all that much. If I live to be ninety I'll never forget that pleasurable moment when I first looked up and saw her.

"Sabella is an extraordinary woman and before I learned the truth, she gave me—for a little while at least—a kind of happiness I had never known before. I didn't know such happiness was possible. So it wasn't permanent. What is? I can look on that interlude as a warm, wonderful season in the sun."

Burt paused, smiled, and said, "And after she's gone, when I'm alone with the empty years stretching ahead, I'll always have that memory of her to warm a lifetime of loveless affairs."

For several minutes he said nothing more. Then finally, "I've forgiven Sabella, but it's clear she hasn't forgiven me. I haven't stopped loving her. I never will and I wish more than anything in the world that she loved me. But she never did and she never will."

Carmelita also talked to Cappy when she took her turn at his bedside.

In a warm, almost motherly tone, she told him, over and over again, that he was not to worry. He would get well. She would see to it.

And in those calm, still hours, she talked to him about something else that was weighing on her mind. The two of them. Not Burt and Sabella. But Cappy and herself.

"It isn't too late for us, you know. We still have some good years left." She clutched his hand to her breast. "I'm not saying I could ever take the place of your Geneva. I know I couldn't; nothing measures up to that first young love. I feel the same. Victor Rivera was a god to me and I adored him. But Victor and Geneva are dead and we're still alive. We're good friends, you and I, and we're content together. At our age, isn't that more than plenty?"

Carmelita suddenly frowned and shook her head. "Oh, Cappy, I do wish I was still pretty. I'd like to be pretty for you. I'm too plump and there's silver in my hair and wrinkles in my face." She laughed then and said, "You told me your eyesight is not what it once was. Maybe you can't see me so good, no?

"I will take good care of you, Cappy. Soon as you're better I'll fix you some of my special *sopapillas*. We'll sit on the south patio in the afternoon and take walks together at sunset. We will enjoy ourselves, *querido*.

"*Por favor*, Cappy, open your eyes," she said patiently, again and again.

At straight up noon on the nineteenth day of March, Carmelita stood at Cappy's bedside, once again asking him to open his eyes. To look at her. To her delight, he did.

It was St. Joseph's Day.

Each year on this day the swallows came back to Capistrano.

This year Cappy Ricks came back as well.

Chapter Forty-six

To the traveler passing by or the occasional visitor who came to call, *Lindo Vista* seemed the same that spring as it always had. The imposing adobe mansion on the cliffs shimmered in the bright May sunshine. A miraculous profusion of fuschia and purple bougainvilla spilled over the whitewashed walls in vivid splashes of color. The wisterias bordering the south patio were heavy with lavender blossoms. And the rose bushes flanking the front flagstone walk were covered with rare pink Castilian gems.

Birds sang sweetly from their perches in the pepper tree beside the kitchen window. Out offshore, peregrine falcons left the safety of their bluffside nests to soar high above the cliffs. The low sounds of the ocean were a placid constant, lulling to the ear and to the soul.

From without *Lindo Vista* was still the picture of pastoral peacefulness. But behind the whitewashed walls of the sprawling hacienda, things were far from tranquil.

Cappy Ricks was well enough to feel guilty about not helping Burt, but was not well enough to do any of the work. He was as weak and helpless as a baby. For a man who had never been sick a day in his life, the helplessness was hard to take. Cappy was irritable and anxious to be up and around. If Burt ever needed him, it was now, and here he was laid up like a beached whale. Carmelita listened to his rantings, sympathized sweetly, and refused to let him get out of bed.

Sabella was even more unhappy than Cappy.

The physical sickness of early pregnancy had passed, but her slim figure was changing and she was beginning to feel clumsy and unattractive. The physical transformation taking place in her body was not the only change. She was more emotional than she had ever been before. She cried at the drop of a hat. She didn't sleep well. She felt so unwanted and unloved, she rashly considered flinging herself into the ocean and swimming out so far she couldn't make it back.

She badly needed to feel a husband's loving arms around her. She rarely saw Burt. He was away from the mansion much of the time and she wondered where he was and what he was doing. When she did see him, he had nothing to say to her.

Looked right through her as if she wasn't there.

He despised her and she was miserable!

Burt was not only unhappy, he was worried.

Lindo Vista was faced with the worst water shortage since the devastating droughts of the sixties. There was no grass. No wheat. No grain. Hundreds of cattle had died and those who had survived were so poor, their ribs showed through their dusty hides.

Not a drop of rain had fallen since early March. Irrigation ditches, ponds, and brooks were so dry their sandy bottoms had become broken, sun-baked clods curled up around the edges.

Burt had given up on rain. The drought continued, so it was useless to hold on to his diminishing herd any longer. He had no choice but to ship them to market and take what he could get for them.

The roundup was hard work, with none of the fun and good times it had been in past years. There was no cash to hire seasonal help and no profits to be realized from the sale of the poor, underfed stock.

So Burt was worried, far more worried than anyone knew.

The pleasantly warm days of May turned into a hot dry June. June dragged torpidly by, finally giving way to a long sweltering July. It was so sultry that even the occasional breeze felt more like the hot dry Santa Annas that blew in off the desert than the cooling winds from the ocean.

There was no relief from the heat.

The very pregnant Sabella found it almost impossible to sleep. No longer able to lie on her stomach, she stretched out each night on her back, a thin batiste nightgown sticking damply to her fevered skin. She wondered why she bothered going to bed. She was far too hot and uncomfortable and unhappy to sleep.

On a muggy night near the end of July, Sabella couldn't bear lying there in the hot darkness a minute longer. Struggling to rise, feeling like a poor old turtle that somebody had cruelly turned onto its back, she finally managed to sit up and swing her legs over the edge of the bed. She sat there for a moment before coming to her feet.

She moved clumsily across the darkened room and stepped out onto the balcony. A hand to her back, she inhaled deeply, hoping for a breath of fresh invigorating air. But even outside, it was hot and still. If she hadn't been pregnant, she thought irritably, she'd go for a cooling dip in the ocean, sans clothes.

Sighing, Sabella trailed a hand along the railing and lumbered slowly toward the south side of the wide balcony. Once there, she leaned cautiously over, peering down across the courtyard, and instantly shivered in the oppressive heat.

She saw Burt.

Bare-chested, perspiration pooling on his heated belly, Burt sat alone in the library, poring over books and worrying about the future. His eyes were bloodshot from so much reading and so little sleep. His head ached dully. He was far too hot and lonely and troubled to sleep.

The *Silver Lining* had been sold more than a month ago. A prospective buyer would examine the *California Cloud* sometime next week. Then what? Sell off some of the land? Start whittling down a vast *rancho* that had been intact for a hundred years?

The prospect of letting one acre of the prized *Lindo Vista* go to an uncaring stranger was almost more than he could face.

But then he reminded himself, this *rancho* wasn't even his. It was his wife's.

No matter. He had to find a way to save it. Even though it didn't belong to him, had never really been his, it *would* be his son's. Nobody could dispute his son's claim to *Lindo Vista.*

Burt sighed and closed a heavy book, dropping it noisily to the floor. He rolled his bare, aching shoulders, then leaned back in the tall burgundy chair and closed his scratchy eyes.

Several minutes passed.

Burt's gray eyes flew open. His sweat-dampened back came up off the chair and he slammed the palm of his hand against his forehead.

"Jesus Christ!" he said aloud. "The answer's been right here all the time. As plain as the nose on my face!"

He recalled three, maybe four years ago he had read in the *Los Angeles Times* that on just one day during the winter floods, enough water ran into the ocean to supply the entire city for a year!

"That's it!" Burt told himself, snapping his fingers and leaping to his feet.

Not longer tired, he hurried to the tall bookshelves, withdrew a heavy volume, blew the dust from its spine, and sank eagerly down to the floor on his bare heels. Crouching there, he spread the book on the floor and anxiously flipped through the pages until he found what he was searching for—something he had read about a long time ago.

Finding it, Burt again read about the ancient Nabateans in Jordan during the Roman Empire. Heart beating faster, he read the part about them trenching the dry land so that the rain that occurred once a year all went into deep cisterns, supplying their needs for the rest of the year with that one short season's water.

Starting to smile, pleased with himself, Burt reasoned that while it was too late for this year, now was the time to begin work on developing the cisterns for next year. It would take months to dig the vast deep holes all across the far reaches of the *rancho.* But if they started now—tomorrow—they could have a drainage system in place for when the winter rains came.

"Thank you, God," he said aloud, eyes and arms lifted toward the fretted ceiling.

Despite the scorching summer heat, Cappy Ricks had bounced back to good health remarkably fast. He credited Carmelita. He told anyone who would listen that he hadn't felt so good in years.

They believed him. There was a new sparkle in his eyes and that, too, was credited to Carmelita. Since Cappy's illness, the two had spent many a companionable hour together. For people of their advanced age, they had been remarkably shy and ill at ease in each other's company until Cappy's brush with death. Now they talked about everything under the sun.

But they talked most about Burt and Sabella.

"What can we do?" Carmelita would say to Cappy, though she had asked that question dozens of times before. "We must do something, we must. Sabella loves Burt, I know she does. Can't you speak to Burt, tell him that—"

"Now, Lita, we've been over this a hundred times," Cappy would gently, but firmly reply. "I said all I had to say back when I was sick and thought I'd bought the farm. I told Burt the truth about his father. I told Sabella that Burt was innocent, that he knew nothing about any of it."

"*Sí*, I know, but—"

"I can't do any more. Burt's stubborn as a mule, always was. Anytime I so much as bring up Sabella's name, he shuts me off."

"It is the same with Sabella," Carmelita lamented. "She will not believe that he could care for her after what she did to him. But I do. I see the pain in his eyes and—"

"They're grown, both of 'em," Cappy interrupted. "We can't be telling them how to run their lives."

Carmelita sighed heavily. "But they love each other!"

"Then let them sort it out. We can't go meddling anymore." He smiled then, and added, "We wouldn't want them meddling in our lives, now would we? We wouldn't appreciate their offering advice we hadn't asked for. We wouldn't need their permission if we decided to . . . to"—Cappy needlessly cleared his throat and he reached for Carmelita's hand—"if we wanted to . . . marry."

Carmelita's dark eyes flashed and she smiled at him. "Are you proposing to me?"

"I guess I am." His face flushed and he hurriedly added, "If you'll have me. Now, I figure we should wait 'til the baby comes. See what happens with the kids and all before we say anything to the others."

Carmelita touched his face affectionately.

"You are a very kind and caring man, Cappy Ricks," she said. "*Sí, mi amor*. I will have you." Tears of happiness filled her eyes.

"Aw, Lita, come on now, don't do that," he said and reached for her.

August was a real scorcher.

Constantly concerned for Sabella's comfort and health, Carmelita anxiously watched over her through the long, blistering days. She gave Sabella cooling sponge baths and kept ice-filled tea or lemonade always at hand. She made sure Sabella ate properly. She watched for any sign of pain or danger to the nearly full-term pregnancy.

And each evening, when the burning summer sun had finally set across the ocean, Carmelita would help Sabella down the stairs and out to the south patio. Cappy would join them there after a day of helping dig the deep *acequias*.

Cappy had explained the project to the women when Burt first came up with the plan which he hoped would save the *rancho*. Now as the actual work was in progress on the system, Cappy reported how hard Burt was working. Said some nights Burt didn't even return to headquarters, but slept in one of the line shacks far out on the range.

The information, casually offered, was for Sabella's benefit. Cappy was sensitive enough to know that Sabella wondered where Burt was nights. Women were mighty quick to jump to conclusions. Especially pregnant women. He didn't want Sabella thinking that Burt was out tom-catting around when he wasn't.

Cappy wasn't fooled for a moment by Sabella's seeming disinterest. No more than he was fooled by Burt's indifference when he offered the latest bulletin on Sabella's health. While neither ever made a single inquiry or offered a comment about the other, Cappy saw to it that all their unasked questions were answered.

August finally ended, but not the terrible heat.

Chapter Forty-seven

September sizzled.

On a steamy Wednesday night in mid-September, Burt dined at the Mission Inn with the village's only banker. Tired, hot, and bored, Burt squirmed uncomfortably, eager to finish this necessary business meeting and go home.

At first he had planned to spend the night in Capistrano. But Sabella was too strongly in his thoughts. He had been thinking about her all day. Couldn't seem to get her off his mind. He wondered if it meant something. A faint twinge of alarm stirred in his chest.

He made his excuses and cut the meeting short. Still dressed in his evening clothes, Burt mounted Sam and set out for *Lindo Vista*. The stallion seemed to sense his master's urgency. The big paint went immediately into a comfortable, ground-eating lope and didn't slow the pace until he reached the stables at home.

Burt lunged down off the stallion's back, hit the paint on the rump. "Go on inside, Sam. One of the boys will rub you down."

Sam blew out a breath and obeyed.

Burt could hardly keep from running to the house. He walked very fast up to the darkened hacienda, unable to shake a mounting case of the jitters. He felt edgy. Worried.

He had to know that Sabella was all right. Or, rather, the child she was carrying.

His child. His son.

Burt went directly to the northern wing of the mansion. He climbed the back stairs, taking them two at a time. He knocked softly on the bedroom door. No answer. His apprehension grew. He gently turned the knob, cautiously poked his head inside. The turned-down bed was empty. He was really worried now.

It was after eleven o'clock at night! Where the hell was she?

Maybe she was still downstairs. He had come directly up the back stairs, so he wouldn't have seen her. Burt turned to leave when he heard someone humming.

Faintly. Softly.

Burt opened his mouth to call out. Closed it without making a sound. Noiselessly he crossed the plushly carpeted bedroom to the half open door of the bath-and-dressing room. Curiously, he peered inside.

And his breath caught in his throat.

Her golden hair pinned atop her head, head tilted slightly downward, Sabella sat naked in the glow of the lamplight, smoothing oil over her huge, rounded belly.

"Sabella," Burt softly murmured her name.

Startled, she looked up. Taken totally by surprise, she anxiously reached for a towel, staring at him wide-eyed. Speechless, shaking her head, she hurriedly covered herself.

Burt came slowly to her, fell to one knee before her.

"Will you let me . . . may I touch you?" he asked and it was almost a plea.

He didn't wait for an answer. Sabella swallowed nervously as Burt pulled the covering towel away and tossed it aside. Her face flaming with embarrassment, she took the tanned hands he held out and gently placed them on her oil-shiny belly.

The broad smile that came to his handsome face was the first real smile she'd seen in months. The smile was contagious. Sabella smiled, too. And she cheerfully gave her okay when he asked if he could help. ·

"May I"—his beautiful silver eyes lifted, met hers—

"spread the oil for you? I'll be real careful, I won't hurt you."

"Of course, you may," she said softly, her throat constricting with emotion.

Sabella sat there smiling shyly, naked and vulnerable, while Burt shrugged out of his black dinner jacket, rolled up the sleeves of his white dress shirt, and again went down on his knees before her. She handed him the bottle of oil.

Burt poured a drop into his cupped palm, set the bottle on the floor, and began carefully spreading the oil over her swollen stomach. The touch and the sight of his dark lean hand tenderly rubbing oil over her naked white belly filled Sabella with one of the sweetest joys she'd ever known.

"Does this make you feel cooler?" he asked.

Sabella laughed softly. "No, not really." She then explained, "A pregnant woman spreads oil over her stomach and thighs because it is supposed to keep the stretching skin from breaking."

"Oh. Uh-huh. I'm afraid I'm terribly ignorant about such things," Burt admitted. "But I'm willing to learn." He grinned boyishly and he looked younger and handsomer than he had in ages. His dexterous fingers gently caressing her slick belly, he asked, "Are you feeling well? Are you all right?"

"I'm fine," she assured him, warmed by the unexpected tenderness in his eyes, "even if I am two weeks overdue."

That irresistible Burnett smile flashing, he said, "You sure do look fine." A suggestion of awe and affection in his eyes, his silver gaze moved slowly, lovingly over her enlarged breasts, her rounded belly, her gleaming thighs. "You look ... beautiful."

Her heart racing, Sabella longed to reach out and touch him. To put her arms around his neck and press his handsome face to her naked breasts.

She said, "Thank you. If I am, it's because your son is inside me."

Burt gave no reply, but Sabella saw a muscle twitch in his lean jaw and the flicker of his eyes. He continued to spread the oil over her, not stopping at her stomach, but working on her hips and thighs as well. She sighed and smiled and

began to think that everything between them was going to
be okay.

But too soon Burt was washing his hands, hooking his
discarded jacket over his shoulder, and leaving her. At the
door, he paused, and turned back.

"Sabella," he spoke her name softly.

"Yes?" she said, and held her breath.

Several long seconds passed.

"Nothing," he said finally, shook his dark head, and left.

Sabella's spirits sank. With a sick sensation, she realized
that nothing was changed. That nothing would ever change
if she didn't do something.

It was up to her.

She was the one who had done everything wrong.

So she was the one who must make everything right.

Exhausted from a long, hard workday followed by the evening's business meeting in the village, Burt stripped down to
his skin and fell into bed in a downstairs guest room. Satisfied
that Sabella was okay, he fell asleep almost instantly.

Sometime later, he was roused from a deep slumber by a
strange orange glow lighting the darkened room. The eerie
light shone right through his closed eyelids, awakening him
with a start.

Burt sat up and looked anxiously around. He was up and
out of bed in a flash. He raced to doors standing open to
the courtyard. He blinked in confusion and alarm.

On the summer-dead lawn, not twenty yards from where
he stood, a fire was burning. Bright orange flames shot high
into the night sky. A woman stood between him and the
blaze.

Instinctively, Burt started out the door, caught himself, and
searched frantically for his discarded trousers. He hunched
anxiously into the pants and went out, still buttoning them.
Baffled, he hurried forward, his heart slamming hard against
his ribs.

Twenty feet from the woman and the fire, Burt stopped
and stared.

Perfectly framed by the fire, Sabella was smiling at him.
She said nothing, but she extended her hand toward the

blaze, directing his attention to its source. It was not until then that Burt saw what was on fire.

The Worry Chair.

When his gaze left the burning chair, returned to her, Sabella held up a worn leather journal for him to see. Burt knew in an instant it was the damning Rivera journal he had heard so much about.

He watched, entranced, as Sabella turned and tossed the journal into the flames. She turned back to face him, dusted her hands together, and walked purposely toward him.

Stopping directly before him, she said, "You can't send me away from you, Burt Burnett. I refuse to go. I'm staying right here no matter what happens. This is *our* land, yours and mine. And I'll tell you something else, I love you. I love you whether you like it or not. So there!"

She turned and walked away while Burt, dumbfounded, stared after her, shaking his dark head in wonder. He began to smile. Then to laugh. Burt went after her, caught her arm, turned her to face him.

"I do like it," he said, smiling down at her.

"Well, it's a good thing."

"You," he said, "are a marvel."

"You just now finding that out?" She put her arms around his neck. "Burt, I'm so sorry for everything. Please say you'll forgive me."

Burt's arms went around her. Gently, he drew her close, and as her huge stomach pressed against him, he was overwhelmed by the thought that their child was safely cradled between their embracing bodies.

"Only if you will forgive me, sweetheart."

"You've done nothing wrong," she said, "so that's easy."

"Will it be as easy to love me for the next fifty or sixty years?"

"Lord, I don't know," she teased. "Ask me again in about fifty years."

Burt laughed, then lowered his lips to hers and kissed her. Sabella squealed in surprise when he picked her up.

"You can't carry me," she protested, "I'm too heavy!"

"You feel light as a feather to me," he said and carried her inside.

Watching from inside his darkened bedroom in the hacienda's southern wing, Cappy Ricks exhaled with relief. Having been the one to haul the burgundy leather chair out into the courtyard for Sabella and set it afire, he didn't feel all that guilty about watching to see what happened afterward.

Smiling now, Cappy went back to bed feeling almost as happy as the reunited pair.

But not quite.

In their suite upstairs Burt and Sabella lay side by side in their big bed, Sabella on her back, Burt turned on his side to face her. Sabella's starving lips traveled over his face, her hands searched out the beloved hollows of his leanly muscled body.

Words of love and apology and undying devotion were whispered between the sweetest of kisses.

Sabella went peacefully to sleep in her husband's loving arms.

Two hours later, she was awakened by an agonizing pain in her back. She gritted her teeth and waited for it to pass. It didn't. It got worse.

She turned to look at Burt. He was sleeping soundly. She hated to wake him; he had been working so hard, he needed his rest. She wouldn't bother him.

Sabella eased slowly out of Burt's arms. Grimacing with pain, she struggled toward the edge of the bed. She was up on her elbows when Burt awakened from a nightmare. Heart pounding, his head snapped around.

"Oh, God, no!" he said, seeing the look of pain on Sabella's pale, drawn face.

"Burt . . . help me . . ." she moaned.

"I will, sweetheart, I will."

Stepping into his trousers, Burt dashed into the hall. Shouting loudly enough to wake the dead, he summoned the servants. Terrified, he hurried back to Sabella, cradled her head against his shoulder, and assured her that everything was going to be all right.

Carmelita, in a dressing robe and plaited hair, was the first one there. She nodded worriedly when Burt told her he thought Sabella was going into labor. Blanton and Cappy showed up seconds later, out of breath.

"Get Doc Ledet!" Burt shouted.

Within an hour Doctor Ledet arrived. Sabella's intense pain had grown worse, but she bit her lip and tried not to cry out. Surely it wouldn't last long.

But it did.

At dawn Burt still paced worriedly outside the closed door while Sabella writhed in agony, unable to hold back the moans as one fierce pain after another left her weak and perspiring and frightened.

As the September sun rose higher, the day grew hotter. Carmelita had to change Sabella's sweat-soaked nightgown time and again.

Doctor Ledet talked in low, comforting tones to Sabella, acting as though everything was perfectly normal. In truth, he was terrified he was going to lose both her and the baby. At midmorning, when he stepped out for a breath of fresh air, he had to admit to the questioning Burt that both his wife and his child were in danger.

His face a mask of pain, Burt said, "You *must* save Sabella, even if it means losing the baby. You hear me, Doc? I can't lose her, I can't!"

Leaving the doctor gaping after him, Burt anxiously barged into the room and went to his suffering wife. Her eyes tightly closed against another jolt of wrenching pain, she opened them when Burt softly spoke her name.

"Burt," she murmured barely above a whisper, "I'm scared."

"Don't be," he said, taking her hand and kneeling beside the bed. "I'm right here. I'll be with you every step of the way."

He meant it.

Burt stayed at Sabella's bedside through the terrible ordeal, kissing her damp temples, holding her cold hands, and bathing her pale, perspiring face.

And silently, wordlessly begging her not to leave him.

The agony continued throughout the long hot day as the weak, barely conscious Sabella was unable to expel the child from her pain-weakened body.

His tortured face shiny with sweat, Burt cursed himself for what he had done to her. He prayed for her life, more precious than his own. He murmured over and over again how much he loved her, worshipped her.

Giant thunderheads formed in the east as the long hot day dragged on. The sun disappeared and soon the fresh scent of rain filled the cooling air. Lightning streaked across the sky and thunder boomed, rattling the leaded windows.

When the welcome rain at last began, Sabella finally delivered her child. Tiny, red-faced, perfectly formed, the infant's squalling—loud enough to be heard above the falling rain—assured the worried parents its lungs were strong and healthy.

"The baby will be fine," the doctor told them both. He smiled at Sabella, patted her arm, and said, "And so will you. You've shown your mettle, child. You're a very brave young woman."

A smiling Carmelita brought the tiny, cleaned-up infant to its mother. She carefully placed the crying baby in Sabella's arms.

While Burt and Sabella smiled and stared at their healthy newborn, Carmelita plucked at the doctor's sleeve, motioning him to follow her out of the room.

Cappy looked up anxiously, and then his shoulders slumped with relief when Carmelita nodded reassuringly and smiled.

Left alone with their tiny newborn, the awed parents kissed the squirming baby and each other.

"Sweetheart, I love you. I love you more at this moment than ever before," Burt said to Sabella. "Thank you for giving me such a beautiful child."

She smiled. "You had something to do with it, as I recall."

He smiled too. "I could never live without you. Either of you."

Tears of happiness streaming down her pale cheeks, Sabella said, "You'll never have to, darling. We could never leave you."

Burt kissed her lips. Then kissed the baby's downy head and said, "I'm the luckiest, happiest person on earth."

Sabella's tired lids slipped low over her dark, shinning eyes. She said, "No, you're not. I am."

"You?" Burt said softly, a caress in his voice, brushing a limp strand of blond hair back off her cheek. "Why is that, sweetheart?"

Sabella smiled, sighed, and whispered tiredly, "Because you're mine. Both of you."

Epilogue

From the social page of the *Los Angeles Times* of Sunday, May 23, 1902:

... the groom, a scion of an old California land-grant family was personally decorated by President Theodore Roosevelt for his brave deeds that day on San Juan Hill. The bride ...

"I'm not going! No sir. And you can tell our young hero that. I'm not going to be a part of it!" Burton J. Burnett slammed the newspaper down on the table.

Sabella Burnett merely smiled at her scowling husband and said calmly, "You're going, dear."

His voice rising, he said, "I am *not* going!" And this time it was his fist that slammed down on the table.

The racket startled the aged Cappy Ricks, awakening him from his catnap. Cappy's snow-white head came up off his chest and he looked anxiously around.

"Huh? What is it? What's the trouble, Lita?"

Carmelita patted her eighty-eight-year-old husband's stooped shoulder and murmured soothingly, "Everything's fine, Cappy. We were just discussing the wedding."

"Again?" mumbled the old man, shooting a watery-eyed glance at Burt's scowling face. "I thought that was all settled."

"It is," Sabella said softly, and poured Cappy a fresh cup of coffee.

Burt glared at her. "I will not be bullied in my own home,"
he said, withdrawing a cigar from his shirt pocket. "Everybody had best remember that."

"Everybody?" his wife asked, a perfectly arched eyebrow
lifting accusingly.

"Everybody!" Burt assured her, lighted his cigar, and
again took up the newspaper and began to read, muttering
under his breath.

Sabella smiled fondly as she gazed at her stubborn husband. At fifty-three Burt was still an imposing figure, tall and
lean, with piercing gunmetal gray eyes and a deep booming
voice. He still possessed that special charm, that power to
walk into a room and take total possession.

Sabella sighed with sweet contentment. She was surely the
happiest woman alive. Her affectionate gaze lingering on her
husband's handsome, suntanned face for a time, she sighed
again before she looked away.

Cappy had pushed the fresh cup of coffee aside and fallen
back to sleep. Carmelita was busy buttoning his old blue
sweater over his frail chest.

The four of them had breakfasted this late Sunday morning on the south patio. There they had remained after the
meal had been finished. The broad flagstone terrace had always been one of Sabella's favorite spots. The grounds surrounding the hacienda grew more beautiful with each
passing year.

Improvements had been made regularly on the old place
and Sabella looked with pride and pleasure at the tall old
oaks, their trunks now pristinely whitewashed and lighted at
night. Lush green hedges of seventy-foot-high eucalyptus and
sycamores marched eastward from the ocean cliffs to the
coast road, concealing the many outbuildings and corrals
below the mansion.

Within the sprawling grounds, vast expanses of velvety
green grass sloped downhill, dotted with lemon trees and
framed by patches of marigolds and plots of larkspur. On
one piece of the huge terraced lawn was a tennis court, and
beyond it, Cappy's prized horseshoe pit.

Meandering paths threaded throughout the well-tended
property, the flagstone walks lined with the oaks, olive trees,
oleanders, and tangles of honeysuckle and jasmine.

Precious life-giving water had made this coastal paradise possible. Burt's long-ago dreams of plentiful water were a reality—had been for more than a decade.

There was almost a supernal peacefulness about this beautiful place.

That peacefulness was about to be shattered.

A tall, slender rider sat astride a dancing roan mare outside the white-fenced boundaries of the coastal *rancho*. The rider, squinting into the midmorning sun, was dressed in the unique garb favored by the Mexican *charros*—leather trousers, white shirt, scarlet butterfly necktie, scuffed ankle boots, and a broad-brimmed straw sombrero.

The rider's narrowed eyes lifted to the hammered silver sign mounted from the tall crossbars above the *rancho*'s main front gate. The shimmering silver letters spelled out simply LINDO VISTA—beautiful view.

The rider did not enter the guarded gate, but turned the roan mare about and rode off in the opposite direction.

Then yipping loudly, the rider wheeled the mare about in a tight semicircle and laid the spurs to its flanks. The responsive mount loped down out of the verdant meadow, galloped across the dusty road, and leapt over the high, white border fence as the rider shouted and laughed with joy.

Attracting the immediate attention of those on the south patio, the rider thundered up the palm-lined avenue, came to a plunging, gravel-flinging stop directly before the hacienda, and dismounted, tossing the reins to a waiting groom.

Boot heels clomping, military spurs jingling, the rider hurried around the house, crossed the flagstone patio, stepped up directly behind Sabella's chair, leaned down and kissed her smooth cheek.

Patting the strong young hands resting atop her shoulders, Sabella said, "Dear, your father says he's not going. Perhaps you can change his mind."

"Can't," said the glum Burt, gray eyes clinging to the tall, slim rider. "Nobody can."

The rider simply smiled and rounded the table, running a tanned hand affectionately over the dozing Cappy's white head and pressing a flushed cheek to Carmelita's.

"Nobody?" said the rider, laughing and flinging slender arms around Burt's neck. "Not even me?"

Burt's scowl quickly turned to a wide grin as the rider plopped down on his lap.

"Your momma has spoiled you rotten," he said, reaching up and removing the rider's broad-brimmed sombrero. Smiling with pleasure as an abundance of shimmering blond hair spilled down around his willful daughter's lovely face, he said, "High time I took a firm hand around here."

Her musical laughter showed her total lack of concern. Hugging his neck affectionately, she said, "Don't be hardheaded, Daddy. You *have* to come to the wedding." She gave his tanned cheek a kiss. "After all, you're giving the bride away!"

Coming in August . . .

"Lud, Ethan," Mr. Durwin Harrison said, slapping his plump, satin-clad knee, "I am glad you have abandoned your estates and that school business, if only for a short while. You are too serious by half since your father's demise, and this is a great time to come up to town, even though it is summer. The place is abuzz with the frantic machinations of the royal dukes, all of them suddenly in a race to see who can marry first and produce the heir to the throne."

Mr. Harrison's ruddy face creased with laughter. "The Duke of Clarence is especially amusing and has made himself the butt of half the jokes at the clubs. After having proposed marriage to the exquisite Miss Tylneylong, then Miss Mercer Elphinstone, and then that heiress, Miss Wykeham—and been spurned by all three—now he has agreed to this arranged betrothal to some obscure German princess."

Ethan Delacourt Bradford, the sixth Baron Raymond, leaned against a handsome Adam mantel, his muscular arms folded across his chest, and stared unseeing at some object across the candlelit book room. For all the attention he paid the chatter of his dinner companion and lifelong friend, he might as well have been alone.

"I tell you, Ethan, the betting book at White's is filled with wagers on how soon after clapping eyes upon her betrothed, the princess Adelaide turns and flees the country." His loud guffaw resounded in the late-night quiet of the room. "I laid a pony she would balk on the evening of the third day. Wanted to lay my blunt on the first evening, but old Coruthers was there ahead of me, already had a monkey on it."

Noticing that his friend had not shared in his laughter, Mr. Harrison gave his attention to the crystal decanter that had been placed on the Pembroke table at his elbow by Ethan's estimable butler, Yardley. He filled his glass, sniffed the excellent bouquet of the brandy, then tasted the smooth liquid, letting it glide slowly down his throat.

As he resettled himself in the leather-covered wing chair, one plump leg draped negligently over the chair arm, he eyed a plate of freshly baked cakes. His friend's wine cellar, second to none in London, was only one of the delights of Raymond House. Ethan's chef was coveted by half the hostesses in London.

"Not that I blame Prinny for giving his support to this scheme to marry off his brothers," he continued, a macaroon halfway to his mouth. "The country must have an heir. But watching the royal dukes—all of them middle-aged, and at least one of them distressingly corpulent—scouring Europe for eligible, nubile princesses is more than a sensible man can endure with a straight face."

When Lord Raymond vouchsafed no reply, Mr. Harrison set the macaroon aside and licked an errant crumb from his full bottom lip. "If I am keeping you from your bed, dear boy, just say so. I can take myself back to my lodgings in a trice. Wouldn't want to overstay my welcome."

"Your pardon," Ethan replied, pushing away from the mantel and stretching to his full six feet. "I am afraid my mind was wandering." A smile played at the corners of his well-shaped lips, softening the angular face that one disappointed young lady had stigmatized as too forbidding by half. "Blame it on my advanced age."

"Certainly," Mr. Harrison replied affably, wistfully eyeing the cut of Lord Raymond's blue evening coat and the way it fit so smoothly across his friend's broad, athletic shoulders. "I will blame it on anything you like. Although for a man of your advanced years—thirty, is it not?—you seem remarkably fit."

Ethan's smile vanished. "The guardianship of a harebrained younger brother obliges me to keep fit."

"I might have known your preoccupation would have something to do with that young paperskull. Ever since the Bag Wig sent him down from school, Reggie's been up to every rig. Been amusing himself boxing the watch, has he?"

"I wish it were that simple."

"Well, I remember you threatened to draw and quarter

the lad if he ever again visited one of those havy-cavy gaming hells, so that cannot be what has got you blue deviled." Sitting up, Mr. Harrison brushed stray morsels of cake from his silver brocade waistcoat, then took a sip of his brandy. "So if it ain't pranks, and it ain't gambling, that leaves only the fair sex." He chuckled. "Never tell me the lad has taken a page out of the royal book and gotten himself betrothed?"

"You are too sharp for me, Winny."

"Egad, Ethan! I was merely funning. Reggie cannot be above eighteen." He shook his head, then was forced to rearrange a carrot-colored lock of his carefully pomaded Brutus. "The lad's attic must be to let."

"No. Reggie is just heedless. He rushes his fences, then considers the consequences later. Much later."

"But some consequences will not wait for later, betrothals being among that number. They have a nasty way of catching up with a fellow."

Ethan's thick, dark eyebrows lifted in displeasure. "As you say, it has caught up with him."

"Naturally. And might one hazard a guess that in the light of day, the parson's mousetrap lost the allure it held by candlelight?"

"I can always depend upon your grasp of the central point, my friend."

Mr. Harrison rolled his slightly protuberant eyes heavenward. "And now, I presume, your brother wishes you to extricate him from his latest folly."

"That is his wish . . . hopefully before word of it reaches our mother."

Ethan walked over to the massive desk that dominated the far end of the room. Once there he withdrew a piece of paper from the top drawer, then returned to his place beside the empty fireplace. "Of course, there can be no question of legalities in this matter. Reggie has not obtained his majority and could not enter into a formal betrothal contract without my consent." He stared at the paper with its broken wafer. "Unfortunately, there is a further complication."

"If you are worried about tittle-tattle, dear boy, I should not think the story would be more than a nine-days' wonder.

Not with the royal dukes supplying the ton with *on dits*
around the clock. Compared to royal betrothals, the near
betrothal of a mere lad should prove rather insipid fare for
the gossipmongers."

"I hope you are right, Winny. However, the complication
to which I refer is of another nature." Ethan ran his hand
through his midnight black hair. "It seems my brother sealed
the bargain with the family betrothal ring."

Mr. Harrison choked on his brandy. "The Bradford Diamond! Egad, Ethan, you cannot be serious. The demmed
ring is worth a king's ransom." In deference to his friend's
feelings, he made no mention of the fact that the ring's rightful owner was the Bradford heir—Ethan.

"Reggie knows he had no right to the ring," he said, as
though reading his friend's thoughts, "and he has begged
my pardon."

Mr. Harrison kept his tongue between his teeth on the
subject of heedless cubs who acted badly, then expected pardon for the mere asking.

"The important thing now, Winny, is getting the ring
back."

"I should rather think it would be. But what of the young
lady? Has she a *tendre* for the lad, do you think?"

Ethan shook his head. "That I cannot answer."

"Do we know the chit?"

"*I* do not, and that worries me. I have asked a few discreet
questions here in town, but no one appears to be acquainted
with the family."

Pondering this new information, Mr. Harrison asked,
"Might the lad have got himself entangled with some demi
rep? Some seasoned adventuress who would entrap him
thinking to extract money from the Bradford coffers?"

Ethan's face was grim. "That could be her design. Anything is possible. I do not even know the person's given
name."

"But surely Reggie told you—"

"All I know is that she is a Miss Sommes, from a village
near Canterbury." He unfolded the piece of paper he held
in his hand. "Her first name is illegible."

Mr. Harrison stared at the paper that had been abused by
repeated folding and unfolding. "Am I to assume that your

brother took the course of least resistance and opened his budget in a letter?"

Ethan nodded. "It was delivered this morning to Raymond Park. I left for town within the hour, but by the time I got here, Reggie and that addlepated school chum of his had already taken themselves off on a repairing lease, their destination unknown."

He passed the mangled letter to Mr. Harrison. "See what you make of the chit's name. It is there in the last paragraph."

Mr. Harrison held the paper close to the branch of candles nearest his chair and attempted to decipher the youthful scratches on the page. "Demmed scrawl," he muttered, "and half the words have been crossed out or written over."

He moved the candelabra closer and reread the paragraph. "The letters are difficult to make out, but it looks like the name might be Gilly, or Milly. No, wait. It is Molly. No ..." He returned the letter to Ethan. "Sorry, dear boy, it could be anything."

Ethan held the letter over one of the candles until yellow-blue flames licked the edge of the paper. When it was well caught, he tossed the paper into the empty fireplace. The flames devoured the missive in a matter of seconds. "Whatever her name, I must find her."

"Of course. But how do you plan to do that?"

"Since my only lead is Canterbury, I will have to go there. My mother has an elderly cousin who resides in the town; I will stop by the old girl's place and see if she is acquainted with the Sommes family. Once I locate the family and pay them off if necessary, I will tell Miss Gilly-Milly-Molly to hand over the Bradford Diamond."

"And what if there is no Sommes family? What if the person is, in fact, an adventuress who has taken the ring and bolted to the Continent? One might live a luxurious life on the proceeds from such a stone."

A flash of anger darkened Ethan's brown eyes, making them appear cold and dangerous. "If she has run, I will find her. And if she has sold the ring, I will make her rue the day she decided to cheat Ethan Bradford."